THE GLORIOUS SALVATION MACHINE

PART ONE
OF

THE CHRONICLES
OF
PEREGRINUS
AND
PLOWMAN

© 2012 Lee W. Brainard

Soothkeep Press

Scripture citations are either KJV, or my own translation from the original Greek, or my own paraphrase based on either the KJV or the original Greek. If any citation happens to concur with a copyrighted translation, I offer my sincerest apologies.

ACKNOWLEDGEMENTS

I thank my wife Nita for reading through the book at various steps of the project, catching errors and offering suggestions on how I might make the story easier to read. I also thank her for her amazing support the past two years, especially during those long stretches when I logged many hours burning the candle at both ends, trying to finish this book while working 45 to 60 hours per week.

I thank John and Kathy Morell for the many hours they put into the first six chapters of this book. We spent many pleasant hours together in their living room, reading through early drafts of the first six chapters, fellowshipping in the things of God, laughing, and drinking coffee. Their help in developing the characters, refining the terminology of the story, and polishing my grammar and diction was a tremendous blessing.

I thank Steve Rusk for his savvy editorial work on the entire book toward the end of the project.

I thank George and Kathy Lemelin for their encouragement in the project and for their helpful comments on the rough draft of the first four chapters. Their e-mail on what I needed to do to improve the readability of the book was kept on my clipboard for years and referred to regularly.

I thank Tara Bulow for the cover artwork. She dared to try her hand in a new field — illustration — and the Lord honored.

I thank the saints at Harvey Gospel Chapel for their continual encouragement in this project and their prayers for it over the past fourteen months.

I thank a host of family members and friends who kindly read the first four chapters in rough draft and forwarded to me their helpful observations, positive feedback, and encouragement to keep going with the project.

ABOUT THE AUTHOR

Mr. Brainard is married and has four children, all of whom are born-again, and three of whom are married. Currently, he and his wife, Nita, live on a farmstead near Harvey, ND. They are in happy fellowship with the believers at Harvey Gospel Chapel where Mr. Brainard frequently teaches and preaches.

His areas of interest and study are diverse: Bible languages, textual criticism, the authority and inspiration of Scripture, conservative evangelicalism and the forces which threaten it, the major doctrinal controversies, eschatology, apologetics, Bible chronology, ancient history, ancient religion and mythology, ancient cosmology, and post-flood catastrophism.

TABLE OF CONTENTS

PREFACE 9
ONE — THE BIG EMPTY 11
TWO — REVEREND QUACKSALVER 21
THREE — JUMPING JACK HALLELUJAH...................51
FOUR — THE PROVIDENTIAL MEETING...................73
FIVE — THE STEAMING JOE 113
SIX — QUACKSALVER RELOADED..........................149
SEVEN — LUKE W. ZEAL RETURNS........................185
EIGHT — MORE STEAMING JOE 211
NINE — STRAWBERRY NOSTRUM 261
TEN — WILLY RUSH FORWARD 285
ELEVEN — THE GOD MAGIC MENACE 305

PREFACE

The theme of this book can be summed up in one question, "How does a man enter into a saving relationship with God?" This is the most important question in the world. Does he enter into a saving relationship through a religious form? Or does he enter into a saving relationship by engaging in a relationship, through faith, with the Lord Jesus Christ, who is "God manifest in flesh"? Many profess to be Christians and pretend to have a relationship with God, but they neither know God, nor are they known of God. All they have is religion. (See Matt. 7:21-23.)

Peregrinus is Latin for *pilgrim*, alluding to the fact that this world is not the Christian's home, heaven is. He is only passing through. The name is also a reverent allusion to Pilgrim in John Bunyan's *Pilgrim's Progress*, though this work of satire differs quite widely from his beloved allegory.

Plowman alludes to William Tyndale's prophecy that before he was done with his work of putting the Bible in the hands of the common man in the language of the common man, the plowboy would know the Bible better than the priest. This is a timeless principle. The working man who gives himself to the study of the Bible and its teachings can know the Bible better than educated preachers steeped in popular religion.

Astute readers will observe that several undeveloped themes interweave with the tale unfolded in these pages. These are vital parts of the whole Peregrinus and Plowman saga of which this volume is but the introduction. The Lord willing, further volumes will be penned which will develop these themes.

Lee W. Brainard
Harvey, ND
October 5, 2012

CHAPTER ONE

THE BIG EMPTY

Peregrinus Had a Big Empty

A young man by the name of Peregrinus lived in the Big Here & Now. Like men everywhere, he had a Big Empty. He felt unfulfilled. Something was missing. Life didn't satisfy like his heart wanted to be satisfied. His happiness was sporadic and mingled with disappointment.

Like everyone else, Peregrinus worked hard to fill his Big Empty. He shoveled away day after day, week upon week, year upon year with the biggest shovels he could find, from the best piles of fun stuff he could find. He shoveled until everything hurt, from his head to his heart to his conscience. But his Big Empty was as empty as ever.

His failure left him discouraged and frustrated. He began to be nagged by doubts. Was it even possible to fill his Big Empty? Why even try? But he couldn't and wouldn't give up. To do so guaranteed that it would remain empty.

So he pressed on in his quest to fill his Big Empty. What else could a man do? He searched for bigger and better shovels. He searched for new and better piles of fun stuff. Despite frequent bouts of discouragement, he never stopped hoping and seeking. He was determined to find — somewhere, somehow, some day — whatever it was he needed to fill his Big Empty and give him the abiding fulfillment and happiness that he craved.

THE GLORIOUS SALVATION MACHINE

Peregrinus Reads a Motivational Book

One day a coworker handed Peregrinus a book and insisted that he read it. Peregrinus looked at the cover. The title was provocative — *How to Fill Your Big Empty to the Brim*. The author was a man named Johnny Hotstuff, who claimed to have filled his Big Empty three times over.

On the back cover he read the following blurb: "Do you want to fill your Big Empty? Of course you do. You are a human, and all humans want to fill their Big Empty. The desire to fill the Big Empty is so universal that it is called the Universal Quest by psychologists.

So how do you fill your Big Empty? In this award winning book — Narcissism International's *Motivational Book of the Year* — Mr. Hotstuff explains step-by-step what to do and how to think, so you can fill your Big Empty to the brim."

That evening, after he had eaten supper, he settled into his favorite chair and read the book cover to cover. He highlighted a few passages that really stood out to him.

In the first chapter, *Naughty Stuff Doesn't Work*, he marked, "Why try to fill the Big Empty with naughty stuff? That won't work, no matter how big the shovel, no matter how big the pile. Only clean stuff can fill the Big Empty."

In the second chapter, *You Need a Big Dream*, he underlined, "You need to get yourself a big dream. Only a big dream can fill the Big Empty. What is a big dream? It is picturing the fun stuff that will make you happy. What do you really want to do, have, and be in the Big Here & Now? If you can't picture it, you can't pursue it. If you can't pursue it, you can't possess it. So picture it. Bring it into focus. Then pursue it with all your heart."

In the third chapter, *The Importance of Meaningful Stuff*, he was impressed with the statement, "Don't make the mistake of thinking that entertainment and recreation alone will fill your Big Empty. This mistake leads to disappointment. We are wired to find more satisfaction in purpose than in pleasure. We need meaningful fun stuff in our life — noble stuff, helping stuff, giving stuff. Make sure that you have some meaningful fun stuff in your big dream.

In the fourth chapter, *Basic Principles*, he highlighted, "There are several basic principles you must follow if you want your big dream to come true. *Set goals*. If you don't aim at definite things, you won't hit anything. *Work hard*. Rome wasn't built in a day, you know. *Give*. But only give enough to look good. You don't want to undermine your big dream. *Keep the Golden Rule* — except where it threatens the big dream. *Give credit to the big guy in the sky*, or the higher power, or mother earth, or the cosmos, or whatever concept of divinity you please. *Love all men* — especially YOURSELF."

In the last chapter, *Winners and Quitters*, he underlined, "You need to be a winner. Winners have grit. Grit is what it takes to lasso your big dream and drop it into your Big Empty before you kick the bucket. Grit won't quit. If you have grit and never quit, you will, shovel by shovel, fill your Big Empty right up to the brim. Winners continue shoveling until their last breath. Whiny, little crybaby quitters quit.

So never, never, never quit. Never. Drive yourself with whips if you need to. When you grow tired of whipping yourself, encourage yourself by reminding yourself how good it will feel when your Big Empty is filled to the top and sloshing over the sides. Never take your eyes off your big dream. Keep chasing your big dream. Happiness and fulfillment can be yours — if you don't quit."

Peregrinus finished the book and set it down. The possibilities warmed his heart. He had been going about it all wrong. He hadn't had a plan. His efforts had been haphazard. Now he was on the right track.

Peregrinus Pursues His Big Dream

Over the next few weeks, Peregrinus formulated a big dream for himself. Then he went after it with gusto. He became a model big-dream-chasing person. He replaced the naughty fun stuff in his life with clean fun stuff. He took up some noble fun stuff. He set himself goals to help him see his big dream come to pass. He worked hard. He crossed goals off his list. He made positive changes. He felt better about himself. People even said he was a better person. He was well on his way to the promised land of a Big Empty filled to the top and sloshing over the sides.

The Big Dream Belly Flop

After a few years, however, Peregrinus came to a painful realization. Big-dreaming had gained him nothing. His Big Empty was just as big and just as empty as ever.

This left him confused. Was quitting the only reason that a man failed to fill his Big Empty? Maybe it required lots of luck as well as lots of pluck. But if that was the case, then all the pluck in the world was no guarantee that a man could lasso his big dream and fill his Big Empty.

This led him to reexamine the lives of the big-dreamers that he knew. When he did so, he noticed something he had missed before. Not one of them had filled their Big Empty. Those that claimed they had were living a lie — they were practicing a sanctimonious dishonesty to uphold the theory and their pride. But they couldn't maintain the lie with consistency. The truth, as it always does, managed to come out here and there. A slip of the tongue. A moment of frustration. A little too much transparency.

Peregrinus awoke from his fantasy. The truth became crystal clear. It is extremely difficult to lasso a big dream. Very few succeed despite years of striving. The few that do somehow manage to rope their big dream, wrangle it to the ground, and drop it with great fanfare into their Big Empty always discover within a short time, to their sorrow, that their Big Empty is empty again. Filling it is a short-lived illusion.

And so Peregrinus concluded that his attempt to fill his Big Empty with a big dream was a big belly flop, not because he was a failure, but because the theory was bogus.

THE BIG EMPTY

Only God Can Fill the Big Empty

A few weeks later Peregrinus was channel surfing on the radio during his commute home from work. For some reason he stopped on a religious station, something he normally didn't do. He caught the last few minutes of a message by Mr. Radio Preacher on a program called the *Old Time Sacred Trust Hour*.

"Only God can fill the Big Empty. A big dream can't fill it. Success, careers, fame, and fortune can't fill it. Money, houses, cars, land, and possessions can't fill it. Adventures, vacations, and experiences can't fill it. Health food and yoga can't fill it. Friends and family can't fill it. Love and marriage can't fill it. Nice girls and guys can't fill it. Bad girls and guys can't fill it. Parties and good times can't fill it. All these things are way too small. Only God is big enough to fill your Big Empty."

Instinctively, he knew this was true. The message struck him as a hammer-blow to his heart. Yet it also made him a little nervous. After all, isn't God the one who is trying to keep us from filling the Big Empty? Isn't he the one that is trying to keep us from having fun, from having a good time, from doing what makes us happy? He was a little ashamed that he thought that way. But everyone he knew thought that way, even those that tried to pretend they didn't. God didn't have a very good reputation.

Peregrinus Gives God a Chance

Despite his fears, Peregrinus decided to give God a chance. He didn't really know where to start, but he was determined to do whatever was necessary. He suspected that he needed to be more serious about going to church and reading the Bible.

These new God-thoughts captivated his mind like a majestic mountain or a glorious sunrise. How could he have overlooked such a wonderful possibility? Who was more likely to be able to fill his Big Empty than God? For the first time, real hope rose in his heart. Not the vain kind of hope men entertain when they chase Shimmering Elusive, but the kind they have when dealing with settled facts, like the fact that if a man plants good seeds in good soil and waters them, he will be rewarded with plants that bring him blessing.

But Peregrinus also felt ashamed. He had been so busy trying to fill his Big Empty with Big Here & Now stuff that he had — to be blunt — callously ignored God. He had given a string of mundane things their turn at trying to fill his Big Empty. Now he was giving God a turn? The irony of the thought struck him. It had been God's turn all along, and he had been ignoring him. He had been ignoring the only path that leads to fulfillment, to meaning, to purpose, to lasting happiness.

The Old Time Sacred Trust Hour

After that day, Peregrinus listened to the *Old Time Sacred Trust Hour* during his commute home from work. He usually picked up the program partway through, so he missed some of it, but he thoroughly enjoyed what he did hear. Mr. Radio Preacher preached like no preacher he had heard before — with absolute confidence in the plain statements of the Sacred Trust on important themes like unbelief and sin, salvation by grace through faith, the cross, the freshbirth, Sweet Everlasting and Awful Everlasting, discipleship, prayer, reading the Sacred Trust, and seeking fulfillment in the things of the Crucified One.

Sweet Everlasting and Awful Everlasting

One evening while Peregrinus was driving home from work, he tuned in to the *Old Time Sacred Trust Hour* and heard Mr. Radio Preacher deliver a powerful message titled "All Men Live Forever." The message drove home three thoughts. *One*, all men will live forever. *Two*, some men will live forever in Sweet Everlasting and some will live forever in Awful Everlasting. *Three*, a man's response to the Wonderful Message of salvation in the Crucified One determines where he will live forever.

As Peregrinus listened, his heart was awakened to the awful reality of Sweet Everlasting and Awful Everlasting. Mr. Radio Preacher taught that these two eternal destinies are not mere religious stories that teach vague moral lessons, but real places that can be experienced like any other real place. They are as real as the city you live in and the bed you sleep on. Moreover, the day of reckoning is coming down the highway fast. And when it gets here, it will be really sweet for a few and really ugly for most. Men had better be ready.

Peregrinus was stunned. He reflected, "I have known about Sweet Everlasting and Awful Everlasting since I was a kid. I would have said they were real if anyone had asked me. Yet they made no difference in my life. They had zero effect on what I did or didn't do. I kept pushing them out of my mind whenever they tried to interfere with my life. I didn't want them in my Daily Grind. They were only religious concepts that you occasionally heard about when you did the Weekly Duty."

The situation reminded him of cappuccino. He had known about it for a long time. His friends had tried to get him to try it, but he had refused. "I don't like coffee," he would say. "Oh, but it's good," they would answer. Then one day he put a cup to his lips and he was hooked. He couldn't believe that he had been passing up the good stuff all these years. Since then, he had also grown to like straight coffee.

In the same way, he had been passing up God's good stuff. It had been right at hand the whole time. He could have tried it any time he wanted, but he would never put the cup to his lips. People would hand him the cup, and he would say, "Naw, that God stuff isn't for me." But now he had lifted the cup to his lips and tasted that God is good. For the first time in his life, he really-truly wanted to go to Sweet Everlasting and really-truly wanted to not go to Awful Everlasting. He was awakened.

THE GLORIOUS SALVATION MACHINE

The Wonderful Message

Two weeks later, Peregrinus heard Mr. Radio Preacher teach on the Wonderful Message. His summary at the close of the message was succinct and powerful:

"Take to heart the three points of this message. Think about them. Get serious about them.

The *first* point was the *big choice*. Every man must choose between living for the Big Here & Now and living for Sweet Everlasting. You cannot live for both. Those who say they live for both are really living for the Big Here & Now. They have merely brushed a coat of religious paint over their life.

Besides, why would anyone want to live for the Big Here & Now? Men cannot keep the few gains they make in this life, if they make any. They give them up at death, if not sooner. Even if a man somehow managed to gain the entire Big Here & Now, it would be a worthless gain. As the Sacred Trust says, 'What good would it do a man if he gained the whole Big Here & Now and yet lost his soul?'

The *second* was the *big city*. Sweet Everlasting isn't merely a religious veil to throw over the coffin of a loved one. It is real. Those who inherit Sweet Everlasting will live in a city built by God himself — a real city in real space and real time — which is called the New Jerusalem. It is beyond description. It is wonderful multiplied by amazing multiplied by incredible.

This wonderful city is built for man as man. It is designed to provide man all that he needs to fill his Big Empty perfectly and permanently. Believers shall live there in the presence of God as the children and heirs of God. They shall be surrounded for all eternity with such heavenly treasures as love, joy, peace, laughter, friends, beauty, and music. They shall never again experience sorrow, tears, death, or disappointment.

The *third* was the *big change*. No man shall enter and enjoy Sweet Everlasting unless he is born afresh. Baptism can't make you freshborn. Going to church can't make you freshborn. No religious experience can make you freshborn. No man can give you the freshbirth. And you can't make yourself freshborn. The freshbirth is not of man, nor of the will of man, nor of the will of the flesh. The freshbirth is a work of God. And how does a man become freshborn? By believing the Wonderful Message of salvation in the Crucified One. If you really believe, God will honor your faith in his Son and freshbirth you."

Peregrinus was still pondering the third point when he turned the corner near his house. He parked in his driveway, put his elbows in his steering wheel, propped his head in his hands, and sat there, his mind still whirling. What was this born afresh stuff? It didn't sound like anything he had ever heard in his church. Why didn't his church teach this stuff? How did a man get freshborn? All he knew was that it had something to do with believing the Wonderful Message. He decided to look into the matter right away. But who should he talk to? The only person he could think of was the pastor of the family church. So he decided to drop in on him next Saturday morning.

CHAPTER TWO

REVEREND QUACKSALVER

Peregrinus Drops In on Quacksalver

On Saturday morning Peregrinus rushed around the house getting ready. He was excited that today he was going to drop in on Quacksalver and get his questions answered. He raced through his shower, wolfed down his breakfast, slammed a cup of coffee, brushed his teeth in about fifteen seconds, whisked a comb through his hair, ran out the door, hopped in his car, raced to Quacksalver's house, parked in a haste, bolted out the car door and down the sidewalk, bounded up Quacksalver's porch stairs, knocked on the door, noticed the rapper and rapped it, and then noticed the doorbell and rang it. While he stood there waiting, he saw Quacksalver through the side glass walking to the door. He was both nervous and expectant.

Peregrinus Spills His Heart

Rev. Quacksalver—Good to see you Peregrinus. Your mom said you might be stopping by.

Peregrinus—Hi, Reverend. Good to see you.

Rev. Quacksalver—Well, come on in and have a seat. I've got a few minutes before the ball game starts. What brings you by today?

Peregrinus—Well, I've been wrestling with questions about stuff like the Big Empty, Sweet Everlasting, and the freshbirth.

Rev. Quacksalver—Those are some deep questions. I have been wrestling with them all my life.

THE GLORIOUS SALVATION MACHINE

Peregrinus—How does a man get his Big Empty filled? I have begun to wonder if it's even possible. The Big Here & Now doesn't fill it. Chasing the Big Dream is a big flop. I don't know a single person who has filled his Big Empty.

Not to mention, what do we gain even if we do manage to fill the Big Empty? Everybody dies. Why play a game which is difficult to win and which, even if we happen to win, strips all our winnings out of our hands at the end of our life?

Rev. Quacksalver—Ah yes, the game of life.

Peregrinus—Life can be so painful. Dreams spring up in our hearts promising to fill the Big Empty if we lay hold of them. Yet we live unfulfilled and die unfulfilled, no matter how hard we try. Most people never even come close to having their dreams fulfilled. The few that do generally see them unravel again. What doesn't unravel in life slips away in death. What's the purpose in that?

Rev. Quacksalver—Ah yes, life is full of mysteries.

Peregrinus—What about Sweet Everlasting? Will it fill the Big Empty? Will we find satisfaction there? What about the freshbirth? I heard on the radio that we must be born afresh if we would have Sweet Everlasting. What is this freshbirth?

Don't Get So Worked Up About Religion

Rev. Quacksalver—Slow down. That is my first piece of advice. Slow way down. Don't get yourself so worked up about religious questions.

Peregrinus—But I thought we were supposed to diligently search for answers.

Rev. Quacksalver—Answers won't do you any good if your heart and brain are spinning like the blades in a blender. Think *slow* — S-L-O-W. The Christian life is not a race. It is a casual walk. It is more important to stop and smell the flowers, and revel in the experience, than it is to know exactly what it is that we are experiencing and where it is that we are going.

Peregrinus—But I have questions that need answers.

Rev. Quacksalver—Peregrinus, there are no questions so important that they need answers now. If answers were that important, you would have been born with an answer book in your back pocket. You just need to take things in Deep Faith.

Peregrinus—Take them in Deep Faith?

Rev. Quacksalver—That's right. You need to Deep Trust the Foggy One. You need to Deep Trust that where you are at now is his ideal place for you. This takes the pressure off you and allows you to search for truth at your leisure. If your don't get around to the search for years, the Foggy One understands. He knows how busy we get down here, and he has us covered. He gives those who Deep Trust him the answers they need in his time, if they really need them. He loves to be trusted.

Peregrinus—But I don't want to wait for years to get answers.

Rev. Quacksalver—If you are not careful, you are going to get yourself in a panic.

Peregrinus—Get myself in a panic?

Rev. Quacksalver—When men get worked up about things like Sweet Everlasting, Awful Everlasting, and the freshbirth, they end up in a panic. They start looking for answers in the Sacred Trust. The next thing you know, they start trusting its statements in a simplistic, literal way and start tossing the Invincible Dogmas and Ironclad Interpretations of the Glorious Salvation Machine in the scrapheap. They claim they don't need the Glorious Salvation Machine to hold their hand and tell them what to believe. They think they can understand the Sacred Trust on their own — even hard stuff like the parables and prophecies. Before you know it, they turn their backs on the church that the Foggy One — in his loving providence — put them in and they walk away. After that their Big Here & Now crumbles into a heap of rubble. Getting worked up about things like the freshbirth, Sweet Everlasting, and Awful Everlasting is just plain unprofitable.

Peregrinus—Say, why do we call God the Foggy One?

Rev. Quacksalver—Because he has hidden himself behind a Sacred Trust so difficult to understand that we ignore most of it and a Big Here & Now so pleasant to the eye that it distracts us. If it weren't for the Important Formality, which we do Sunday morning, I doubt we would even know he was there.

Religious Questions Both Important and Unimportant

Peregrinus—It sounds like you believe that religious questions are not that important and that it doesn't really matter whether or not we find answers.

Rev. Quacksalver—That is exactly what I believe. One of the most important pieces of Deep Significance you will ever learn is that religious questions are, in the overall, big-picture scope of things, just not that important.

Peregrinus—But I thought they were important.

Rev. Quacksalver—Well, yes and no.

Peregrinus—Yes and no? How can they be both?

Rev. Quacksalver—In many ways.

Peregrinus—Okay, so in what sense are they important?

Rev. Quacksalver—They are important because they touch on the God question. That is a wonderful mystery that we must all grapple with.

Peregrinus—If we grapple with it long enough and hard enough, will we find answers?

Rev. Quacksalver—I hope not. That would be tragic. Can you imagine religion with answers?

Peregrinus—But that's what I'm looking for.

Rev. Quacksalver—Trust me, young man. You don't want answers. Answers take the mystery out of religion. If you take the mystery out of religion, then you take the purpose out of religion. If you take the purpose out of religion, you don't have religion anymore. Where would man be without religion? You don't really want to overthrow religion, do you?

Peregrinus—Definitely not.

Rev. Quacksalver—Then you don't want answers.

REVEREND QUACKSALVER

Peregrinus—Okay ... in what sense are religious questions unimportant?

Rev. Quacksalver—They are unimportant for two reasons. *One*, compared to the far more important things of the Big Here & Now which demand our attention, religious questions are just not that important. *Two*, the Foggy One has given us an obscure tome of a book that the colossal intellect in the pulpit only partially understands and the meager minds in the pew cannot understand at all.

Peregrinus—In other words, we don't have time to search for answers to our questions. And even if we did have the time, we can't understand the answer book — the Sacred Trust.

Rev. Quacksalver—That's exactly right. And the Nice God knows our dilemma and understands.

Peregrinus—But what if a man makes the time and looks for answers for himself in the Sacred Trust? Mr. Radio Preacher says that the man in the pew can read and understand it.

Rev. Quacksalver—If the man in the pew attempts to answer religious questions for himself, he will make a mess of things. He will flounder in the Sacred Trust like a hippo in quick sand, striving to make sense out of what he can only make nonsense out of. It is okay to dabble in religious questions once in while, but you absolutely must leave the answers to the experts. Your duty is to sit through the Important Formality every week.

Peregrinus—I understand the part about going to church. But I don't understand the part about not seeking answers.

Rev. Quacksalver—The more answers you get, the more you will realize that answers don't matter. But you had several questions. How about we tackle them one by one?

Don't Worry About the Big Empty

Rev. Quacksalver—Lets start with everybody's favorite, the Big Empty. My advice — don't worry about it. Nobody fills it. All men search for meaning and fulfillment. That's the glory of the mystery of life. It is all about the quest. If there were no quest, there would be no meaning, no mystery, and no purpose.

THE GLORIOUS SALVATION MACHINE

If man found fulfillment, there would be no more purpose in life. Life is a journey. Life is a quest. Go sail your ship on the big ocean of life, looking for meaning and fulfillment. Don't stop looking. It is out there, somewhere, elusive and beautiful. Sail big. Sail bold. Sail till you're old. Sail until your dying breath. Sail. Sail. Sail.

Peregrinus—But doesn't it seem kind of odd for God to make us with a Big Empty and not intend to fill it?

Rev. Quacksalver—Don't let yourself get caught up with theoretical questions on the matter. I deal with hard, cold facts. I've been pastoring in the Glorious Salvation Machine for over forty years, and I have yet to see a single person who actually filled their Big Empty. Oh, I've seen quite a few make great professions, but without exception their professions were vastly superior to their possessions.

Peregrinus—Well, I can't argue with your observation, but I still have this hunch that God wants to fill it. Maybe we are doing something wrong, and that's why we aren't filling it.

Rev. Quacksalver—Facts are facts, and I don't deal in any kind of speculation. I like to be practical. Don't you think that if the Foggy One intended for men to have their Big Empty filled, that there would be lots of people in the Glorious Salvation Machine who no longer had a Big Empty?

Peregrinus—Well, that does sound reasonable.

Rev. Quacksalver—It is beyond reasonable. Consider the ugly alternative. If we start with the assumption that the Foggy One intends to fill our Big Empties, and then look at the fact that nobody in the Glorious Salvation Machine fills their Big Empty, we're forced to conclude one of two things. Either God is unable to fill the Big Empty, or the Glorious Salvation Machine is so far departed from God that it cannot minister unto men the things designed by God to fill the Big Empty.

Peregrinus—That's definitely an ugly alternative.

Rev. Quacksalver—Don't worry about the Big Empty. It can't be filled. Get over it. Personally, I believe the Big Empty is nothing but a big motivator to inspire us in our quest. It is just wind for our sails, so we can sail the wide open seas of the Big Here & Now in search of meaning and purpose.

Peregrinus—A motivator?

Rev. Quacksalver—Yes, a motivator. So be motivated. Give yourself to the quest to find purpose in the Big Here & Now. Search for those elusive and mysterious answers that are hard to find and even harder to understand. Learn to rejoice in the mystery. Only then will the quest and the answers make sense.

Peregrinus—So I won't ever fill my Big Empty?

Rev. Quacksalver—I'm afraid not. The fullness of the Big Empty exists only as a theoretical construct on the frontiers of the Mystic Plane.

Peregrinus—That seems like such an empty answer for such a big question.

Rev. Quacksalver—It only looks empty. If you peel back the outward emptiness, you will discover that it is filled with Deep Meaning.

Peregrinus—But years of ministry filled with Deep Meaning haven't given me any meaning or purpose.

Rev. Quacksalver—Whose fault is that? Am I to be blamed if people don't appreciate Droning like they used to? Is it my fault if they fail to see how much Deep Meaning there is in it? Nobody takes Glorious Salvation Machine preachers seriously anymore. People show up on Sundays to do their Weekly Duty and just sit there, fidgeting, yawning, and watching the clock.

Don't Worry About Sweet Everlasting

Peregrinus—How about Sweet Everlasting?

Rev. Quacksalver—Ah yes. Sweet Everlasting. One of the most endearing, heartwarming doctrines in the creed.

Peregrinus—So what is it? How do I get there?

Rev. Quacksalver—Peregrinus. You need to relax. Worrying about these things doesn't change anything. Sweet Everlasting isn't going anywhere. It will still be there. So do yourself a favor and stop worrying about Sweet Everlasting.

THE GLORIOUS SALVATION MACHINE

Peregrinus—Don't worry about it? Is that your answer for everything? I thought we were supposed to set our hearts on Sweet Everlasting and focus on it and make a big deal about it? I heard on the radio a couple weeks ago ...

Rev. Quacksalver—Getting your religion from the radio is dangerous. Mr. Radio Preacher has a reputation for majoring in the minors and minoring in the majors. We need to major in the majors. That means the important Big Here & Now stuff that demands our attention. As for the minor stuff, like Sweet Everlasting, we need to "Let go and let God." We need to put it in the back seat and quit worrying about it. If we get around to it, we get around to it; if we don't, we don't.

Peregrinus—Okay, let's say we make the Big Here & Now our main focus and put Sweet Everlasting in the back seat. But still, shouldn't Sweet Everlasting get some serious attention from time to time? Like once a week? Or once a month?

Scholarly Doubts About Sweet Everlasting

Rev. Quacksalver—Your approach is too simplistic. Merely putting Sweet Everlasting in the back seat will not give you a proper perspective on the subject. You also have to deal with a serious information problem.

First of all, there is a significant lack of information on Sweet Everlasting in the Sacred Trust. There are only a few, scattered bits and pieces that touch on the subject.

Secondly, the scant information we do have is beset with difficulties. The most brilliant theologians in the Glorious Salvation Machine cannot reach a consensus on what we should conclude from the discordant, confusing mishmash of source material. Chew on the ramifications of that for awhile. If the Foggy One intended for us to make a big deal out of Sweet Everlasting, don't you think he would have made things a little easier to figure out?

Peregrinus—But isn't it reasonable to think that God intended the Sweet Everlasting passages to be understandable to the average working man like myself?

Rev. Quacksalver—You treat this matter as if a smart kid with a copy of the Sacred Trust could figure it out. That's a slap in the face to the Glorious Salvation Machine and the Big Cheese. The fact is, there are many subjects in the Sacred Trust on which God, for reasons known only to himself, has revealed his mind in a way which veils his mind. It is not your job to find clarity, order, and reason in this obscurity. It is your job to accept the fact that the Foggy One has communicated his Deep Significance to us in a Sacred Trust veiled in fog.

Peregrinus—But is it possible that God intended for us to fill our Big Empties with Sweet Everlasting, even if it is veiled in fog, and we can't know anything about it clearly?

Rev. Quacksalver—I can't say anything on the subject with certainty. I can't say *yes* because that assumes that there is some sort of literal Sweet Everlasting which could fill the Big Empty and that in our future existence we will still be people with a Big Empty capacity — of which I am skeptical. I can't say *no* because that too obviously tramples on the universal hope that the Big Empty will be filled in the next life. If we openly deny future hope, men will begin to wonder if there is any purpose in going to church and doing the Weekly Duty. So I'll just have to give you my unbiased, scholarly, skeptical doubt that we can know anything with certainty about Sweet Everlasting.

Peregrinus—Why do I get the feeling that in the Glorious Salvation Machine intellectually dressed doubts are more esteemed than plain knowledge of what the Sacred Trust says?

Rev. Quacksalver—Because they are. Apart from doubting the plain statement and meaning of the Sacred Trust, there is no scholarship. Scholarship starts with the question, "Hath God said?"

As one of my professors used to say, "Scholarship is dripping with doubt. Those that know, really don't know; and those that don't know, really do know." The less you know for sure about God, the more you own him for what he really is — the great mysterious Foggy One. The less you know for sure about what the Sacred Trust means, the more you own it for what it really is — a mysterious book designed to communicate Deep Significance about the Foggy One and his Foggy ways.

Rightly Deep Significating the Sacred Trust

Peregrinus—I still think we should be able to know some things about God and Sweet Everlasting with certainty — at least some basic things.

Rev. Quacksalver—Be careful. You are definitely fixated on understanding the Sacred Trust. All fixations are dangerous. They lead to instability and extremes. And no fixation is more dangerous than fixation on the Sacred Trust. When men get fixated on the Sacred Trust and start reading it earnestly and start taking what it says literally, they lose their excitement for maximizing the wonderful opportunities which the Big Here & Now holds out to them.

Peregrinus—Well, I have spent a lot of time thinking about Sweet Everlasting lately.

Rev. Quacksalver—Why would you spend lots of time thinking about a subject we know almost nothing about and can know almost nothing about?

Peregrinus—A while back I heard Mr. Radio Preacher quote a verse from the Gospels which said I should quit laying up treasure in the Big Here & Now and start laying up treasure in Sweet Everlasting. That verse went home to my heart. I have not been able to quit thinking about it. Since that day, I have spent a lot of time reading the Sacred Trust, trying to find out more about Sweet Everlasting and how to get there.

Rev. Quacksalver—How can you possibly understand the things you read in the Sacred Trust? Have you been to a Deep Signification Indoctrination Institution?

Peregrinus—No.

Rev. Quacksalver—Then you don't have the tools you need to rightly Deep Significate the Sacred Trust. You need to be able to rightly eviscerate, manipulate, twisticate, and evaporate it from beginning to end. This cannot be done without proper training and indoctrination.

Peregrinus—Well, I'm not trying to intrude on the place of the Big Cheese.

Rev. Quacksalver—Oh, but you are.

Peregrinus—But what if the Glorious Salvation Machine has over-sophisticated things?

Rev. Quacksalver—I have my highly educated doubts about that. From time immemorial, the biggest danger has been over-simplifying the Sacred Trust, not over-sophisticating it.

Sweet Everlasting Is Only a Religious Concept

Peregrinus—But what if Sweet Everlasting is supposed to fill the Big Empty? What if God really intended for us to find meaning, purpose, and fulfillment in Sweet Everlasting? Isn't it possible that somehow, someway, someday God will fill the Big Empty with good stuff in Sweet Everlasting?

Rev. Quacksalver—Your problem is that you are confusing reality and religion. The stuff of the Big Here & Now is reality. Stuff like Sweet Everlasting is religion. If the Big Empty can be filled, it can only be filled with reality.

Peregrinus—But why can't Sweet Everlasting be real in the same way that everything in the Big Here & Now is real? Why can't it be as real as the things we touch, see, smell, and taste every day in our Daily Grind?

Rev. Quacksalver—Because Sweet Everlasting is only a religious concept. It is only religion.

Peregrinus—Only religion? You mean it isn't real?

Rev. Quacksalver—I didn't say it wasn't real. I said it was only religion. Religion is real in its own way. But it is not real in the same way that reality is real.

Peregrinus—If Sweet Everlasting is real, but not real in the same way the Big Here & Now is real, then how can it really be real?

Rev. Quacksalver—These kinds of questions are why men go to Deep Signification Indoctrination Institutions. You will just have to take my word for it.

The things we can touch, see, hear, smell, and taste down here in the Big Here & Now belong to *real reality*. They are everyday facts that we believe with everyday faith. This reality we refer to as the *Daily Grind*.

The teachings of religion belong to *religious reality*. This is a very different kind of reality in which things are real in a very different way. Matters of religious reality need no proof. In fact, they may defy proof and fly in the face of facts. They are independent of actual history and actual science. These realities must be accepted by Deep Faith. This reality we refer to as the *Mystic Plane*.

Peregrinus—So there are two completely different realities?

Rev. Quacksalver—That's right. You just have to grow up and deal with ambiguity.

Peregrinus—So I can't take what the Sacred Trust says about Sweet Everlasting at face value? I can't treat Sweet Everlasting as a future Daily Grind reality every bit as real as the things in our present Daily Grind like horses, rivers, mountains, trees, campfires, and trout fishing?

Rev. Quacksalver—I'm afraid not, Peregrinus. I'm sorry. I admire your strong spiritual inclinations. I empathize with your vibrant aspirations after Sweet Everlasting. But you are in over your head. Sweet Everlasting must not be conceived of as a real existence in a real universe made up of real matter where real people will touch, see, smell, hear, and taste real stuff in the same Daily Grind way that they do now. Sweet Everlasting is a matter of the Mystic Plane, not the Daily Grind. To import Daily Grind into Sweet Everlasting is theological taboo.

The Significance and Substance of Sweet Everlasting

Peregrinus—What are we supposed to do, then, with Sweet Everlasting?

Rev. Quacksalver—We use it the way that the Foggy One intended for us to use it — as a religious security blanket. That probably is, after all, its most likely significance. It was given to us as a security blanket to help us endure the disappointment and pain we face every day in the Big Here & Now.

Peregrinus—Are you saying, then, that there really isn't a Sweet Everlasting?

Rev. Quacksalver—No, I am not saying that. The existential reality of Sweet Everlasting is not in question. It is the nature of Sweet Everlasting that gives us trouble. We know very little about what it is and what it will be like. But we do, thankfully, know two things.

One, we know that the religious and sentimental significance of the Sweet Everlasting passages in the Sacred Trust can most likely be retained relatively intact, at least in most instances, with a high degree of probability.

Two, we know that it is probably reasonable for us to infer that Sweet Everlasting will be more Nirvanic than classically Heavenic. It will be more a state of existence than a place. It will be more nothing than something. There will probably not be any manifestation or recognition of personality. There will probably not be a bodily resurrection, but rather freedom from the limitations of the physical and the mental. We will likely enjoy unadulterated freedom from feeling and thinking.

Peregrinus—That doesn't sound real inviting to me.

Rev. Quacksalver—Well, we have to learn to accept things for what they most probably could well likely be, based on the assumptions and inferences of accepted authorities, who have demonstrated a healthy dose of rationalistic skepticism when it comes to matters of religion. We can't just decide that Sweet Everlasting is a Daily Grind reality, just because the apparent Daily Grind treatment it gets in the Sacred Trust appeals to us. That is getting our doctrine from our feelings.

THE GLORIOUS SALVATION MACHINE

Good People Go to Sweet Everlasting

Peregrinus—Well, whatever Sweet Everlasting is, I want to make sure I go there. I don't want to go to Awful Everlasting.

Rev. Quacksalver—You don't need to worry about that. Regardless of what Sweet Everlasting is, you will be there.

Peregrinus—What makes you so sure?

Rev. Quacksalver—Because good people go to Sweet Everlasting and bad people go to Awful Everlasting. That is a universally accepted axiom.

Peregrinus—But ...

Rev. Quacksalver—But nothing. Good people go to Sweet Everlasting. That means almost all of mankind will go to Sweet Everlasting. Since you belong to almost all of mankind, that means you will be in Sweet Everlasting. This is simple logic. This is like the ABC's. We're not talking rocket science here.

Peregrinus—But ...

Rev. Quacksalver—Not to mention, many of our scholars suspect that there is no Awful Everlasting and that everyone will go to Sweet Everlasting. That increases your odds even more.

Peregrinus—I thought the Sacred Trust taught that few are saved and most are lost. Doesn't it say that the road which leads to Sweet Everlasting is narrow and the road which leads to Awful Everlasting is broad? I have heard Mr. Radio Preacher quote that verse a few times.

Rev. Quacksalver—Listening to Mr. Radio Preacher is a moral hazard. He makes vigorous appeals to the Sacred Trust, trying to get people worked up over Sweet Everlasting and Awful Everlasting. That isn't good. When people get worked up about such things, they quit maximizing the Big Here & Now. They become so Sweet Everlasting minded that they are no Big Here & Now good.

Peregrinus—But shouldn't we be concerned about Sweet Everlasting and Awful Everlasting?

Rev. Quacksalver—I might say *yes* if we were talking about really bad people like serial killers, but we're not. We're talking about good people who were raised in the Glorious Salvation Machine and sit through the Important Formality at least once in a blue moon.

Peregrinus—So I don't need to worry?

Rev. Quacksalver—Not in the least. I have known your parents for years. They are good people. Your father is a prominent businessman who is active in civic matters and often sits through the Important Formality. Your mother is a devout woman who faithfully does the Weekly Duty. As for you, you were born and raised in the Glorious Salvation Machine. I administered the Sprinkle Form to you myself. What do you have to fear?

Keeping God Out of the Daily Grind

Peregrinus—But what about the freshbirth? Don't we have to be born afresh to be saved? Mr. Radio Preacher says no man will obtain Sweet Everlasting who is not freshborn. He quotes verse after verse straight out of the Sacred Trust to prove this point. His favorite verse is, "Unless a man be born afresh, he cannot see Sweet Everlasting."

Rev. Quacksalver—You are walking on thin ice. Such verses in the hands of reckless men like Mr. Radio Preacher are dangerous. They can lead you into serious error. They can hurt you.

Peregrinus—How can believing what the Sacred Trust says lead a man into error?

Rev. Quacksalver—The problem isn't believing what the Sacred Trust says. We all agree that it teaches that salvation is through the freshbirth. The problem is understanding what the Sacred Trust means. What is the freshbirth and how does a man obtain it?

Mr. Radio Preacher entices the gullible to believe that the freshbirth is a powerful work of God that can only be obtained by heart-believing the Wonderful Message. But you can't go down this Daily Grind road — actually requiring heart-faith, which actually results in a real work of God in the heart, which actually makes significant changes in a man's Daily Grind — without dire consequences.

Peregrinus—Well, Mr. Radio Preacher says that the Daily Grind approach really works.

Rev. Quacksalver—Do you believe everything you hear? Are you really that gullible? Do you want false religion or true religion? False religion is based on something *man does* in the Daily Grind: like heart-believing the Wonderful Message. True religion is based on something *God does* on the Mystic Plane: like pouring out God Magic in the Sprinkle Form.

I am sick and tired of men like Mr. Radio Preacher getting folks worked up about Daily Grind religion where men are supposed to *do, do, do*. Men are supposed to heart-believe in the Crucified One. Men are supposed to manifest a freshbirth which is a real renewal of their heart. Men are supposed to actually walk with God, talk with God, serve God, and obey God in their Daily Grind. This Daily Grind message reminds me of hucksters peddling snake oil.

Peregrinus—But don't we want God in our Daily Grind? Don't we want to know him in a Daily Grind way like we know all the people we know?

Rev. Quacksalver—Trust me. You don't want God in your Daily Grind. When you let him in, he can't stay out of trouble. You wouldn't believe the mess you will get. Your right-side up will get turned upside down. The Big Here & Now around you will get stirred up like a swarm of hornets, angry because you disturbed their nest. This is why we refer to God as the Big Troublemaker when he gets involved in our Daily Grind.

Life is much more pleasant when we keep God out of the Daily Grind and in the Mystic Plane. When we exclude him from our Daily Grind, he behaves himself and doesn't cause any problems. He meekly presides over the Sprinkle Form, the Important Formality, weddings, funerals, potlucks, bake sales, annual picnics, softball games, and other church functions, and other than that pretty much minds his own business. This is why we refer to God as the Nice God when we keep him in the Mystic Plane.

The Sacred Trust Is Deep and Dangerous

Peregrinus—I have a hard time believing that we will hurt ourselves if we take the Sacred Trust at face value.

Rev. Quacksalver—A little clear thinking will dispel that nonsense. Is the Sacred Trust a sword?

Peregrinus—Yes.

Rev. Quacksalver—Is a sword like a knife, except that it is bigger and more dangerous?

Peregrinus—Yes.

Rev. Quacksalver—Didn't your mother tell you that children shouldn't play with knives because they can hurt themselves?

Peregrinus—Yes.

Rev. Quacksalver—Aren't you a child when it comes to understanding the Sacred Trust?

Peregrinus—Yes.

Rev. Quacksalver—Then why aren't you afraid to pick it up and play with it?

Peregrinus—I don't know how to answer that argument. But I have a hard time believing that reading and studying the Sacred Trust on my own will hurt me.

Rev. Quacksalver—For crying out loud, the Sacred Trust is Deep and dangerous. How can it not hurt you? You either need professional training or guidance by men with professional training. You just can't rush into the Sacred Trust and interpret its names, dates, places, events, facts, and stories as if you were interpreting the Sports page in the newspaper.

Peregrinus—Why not? What's the difference?

Rev. Quacksalver—The names, dates, places, events, facts, and stories in the Sports section are Daily Grind real. But the names, dates, places, events, facts, and stories in the Sacred Trust are a mixed bag. Some are Daily Grind real; most are Mystic Plane real. And there are no clear rules to determine which are which. Even the experts have a hard time classifying most of the material. To complicate matters further, most of the material that is Daily Grind real has been so colored by Mystic Plane reality that we have a hard time figuring out what to do with it. How can you face this discombobulation honestly and claim that reading and studying the Sacred Trust on your own can't hurt you?

Mystic Plane Material Increases the Value of the Sacred Trust

Peregrinus—But if much of the Sacred Trust is Mystic Plane real and not really-truly real like the stories in the Sports page, then why waste our time with them? If they aren't real events that really took place in the Daily Grind, aren't they worthless?

Rev. Quacksalver—Absolutely not. Mystic Plane material does not decrease the value of the Sacred Trust. It increases it.

Peregrinus—How's that?

Rev. Quacksalver—Every departure from historic fact and strict truth is an intentional Deep Illumination to help us get a better handle on the Deep Significance that the Foggy One wants to communicate to us.

For instance, many of the people, dates, places, and events in the Sacred Trust are invented, altered, or embellished to better bring out the Deep Significance. And most of the beliefs and teachings found in the Sacred Trust are either partly or purely the imagination of man, which again better brings out the Deep Significance.

Peregrinus—It sounds to me like you're saying that the Sacred Trust is a collection of myths and legends.

Rev. Quacksalver—That is putting the Mystic Plane material in negative light. When we view the Mystic Plane material in its proper and positive light, it is not mere myth and legend. It is Deep Illumination consecrated by the Foggy One for the communication of Deep Significance. You have to look beyond the story to get the real story.

REVEREND QUACKSALVER

What We Don't Like or Don't Believe Is Mystic Plane

Peregrinus—So if the Sacred Trust is a confusing mixture of Daily Grind real and Mystic Plane real, how are we even supposed to use it?

Rev. Quacksalver—Despite the difficulty of the subject on the scholarly level, it isn't that difficult on the practical level.

Any passage that we don't like or don't believe, we are free to regard as Mystic Plane content. Some of this Mystic Plane material we can still use — as we use Aesop's Fables — for lessons on things like morality or hope. But most of it has no practical value, so we do very little with it aside from admiring its Deepness, Deep Trusting that if the Foggy One wanted us to do more with it, he would have made it easier to understand and apply.

Most of the Daily Grind material has no practical application either. It just doesn't have a lot to say to the modern man in the modern world. That was then. This is now.

But we are happy to use any passage, whether Daily Grind or Mystic Plane, that lends itself to the promotion of hallowed Big Here & Now purposes as business, politics, sports, success-motivation, Innocuous Minimum religion, and the Glorious Salvation Machine.

Peregrinus—Well, Mr. Radio Preacher says that the entire Sacred Trust is Daily Grind true, that all of is profitable for the modern man, and that the average man can understand all of it.

Rev. Quacksalver—The Big Cheese have devoted their lives to the pursuit of Deep Scholarship, so they can rightly Deep Significate the Sacred Trust. Doesn't it seem a bit arrogant for you to think that you can understand the Sacred Trust on your own without the help of such scholarship? I suppose you think you can build your own spaceship and fly to the moon too?

If you keep listening to Mr. Radio Preacher, thumbing your nose at Deep Scholarship, and reading the Sacred Trust in the same Daily Grind way that you read the Sports section in the newspaper, you will end up joining a Haven where simplistic confidence in the Sacred Trust is everything and the wisdom of the Big Here & Now is nothing.

The Sprinkle Form and the Freshbirth

Peregrinus—Can we go back to the freshbirth? Somewhere along the line we got sidetracked. The Sacred Trust says I have to be freshborn. How come I have never heard you talk about the freshbirth?

Rev. Quacksalver—Yes, men do need to be freshborn. But you have nothing to worry about. You are freshborn. You were freshborn when you went through the Sprinkle Form as a baby. And the reason I don't talk about the freshbirth is because it is counterproductive. When people start thinking about, talking about, and worrying about the freshbirth, they usually end up in a Haven. That is not good.

Peregrinus—But …

Rev. Quacksalver—There are no buts. Your freshbirth is a settled matter. It is a simple fact of history. The Nice God has chosen to freshbirth men by God Magic in the Sprinkle Form. You did the Sprinkle Form when you were a baby. Therefore, you are freshborn by God Magic. It is as simple as that.

Peregrinus—But Mr. Radio Preacher says that the freshbirth comes through heart-faith in the Wonderful Message.

Rev. Quacksalver—Nonsense. The freshbirth is the Free Gift of the Nice God. There is no connection between it and human effort. No human effort can obtain the freshbirth, not even something as apparently noble as heart-faith.

Peregrinus—But Mr. Radio Preacher says that the freshbirth changes people in a way that makes them a new person. They lead a new life in the Big Here & Now. I am not a new person. I haven't been changed. I am not leading a new life.

Rev. Quacksalver—Again, I must emphasize that fact that the freshbirth is the Free Gift of the Nice God. There is no connection between it and human effort, not even noble effort like heart-faith. Effort does not belong in the freshbirth equation at all: not as a condition of salvation; not as an evidence of salvation. We don't have to see a person leading a new life to know that he has been born afresh.

Peregrinus—So my lack of change doesn't call the reality or validity of my freshbirth into question?

Rev. Quacksalver—That's right. In the Sprinkle Form the Nice God pours out his God Magic and — Shazam! — the infant is freshborn. We just have to trust the Nice God in this matter and take our freshbirth as a matter of Deep Faith.

Peregrinus—But what about having a real relationship with the Crucified One? Mr. Radio Preacher says men need to have a real relationship with the Crucified One and that they can only have that if they have been born afresh by heart-faith.

Rev. Quacksalver—Don't let yourself get bamboozled by spiritual sounding talk about having a real relationship with the Crucified One. This message sounds reasonable, but it tramples on the truth of salvation by God Magic without human effort. Make no mistake, heart-faith is human effort. Heart-faith is Dead Works. Only in the Sprinkle Form do we find God Magic without human effort. Therefore, only in the Sprinkle Form do men receive the freshbirth without human effort.

God Magic vs. Real-Relationship Grace

Peregrinus—I get the feeling that the concept of God Magic you are defending is not the same concept as the grace that Mr. Radio Preacher teaches.

Rev. Quacksalver—You are right. They are not the same thing. Why do you think I have been ranting and raving for the past half hour? Mr. Radio Preacher and the Havenmongers teach the bad, bad, nasty-bad heresy that the freshbirth comes through *real-relationship grace*. We in the Glorious Salvation Machine, on the contrary, believe and teach that the freshbirth comes by *God Magic*.

Peregrinus—So there is more than one kind of grace?

Rev. Quacksalver—Think God Magic, son, not grace. God Magic is a definite concept. Grace is an indefinite concept. There are many false notions of grace out there. God Magic is

THE GLORIOUS SALVATION MACHINE

the only concept of grace that is right. It is the true grace of the Nice God.

Peregrinus—So what's the difference between God Magic and real-relationship grace?

Rev. Quacksalver—In the real-relationship grace system, men are freshborn by grace (the favor and kindness of God) through heart-faith in the Crucified One, which brings them into a real-relationship with him.

In the God Magic system, men are freshborn by God Magic (a mysterious outpouring of a mysterious elixir) in the Sprinkle Form, which brings them into a real-religionship with the Nice God.

Peregrinus—But why do you prefer God Magic over real-relationship grace?

Rev. Quacksalver—Because we dislike real-relationship grace.

Peregrinus—Why do you dislike real-relationship grace?

Rev. Quacksalver—For several reasons. *One*, we don't want a real-relationship with God; we want religion. We already have more relationships than we know what to do with.

Two, real-relationship grace bulldozes its way into a man's Daily Grind, changing the way he thinks and lives, and creating an uproar around him. This is totally unacceptable. Religion is supposed to be a personal matter, not a public matter.

Three, when folks under the influence of the real-relationship grace message don't see change in a man's heart and life, they conclude that he is not born afresh. That is requiring men to do stuff. That is the bad, bad, nasty-bad heresy of Dead Works.

Peregrinus—And why do you like God Magic?

Rev. Quacksalver—For several reasons. *One*, it gives us the religion we crave — a religious-relationship with the Sweet One in the Mystic Plane, which we are able to maintain with even the feeblest efforts at the Innocuous Minimum.

Two, it doesn't create an uproar in our Daily Grind because it doesn't make significant changes in our hearts and lives, unlike the disastrous results men experience when they pursue a real-relationship with the Crucified One.

Three, it maintains a consistent stand against Dead Works because it doesn't require heart-faith as either a condition or an evidence of the freshbirth.

Peregrinus—I can definitely see why men prefer God Magic over real-relationship grace.

Rev. Quacksalver—I'm glad to hear that. The difference between real-relationship grace and God Magic is paramount. It is the most important difference between the Havens and the Glorious Salvation Machine.

Religious Effort and Activity Is Okay

Peregrinus—So if we see any effort or activity on man's part, that short-circuits God's design to dispense salvation by God Magic apart from works?

Rev. Quacksalver—Not quite. The problem doesn't lie in the *fact* of effort and activity. The problem lies in the *kind* of effort and activity. Do the efforts and activities promote real-relationship grace? Or do they promote God Magic?

The fact is, there must be religious ceremonies and forms, or there is no religion. This is axiomatic. And the Sprinkle Form — technically known as the Passive Form because those going through it are not doing anything to obtain salvation — is the most important religious ceremony of all. Babies must get Wet Sprinkled in a special moment of Passive Exposure, or there is no Sprinkling of God Magic. And where there is no God Magic, there is no salvation.

The efforts we are trying to avoid are things like seeking God in dead earnest, pursuing God like your eternal destiny depends on it, turning to God with a whole heart, taking the Word of God dead-serious, and searching for understanding as for hid treasure. These things promote real-relationship grace. And real-relationship grace is taboo, for it turns a man's Daily Grind upside down and tramples on the Innocuous Minimum.

THE GLORIOUS SALVATION MACHINE

The Passive Form Is Religion

Peregrinus—It sounds like the Passive Form is an important part of religion.

Rev. Quacksalver—The Passive Form is not merely a vital part of religion; it *is* religion. The Invincible Dogma which we know as the Great Illumination says that all effort is sin. And *all* means *all*. Even the apparently noble effort of heart-faith is sin. This means that man's only legitimate option for salvation is God Magic in the Passive Form.

Peregrinus—And that's why you use the Sprinkle Form.

Rev. Quacksalver—Correct. Consistency with the passivity of the Passive Form is why I belong to a Sprinkle Form church. There is zero chance that the infant undergoing the Sprinkle Form is going to do anything unto salvation — with his hands or his heart — and thus undermine the required passivity.

Peregrinus—I'm sorry, but requiring men to be passive in a Passive Form to obtain salvation makes no sense to me.

Rev. Quacksalver—It doesn't have to make sense to you. Whether or not something is true is not determined by man's sense and reason. It is determined by comparing it to known truth. The truth has been handed down to us in the Invincible Dogmas. Whatever agrees with these Dogmas is true; whatever disagrees with them is false.

Peregrinus—Well, I certainly understand why men prefer Passive Form salvation.

Rev. Quacksalver—The Passive path is no mere preference. It is the Deep Truth of the Nice God. And how glad we are that Deep Truth is easy to find and pleasant to follow — it tickles men's ears. That's why men prefer it. Just follow the tickle and you can't go wrong.

The Innocuous Minimum

Peregrinus—Well, I must admit that the difference between the God Magic which the Glorious Salvation Machine preaches and the grace that Mr. Radio Preacher preaches is so great that if you are right, he is wrong.

REVEREND QUACKSALVER

Rev. Quacksalver—You're right. He is wrong. And don't think for a moment that salvation by God Magic is the only subject where Mr. Radio Preacher tramples on the truth. He ridicules the Innocuous Minimum, too, and claims that it is not a legitimate expression of Christianity. He slams it as a death-trap for the religious and a dearth-trap for real believers. He says real believers who fall into the Innocuous Minimum mode need to repent of their lukewarmness, or they will face the disciplining hand of God for their lack of fruit.

Peregrinus—I know that I should know what the Innocuous Minimum is because I've heard you mention it in your Sunday morning Dronings. But I must confess that I never paid close attention when you were Droning. Can you refresh me?

Rev. Quacksalver—I would be offended by your admission, but I have long since come to grips with the fact that most folks only go through the motions of the Weekly Duty. They sit in the pew like bumps on a log and let the content of the Droning go in one ear and out the other.

The Innocuous Minimum was given to us by the Nice God as a proxy for discipleship. It enables men to meet their God-obligations in a Big Here & Now that demands virtually all of their time and attention. It consists of two parts: the Passive Form and the Important Formality. Those who have done the Passive Form and sit through the Important Formality at least once in a blue moon are accepted by the Nice God as faithful Christians.

Peregrinus—But maybe we're not supposed to go down the Innocuous Minimum path. Maybe we're supposed to go down the path of devotion and diligence. Maybe we're supposed to live as if what we get in the next life depends on how we live in this life.

Rev. Quacksalver—Are you going to let the fearmongers run your life? Are you going to let them scare you into going through life with an extreme focus on the life to come? Listen, Awful Everlasting and Sweet Everlasting are not Daily Grind realities, they are Mystic Plane morality themes.

THE GLORIOUS SALVATION MACHINE

Peregrinus—But how do you know for sure?

Rev. Quacksalver—The proof is in the pudding. We don't like the fruit we see when men treat Awful Everlasting and Sweet Everlasting as Daily Grind realities. They become fanatics. For instance, they say *good-bye* to the Nice God and *hello* to the Big Troublemaker. They start preaching to family, relatives, friends, neighbors, grocery clerks, coworkers, strangers, and anyone else they can find that the Passive Form is a scam, that the Innocuous Minimum is a sham, and that men must believe in the Crucified One with real-relationship faith.

The God Box

Peregrinus—Well, I can identify with the fanatics who talk about a real-relationship with the Crucified One. My present life and religion don't satisfy. I follow Innocuous Minimum religion, I indulge the fun stuff of the Big Here & Now, and I am not satisfied.

Rev. Quacksalver—The fact that you are dissatisfied with your religious experience doesn't mean that you don't have genuine religion. Religious experience and the genuineness of religion are two different things. Genuine religion is based on God Magic in the Passive Form, not feelings. You did the Sprinkle Form, therefore you have genuine religion. So your present problem is an *experience* problem, not a *genuineness* problem; it concerns your *satisfaction*, not your *salvation*. If you are not satisfied with your present experience, then you need to go Deeper. Do you want to go Deeper?

Peregrinus—Well, yeah. I guess so.

Rev. Quacksalver—If you really want to go Deeper, then I suggest you try the God Box.

Peregrinus—The God Box? What's that?

Rev. Quacksalver—The God Box is an unobtrusive display of religion that the Deeply religious carry around with them as they go about their daily business in the Big Here & Now. It allows them to inoffensively display their religiousness.

Peregrinus—Okay, so how do I get a God Box?

REVEREND QUACKSALVER

Rev. Quacksalver—You make one. People customize their own God Boxes according to their own tastes. I suggest you start with the extended model and add a couple common bells and whistles.

Peregrinus—What's the extended model?

Rev. Quacksalver—It is the basic model of attending the Important Formality faithfully every week plus the addition of a weekly Dabble Study.

Peregrinus—What's a Dabble Study?

Rev. Quacksalver—A Dabble Study is when folks get together to study the Sacred Trust in an Innocuous Minimum environment. There are three rules they must follow to ensure that they only dabble in the Sacred Trust. *One*, they must avoid subjects that might rock the boat. *Two*, they must conduct the study with the same superficial spirit and social-club levity that characterizes the Important Formality. And *three*, they must employ an Innocuous study guide that has them look up a few isolated verses in the Sacred Trust, rather than actually reading and studying it. We absolutely cannot have men handling the Sacred Trust in a way that strays beyond the permitted trifling.

Peregrinus—What bells and whistles do you suggest?

Rev. Quacksalver—You should get yourself one of the racy new paraphrases of the Sacred Trust, start wearing a Sweet One bracelet — the most common variety says, "WWSOD" — and drop generic God-phrases from time to time.

If you want to add a little more ostentation, you can wear a Sweet One t-shirt. My favorite one shows a bottle of soda and says, "Thirsty? Nothing satisfies like a Sweet One."

Perhaps you could even carry a hot new bestseller and set it in conspicuous places — something like *How To Keep God in Your Pocket and Still Have Room For Your Cell Phone*.

Peregrinus—Will that fill my Big Empty?

Rev. Quacksalver—Probably not. But it should satisfy your religious desires and salve your conscience a little.

Peregrinus—Well, I'll give it a shot. I don't have anything to lose.

THE GLORIOUS SALVATION MACHINE

Rev. Quacksalver—Oh, my-oh-my, the time has flown by. My ballgame is going to start in a couple minutes. But I want to say one more thing real quick.

Peregrinus—Yeah, what's that?

Rev. Quacksalver—Don't let God out of the box.

Peregrinus—What do you mean by that?

Rev. Quacksalver—Many who start carrying a God Box are disappointed when those around them disapprove. They get shook. Their religion takes a hit. But the problem is not the Box. The problem is opening the Box and letting God out. When you let him out, he offends people. He just does not know how to keep his mouth shut. He starts telling people what they are supposed to believe and how they ought to live. Things can get ugly in a hurry.

Trust me. Opening the Box is counterproductive. You'll shoot yourself in the foot. You'll undo what you are trying to do with the Innocuous Minimum — which is to be serious about religion without offending your fellow man. Never forget the Platinum Rule: "It is the ultimate taboo to offend people or make them uncomfortable with your religion." Men want the Nice God. We give them the Nice God.

Peregrinus—Well, thanks for your time, Reverend. I'll see you on Sunday.

Peregrinus shook his hand and headed out the door. Before he reached his car, however, a wave of discouragement overcame him. Quacksalver had shed more murk than light on his questions. Mr. Radio Preacher was far more helpful. This left Peregrinus feeling torn. He felt like he ought to follow the simple teaching of the Sacred Trust, like Mr. Radio Preacher encouraged his listeners to do. Indeed, he wanted to. On the other hand, he felt obligated to give the family pastor the benefit of the doubt. He decided — with a sigh — to try Quacksalver's advice and see what happened.

REVEREND QUACKSALVER

Disillusionment with the God Box

Despite being skeptical, Peregrinus made himself a God Box. He went out of his way to attend the Important Formality every week. He started going to a Dabble Study led by one of the leading men in the church. He bought himself a bestselling paraphrase of the Sacred Trust called the *Groovy Cool Book*. He got himself a "Smile if you love the Sweet One" bracelet. He made a conscious effort to let people know in subtle little ways that he was religious. Of course, he kept the lid on the God Box carefully latched.

As the weeks went by, however, his doubts about the God Box turned into full-blown disillusionment.

The Important Formality? Listening to Reverend Quacksalver Drone was as boring as watching grass grow. How many times can a man count the tiles on the ceiling or the panes in the stained-glass windows?

The Dabble study? Nobody seemed to know or care what the Sacred Trust actually taught. In fact, serious study was against the unwritten rules. If men displayed too much knowledge or asked pertinent questions too often, that actually eroded their credibility. The true badge of spirituality was humility, and this was demonstrated by frequent professions of ignorance. If you truly were ignorant, that was even better. Then there was the ever-present political jousting and sports talk which were given far more time and attention than the Sacred Trust.

The *Groovy Cool Book*? He just wasn't impressed with the modern paraphrases that everyone was raving about. He vastly preferred the older, literal translation he had been given in Sunday School many years ago. Besides, he just couldn't picture the Lord sitting on the Mount of Olives talking Groovy Cool with his disciples.

The Sweet One bracelet? He actually only wore it once, and it was an unpleasant experience. It made him feel conspicuous. He might as well have been wearing one of the outlandish hairstyles that teenagers sometimes wear.

THE GLORIOUS SALVATION MACHINE

Peregrinus Lays Awake Thinking

A few days later Peregrinus lay awake in bed thinking. He was disillusioned with the God Box and the Glorious Salvation Machine. He was dissatisfied. His Big Empty was still empty. What was he going to do about that? He was convinced that God wanted to fill it.

His mind wandered to Mr. Radio Preacher. Peregrinus had continued to listen to his programs regularly even though Quacksalver disapproved. The other night he had heard him say that the freshborn man would never thirst again. That sounded like filling the Big Empty. After all, what difference was there between quenching a thirst that couldn't be quenched and filling a hole that couldn't be filled?

Deep in his heart he knew that the answer was the freshbirth. But how did a man get freshborn? He knew it had something to do with believing the Wonderful Message of salvation in the Crucified One, for Mr. Radio Preacher quoted many verses from the Sacred Trust which proved that. But he wasn't quite sure what to do with these verses. He already did "kind of" believe in a go-to-church, lip-service way. Yet his faith was missing things that faith was supposed to have.

One thing in particular bothered him. He lacked *assurance* of salvation. Mr. Radio Preacher loved to quote the verse, "I write these things unto you that you may *know* that you have Sweet Everlasting." He always added the comment, "Salvation is not hope so or think so, but *know* so. You can know for sure that you have eternal life and will be in Sweet Everlasting." This he did not have, and this he desperately wanted.

So where was he going to get the help he needed to find the faith he needed? He didn't know. But one thing he did know, he wasn't going to give up searching for answers. He would press on no matter what the cost. With this fresh resolve, a warmth flooded his heart and encouraged him. Right then and there he knew that God would somehow, someway, someday show him what he needed to know.

CHAPTER THREE
JUMPING JACK HALLELUJAH

Luke W. Zeal Calls

After some serious soul-searching, Peregrinus laid aside his God Box and started looking for answers that had substance. He was tired of dead religion. Shortly afterwards, he received a phone call from an old friend he hadn't heard from in a while. They talked about old times and old friends. They talked about their jobs and the economy. Then the conversation turned to spiritual matters.

Luke W. Zeal—I know that you're not particularly religious beyond doing the Weekly Duty in one of the dead churches of the Glorious Salvation Machine, but I've got to tell you, I've found God. I'm living for the Sweet One now. It's great! It's incredible. He makes life so sweet.

Peregrinus—Well, that's interesting. I've been thinking a lot about spiritual matters myself lately.

Luke W. Zeal—Really? Tell me about it.

Peregrinus—For a few months now, I have been thinking quite a bit about stuff like the Big Empty, the freshbirth, and Sweet Everlasting. The Big Empty gnaws away every day. I've tried to fill it with the Big Here & Now, but that doesn't work. I've tried to fill it with Innocuous Minimum religion, but that doesn't work either. Every time I think I've found something to fill the Big Empty — whether purpose, pursuit, or pleasure — I face the Big Let Down. The Big Empty is just way too big and way too empty. I suspect that the freshbirth and Sweet Everlasting have something to do with filling the Big Empty, but I feel like I'm groping in the dark.

THE GLORIOUS SALVATION MACHINE

King Sugar and the Big Empty

Luke W. Zeal—You need to ask King Sugar into your heart. If you do, you will be freshborn, and King Sugar will fill your Big Empty.

Peregrinus—Just ask King Sugar into my heart?

Luke W. Zeal—That's right. That's all you have to do. He will do the rest.

Peregrinus—That seems too easy.

Luke W. Zeal—It works every time. When we ask King Sugar into our heart, he comes and lives in us. That is called the Sweet Presence.

Peregrinus—I thought I heard somewhere that we must give stuff up and surrender, or something like that.

Luke W. Zeal—That's true in a sense. We do have to give up our sins. But we really don't give them up. King Sugar takes them from us. Sometimes fast. Sometimes slow. Always in his sweet time. We also have to give up the Altar of Worthy Self. But bless Sugar Daddy, he gives it right back. It's not his intention to make us unhappy. He only wants to see that we mean business and that we really love him.

Peregrinus—My Big Empty will get filled too?

Luke W. Zeal—Faster than fast and fuller than full.

Peregrinus—So how does my Big Empty get filled?

Luke W. Zeal—King Sugar will fill it. He Sugar Fills those who ask him into their hearts by giving them a Triple Blessing of Big Here & Now fun stuff to pile on the Altar of Worthy Self. Tons of money. Tons of toys. Tons of fun. His Sugar Kids walk through life enjoying fun stuff blessings like a kid licking on a triple-dip ice cream cone. There is nothing like it. Bless Sugar Daddy.

Peregrinus—I tried filling my Big Empty with the fun stuff of the Big Here & Now and it didn't work.

Luke W. Zeal—But you're not Sugar Daddy. Trust me, Sugar Daddy knows your Big Empty like the back of his hand. He knows what fun stuff will fill your Big Empty. If you ask the Sweet One into your heart, he will take you by the hand, walk you around the Playground of the Big Here & Now, and take you to the fun stuff he knows will fill your Big Empty right to the top. Life was meant to be exciting, you know. Just trust him. His way is best, it leads to zest.

Of course, we need to keep our fun stuff clean. We must avoid the dirty stuff on the edges of the Playground where the naughty kids hang out.

The Faith Form and the Freshbirth

Peregrinus—Tell me more about the freshbirth. You said that if I asked the Sweet One into my heart, I would be born afresh. What happens that makes me freshborn?

Luke W. Zeal—When we ask King Sugar to come live in our heart, we do what is technically called the Faith Form. The Faith Form is the official, heaven-authorized way to believe. When we pray the Faith Form prayer, the Sweet One comes and lives in our heart. His presence in our heart — we call it the Sweet Presence — is the freshbirth.

Peregrinus—That sure is different than the church I grew up in. We didn't have anything like the Faith Form. All we had was the Sprinkle Form.

Luke W. Zeal—The Sprinkle Form is nonsense. How can any intelligent man honestly think that sprinkling a little water on a baby gives it the freshbirth?

Peregrinus—No kidding. That's way messed up.

Luke W. Zeal—What's sad is how much light men can have and still be wrong. The Sprinkle Form churches are right that man is saved by God Magic in a Passive Form and not by Dead Works. But their understanding of the Passive Form is really goofed up.

The Sacred Trust plainly teaches that a man must believe to be freshborn. This means that salvation by God Magic is a two-way street. Sugar Daddy invites and man answers. And man must answer for himself. He must move his own lips. Nobody else's lips will do. He must ask the Sweet One into his heart. A baby can't do this. This means that the Faith Form is the only God-ratified, fully-*bona-fide* expression of the Passive Form.

Peregrinus—How about change? Where does that fit in? Mr. Radio Preacher says that if we are truly freshborn, we will be new creations. We will be changed. And our life will reflect this change.

Luke W. Zeal—We become new creations when King Sugar comes and lives in our hearts. His Sweet Presence is the new creation. As for change, we are not the same after we ask King Sugar into our heart. He becomes our whole life. We pursue him with our whole Sugar-loving heart in Sugar meetings and in Sugar blessings in the Big Here & Now, especially in the Sugar blessings.

Peregrinus—Is Sugar gain the only kind of change there is?

Luke W. Zeal—We need to be careful when we talk about change. We don't want to fall into legalism. King Sugar came to set us free, not put us in bondage. What a lot of people don't understand is that the freshbirth is not a change in our heart that leads to obvious discipleship in our Daily Grind. It is the Sweet Presence of the Sweet One in our heart. As we like to say: the freshbirth is King Sugar in the heart, not change in the heart.

Now change does sometimes come — generally later rather than sooner, and normally more lukewarm than fervent — but at least it does come sometimes. We just have to be patient. We need to make sure that we don't take matters into our own hands and try to change ourselves. Change is his job. Our job is to graciously take whatever change he gives, when he gives it, if he gives it.

King Sugar and Sweet Everlasting

Peregrinus—So where does Sweet Everlasting fit in?

Luke W. Zeal—I'm sure it will be wonderful, but we need to keep things in their proper place and time. King Sugar wants us to concern ourselves with the present and not worry about the future. We need to focus on filling our hearts right now with the Big Here & Now and quit worrying about filling our hearts with Sweet Everlasting until we actually get there.

Peregrinus—But wouldn't men be more likely to seek the filling of their Big Empty in Sweet Everlasting if they weren't filled with the Big Here & Now? Think of kids, for example: when their bellies are full of candy and junk food, they have no interest in supper.

Luke W. Zeal—Actually, I think it's the other way around. I wouldn't trust a God that offered to fill my Big Empty in Sweet Everlasting, but couldn't prove himself by filling it right now with the fun stuff of the Big Here & Now. Faith is based on facts that can be seen and touched and felt. It isn't based on fantasy or pretend. I want proof. I want facts. I want a God who is able. That's why I serve Sugar Daddy.

Peregrinus—But what about the verse that talks about losing our life in the Big Here & Now for the sake of the Crucified One and his Wonderful Message? That has been burning in my heart. I feel like I ought to be going in that direction.

Luke W. Zeal—You can't lean on your own understanding of the dead letter of the Sacred Trust. We need the Deep Truth of the Sweet Spirit.

Let me give you an example. We read in the Sacred Trust that our Sugar Daddy in heaven sent the Sweet One to give us "life more abundantly." Now the translation "life more abundantly" fails to bring out the Deep Significance in the original Greek. A consistent Deep Adjustification based on the Sweet character of Sugar Daddy suggests that the true sense of this verse is that the Sweet One came to give us "life in the Big Here & Now far more Big Here & Now abundantly."

I just love this verse. It proves that our Sugar Daddy wants to fill our Big Empties with the fun stuff of the Big Here & Now. He wants our journey to go from full to full, not from empty to full. In other words, he wants the first leg of our journey in the Big Here & Now to be just as filling as the second leg in Sweet Everlasting.

Peregrinus—Well ... that does sound kind of logical.

THE GLORIOUS SALVATION MACHINE

Luke W. Zeal—Logical? That's an understatement. The Deep Logic of the Sugar Kids is light years beyond the dead letter logic which the Havenmongers use to defend an empty discipleship that leaves the Big Empty empty.

Invitation to Hear Jumping Jack Hallelujah

Luke W. Zeal—Any chance you'd be interested in going to a Sugar Kids meeting this evening? I'd like you to meet Jumping Jack Hallelujah and hear him preach. He can blow the doors off of any preacher you've ever heard.

Peregrinus—That sounds cool.

Luke W. Zeal—I guarantee you, if you come tonight, you will sense the power of Sugar Daddy, and King Sugar will come down and touch you, and you will be born afresh, and your Big Empty will be well on the way to being filled.

Peregrinus—Hey, whatever it takes. I'm willing to swim the Amazon crawling with crocodiles. I just want to get my Big Empty filled and lay hold of Sweet Everlasting.

Luke W. Zeal—That's the spirit. I'll pick you up at your house at six-thirty sharp. Be there.

Peregrinus—Don't be late.

Luke W. Zeal—Don't you be late.

Peregrinus Meets Jumping Jack

At six-thirty sharp, Luke W Zeal pulled up to Peregrinus' house, Peregrinus hopped in, and they raced off to the meeting. They were giddy with anticipation and talked excitedly about what God might do that evening. They were so pumped when they arrived that they ran from the parking lot. When they barged through the front doors of the Triple Blessing Power of God Tabernacle, Luke caught sight of Jumping Jack talking to a group of Sugar Kids in the foyer, and he headed straight for him to introduce Peregrinus to him.

Luke W. Zeal—Hey, Brother Jumping Jack, I want you to meet my friend Peregrinus.

Jumping Jack Hallelujah—Glad to meet you, Peregrinus. Are you one of King Sugar's Kids?

Peregrinus—I would like to be. I really want to spend Sweet Everlasting in the Wonderful Place.

Jumping Jack Hallelujah—Well, do your part and you will enjoy Sweet Everlasting.

Peregrinus—What is my part?

Jumping Jack Hallelujah—Your part is to accept the Triple Blessing that Sugar Daddy wants to give you. If you do that, he will give you his Triple Blessing in the Big Here & Now and Sweet Everlasting in the life to come.

Peregrinus—What do I do to accept this Triple Blessing?

Jumping Jack Hallelujah—Simple. Just ask King Sugar to come live in your heart. He will come and live in you. He will take away the Altar of Worthy Self and give it right back again with a blessing so big it will blow your mind. But you can't please him if you don't bask in his love. The only way to bask in his love is to enjoy his Sugar blessing in this life and let him fill your Big Empty with the clean fun stuff of the Big Here & Now. Doesn't that just tickle your ears?

Peregrinus—What do I do about my sins?

Jumping Jack Hallelujah—Not your job. That's God's job. You need to stand down and disengage yourself. Sugar Daddy will take away all your sins in his sweet time. If you start trying to do God's job, if you start trying to play God, it won't be pretty. Believe me, you don't want to play God. Sugar Daddy will not appreciate that. But hey, it was nice talking to you. I have to scoot. I'll be sharing King Sugar's love in a little while.

Praise and Worship Time

The group broke up, and Luke and Peregrinus made their way to the auditorium where they found seats in the back row. The worship-band was still warming up, playing riffs from songs with a little more zing than he was used to. This continued for several minutes. Then the music faded as the song leader strolled to the microphone. He spoke briefly on how he loved

THE GLORIOUS SALVATION MACHINE

to be in the Triple Blessing Power of God Tabernacle on Sundays and how he loved to praise King Sugar. Then he gave out the first song, the worship-band cranked up the music, and for the next twenty minutes he led the congregation in rowdy sing-and-sway music, punctuated with short thoughts on the blessings of being a Sugar Kid. When the praise and worship time drew to a close, he motioned for Jumping Jack — who bounded to the pulpit full of energy — and turned the meeting over to the preacher.

Jumping Jack Live on Stage

Jumping Jack Hallelujah—Glad to see an auditorium full of shouting, swaying Sugar Kids. There is no life in the Big Here & Now like the life of a Sugar Kid. King Sugar wants us to have bigger, better, faster, louder, and more than the children of the Mad Spirit. Do you believe that? I do! Whatever clean Big Here & Now fun you want can be yours if you trust King Sugar and praise him.

Well, we're not here merely to get stuff from Sugar Daddy, but also to give stuff to him. So let's open up with a time of prayer and give him the recognition that he deserves.

Jumping Jack then alternated back and forth between talking to the audience in a loud voice and praying in a booming voice that could have roused the dead.

Jumping Jack Hallelujah—Would you like to get your very own personal Mega-Blessing tonight from Sugar Daddy? OH, SUGAR DADDY, DROP YOUR SUPER-DUPER BIGGEST MEGA-BLESSING SUGAR-BOMB ON THIS BUILDING TONIGHT! Would you like to see Sugar Daddy move tonight? SWEET SUGAR DADDY, MOVE UNSUGARED HEARTS TONIGHT! MOVE THEM TO SUGAR-BELIEVE IN KING SUGAR. Would you like to have your Big Empty filled? OH, SWEET SUGAR DADDY, SUGAR-FILL EVERY LAST BIG EMPTY HERE TONIGHT! Would you like to see a Sugar Spirit revival here tonight? OH, SUGAR DADDY, SUGAR-

SHAKE THIS HERE BUILDING TONIGHT! POUR OUT YOUR SPIRIT LIKE YOU HAVE NEVER POURED HIM OUT BEFORE AND GIVE US THE WARM FUZZIES LIKE WE HAVE NEVER HAD THEM BEFORE.

He went on in this stentorian manner for about five minutes until his voice started to crack. Then he shifted gears, dropped into a more reserved voice, brought the prayer to a close, and began to share.

Humble Money Pipes

Jumping Jack Hallelujah—Before I get to my message, I want to thank all of you for supporting this Sugar ministry. I thank you for allowing yourselves to be humble money-pipes in Sugar Daddy's hands, so he can transfer the green stuff from your pockets to mine — my ministry pocket and my personal pocket. The Sweet One just loves it when you reach for your checkbook. It touches his heart. If you could somehow see just how much it touches his heart, you would reach for your checkbook every time you walked through these doors.

Praise the Sweet One that we do not have to beg for money around here like they do in some churches. You are all so in tune with the Sweet Spirit that we don't need to beg.

The Blessings of Being One of King Sugar's Kids

Jumping Jack Hallelujah—As I said a few minutes ago, there is no life in the Big Here & Now like the life of a Sugar Kid. Are you one of King Sugar's Kids? If not, all you have to do is ask King Sugar to come and live in your heart. GLORY! He will come down from the Wonderful Place. GLORY! He will come into your heart. GLORY! He will take away all your sins and demons in his own sweet time. GLORY! He will give you victory that you may or may not be able to see. GLORY! You shall be holy, whether anyone else can see it or not. GLORY! He will take away the Altar of Worthy Self to test you and see if you mean business. If you make it past two seconds — that's all he asks is two seconds — he will give it

THE GLORIOUS SALVATION MACHINE

right back with his Triple Blessing of fun stuff and money. HALLELUJAH!

Oh, I almost forgot. We also get to spend Sweet Everlasting in the Wonderful Place. Isn't that cool? But I understand how hard it is to get excited about Sweet Everlasting. We have so much blessing from King Sugar right now in the Big Here & Now that we sometimes forget that there is another time and place. But GLORY!, we are not like the typical Christian who only gets pie in the sky in Sweet Everlasting. We get pie in this life too! We don't have to wait for Sweet Everlasting to live like king's kids. We reign in this life! We get Sugar Filling fullness right here and now in the Big Here & Now!

Jumping Jack went on in this vein for about thirty minutes, sharing thoughts on the Sugar Kids life and mushy-gushing about how much he loved playing with the expensive toys that King Sugar had given him.

Then he closed with an opportunity for those who wanted to become a Sugar Kid to join him in prayer. At this point the worship-band struck up some appropriate music — conducive to the production of the warm-fuzzies.

Jumping Jack Leads in Prayer

Jumping Jack Hallelujah—Everyone bow your heads and close your eyes. No peeking. In a moment I'm going to lead in a Faith Form prayer. If you want to be one of King Sugar's Kids and have your Big Empty filled, just repeat the words of this prayer after me. If you pray this prayer, you will get the warm-fuzzies. The warm-fuzzies are the Sweet One coming into your heart. They are proof that you have been freshborn and adopted by Sugar Daddy into the Sugar Daddy family, so you can bask in his Sugar Daddy love and go through this life having tons of Sugar Daddy fun under the sun.

By the way, don't nitpick yourself about whether or not you really mean the words you pray. Sugar Daddy doesn't nitpick your efforts at the Faith Form. Neither do we. Your profession of faith will not be judged, scrutinized, or challenged.

Well, let's turn to the Sweet One:

Dear King Sugar ... Come into my heart ... Take my sins in your sweet time ... Thank you for saving me from the penalty of sin without regard to the practice of sin ... Take the Altar of Worthy Self and give it right back again with your Triple Blessing ... Sugar Fill me to overflowing with the fun stuff of the Big Here & Now ... Thank you for hearing and answering these prayers ... Oh, I almost forgot ... Thank you for Sweet Everlasting too, though we're a little afraid that it'll be boring compared to the fun stuff of the Big Here & Now. Amen!

Peregrinus Gets the Warm-Fuzzies

The buzz in the Tabernacle had gotten louder and louder as Jumping Jack prayed, until it reached a crescendo of shouts. When Jumping Jack said *AMEN!* at the end of his Faith Form prayer, the crescendo climaxed with a roar that seemed to shake the building. At that moment Peregrinus felt a powerful, electric-like energy enter his body, giving him the tingles from the top of his head to the tips of his toes. He turned excitedly to Luke.

Peregrinus—Wow! I feel the warm-fuzzies running up and down my spine. My body feels warm all over.

Luke W. Zeal—Yea, I got them too. Sugar Daddy is really moving and working tonight.

Peregrinus—This is so amazing.

Luke W. Zeal—GLORY! I am so excited that I can hardly stand it. Now we're both Sugar Kids. Now we can whoop it up together, indulging tons of good, clean fun under the sun in the Big Here & Now. I just love the Big Here & Now. It's hard to imagine that Sweet Everlasting could be even half as fun. But we don't need to worry about that now. All we have to worry about now is indulging the fun stuff of the Big Here & Now for the glory of Sugar Daddy and his son King Sugar ...

THE GLORIOUS SALVATION MACHINE

Right in the middle of Luke's thought, their conversation was drowned out by Jumping Jack's voice booming out from the powerful speakers.

Welcome to King Sugar's Family

Jumping Jack Hallelujah—Congratulations to all of you who joined me in the Faith Form and asked the Sweet One into your heart. Welcome to King Sugar's family. You are now a Sugar Kid. You are now a child of the King. You can probably already feel the first waves of the Sugar Filling rolling in and splashing around down at your ankles. This, Kids, is just the beginning. Keep going forward in Triple Blessing truth in the Big Here & Now, and before you know it, you will be in the river of Blessing up to your knees, then your waist, then your shoulders, and then over your head. HALLELUJAH!

At this comment the crowd cranked up a thunderous round of praise and clapping. Peregrinus sat on the edge of his chair stunned. He was amazed by this meeting. He was amazed by the electricity in the air. He was amazed by his warm-fuzzies. He was amazed by the preaching and singing. He had gotten more excitement in just one Faith Form meeting than he had gotten in his whole life in Sprinkle Form meetings. This stuff was addicting. No wonder Luke liked it so much.

Jumping Jack let the crowd pulsate and enervate for a few minutes, then hushed them with a wave of his hand, so he could continue.

The GIMME Principles of Faith Talk

Jumping Jack Hallelujah—I want to share with you five powerful principles of spiritual warfare. They cover the *tactics* that the Mad Spirit will use to rob you of your Triple Blessing and the *weapons* that you have been given to overcome these tactics. These principles spell the difference between success and failure as a Sugar Kid in a world designed by the Enemy to keep your Big Empty empty. Those of you who recently did the Faith Form really need to pay attention.

I have arranged these principles into the acronym GIMME. This stands for: the *Grinch* that hates fun stuff, the *Icky lies* of the Mad Spirit, the *Mighty shield* to resist the Mad Spirit, the *Mighty sword* of Faith Talk, and the *Easy faith* of the spiritual wimps who can't hang with the big dogs.

The Mad Spirit is a mean, old grinch that hates the teaching of the Triple Blessing. He does not want believers to fill their Big Empty with the clean fun stuff of the Big Here & Now. He does not want them to enjoy life in the Big Here & Now more fun-stuff abundantly. There is no depth of low-down, dastardly dirtiness that he will not stoop to in his efforts to snuff out the Deep Faith necessary to obtain the Triple Blessing and thereby rob believers of its bounty. But this is all in keeping with his character, for the Mad Spirit is a thief: he came only to rob, steal, and kill.

The Mad Spirit will try to get into your head and fill it with icky lies that will keep you from the Triple Blessing. He will tell you that it is impossible to fill the Big Empty with the Big Here & Now. He will tell you that you are not supposed to fill your Big Empty with the Big Here & Now, but are supposed to fill it with Sweet Everlasting. He will point his bony finger at your experience and tell you that your Big Empty is really just as empty as it Daily Grind looks and feels. But this is all in keeping with his character, for the Mad Spirit is the father of lies. Lies are his most effective weapon for keeping men from the path of fullness and blessing.

But you don't have to be beaten in battle, for you have been given a mighty shield. I'm not talking about the worthless shields that most Christians carry about. You know what I'm talking about: wimpy shields that don't stop any of the lies that the Mad Spirit spreads against the Triple Blessing. And what is the believer's mighty shield? His index fingers and lungs. When you hear the Mad Spirit's perfidious lies, you must stick your fingers in your ears and holler, "Lies! Lies! Lies!" at the top of your lungs. If you resist the Mad Spirit, he will flee.

THE GLORIOUS SALVATION MACHINE

You have a mighty sword too. I'm not talking about the toy sword that the dead folks in the Havens carry around: that piece-of-junk, plastic sword which couldn't get a blessing out of a piñata, much less the Triple Blessing out of King Sugar. I'm talking about the powerful Faith Talk sword. The sword that actually gets the job done. The sword that slices through the paper-mache of lies like hot butter and HALLELUJAH! — it's Faith Talk party time, with cool stuff flying everywhere.

Don't give in one inch to the easy faith of spiritual wimps who defend their wimpiness with the argument that believers are supposed to walk in the same kind of Big Here & Now emptiness that we see in the Crucified One. They don't really believe that. They know that the Sweet One came down here to live and die for us in Emptiness Bondage, so we don't have to live in Emptiness Bondage. They know he came to give us life more fun-stuff abundantly. They are just spiritual wimps looking for easy faith and making excuses. Faith Talk is too hard for them. They can't run with the big dogs.

Baby Steps for Spiritual Giant Wannabes

Jumping Jack Hallelujah—Now you can't run with the big dogs until you learn to walk. So — for all of you spiritual giant wannabes — here are the baby steps of Faith Talk. You must learn to walk this way, or you will be defeated in the Sugar Kids life and your Big Empty will stay empty. Just professing to believe the Sugar Kids teaching is not enough. You must learn to Faith-Talk walk the Faith-Talk talk.

Faith Talk *confesses*, despite all evidence to the contrary, that it's Big Empty really is filled in the Mystic Plane with a Triple Blessing of fun stuff that is out there, somewhere.

Faith Talk *knows* that if it keeps on Faith Talking, sooner or later the mystical filling in the Mystic Plane will be alchemized into a Triple Blessing in the Daily Grind.

Faith Talk *believes* that it has the creative power of Sugar Daddy at its disposal for Sugar Kid purposes — kind of like having one's own private magic wand — and that it can speak what does not exist into existence.

Faith Talk *scoffs* at every challenge raised against the validity of the Sugar Kids teaching: whether facts, evidence, common sense, experience, or arguments from the Sacred Trust.

Most of those who ask King Sugar into their heart never get past these baby-step battles against the baby-size lies. They just lay down their sword and shield and beg the thief to rob them. They surrender before they ever get to the really big and really devious lies of the Mad Spirit. You that are mature, battle-hardened soldiers know exactly what I am talking about.

Faith Talk Isn't Pretending

Jumping Jack Hallelujah—Now some ridicule Faith Talk as pretending. They claim that those who are trying to Faith Talk their Triple Blessing into existence have been duped into indulging a fantasy that is just as silly as believing in a pot of gold at the end of the rainbow. They claim that no matter how strongly men Deep Believe, no matter how heartily they Faith Talk, they will never see their Triple Blessing materialize. These claims are bogus. Faith Talk is not pretending.

Take a look at my life. The wealth and the toys that I enjoy are not fantasies. They can be touched and handled. And if Faith Talk worked for me, it can work for you. I was nothing special until the Sweet One got a hold on me. Eight years ago I was flipping hamburgers in a fast-food joint.

So don't let the Mad Spirit discourage you. Don't throw in the towel on Faith Talk just because it doesn't seem to be working for you. Sometimes men fight the Good Fight of Faith Talk for years before they see the first significant signs of their Triple Blessing. Whatever you do, don't give up. That is bad, bad, nasty-bad surrender to the lies of the Mad Spirit. Millions have given up on Faith Talk after struggling valiantly for years when they were only days or hours from their Sugar Filling. It was on the very next train. I could just cry. It breaks my heart. There is no song sad enough.

THE GLORIOUS SALVATION MACHINE

The Possibilities Are Mind-Boggling

Jumping Jack Hallelujah—Well, lets close this meeting on a positive note. What do you want to Faith Talk into your life? What would you like to fill your Big Empty with? Wealth, success, fame, fortune, mansions, toys, yachts, luxury cars, expensive watches? King Sugar wants to give it to you, but his hands are tied behind his back. It's all up to you. What will you do? Will you leave him tied and bound? Or will you untie his hands with Faith Talk? The possibilities are mind-boggling. If you can Faith Talk it into existence, then it's yours. Yours! Yours!! YOURS!!!

Won't that be a wonderful day when you finally Faith Talk your Triple Blessing into existence? Not only will you enjoy the pleasure of having your Big Empty filled to the brim with the fun stuff of the Big Here & Now. But you will enjoy the pleasure of a big dollop of "I told you so" whipped cream on top. On that day all those unbelieving folks in the Havens who scoffed at your gullibility will have to choke down a big piece of humble pie. Won't that be fun to watch!

Then Jumping Jack closed the meeting with his favorite chorus, which the crowd heartily sang a dozen times.

Eating Sugar night and day,
Worldly fun stuff, worldly play.
This is Sugar Daddy's will,
So his Sugar Kids can fill
Their Big Empty all the way—
Triple Blessing bliss each day.

The Excitement Starts to Wear Off

After that evening Peregrinus began attending Jumping Jack's church every time the doors were open for meetings. He loved going there. The meetings were more exciting than the boring meetings in his old Glorious Salvation Machine church. They sang fun songs instead of boring songs. They heard riveting preaching instead of dead Droning.

After a few months, however, his excitement started to wear off, and he noticed that the same old empty and the same old ugly were still raging in his heart. His heart problems hadn't been fixed. They had only been covered up. And the frequent doses of excitement that he got from the Sugar Kids meetings were no longer able to cover them up. As he pondered the situation, he realized that several things in the Sugar Kids Message just didn't add up.

The Sugar Kids path was supposed to sanitize and legitimize the Altar of Worthy Self. Why did his conscience still bug him about it? Why did it bring up Sacred Trust verses that seemed to teach that he should tear it down?

The Sugar Kids path encouraged him to fill his Big Empty with the clean fun stuff of the Big Here & Now. Yet indulging fun stuff had not given him satisfaction and meaning. It gave him fleeting moments of pleasure while he drifted in a sea of emptiness.

The Faith Form was supposed to take care of his sin problem. Why did he still feel like a guilty sinner? Why *was* he still a guilty sinner? Where was his victory? Wasn't the Sweet One supposed to take care of his sins?

Peregrinus Writes to His Friend Luke

In his discouragement Peregrinus wrote a letter to his friend Luke and poured out his heart. He would rather have visited with him face to face, but Luke was enrolled in a prestigious Deep Signification Indoctrination Institution in a distant city, studying to become a Faith Form preacher.

> Dear Luke:
>
> I tried to fill the Big Empty by trusting King Sugar and living the life of a Sugar Kid in the Big Here & Now. But that big old hole is not filled. The ache is not satisfied. Are you sure that the Sugar Kids path is the right way to fill the Big Empty?

THE GLORIOUS SALVATION MACHINE

I also have questions about the Faith Form. Are you sure that it's the right way or the best way to get freshborn? It didn't seem to work for me. I just don't want to miss out on Sweet Everlasting.

Hungry for reality,
Peregrinus

Luke Writes Back to Peregrinus

Luke's response was no help at all. He was a cheerleader for the official position, not a man who sought to understand exactly what the Sacred Trust taught.

Dear Peregrinus:

Is the Sugar Kids path the right way to fill the Big Empty? You sound like a Havenmonger preaching their "empty" message — God's best is Sweet Rest in Sweet Everlasting. That view is way wrong. How can we honor the Sweet One if we turn our backs on his promised blessing of life way more fun-stuff abundantly in the Big Here & Now?

Why hasn't your Big Empty been filled? It never will if you give up.

Is the Faith Form the right way to get freshborn? You're walking on thin ice. The Sacred Trust plainly states that salvation is by God Magic alone in the Faith Form alone. How could you even question the Faith Form?

As for Sweet Everlasting — one thing at a time, dude. Take care of the present, then worry about the future. Lay hold of Sugar Daddy's blessing right now in the Big Here & Now and worry about his Sweet Everlasting blessing when you get there. You are really missing it here. No preacher I respect is concerned about Sweet Everlasting. They are all focused on getting filled right here and now in the Big Here & Now with Sugar Daddy's fun-stuff best.

Eating Sugar night and day,
Luke W. Zeal

The Collapse of the Sugar Kids Scheme

Peregrinus tried hard to bring back the excitement and find answers for his emptiness and ugliness. He listened carefully to every word Jumping Jack said in case he might disclose some magic key that would unlock his difficulties and reveal their solutions. He doubled his efforts in Faith Talk prayer, seeking the Deep Faith that everyone said would fix his problems. He read and reread the Sacred Trust, returning again and again to those passages which supposedly taught the Sugar Kids life.

But neither Jumping Jack's ministry nor Faith Talk gave him any help at all. The only help he got was from the Sacred Trust; and to his dismay, it wasn't the help he was looking for. The more he read the Sacred Trust, the more it fed his doubts on the Sugar Kids scheme.

After a few weeks of struggling and searching, the Sugar Kids scheme collapsed. It had gone from sweet jam to body slam. It had picked him up with sweet promises, let him struggle with pretending, then slammed him to the ground when he couldn't maintain the charade any longer. He was tired of pretending. He wanted reality.

Worse, he was ashamed that he had let himself get sucked in by the Sugar Kids teaching. He should have known better. The Johnny Hotstuff fiasco had already taught him that nothing in the Big Here & Now could fill the Big Empty. But the Sugar Kids Message had seemed different. It had made it seem like God looked with favor upon the Altar of Worthy Self and the clean Big Here & Now— at least for the believer.

More than ever he suspected that he was supposed to fill his Big Empty with the lasting things of Sweet Everlasting, not the fleeting things of this life, that true meaning revolved around God's eternal plan, not man's petty temporal plans, and that his heart should be wrapped up with pleasures forevermore at the Father's right hand, not the passing pleasures of this sin-cursed, sin-ravaged world.

THE GLORIOUS SALVATION MACHINE

Peregrinus Lacks the Evidences of the Freshbirth

Despite the collapse of the Sugar Kids scheme, Peregrinus still wanted to believe that he was freshborn because he had done the Faith Form. But he didn't find a lot of ground to stand on. His main concern was that he lacked the evidences Mr. Radio Preacher taught should accompany the freshbirth.

One, he was not an overcomer. Like most who trusted the Faith Form, he didn't live much differently than those who trusted the Sprinkle Form. Sure, he had given up a few of his dirtier fun stuff endeavors, but he did not have victory over his sin and the Big Here & Now. He was still playing games. The Altar of Worthy Self was still standing.

Two, he had no assurance that he was right with God. He was not certain that his sins were forgiven. He did not know for sure that he had eternal life.

Three, his Big Empty was not filled. As Mr. Radio Preacher loved to say: "If a man is freshborn, then he has embraced the infinite, eternal God and his promise of infinite, eternal reward. And if he has embraced the infinite, eternal God, then his Big Empty is filled. But if his Big Empty is not filled, then he has not embraced the infinite, eternal God. And if he has not embraced the infinite, eternal God, then he is not freshborn."

But if he wasn't born afresh through the Faith Form, then how was he supposed to get born afresh? He knew it involved believing on the Crucified One. But what did it mean to believe on him? And to what church or preacher should he turn to find out what it meant? He had no idea. All he could do was to look to God in prayer and in his Word.

God at Work Behind the Scene

Little did Peregrinus know that help would soon arrive. For God was at work behind the scene — managing his spiritual awakening — and would soon bring him through the strait gate of the freshbirth and place him on the narrow path of faith that leads to Sweet Everlasting. In a few days Peregrinus would no longer be a citizen of the Big Here & Now, but a pilgrim seeking a better land. As the Sacred Trust says, "If you seek him with all your heart, you shall find him."

CHAPTER FOUR
THE PROVIDENTIAL MEETING

A Providential Meeting

Peregrinus had been searching for weeks. He was troubled by questions regarding the freshbirth, Sweet Everlasting, and Awful Everlasting. He was troubled by temptations he had no power to resist. He was troubled by the emptiness of religion — both boring and exciting. And he was troubled by his Big Empty. How was a man supposed to fill his Big Empty when the world is a barren desert filled with empty mirages that tantalize men with glimmering promises, then fill their cups with sand?

When he was feeling stressed out, he liked to drive to a local park and go for a walk on one of the trails. As he walked, he would think through things and pray, asking God for direction and help. Then he would stop somewhere along the trail and read from the Sacred Trust. These walks refreshed him, helped him to refocus, and gave him the strength to keep going in the search for truth and answers.

Several days after he had read Luke's letter, Peregrinus went for one of his walks. His heart was heavy over his differences with Luke and his ever-increasing sense that he was lost. He pondered what he had read in the Sacred Trust regarding the freshbirth and following the Crucified One. He prayed as best as he knew how that God would show him the right way.

Deep in thought and oblivious to his surroundings, he was startled to find himself at one of his favorite places to stop and read — a flat rock under a gnarled, old pine tree overlooking the valley. He looked up and saw a man sitting under the tree with a book in his hands. But this was no ordinary meeting and no ordinary man. This was the providence of God meeting the needs of man — as it so often does — in a way unexpected, in a place least expected, at a time not expected.

How to Understand the Sacred Trust

Peregrinus—Hi there. Is that the Sacred Trust?

Plowman—It sure is. The Sacred Trust is my favorite book. I read it every day and study it often.

Peregrinus—Every day? I've been trying to do that, but I get discouraged because I don't understand a lot of what I read.

Plowman—I know what you're talking about. I too found the Bible difficult to understand when I first started reading it.

Peregrinus—How did you get through the discouragement and difficulties?

Plowman—A brother once shared with me that I needed to do three things if I wanted to understand the Sacred Trust.

Peregrinus—I'm all ears.

Plowman—The *first* thing was to lay aside everything I had been taught in the Glorious Salvation Machine or Half-Havens and start over, taking the Sacred Trust alone as my teacher.

Peregrinus—The Sacred Trust alone? That makes sense to me. The past few months have been sheer confusion. I would read the Sacred Trust and cling to what it said. Then my friends would tell me that my view was nonsense and pressure me to believe Invincible Dogmas and Ironclad Interpretations that conflicted with what the Sacred Trust seemed to say. It was confusing. Was I screwed up, or were they?

Plowman—Everyone who attempts to take the Sacred Trust at face value will face such opposition.

Peregrinus—So what was the *second* thing?

Plowman—He advised me to start reading in the Gospels and not move on to the rest of the Sacred Trust until I had read them through a few times.

Peregrinus—Why start there?

THE PROVIDENTIAL MEETING

Plowman—Because they give us the meat and potatoes of the Wonderful Message: the incarnation, birth, life, ministry, message, death, burial, and resurrection of the Crucified One. They teach us the basics of what it means to believe on and follow the Crucified One. They teach us the difference between true religion and false religion. This foundation makes it easier to understand the rest of the Sacred Trust.

A Single-Focus Heart

Peregrinus—So what was the *third* point?

Plowman—He encouraged me to have a single eye, that is, a single-focus heart.

Peregrinus—So what's a single-focus heart?

Plowman—The single-focus heart has made the truth — the revealed mind of God in the Word of God — its chief passion. It searches for this truth as for hid treasure.

Peregrinus—That would make a big difference in how a man handles the Sacred Trust.

Plowman—It does. Such a man submits to the authority of the Sacred Trust as the very words of God, believing its testimony, obeying its commands, and applying its teachings — with no exceptions. He cannot be turned from the plain understanding and plain implications of the statements of the Sacred Trust — not for any consideration.

Peregrinus—Such a man would not be swayed by Invincible Dogma and Ironclad Interpretations.

Plowman—That's right. Because he holds nothing sacred but the Sacred Trust, he rejects the concept of Invincible Dogma. No supposed truth is regarded as self-evident. No supposed truth is received upon a superficial examination. No creed, no statement of faith, no system of theology, no point of doctrine or practice, no interpretation of a verse or passage, no tenet of psychology or science falsely so-called, and no sentiment of public opinion or political correctness is allowed to escape a rigorous trial in the court of the Sacred Trust. Every supposed truth and every supposed correct interpretation is rigorously cross-examined by every passage in the Sacred Trust which touches on the subject.

Peregrinus—Dude! That's radical.

Plowman—It is radical. It is the root of every real gain we make in our knowledge of God's will and ways.

Peregrinus—What happens when men don't have a single eye?

Plowman—That makes it virtually impossible for them to be free from false doctrine. Without a single eye, a man can read the Sacred Trust for years and still be wrong on important issues. For such men the Sacred Trust is, to a greater or lesser degree, merely a sourcebook that provides them with Ironclad Interpretations that support their Invincible Dogmas. They read and study the Sacred Trust, so they can be strong in their Invincible Dogmas.

Peregrinus—Wow! Men can read the Sacred Trust for years and still not see truth that they should be able to see.

Plowman—Yep. Submission to light is one of the principles of God's dealings with man. Men must submit to the authority of any particular revelation before they can understand it. As we read in John, "If any man will do his will, he shall know the doctrine, whether it be of God." If a man's heart is single-focused, he will receive the testimony of the Sacred Trust regardless of what it does to his doctrine or his desires. But if his heart is committed to Invincible Dogma or worldly wisdom, he will reject it. The Sacred Trust will not conform him to the mind of God. He will conform the Sacred Trust to his Invincible Dogma and worldly wisdom — he will Sanitize the Sacred Trust.

The Chameleon Heart and the Tradition Heart

Peregrinus—I can't imagine Christians not having truth as their highest priority.

Plowman—Sadly, most professed followers of the Crucified One don't really care what the truth is. These truth-challenged followers fall into one of two camps: those who have Tradition Hearts and those who have Chameleon Hearts.

Peregrinus—What's a Chameleon Heart?

Plowman—A Chameleon Heart conveniently conforms to the surrounding environment like a chameleon. Such people have few, if any, strong convictions or settled beliefs. They are happy to conform to the world and to churches that pursue conformity to the world. They feel comfortable in a broad array of churches, for they are not concerned about negative things like doctrine and error. They just want to love the Sweet One and love on those who love the Sweet One.

Peregrinus—And what's a Tradition Heart?

Plowman—A Tradition Heart is committed to the religious traditions of man. This problem often befalls people who show concern about spiritual matters. The defenders of Invincible Dogma pressure them saying, "If you are spiritual, if you care about truth, if you have a single eye, if you love God — blah, blah, blah — you will believe that such and such an Invincible Dogma is the truth." Most men cannot withstand this pressure. They can't handle having their sincerity or spirituality doubted merely because they question Invincible Dogma. So they cave in and embrace the Invincible Dogma.

Head Pounding

Peregrinus—So men are pressured and hounded until they get tired, give up, embrace an error as truth, and quit thinking for themselves in that area.

Plowman—Yep. We call it Head Pounding.

Peregrinus—That's scary.

Plowman—It's beyond scary. When men embrace Invincible Dogma, they void their obligation to test and prove all things — carefully considering context and weighing every passage in the Sacred Trust which touches on the subject. All they have to do is look up a few proof texts and say "Wow! Invincible argument."

Peregrinus—What do they do with the passages that pose a challenge to Invincible Dogma?

Plowman—They are taught to use Ironclad Interpretations which neutralize them and bring them into harmony with Invincible Dogma. After all, it is axiomatic that the proper interpretation of a passage cannot contradict Invincible Dogma.

Peregrinus—How do I keep from being deceived by Head Pounding?

Plowman—*First of all*, determine that you will never, never, never twistify, emptify, alchemize, or silly-puttyize a passage to bring it into harmony with a doctrine you are taught or believe. Adjust your beliefs, not your Bible.

Secondly, determine that you will give the Sacred Trust free recourse to balance, guard, qualify, modify, or overthrow every doctrine you believe — no exceptions. On every subject you take up for study, every passage that touches on it —directly or indirectly — must be given free recourse to speak its mind.

Thirdly, determine that you will never rest satisfied with a solution to a doctrinal question that does not harmonize every passage in the Sacred Trust that touches on the subject.

If you do these things, you will recover yourself from the errors you hold and protect yourself from future errors.

The Truth Transcends Our Doctrine

Peregrinus—It sounds like you're saying that the truth is something that transcends our doctrine.

Plowman—That's exactly what I am saying. We need to regard the doctrines we hold as the fallible efforts of fallible men to portray the truth that God committed to us in the Sacred Trust. If we equate the doctrines we hold with the truth as it is in heaven, we lock ourselves into the dark dungeon of revering error as truth and resisting truth as error, and we shut the door that would let in further light on the subject.

For some men, this practice keeps them under a dark shadow in one or two areas of Christian doctrine, though they walk in bright light in the rest of their testimony. For most men, it keeps them in that great darkness that herds mankind down the road to Awful Everlasting.

Peregrinus—Are there churches that hold the truth on every important point of doctrine?

Plowman—Absolutely. But even if the body of doctrine we hold is true on every point, that does not mean that we uphold the truth as well as we could. We can be on the right side of an issue and still stand in need of correction. For instance, we may hold the truth in a way that needs to be guarded or balanced. Or we may mar the truth by associating it with lesser errors. As a poet once wrote:

> Even though we know a lot,
> We know nothing as we ought.

He also wrote:

> A man the truth may truly hold,
> Yet stand in need of purer gold.

Studying the Sacred Trust

Peregrinus—Now you said a few minutes ago that you study the Sacred Trust. I don't personally know anyone that studies the Sacred Trust.

Plowman—There is very little studying of the Sacred Trust in our day. Some folks follow a daily devotional that gives them a daily "feel good" thought. Others use a few favorite passages as proof texts for errors like the Sugar Kids Message. Others lean on a few favorite passages as success-motivation slogans. And others yet use the Sacred Trust like a Christian horoscope, seeking tidbits that encourage them in their pursuit of happiness. But few go beyond the Innocuous Minimum. They don't have the time or the interest. Their Big Here & Now is way too important.

Peregrinus—I've seen a bit of that lately.

Plowman—I don't understand "Christians" who don't have an unquenchable hunger for studying the Sacred Trust, but seem content with trifling. John says, "My sheep hear my voice and follow me," and Romans informs us that, "hearing comes by the Word of God." In other words, believers hear the voice of the Crucified One in the Sacred Trust and follow him by following his Word. How can a man be a real Christian if he shows little interest in walking with the Redeemer in his Word?

Peregrinus—So believers don't dabble in the Sacred Trust; they diligently read and study it?

Plowman—That's right. In John we read, "If you continue in my Word, then you are my disciples indeed." This diligence is no mere religious toil or academic exercise. It is a practical effort that is a huge blessing for the believer. As John says, "in the Sacred Trust you will discover the truth, and the truth will set you free": free from error, free from sin, free from self, and free from the Big Here & Now. Dabbling in the Word of God never leads to this discovery and deliverance. Only diligence in it does.

The Three Components of Serious Studying

Peregrinus—I noticed you were taking notes when I walked up. Do you always take notes when you study?

Plowman—I sure do. There is no serious studying that does not involve taking notes. It is one of the three main components of serious studying.

Peregrinus—So what are the three?

Plowman—Breadth and depth, note taking, and drawing conclusions.

Peregrinus—So what do you mean by breadth and depth in our studies?

Plowman—God has clearly revealed his mind in the Sacred Trust on every important matter like the freshbirth and Sweet Everlasting. But the Sacred Trust isn't an encyclopedia which gives us a full understanding of a subject in one passage. It is a marvelous tapestry whose handling of subjects is piecemeal and progressive. The only way to fully uncover God's mind on any matter is to study the entire Sacred Trust and find all the material from Genesis to Revelation that touches on the subject and take all of it into consideration. The broader and deeper our study, the less likely we are to confuse the thoughts of man with the thoughts of God.

Peregrinus—What's the purpose of taking notes?

Plowman—Taking notes helps keep track of the conclusions you have reached on the subjects you have studied. Is also helps you to refine your thoughts.

Peregrinus—I take notes once in a while, but it doesn't help me keep track of anything. I can never find them again.

Plowman—Occasionally scratching out a few notes on any handy scrap of paper — including old envelopes and grocery receipts — doesn't count as note taking. Such notes are usually tossed in a pile or a drawer and forgotten.

Peregrinus—What about drawing conclusions?

Plowman—We don't fulfill our responsibility merely by knowing the letter of Scripture. The Pharisees had that. Nor do we fulfill it with hazy notions about vital subjects as grace, faith, and the freshbirth. We must gather passages, compare them, and draw conclusions from them. God wants us to think.

Peregrinus—But what if our conclusions are wrong?

Plowman—They will be sometimes, especially early in our studies. There is no such thing as thinking without being wrong sometimes. But the honest man who thinks and draws wrong conclusions can rethink the subject and correct his conclusions. This is better than the ugly alternative. If men choose not to think, they are choosing to let someone else think for them. That is dangerous. It guarantees that they will be susceptible to Invincible Dogma and the Ironclad Interpretations used to defend it.

Peregrinus—Serious studying sounds like hard work to me.

Plowman—It is hard work. But the reward is well worth the effort. If men search for understanding as for hid treasure and seek after wisdom as after silver, they will find it. And it is far better to find wisdom and understanding than silver and gold.

THE GLORIOUS SALVATION MACHINE

Repentance and the Hard Sayings

Peregrinus—So what are you studying now?

Plowman—I am studying what the Sacred Trust teaches on repentance — for the fourth time actually.

Peregrinus—Really? I have wondered about that subject myself. It seems to me that the Sacred Trust commands men to repent, but my friend Luke W. Zeal and the folks in the Sugar Kids church I attend tell me that men can't repent. They insist that all we can do is feel bad about our sins and ask the Sweet One to take them from us. If we toss them aside ourselves and walk away from them, that is bad, bad, nasty-bad Dead Works. It is trampling on God Magic and trying to save ourselves.

Plowman—Yep. I've heard that a thousand times myself.

Peregrinus—What do you think?

Plowman—They are dead wrong. They have been Head Pounded. We read in the Sacred Trust that the law was until John the Baptist, but grace came by the Crucified One. And the bringer of grace was a preacher of repentance. His constant message was "Repent and believe the Wonderful Message." He warned men that they would perish if they did not repent. The only reasonable conclusion we can draw is that the preaching of repentance belongs to grace, not law. And this should not surprise us. Law is unmerciful. It doesn't forgive. It doesn't give second chances. But the message of repentance, on the contrary, offers a second chance, and a third, and a fourth, and so on. This speaks of grace.

Peregrinus—What about the other hard sayings in the Gospels like "Take up your cross and follow me," "Strait is the gate and narrow is the way that leads to Sweet Everlasting," and "He that would save his life must lose his life for my sake and the sake of the Wonderful Message"?

Plowman—They mean exactly what they say. There is no more contradiction between grace and taking up the cross, or grace and passing through the strait gate, than there is between grace and repentance. The Sacred Trust plainly says, "The grace of God that brings salvation to all men has appeared, teaching men to deny ungodliness and Big Here & Now lust, and to live soberly, righteously, and godly in the present Big Here & Now." Grace holds out to men deliverance from the *practice* of sin as well as deliverance from the *penalty* of sin. The two are inseparable. You can't receive grace's ministry of justification and reject its ministry of sanctification.

Peregrinus—Dude! I never heard that before. Not in my old Sprinkle Form church. Not in my new Faith Form church. It always seemed to me that we should take the hard sayings at face value. But who was I to challenge the Big Cheese.

Salvation Is by Faith Alone

Peregrinus—This brings up another question. I was under the impression that salvation was by faith alone. That's what everyone tells me anyway.

Plowman—They are absolutely right. Salvation is by faith alone. When we introduce works into the salvation picture, we make it impossible for man to be saved. The principle of works puts salvation on a shelf so high that man cannot reach it. He can never do enough, and he can never do well enough. The very best efforts of the very best men that have ever lived fall vastly short of the praise of God. Trying to approach God on the principle of works is trying to do the impossible. You may as well try filling the Grand Canyon with a teaspoon.

Faith and the Obligation to Turn

Peregrinus—So how do you go about reconciling salvation by faith alone with the many *do* requirements that we find in the Wonderful Message passages — like repent, pass through the strait gate, and take up the cross? I thought *doing* stuff to obtain salvation was always in conflict with faith?

Plowman—*First of all*, there are not many *do* requirements in the Wonderful Message, there is only one — the obligation to *turn*. All such things as repentance, passing through the strait gate, and taking up the cross are one and the same motion of the heart — turning from our rejection of God and his way and turning to God and his way. The diamond of turning has been cut on the pages of the Sacred Trust with many facets, each facet viewing the necessary turn from a different perspective.

Peregrinus—Okay, so we lump all such *do* requirements into one *turn*. Man is still required to *do* something other than believe. He is required to *turn* as well as believe. That makes two things, right? And since everything other than faith is works, we can only conclude that turning is works.

Plowman—The problem is, there is a flaw in your argument. Turning is not a distinct condition of salvation that man must do in addition to faith. Turning is, in its essence, turning from one's own way — the way of unbelief — to the way of faith.

Peregrinus—Can you expand on that thought?

Plowman—Absolutely. The only reason that ungodly men have ungodly things in their lives that they need to turn from is because they have unbelief in their hearts that they need to turn from. You see, man does not trust God. He does not believe that God is good or fair. He does not believe that God's way is the best way to find happiness and fulfillment. So he goes his own way, the way of unbelief. And on this path, fueled by the fires of unbelief, he seeks happiness and fulfillment in sins that are contrary to the revealed will of God.

But when a man tastes that God is good and his way best, he turns in his heart from his own unbelieving way and turns in faith to God's way. And the faith-turn in his heart produces an outward lifestyle-turn in his Daily Grind.

Faith Is a Matter of the Heart

Peregrinus—That makes a lot of sense. If faith is a heart-turn that manifests itself with a lifestyle-turn in one's Daily Grind, then there is no contradiction between the hard sayings in the Gospels and salvation by faith alone.

Plowman—That's right. Having some Innocuous Minimum religion in your life is not faith. Nor is it faith to do a religious form and believe that it saves you by God Magic. Faith is a heart-turn from unbelief in the goodness of God to faith in God and his goodness. This turn is just as amazing as a man rising from the dead. Faith changes people in a way that amazes people.

Peregrinus—What about the common view that faith is the presence of a few facts in the head?

Plowman—Faith is not the head holding a few notions, even if those notions are correct. That is bogus. If faith is simply the head holding a few correct notions, then there is no distinction between profession and possession. All who profess salvation really do possess salvation — and no amount of sin, rebellion, or unbelief can invalidate that profession. But that is far from the truth. Faith is the heart committed to the Crucified One. And all who are committed to the Crucified One are committed to his commandments and teachings.

Peregrinus—So faith is a matter of the heart?

Plowman—Absolutely. Nothing is more clearly taught in the Sacred Trust. For instance, we read such statements as "With the heart man believes unto justification" and" "Keep your heart, for out of it are the issues of life."

Peregrinus—How come men can't see the truth on faith?

Plowman—They don't want to see the truth on faith. They don't want faith to be a heart matter. That would intrude on their heart commitment to the Big Here & Now. So they embrace Innocuous Minimum systems where faith is confidence in a Faith Form and a few notions rattling around in the head.

Peregrinus—Dude! This is mega-helpful. Your observations have turned the lights on for me.

Plowman—Glad to hear it. One of the biggest needs of our day is a clear understanding of faith.

God Works Faith in the Heart

Peregrinus—Speaking of faith, where does it come from?

Plowman—Definitely not from man. Faith is not something that we can work up, whip up, or draw up from some deep well in our heart. It is wrought in a man's heart by God.

Peregrinus—So how does God work faith into a heart?

Plowman—By his Word. As the Sacred Trust says, "Faith comes by hearing, and hearing by the Word of God."

Peregrinus—And where does faith get the power to turn from stuff, like sin and the Big Here & Now, and turn to God?

Plowman—From two sources: the Word of God and the love of God.

The Sacred Trust tells us that the Word of God is living and powerful. And because the Word is living and powerful, so the faith wrought by it is living and powerful. As the seed, so the fruit.

We also know from the Sacred Trust that faith works by love. Not by mere human love, but by divine love. The love of God is shed abroad in our hearts. This love wins us to God, draws us to God, conforms us to God, and empowers us for God. There is no motive on earth more powerful than love. And there is no love more powerful than God's love.

Peregrinus—So the power does not originate in us?

Plowman—That's right. The power is not drawn from human resources, but heaven's. Just as appliances get their power by being plugged into an outside energy source, so faith gets its power by being plugged into God himself.

Peregrinus—If that's how faith works, then how can a man believe and not turn from the stuff he ought to turn from?

Plowman—He can't. That's impossible. Faith plugs into the amazing power of the Almighty God, who has predestined all who believe in his Son to be conformed to the image of his Son — the Crucified One. The power to turn and walk in victory is, therefore, inherent in faith. That is why the Sacred Trust says faith is the victory that overcomes the Big Here & Now. Not great faith. Not exceptional faith. Not perfect faith. Just faith.

God Works the Willing and the Doing in Us

Peregrinus—This is so different from what I am used to hearing. Men talk about faith being from God, but it's a wimpy faith that doesn't amount to much. No one is expected to walk in victory over sin and the Big Here & Now. Those who exhort men to do so are accused of preaching Dead Works. And those who take these exhortations to heart and walk in victory are charged with vain human effort.

Plowman—That is backwards. We can't have victory in our own effort and strength. The greatest effort that could possibly be mustered by this clay-vessel heart is no match for the wiles of the Mad Spirit and the deceitfulness of sin.

But believers are not left to their own efforts and strength. God strengthens us with might according to the exceeding greatness of his mighty power, which he wielded in his Son when he raised him from the dead, that we might walk worthy of him — both willing and doing his good pleasure.

Peregrinus—Dude! If that's the case, if help from heaven is part of faith, enabling all who believe to turn and obey, then the opposite is true too. Those who do not turn and obey have not been enabled by God, which indicates that they have not believed on God. They are just religious.

Plowman—That's exactly right. When men truly believe the Crucified One and his Wonderful Message, they find strength and help to obey the Wonderful Message, including the hard sayings. They tap into power that enables them to live a godly, obedient life. Those who have a form of godliness, but not the power to live a godly life, are children of the hypocrisy of the Passive Form. When men fail to manifest the life and fruit of the vine, they are not in the vine, no matter how loud they protest. You can know believers by their fruits.

Faith Is Really Having a Relationship with God

Peregrinus—I think I understand. Faith isn't confidence in a Passive Form mixed with a little Innocuous Minimum religion. Nor is it having a few notions about God and his salvation, even if correct, rattling around in the head. Faith is really having a relationship with God.

THE GLORIOUS SALVATION MACHINE

Plowman—Yep. Faith is coming to God in the person of the Crucified One to have a real relationship with him — to walk with him, talk with him, learn of him, and be molded by him.

Peregrinus—Coming to God in the person of the Crucified One. I like that. It puts faith in clear perspective.

Plowman—It sure does. And there are three aspects of faith that are evident in the life of every man that has actually come to God. He is *transparent* before God; he is *pliable* in the hands of God; and he is *confident* in God. Those who lack these things have never come to God. They are still walking with an evil heart of unbelief, seeking their fulfillment in the wicked ways, polluted pleasures, and tainted treasures of the Big Here & Now.

Peregrinus—Can you help me out a bit with those terms?

Plowman—*Transparent* implies that a man is comfortable in the presence of God. In other words, he is comfortable in the presence of penetrating light that reveals everything. God is, after all, light — marvelous light far above all created light. The transparent man is repentant, wanting this light to reveal all his sins, so he may forsake them, and all his faults, so he may fix them. Moreover, he is humble, not trying to maintain a facade, but allowing men to see him in public as God sees him in private. He really is what he appears to be.

Pliable implies that a man is workable clay in the Potter's hands. He may throw a fuss or get discouraged from time to time, even as we see in the men of God in the Old Testament. But when all is said and done, he always gives in. He is willing to be taught, willing to be led, willing to be molded, willing to wait, even for years in the backside of the desert. He is willing to accept the will of God, whatever it may be, and willing to pay the price of faithfulness, no matter what the cost.

Confident implies that a man trusts God. He trusts that God will give him a better deal than he can get from the Big Here & Now, so he tears down the Altar of Worthy Self and follows the Crucified One. He trusts that the pleasures prepared for him in Sweet Everlasting will far outweigh the discouragements of this life. He trusts that every instance of bad that comes his way is ordained of God and that all bad things will ultimately work out for his own good. He trusts that God will fulfill every one of the promises he has made to his people in the Sacred Trust, despite circumstances that seem to imply otherwise.

Tear Down the Altar of Worthy Self to Fill the Big Empty

Peregrinus—Speaking of the Altar of Worthy Self, Jumping Jack teaches that we don't have to tear it down. He says that if we ask the Sweet One into our heart, we are allowed to keep it. We just need to make sure that we only offer clean stuff on it.

Plowman—Well, he is dead wrong. The Sacred Trust clearly teaches that we are supposed to tear the Altar of Worthy Self down.

Peregrinus—But if we pull down the Altar of Worthy Self, how are we supposed to fill the Big Empty? I know by hard experience that I can't fill the Big Empty no matter how much stuff I pile on the Altar. Yet it still seems counterintuitive to tear it down. Everything inside me screams out to keep the Altar of Worthy Self at any cost.

Plowman—Believe me, I understand. Been there, felt that. But if we want to fill the Big Empty, we absolutely must tear down the Altar of Worthy Self. It cannot stay.

Peregrinus—How does tearing down the Altar of Worthy Self help fill the Big Empty? It sounds like you're saying that we must quit trying to fill the Big Empty if we want to fill the Big Empty. That sounds a little Eastern religionish to me. I can picture some wrinkled, old sage in an incense filled temple gravely stating, "Self has a Big Empty. The Big Empty is a big problem. How should we fix the problem? By filling the Big Empty? No. By taking Self out of the picture. If we take Self out of the picture, there is no more Big Empty problem." True. But there is no Self either. I don't want to cease to exist. I want to be fulfilled.

Plowman—Well, there's no mystical nonsense here, only a stiff dose of common sense. Tearing down the Altar of Worthy

Self isn't esoteric religion that would have men try to fix their Big Empty problem by trying to lose themselves and their Big Empty in infinite nothingness. Tearing down the Altar is one of the first steps in cultivating a real relationship with God. God has no interest in man serving two masters: himself and God. God wants man to serve one master: God.

But God is not merely into receiving. He is also into giving. And he wants to fill our Big Empties. We just need to trust him. We need to quit trying to fill them with stuff that can't fill them and let God fill them with stuff that can fill them.

Peregrinus—I'm all ears.

Plowman—The Sacred Trust says that God has put eternity in our hearts. This means that the Big Empty is an infinite hole. Now an infinite hole can only be filled with infinite things like the infinite God and his infinite reward. And this means that no amount of Big Here & Now stuff could fill the Big Empty, not even if we were given ten thousand years, ideal circumstances, and a magic wand. But the Big Empty can be filled with the stuff of Sweet Everlasting: the joy of worshipping the Giver face to face; the joy of life without end or limitation; the joy of stuff that cannot wear out or break; the joy of living where there are no thieves, or taxes, or fees, or fines.

The Altar of Worthy Self Is the Big Here & Now Interface

Peregrinus—I understand that we cannot fill the Big Empty by putting Big Here & Now stuff on the Altar of Worthy Self. But does that necessitate that we tear down the Altar? Couldn't we keep it and determine only put truly good stuff on it, like Wonderful Message stuff?

Plowman—What you need to understand is that we do not need the Altar of Worthy Self to find happiness and fulfillment. We have identified our happiness and fulfillment with it for so long that the thought of tearing it down seems like death. But the Altar of Worthy Self is not you. You are distinct from the Altar.

Peregrinus—If the Altar of Worthy Self isn't me, what is it?

Plowman—It is the interface with the Big Here & Now that men use when they want to exploit the Big Here & Now for Big Here & Now purposes. It stands in stark contrast to the cross of the Crucified One, which is the interface with the Big Here & Now that men use when they want to invest their time in the Big Here & Now for Sweet Everlasting purposes.

Peregrinus—What do you mean by an interface?

Plowman—An interface is a tool that enables us to interact with something. For instance, operating systems and keyboards enable us to interact with computers, instrument panels enable us to interact with airplanes, and control panels enable us to interact with machines. These are all interfaces.

Peregrinus—If it's only an interface, how did it get the name Altar of Worthy Self?

Plowman—Because the spirit of its use boils down to, "Me. Me. Me. What I want, the way I want it, right here, right now."

The Two Interfaces

Plowman—When it comes to computers, we have our choice of different operating systems to interact with our computer. So man has two choices for interacting with the Big Here & Now. He can interact with it through the Altar of Worthy Self, or he can interact with it through the cross of the Crucified One.

Peregrinus—Two choices? Is that like the broad road and the narrow road?

Plowman—You got it. The Altar of Worthy Self is referred to as the Interface of Sight because those who use it live and labor for gain they can see in the Big Here & Now. They strive for profit, pleasure, praise, honor, and glory that they get right here, right now in the Big Here & Now from the men and institutions of the Big Here & Now.

The cross of the Crucified One is referred to as the Interface of Faith because those who choose it live and labor for gain that they cannot see in the Big Here & Now. They strive for profit, pleasure, praise, honor, and glory they shall receive from God in Sweet Everlasting.

THE GLORIOUS SALVATION MACHINE

Peregrinus—So every man has to choose between these two interfaces? He has to decide whether he is going to go through life in the Big Here & Now making his decisions and choices with the Interface of Sight or with the Interface of Faith?

Plowman—Exactly. The followers of the Mad Spirit, the god and ruler of the Big Here & Now, utilize the Interface of Sight. They are not merely *in* the Big Here & Now; they are *of* the Big Here & Now. Their life is characterized by a *my heart is in the Big Here & Now* decision-making process that chooses Big Here & Now considerations over considerations of faithfulness to the Sacred Trust and the Wonderful Message.

The followers of the Crucified One, on the other hand, use the Interface of Faith. Though they are *in* the Big Here & Now, they are not *of* the Big Here & Now. Their life is characterized by a *my heart is in heaven* decision-making process that chooses considerations of faithfulness to the Sacred Trust and the Wonderful Message over Big Here & Now considerations. They are as diligent as any worldly man in their sweat-of-the-brow responsibilities. They can hustle and bustle with the best. But they have a heavenly aura about them. Their priorities are different. The way they think is different. The way they make decisions is different.

Dark Light and the Altar of Worthy Self

Peregrinus—So how do men justify choosing the Interface of Sight over the Interface of Faith? How do they justify taking the Altar of Worthy Self over the cross of the Crucified One? That seems like such an obviously poor choice that you would think that everyone's conscience would beat him to death.

Plowman—They use Dark Light.

Peregrinus—What's that?

Plowman—Dark Light is darkness that is passed off as light. It is used to hide what men do not want to see and dim what they do not want to emphasize. Using it is like doctoring up a picture with photograph software. When the Crucified One said, "If the light that is in you be darkness, how great is that darkness," he was referring to Dark Light.

Peregrinus—So Dark Light allows men to pretend that they don't see what they really do see and make-believe that they see what they really don't see.

Plowman—That's right.

Peregrinus—So how do men use Dark Light to get rid of the fact that they are supposed to choose between the Interface of Sight and the Interface of Faith?

Plowman—They beg the question. They use Dark Light to make it look like there is no choice to be made. They pretend that the Altar of Worthy Self is the only Big Here & Now interface that exists, that it has no intrinsic moral reference, and that its value hinges entirely on the manner in which it is used: good or bad, right or wrong, clean or dirty.

Peregrinus—So Dark Light allows men to trample on the hard sayings in the Sacred Trust that require men to tear down the Altar of Worthy Self and pretend that the only choice they face is what to put on the Altar.

Plowman—Yep. It is unnerving to watch men use Dark Light to deny the obvious and believe the ludicrous, so they can cozy up with Innocuous Minimum religion, condone the Altar of Worthy Self, and close their eyes to the soon coming day of judgment, which shall destroy the entire Big Here & Now — the entire corrupt, God-rejecting world system.

The Altar of Worthy Self Cannot Be Salvaged

Peregrinus—If the Altar of Worthy Self is the Big Here & Now interface for Big Here & Now purposes, then there really is no way to salvage it and use it for God.

Plowman—That's right. Many men have tried to salvage the Altar and dedicate it to God, but such efforts always fail, no matter how strong their resolve at the beginning. The Altar of Worthy Self is dedicated to the Big Here & Now, therefore no matter how hard you try, you will keep drifting back to using it for Big Here & Now purposes.

Peregrinus—Then the Altar must come down.

Plowman—That's right. As long as the Altar of Worthy Self stands, it will undermine a man's best efforts to seek the Crucified One's purposes in the Big Here & Now. It will sidetrack him with Big Here & Now hopes, plans, and goals which get in the way of serving and following the Crucified One the way he wants to be served and followed.

The Way of the Cross Is the Way of Filling

Peregrinus—So, a few minutes ago you said that the way of the cross is the way of filling.

Plowman—That's right. The way of the cross is the only way to fill our Big Empty.

Peregrinus—Okay, then what does it mean to take up the cross of the Crucified One?

Plowman—To take up the cross means to believe on the Crucified One. And to believe on the Crucified One implies that we follow him, that we give up living our lives for Big Here & Now purposes and start living them for the Crucified One's purposes in the Big Here & Now. In the language of the Sacred Trust, we lose our lives for the sake of the Crucified One and his Wonderful Message.

Peregrinus—That sounds like dying to me.

Plowman—It is death in a sense. The cross is an instrument of death. Paul wrote in one of his epistles, "I am crucified with the Crucified One. It is no longer I who live, but the Crucified One lives in me. The life which I now live in the flesh, I live in the faith of the Son of God who loved me and gave himself for me." So we do stop living — for ourselves.

Peregrinus—So how does taking up my cross and losing my life in the Big Here & Now fill my Big Empty?

Plowman—Those who lose their lives for the sake of the Crucified One and his Wonderful Message will receive their lives back in Sweet Everlasting with infinite interest. They shall receive a far more exceeding and eternal weight of glory, which shall more than fill their Big Empty.

THE PROVIDENTIAL MEETING

Peregrinus—So if we say *yes* to the call of the Crucified One to make his business in the Big Here & Now our own business in the Big Here & Now, he will make it his business some sweet day in Sweet Everlasting to fill our Big Empty?

Plowman—That's right. He will not overlook our service of faith or labor of love. The interest we receive in eternity will infinitely surpass the investment we make in time.

The Big Empty Filled with Rock-Solid Hope

Peregrinus—If God's plan is to fill our Big Empties some sweet day in Sweet Everlasting, does that mean that they don't actually get filled now?

Plowman—Oh no, they do get filled now. The Sacred Trust promises that those who drink of the water the Crucified One provides shall never thirst again. I have found this to be true in my experience and so has every man who has ever believed. The Big Empty is filled by faith in this life and by sight in the life to come. Right now we enjoy the promise of life in Sweet Everlasting. Some day we will enjoy the possession of it.

Peregrinus—Well, after some of the experiences I've had, I'm a little nervous about filling my Big Empty by faith.

Plowman—I'm not talking about pretending that your Big Empty is full or pretending that you can fill it with the junk of this world — whether by success-motivation techniques or by Faith Talk. I'm talking about really filling your Big Empty in a way you can really know and feel. The believer can wend his weary way through the barren wasteland of this world filled to overflowing with the promise that he shall be fulfilled in Sweet Everlasting.

Peregrinus—So our Big Empty is filled with hope?

Plowman—That's right. But not the kind of hope that the men of the Big Here & Now have. We don't cross our fingers and hope for the best against long, if not impossible, odds. Our hope is rock-solid, being founded upon unbreakable promises made to us by the Everliving God who cannot lie. We wait in blessed hope for that wonderful day when we shall pass from the good fight of faith to the sweet sight of glory. Our hope is a living hope, even a living Saviour who has given us his Word that he shall come again.

Peregrinus—And this hope actually fills the Big Empty?

Plowman—Absolutely. Our heart and mind are so filled with anticipation of the joy that is set before us that we do not turn aside, though we are footsore and weary in our journey to the Promised Land, and we do not hanker for the leaks and onions of Egypt, though our only food be the heavenly manna of the Word of God.

Apparent Big Here & Now Fillings of the Big Empty

Peregrinus—What about those people that appear to have filled their Big Empty with Big Here & Now stuff?

Plowman—A small percentage of men, at any given time, appear to have filled their Big Empties with the pleasures and treasures of the Big Here & Now. But their filling is a lie that will be exposed. The plug at the bottom of their Big Empty will be pulled sometime down the road, and they shall be emptier than empty. Some get their plug pulled while yet young. Some while in their golden days. Some on their death bed. But every apparently filled man will have his plug pulled as surely as the sun sets in the evening. Every single one will come face to face with harsh reality and discover that his filling was no more real and lasting than a dream.

Peregrinus—So every instance of a Big Empty that is supposedly filled with Big Here & Now stuff — be it honor, fame, success, riches, or pleasure — is a lie.

Plowman—That's right. Attempting to fill the Big Empty with the Big Here & Now is a mad endeavor. It is chasing Shimmering Elusive. Very few men succeed; and those that do will, without fail, watch their gains slip through their fingers. They cannot keep them. It is vanity and insanity to try and fill the Big Empty with stuff that will be stripped from your grasp.

Peregrinus—Then there is no advantage when men "have it made" in the Big Here & Now.

THE PROVIDENTIAL MEETING

Plowman—That's right. No matter what a man has in life — painful poverty or insane wealth — the end is the same. We all leave the world as we came into it, naked and destitute. We all leave all of our Big Here & Now stuff behind. So we ought to use our time down here with our eyes on eternity.

Chasing Soap Bubbles

Peregrinus—If that's the case, then pursuing the stuff of the Big Here & Now is like chasing soap bubbles.

Plowman—You know it. Soap bubbles are hard to catch and harder to keep. Not to mention, they don't have much value. That's exactly the way it is with the shiny baubles of the Big Here & Now. They are hard to catch and harder to keep. Even if we manage to gather up a pile, they will not and cannot last. They will vanish like soap bubbles.

Peregrinus—Dude! What a freeing thought. I don't have to join in the rat race of trying to chase down soap bubbles to fill my Big Empty. This is so different — refreshingly different — from the teaching I heard in the Glorious Salvation Machine and in Jumping Jack's church.

Plowman—Yep. Forget the treasure which cannot be kept. Pursue that treasure which cannot be lost. Get on the path of treasure without measure in Sweet Everlasting — life so vast and wonderful that it is beyond comprehension.

Peregrinus—Why do people keep chasing soap bubbles? It doesn't take a lot of intelligence and experience to see how vain it is.

Plowman—They are living in denial. They have shut their eyes to the undeniable fact that the Altar of Worthy Self gives zero investment return. Putting stuff on it is like putting investment money in the incinerator and burning it up. For when death comes knocking, there is nothing left of the things placed on the Altar except ashes and bitterness.

Peregrinus—Men want fulfillment right here and right now.

Plowman—Exactly. They are living for the moment: for the pleasures of sin for a season; for treasure they cannot keep; for

THE GLORIOUS SALVATION MACHINE

praise and honor that cannot last. They fuss like spoiled, rotten kids saying "Gimme! Gimme! Gimme! Now! Now! Now!" They frantically chase and pile their shiny, little soap bubbles. It's all about now. They won't wait for tomorrow. They won't invest in tomorrow.

Sweet Everlasting Fictionalized or Marginalized

Peregrinus—It seems odd that so many of those who profess to believe in the Crucified One and his Wonderful Message are completely focused on the Big Here & Now. You would think that five minutes of thinking on the matter is all they would need to see the error of their way, get their bearings straight, and start living for Sweet Everlasting.

Plowman—You would think. But man, to his own undoing, has learned how to use rationalizations to justify his wayward love affair with the Big Here & Now.

Peregrinus—Rationalizations?

Plowman—Men have their choice of two rationalizations to get Sweet Everlasting out of their way. They can *fictionalize* it with the "Sweet Everlasting is a fairy tale" option. This option says the Big Here & Now is the only thing that can be pursued. There is no Sweet Everlasting.

Or they can *marginalize* it with the "God wants to minister to our whole person" option. This option insists that God cannot minister to our whole person unless we pursue the Big Here & Now. Walking in the footsteps of the Crucified One and his disciples, as pilgrims in a barren land, is regarded as a path that does not minister to the needs of the whole man.

Those of a secular mindset or a liberal religious mindset favor fictionalization. Those of a more traditional religious mindset favor marginalization.

Peregrinus—If men fictionalize Sweet Everlasting, then they don't really believe in it, do they?

Plowman—How could they believe in it? It's just a happy ending to a fairy tale.

Peregrinus—What about the marginalizers?

Plowman—They don't deserve much more credit than the fictionalizers do. They are guilty of less intellectual dishonesty in the matter, but they are guilty of the same unbelief. They are just as bound and determined to live for the Big Here & Now as their fairy-tale brethren.

Peregrinus—I can't believe how bad we humans are. We are so bad that if we want bad things bad enough, we can convince ourselves that bad is good and good is bad.

Plowman—That's why the Sacred Trust says, "There is a way that seems right to a man, and the end thereof is the way of death." Men have the uncanny ability to believe whatever they need to believe, so they can believe whatever they want to believe. And men are determined to love and pursue the Big Here & Now. This sets their Central Integrity Processor on the Gullibility Setting and predisposes them to swallow any semi-plausible rationale that justifies their love affair with the Big Here & Now.

The Religion of the Big Here & Now

Peregrinus—That helps me to understand why the religious man is just as committed to indulging the Big Here & Now as the secular man.

Plowman—There is very little difference in lifestyle between religious folks and secular folks. Frequently they indulge the same pleasures and vices. Even when they live differently, the differences are superficial. They both operate on Big Here & Now principles. They both make decisions based on Big Here & Now considerations. They both live to exploit the Big Here & Now for Big Here & Now purposes — whether secular, or religious, or some combination thereof.

Peregrinus—So even when they appear to be living differently, they are still living the same.

Plowman—You're catching on. It makes no difference at all whether men wallow in dirty mud or clean mud, secular mud or baptized mud. Mud is mud. Those who wallow in the clean mud are just as much children of the Big Here & Now as those who wallow in the dirty mud. Those who wallow in religious mud are just as much the children of the Big Here & Now as those who wallow in secular mud.

Peregrinus—They might as well all be the same religion.

Plowman—They are the same religion.

Peregrinus—Dude! That's bone-chilling.

Plowman—When everything is boiled down to its essence, there is only one religion in the Big Here & Now — the Altar of Worthy Self. This religion has one solitary tenet — man has an obligation to pursue happiness and fulfillment right here, right now in the stuff of the Big Here & Now.

The men of the Big Here & Now, regardless of their religious or political views, are profoundly and equally religious in the only sense that really matters. They all dance with abandon around the Altar of Worthy Self. They are all determined to *do*, *get*, and *be* the best in the Big Here & Now that they can possibly do, get, and be.

Peregrinus—So all the religions and philosophies of the Big Here & Now are really just branches of the same religion?

Plowman—Yep.

Peregrinus—And this religion is all about man?

Plowman—That's right. Man is his own religion. God is an optional piece of furniture. Some take him out of the picture. Some let him be in the picture as long as he stays out of the way. All have joined the Mad Spirit — the god of the Big Here & Now — in his revolt against God. They do not want to be bound by his Word, will, and ways. They do not want to be burdened with his world view, world history, or world plan.

Peregrinus—What emptiness. That seems so crazy.

Plowman—It is crazy. The human race doesn't trust God. They don't believe he will give them a better deal than they can give themselves by pursuing the Big Here & Now. So they invent religions and philosophies that validate their rejection of God and their vain pursuit of happiness and fulfillment in the Big Here & Now.

THE PROVIDENTIAL MEETING

Emboldened with the lies they have invented for themselves, they dance around the Altar of Worthy Self day after day, goal after goal, pleasure after pleasure, pursuit after pursuit. When they grow tired and weary, they numb their pain and re-zing their brain with the Babylonian wine of their favorite Big Here & Now philosophies and religions, which enables them to keep on dancing until their dying breath.

The Incredible Offer

Peregrinus—But God offers man something far better than what the Mad Spirit offers him in the Big Here & Now.

Plowman—Infinitely better. The offer of Sweet Everlasting for believing on the Crucified One is by far the most incredible offer that has ever been made. From the perspective of a worldly-minded man, turning from the pursuit of the Big Here & Now to follow the Crucified One seems like a steep price to pay. But when you compare what we give up with what we get, there is no comparison. It is like trading a handful of sand for a trainload of diamonds, rubies, silver, and gold — only better.

Peregrinus—I'm all ears. What does Sweet Everlasting offer man?

Plowman—Well, to start with, we get eternal life. We get to enjoy the reward that God gives us for all eternity — for endless ages of ages. This is staggering when you stop to think about it. When the redeemed have walked the streets of the New Jerusalem for a million years, eternity will have hardly started. The ages shall roll by — a billion years, a trillion years, a billion-trillion years — and eternity will still be young.

Peregrinus—I can't even fathom that. I think the mainframe in my brain-frame is going to melt down. No wonder Sweet Everlasting is able to fill the Big Empty.

Plowman—You can't make a Big Empty big enough that Sweet Everlasting can't fill it.

Peregrinus—The Incredible Offer seems to give us so much for so little.

THE GLORIOUS SALVATION MACHINE

Plowman—It does. We give God our clay-vessel faith for this short life, and he gives us an infinite weight of glory, the glory of a royal inheritance as the sons of God, that we shall enjoy for the endless ages of eternity.

Peregrinus—And why would he do that?

Plowman—Because it is God's glory to give in such a way that he has no peers, not even if you give the second best giver in the universe a billion point handicap. His giving makes our giving look like stealing. His giving, being an expression of his love and grace, is and always will be as high above our giving as the heavens are above the earth. Indeed, his giving has the essence of infinite in it. An infinite God cannot give finitely.

Sweet Everlasting Is a People Place with People Stuff

Peregrinus—So what sort of stuff will the followers of the Crucified One get for their reward in Sweet Everlasting?

Plowman—They shall receive a royal inheritance in the new heavens and new earth as heirs of God and coheirs with the Crucified One. This includes a home for each believer prepared by the Crucified One himself in the New Jerusalem, a city far more wonderful and beautiful than any city ever built by the hand of man.

Peregrinus—A real city? Do you really think the Wonderful Place is a real place?

Plowman—Absolutely. If we let the Sacred Trust say what it says and imply what it implies, it will be a real city with all the sights and sounds of city life — but untainted by ungodly man. There will be no sin, no crime, no pollution, no run-down neighborhoods, and no ugly. It will be filled with parks, trees, gardens, architecture, buildings, streets, and waterfront. It will be a bustling, beautiful, colorful, metropolitan city far beyond what the world has ever seen. The redeemed from every culture that has ever existed will display their own unique beauties in dress, music, language, architecture, art, food, and drink.

Peregrinus—That sure is a different perspective. I grew up thinking that the Wonderful Place was boring. Nobody talked about it. Nobody got excited about it. Preachers didn't preach on it. Men well semi-exist there in kind-of-there, kind-of-not-there bodies somewhere between angels and ghosts. Not quite the common picture of an angel sitting on a cloud, wearing a halo and holding a harp. But just as dull and unexciting. There will be nothing to own, nothing to do, and nothing to pursue. Just an unappealing existence in an unappealing place passing unappealing time in unappealing insignificance.

Plowman—I know only too well. I grew up thinking similar thoughts. The common conception of Sweet Everlasting is as attractive as a handful of sand. And a handful of sand, even if you get to hold it for all eternity, is just not a lot of incentive to pry a man's heart away from the pleasures of sin, or persuade him to stop dancing around the Altar of Worthy Self, or woo him away from the charm of the Big Here & Now.

Peregrinus—I know the view of Sweet Everlasting I grew up with didn't draw me away from the Big Here & Now. But for that matter, my church didn't make any spiritual matter look important or attractive.

Plowman—Most people have no understanding of the new heavens, the new earth, and the New Jerusalem. These are real places made for real people. God does not need them. The angels do not need them. They are made for people to enjoy the same way people enjoy things in this life. We do not cease to be human beings in the resurrection. We become glorified human beings. Our body is not changed into a non-body. It is transformed into a glorified, spiritual body. We will have a body that transcends our present body in the same way that the Crucified One's body after the resurrection transcended his body before. His resurrection body could walk through a wall or sit in a chair. He could sit at a campfire and enjoy food, but he did not need the food to survive. So in Sweet Everlasting we will touch, taste, see, hear, smell, and handle people stuff the same way we do now, but it will be "a better and enduring substance."

THE GLORIOUS SALVATION MACHINE

Peregrinus—I never in my wildest dreams thought Sweet Everlasting might be a people place with people stuff.

Plowman—There's more. The glorified body we receive in Sweet Everlasting is not susceptible to sickness, injury, or the ravages of time. It cannot wear out, break down, or die. It can feel sensation, but will never feel pain. Moreover, in Sweet Everlasting we will never face disappointment or loss. We will never suffer, sorrow, or weep. God will wipe away our tears forever. Every minute of every day will be sunshine and gladness. Everything will always be ideal.

Removing the Sand from Sweet Everlasting

Peregrinus—Wow! I used to think that Sweet Everlasting, whatever it was, would probably end up being a boring existence in a boring place. But the Sweet Everlasting you describe sounds fulfilling and exciting. I would pay any price to get there.

Plowman—I'm with you. I can remember how excited I was when I first understood that Sweet Everlasting was designed by a people-loving God to bless his redeemed people with ideal-for-people stuff in an ideal-for-people place in the ideal-for-people presence of God — even the presence of the Crucified One, who is God-manifest-in-people-flesh forever.

Peregrinus—There is one thing I don't understand though. The Sweet Everlasting taught in the Sacred Trust, as you have pointed out, is so heart thrilling and Big Empty filling that you'd think the whole world would storm the gate, jostling and shoving, to get on the path that leads to Sweet Everlasting.

Plowman—You'd think.

Peregrinus—What's the holdup?

Plowman—The same-old same-old. In the eyes of men, the ultimate taboo is interfering with Big Here & Now business and pleasure. They do whatever they have to do to protect their Big Here & Now stuff. They forcibly hold their eyes shut to keep out the light that would warn them against living for the Big Here & Now.

THE PROVIDENTIAL MEETING

Peregrinus—Well, I'm not going to close my eyes. I like what I see. When you take the sand out of Sweet Everlasting and replace it with the truth taught in the Sacred Trust, Sweet Everlasting has a very strong draw that breaks the charm of the Big Here & Now.

Plowman—That it does. Truth always sets men free. The doctrine of Sweet Everlasting is no exception. When men have a clear view of Sweet Everlasting towering over their horizon, it overwhelms every temptation to squander time, money, and heart affections on soap bubbles. It breaks the bewitching spell of the Big Here & Now, allowing men to see through its facade of golden opportunity and see the train wreck hiding behind it.

Peregrinus—The call of the Wonderful Message to take up the cross and follow the Crucified One doesn't seem like such a hardship after all. I can feel the cross growing lighter just listening to you talk about Sweet Everlasting.

Plowman—Yep. Truth changes our perception of things. One of my favorite hymns says, "Tell me not of heavy crosses, nor of burdens hard to bear." These lines are precious truth. When we set our sights on the joy waiting on the horizon, the cross is not a heavy burden, and its shame is not hard to bear.

Plowman Gets Personal

Plowman—Well, I'd like to bring this conversation down to a personal level, because I only have a few more minutes before I have to head back to my car.

Peregrinus—Sure.

Plowman—We've talked about faith, the freshbirth, Sweet Everlasting, and filling the Big Empty. What are you going to do about these matters? You see through the Faith Form. You see the necessity of heart-faith in the Crucified One. You see that you must have a real relationship with him. So what will you do? Will you trust him? Will you say *yes* to him? Will you tear down the Altar of Worthy Self? Will you determine to quit going your own way and being your own boss? You can't tear down the Altar on your own. You can't get victory over sin and

THE GLORIOUS SALVATION MACHINE

the Big Here & Now on your own. But you can say *yes*. If you say *yes* and really mean business, he will give you all the help and strength you need. So what will you do?

Peregrinus Hesitates

Peregrinus—I don't know what to say. Up until now I thought I wanted to go to Sweet Everlasting regardless of the cost. But now I find myself hesitating.

Plowman—What holds you back?

Peregrinus—It's scary to think seriously about tearing down the Altar of Worthy Self. It's a big change to quit living my life in the Big Here & Now for my own desires and start living it for the desires of the Crucified One.

Plowman—Like millions of men, you have found the strait gate and are hesitant to pass through it.

Peregrinus—I'm ashamed to admit it, but that's the truth. That's exactly where I'm at. I guess I'm hesitating because I really want to know for sure that this is going to pay off. What if I tear down the Altar of Worthy Self and follow the Crucified One, and my Big Empty never gets filled?

Plowman—It's a simple matter of faith. It's a matter of the testimony of God versus your fears. Are you going to put your trust in your fears? Or will you put your trust in the Word of God? Think about it. What are you better off trusting — the promises of God who cannot lie or the fears of a man who shouldn't trust himself? If you put your trust in the Crucified One, you will tear down the Altar of Worthy Self and follow him down the pilgrim path in this evil Big Here & Now, and your Big Empty will be filled. If you put your trust in your fears, you will leave the Altar of Worthy Self standing and follow your own worldly desires, and you will keep your Big Empty empty.

At this point Peregrinus managed to deftly evade Plowman's pointed questions and turn the conversation to a subject a little less close to home.

THE PROVIDENTIAL MEETING

The Havens and How They Differ from the Half-Havens

Peregrinus—I know you need to get going in a minute, but can I ask another question?
Plowman—Sure.
Peregrinus—What church do you go to?
Plowman—I go to a Haven.
Peregrinus—So what's a Haven? I've heard preachers and other folks rail against them from time to time. Nobody ever says anything good about them.
Plowman—The Havens are churches that reject the errors of the Glorious Salvation Machine and the Half-Havens.
Peregrinus—In what ways are they different?
Plowman—They differ in three main ways. *One*, how a man gets freshborn. *Two*, how they handle the Sacred Trust. *Three*, their relationship to the Big Here & Now.
Peregrinus—How do they differ on the freshbirth?
Plowman—The Glorious Salvation Machine and the Half-Havens practice *formalized* freshbirth by a Passive Form. The Havens practice *internalized* freshbirth by real-relationship faith in the person and work of the Crucified One.
Peregrinus—How about the differences in how they handle the Sacred Trust?
Plowman—The Glorious Salvation Machine and the Half-Havens deal unjustly with much of the Sacred Trust: ignoring much of it and overthrowing much more of it with their Invincible Dogmas and Ironclad Interpretations.

The Havens take the entire book at face value and in dead earnest. They honor it above every consideration, even all the name of God. They believe that every passage is profitable for teaching doctrine and practice, for rebuking men and churches that are wayward, for straightening things that are crooked, and for educating men on how to live right in a wrong-living Big Here & Now.

Peregrinus—How do they differ on the Big Here & Now?
Plowman—The Glorious Salvation Machine and the Half-Havens regard the Big Here & Now as a playground. Some of

THE GLORIOUS SALVATION MACHINE

the deeper thinking folks regard it as a run-down playground that needs to be fixed up. But all regard it as a playground. The Havens, on the other hand, regard the Big Here & Now as a barren desert. For this reason, they often refer to themselves as the "Havens in the wasteland."

The Most Important Question

Peregrinus—Well, that's a vote for the Havens. I know that I want to attend a Haven.

Plowman—Personally, I believe every follower of the Crucified One should attend a Haven. But whether or not you attend a Haven is not the most important question you face at this point.

Peregrinus—Oh, how's that?

Plowman—The most important question you face right now is whether you will say *yes* to the Crucified One. This is not a matter of attending church. It is not a matter of good church, bad church, indifferent church, or wishy-washy church. It is simply a matter of saying *yes* to the Crucified One. Don't put it off. You need to say *yes* today. Saying *tomorrow* is the same spirit of unbelief as saying *no*. It wears a religious cloak and pretends it will do business with God, someday. But it is just a subtle version of the same evil heart of unbelief.

So what will you do with him? Will you say *yes* and follow him? Delay is dangerous. If you had deadly cancer festering in your body that demanded immediate attention, would you procrastinate and put off surgery? Why do men that have spiritual cancer in their heart procrastinate and delay?

Peregrinus—You're right. I can't put it off. I won't put it off. I am going to get right with the Crucified One.

Read the Sacred Trust

Plowman—There is one thing I want to challenge you with before we part.

Peregrinus—Sure.

THE PROVIDENTIAL MEETING

Plowman—You need to spend time reading the Sacred Trust. Get to know it intimately. There is no other way you can get to know God and his will. The Sacred Trust says, "If you are my disciples, you will continue in my Word, and in my Word you will discover the truth, and the truth will set you free." This is a matter of time and effort. Occasional dabbling will not do.

Peregrinus—Well, you have definitely gotten me stirred up to read and study the Sacred Trust. I am going to do as you suggested and start reading in the four Gospels.

Plowman—Good for you. They are the meat and potatoes of true religion. They are the ABC's of serving the Crucified One. They will give you the essence of his character, his salvation, and his ways of dealing with man. They will teach you much about faith. Read them night and day. Read them over and over again.

Seek for Understanding As for Hid Treasure

Plowman—Be diligent in this matter. The Sacred Trust exhorts us to seek understanding with the same passion that we seek hid treasure. Those who search with this passion shall understand the fear of the Lord and find the knowledge of God.

Think about it. If a prospector determined, based on reliable information, where the richest gold vein in the world was located and that it was his for the taking, he would move like there was no tomorrow. He would let nothing stand in his way and would not rest until it was claimed and worked.

Likewise, the man who sees the incredible, immeasurable riches that are offered to him in the Sacred Trust will move with purpose. He will let nothing stand in his way and will not rest, until he has staked his claim in the Crucified One and worked that claim for all its worth.

Invitation for Coffee and Conversation

Plowman—Hey, I need to run. How about getting together again on Friday. Are you free this Friday evening?

Peregrinus—I sure am.

THE GLORIOUS SALVATION MACHINE

Plowman—How about meeting me at seven-o'clock at the Steaming Joe for some coffee and conversation? We can talk more about the Crucified One, the Sacred Trust, the freshbirth, and faithful discipleship.

Peregrinus—I'd love to. You've given me a lot to think about. I'm going to read as much as I can in the Gospels between now and then.

Plowman—Good for you. May God bless you and guide you.

With that they stood up, shook hands, and went their separate ways. Peregrinus returned the way he came. Plowman dropped down the hill in the opposite direction, towards the parking lot on the other side of the park.

Peregrinus' Conversion

When Peregrinus went to bed that night, he was unable to sleep. His heart was stirred. His mind was full. His thoughts raced with the things that Plowman had said.

He was weary of chasing and stacking soap bubbles. He was weary of trying to fill the Big Empty with Big Here & Now fun stuff. He was disillusioned with the Altar of Worthy Self. He was weary of being weary. He knew he could not go back to his old life. He knew he could not go back to pretending that the Sprinkle Form or the Faith Form fixed the problem. But he was hesitant to go forward. Why was he hesitant?

The answer was obvious. To surrender to the Crucified One really meant to surrender. It meant giving up living his life in the Big Here & Now for himself and living it for the purposes of the Crucified One. It meant breaking down the Altar of Worthy Self. Worthy Self cried out for mercy. He begged and pleaded. He presented argument after argument for letting the Altar stand. "You don't have to put a lot of time and money on it. Use it sparingly." "What will your friends and family think when they find out you tore down the Altar to Worthy Self?" "Won't they think that you've gone off the deep end?" "Surely the Nice God isn't opposed to a little good, clean fun, is he?"

THE PROVIDENTIAL MEETING

Peregrinus was barraged with such pleadings and arguments for perhaps an hour, unwilling to go back to where he was, but hesitant to go forward. Suddenly the words of the Crucified One came to mind, "Come unto me, you weary and heavy laden ones, and I will give you rest." Instantly his heart was filled with hope, faith, and courage. He knew that the pleas presented by Worthy Self were shameful and false. They boiled down to one nasty lie from the Mad Spirit — he could not enjoy all the happiness and fulfillment that human beings were made to enjoy if he tore down the Altar of Worthy Self. He knew this was a direct challenge to the goodness of God.

If God told man to tear down the Altar, then the Altar is not in man's best interest. God loves man and truly cares about his happiness. While the Altar stands, man will chase Shimmering Elusive, which is hard to catch and impossible to keep. God wants him to lay up treasure in Sweet Everlasting, which is easy to lay hold of and impossible to lose.

Right then and there he bowed in his heart before God, laid down living his life for himself, tore down the Altar of Worthy Self, and offered himself to the Crucified One to be his and his alone for ever, come what may. Immediately peace flowed into his heart and the weight was lifted off his shoulders. He was free. He was happy. He was able to relax. Within minutes he was sound asleep.

CHAPTER FIVE

THE STEAMING JOE

Steaming Joe Visit Number One

Peregrinus and Plowman got together the next Friday at the Steaming Joe as planned. Peregrinus peppered Plowman with questions about the freshbirth, discipleship, and the Big Empty. Plowman turned him — again and again — to the Sacred Trust for the answers. He wanted him to lean on the Word of God, rather than the opinions of men. Plowman also counseled him on the things that new believers needed to do if they wanted to grow: read the Word of God, cultivate a regular prayer life, and fellowship in a Sacred Trust believing church.

Peregrinus was impressed with Plowman's knowledge of the Sacred Trust and the fact that he took what it said at face value. He had never met anyone before who knew the Bible as well as he or had such confidence in its authority and accuracy.

They lost themselves in pleasant conversation. Before they knew it, ten-o'clock was nearly upon them, and the proprietors were preparing to close the coffee shop. They wrapped up their discussion and gathered up their stuff.

As they walked to the door, Peregrinus remarked that he had been encouraged by the visit and would enjoy getting together every week, if that were possible. Plowman suggested they meet every Friday at seven at the Steaming Joe to study the Sacred Trust together. And so began a friendship that would have enormous ramifications for time and for eternity.

THE GLORIOUS SALVATION MACHINE

Steaming Joe Visits Bring Mutual Encouragement

The Friday evening visits with Plowman at the Steaming Joe became an important part of Peregrinus' growth in the faith. He found them encouraging and stimulating. Plowman walked him through various books and vital subjects in the Sacred Trust, answered questions on difficult passages, and challenged him to faithfully follow the Crucified One no matter what it did to his Big Here & Now.

And follow him he did, for his faith was not merely a Faith Form — not merely a prayer, or a decision, or warm fuzzies — but real-relationship faith. This reality in his heart resulted in many changes in his life, one of the more significant being that he started attending the same Haven as Plowman.

Moreover, Plowman found encouragement in these visits too. Few things are more encouraging to a shepherd than feeding hungry sheep and watching them grow.

Steaming Joe Visit Number Twenty-Nine

Peregrinus could hardly wait for his shift to end, so he could go meet Plowman at the Steaming Joe. They had been getting together for over six months now, and he still found the visits as enjoyable and profitable as the first. He glanced at the clock for the umpteenth time. It hadn't moved ten minutes since the last time he looked. He sighed. Fridays always seemed to go slower than a clogged sink drain.

When his shift finally ended, Peregrinus raced home, quickly changed clothes, wolfed down a sandwich, and hurried off to the Steaming Joe. He nabbed the first parking spot he saw though it was a half block down the street. Plowman had just arrived himself. They met at the door and shook hands.

Peregrinus—Hey, Plowman. Good to see you again.
Plowman—Good to see you again too, Peregrinus.
Peregrinus—I'm buying the coffee tonight.
Plowman—You talked me into it.

THE STEAMING JOE

They went inside, sat at their usual table, and ordered coffee. But they were there for more than coffee. They were men on a mission. Plowman was on a mission to instruct and encourage young men who wanted to be followers of the Crucified One. Peregrinus was on a mission to learn as much as he could as fast as he could about being a faithful follower. They got down to business even before their coffee was poured.

Honing vs. Droning

Peregrinus—I've noticed that the preaching in the Havens is different than the preaching in the Half-Havens. I can't quite put my finger on it. But I prefer Haven preaching even when the delivery is on the boring side. What's the story here?

Plowman—Very simple. You have gotten serious about the Crucified One. You care about the things that he cares about. Therefore, you are drawn to Honing. Droning no longer appeals to you.

Peregrinus—Honing and Droning?

Plowman—Honing is the method of ministry we use in the Havens. Droning is the method used by the Glorious Salvation Machine and the Half-Havens.

Peregrinus—What's the difference?

Plowman—Honing is all about sharpening. It sharpens the heart and keeps it under spiritual exercise. It sharpens the mind, so that it grows in its understanding of the Word, will, and ways of God.

Droning is all about dullening. It dulls the heart, so it isn't under spiritual exercise. It dulls the mind, so it doesn't think too much, too deeply, or too clearly.

Peregrinus—So the difference lies in how *profitable* the ministry is, not how *pleasant*.

Plowman—That's right. The difference between Honing and Droning lies in the Profit Factor, not the Delivery Factor. It lies in *what* is communicated to the heart and mind, not *how* it is communicated.

Peregrinus—That explains why I come away from Haven preaching with something profitable for my walk even when the delivery is as tasty as cardboard, and why I come away from Half-Haven preaching empty-handed even when the delivery is exceptionally dynamic.

Plowman—Yep. Droning is like clouds without rain. The pleasant oratory skills promise blessing, but the messages are barren of spiritual substance or profit. Honing is filled with spiritual substance and profit, regardless of whether the Honer is as eloquent as Apollos or as unimpressive as Paul.

Two Kinds of Droning

Peregrinus—If Droning is the kind of preaching that both the Half-Havens and the Glorious Salvation Machine practice, then there must be two kinds of Droning.

Plowman—That's right. There are two varieties of Droning: Dead Droning prevails in the Glorious Salvation Machine, and Dynamic Droning prevails in the Half-Havens. There are two varieties of Honing too: Honing that is pleasant to listen to and Honing that is painful to listen to.

Peregrinus—This is so different. I grew up thinking, based on the ministry I heard in the Glorious Salvation Machine, that Droning and boring ministry were synonymous. I thought boring ministry was the only kind of preaching there was.

Plowman—That's a fairly common misconception. But tell me about your experience.

Peregrinus—It was a pleasant surprise the first time I heard Jumping Jack's exciting preaching. That changed my thinking. I concluded that there were two kinds of preaching: the boring kind I grew up with in the Glorious Salvation Machine and the exciting kind I heard at Jumping Jack's church.

But after a while I noticed that Jumping Jack's dynamic preaching didn't make much more difference in how men lived than the dead preaching I left behind in the Glorious Salvation Machine. That confused me. Why make a big deal about dynamic ministry if it produced no more change in men's lives than the boring ministry we lampooned as *dead snoozers*.

Plowman—I remember working through the same question myself. It took me a while to figure out that there are two kinds of Droning: snoozifying and electrifying. One is unprofitable ministry that puts men to sleep. The other is unprofitable ministry that keeps men awake and attentive.

Peregrinus—Dude! This is huge. Seeing that Dead Droning and Dynamic Droning are two varieties of the same thing is a piece of discernment no believer can afford to be without.

Plowman—There is no doubt about that. If believers cannot see that dynamic preaching like Jumping Jack's is just as much Droning as the dead preaching in dead churches, they will be deceived by the Great Murky Revival.

Shift in the Identification of Droning

Peregrinus—It seems like the folks in the Half-Havens are oblivious to the dangers that Dynamic Droning poses to their spiritual well-being. How did the Mad Spirit pull the wool over their eyes?

Plowman—They make the same mistake you made: they equate Droning with boring preaching. They figure that if they avoid preaching that is boring, they avoid Droning. This is understandable. For many centuries, churchgoers were forced to suffer through boring sermons preached by boring preachers. These *yawners* and *snoozers* were the only kind of preaching they heard and the only kind there was. It was only natural to associate Droning with boring preaching.

But eventually the religious masses decided they would not put up with boring Droning anymore. They demanded change; and they got change. It was adjust or bust for the Big Cheese and the Glorious Salvation Machine. So Dynamic Droning was introduced. Today it is fairly common in the Glorious Salvation Machine and the predominant style in the Half-Havens.

Peregrinus—So the big change was really a small change. They simply exchanged one form of Droning for another.

THE GLORIOUS SALVATION MACHINE

Plowman—Exactly. And sad to say, this zero-gain exchange is the way that unstable Christians deal with error. When they discover that some teaching they hold is an error, they don't climb out of the valley and up the mountain of truth. They merely trade that error for another one at the same spiritual plateau. They think they have better, but all they have is different. There is no gain in spiritual elevation. They are still slogging knee-deep in the bog of departure from the Sacred Trust.

Peregrinus—So while the outward form has been changed in the modern practice of Dynamic Droning, it is still the same old Droning on the inside.

Plowman—That's right. The differences between Dynamic Droning and Dead Droning are superficial — they are both Droning. The essence of Droning is the power of spiritual sleep induction, which we call stupification. Droning has the ability to rock men to sleep spiritually and keep them in the non-realities of their own dream-world, oblivious to their true spiritual state and to what is really going on in the Big Here & Now: as the advancing iniquity of the mystery of iniquity and the ever broadening and deepening departure (apostasy) of churchianity. The modern practice of Dynamic Droning does this just as effectively as old-fashioned Dead Droning.

Peregrinus—So men shouldn't use *boring* as their test to identify Droning any more.

Plowman—Nope. There was a time when it was a fairly safe assumption that Droning could be identified by *boring*. If you were listening to preaching that put men to sleep physically, it was probably Droning. If you were listening to preaching that kept men awake physically, it was probably Honing.

In our day this is a dangerous assumption, for most of the Droning in the Half-Havens is dynamic. It does not put men to sleep physically. The only way we can consistently identify Droning is to use the stupification test: Does it put men to sleep spiritually?

THE STEAMING JOE

Dynamic Preachers Preferred over Men of God

Peregrinus—It must be a huge advantage for the Innocuous Minimizers to Drone with passion and eloquence.

Plowman—No doubt about it. The introduction of Dynamic Droning adds tremendous leverage to the cause of Innocuous Minimum religion. For decades churchgoers were migrating away from Minimizing churches because they wanted dynamic preaching. Now they don't have to choose. They can have both good old-fashioned Innocuous Minimum religion and dynamic preaching.

Peregrinus—I understand why people prefer dynamic preaching over boring preaching. But I don't understand why they prefer dynamic preaching over truth.

Plowman—In today's world *delivery* is more important than *content*. Churchgoers prefer a man with a good delivery over a man with a solid message. The truth is, they listen to sermons the same way they listen to music — without discernment. They don't get too picky about the words. They don't think too hard about what was said or meant. This is why they don't notice departures from the Sacred Trust and why they take refuge in indifference when departures are pointed out to them. They just don't care. They are there for pleasure, not profit — for tickle, not truth. They just want to enjoy the Weekly Duty.

Peregrinus—Personally, I can't identify with that mentality. While I would rather shout *Amen*! through a rousing Honing than yawn through a dry Honing, yet the choice between the Delivery Factor and the Profit Factor is a no-brainer. I want profit. I want truth. I want light. I want sound teaching.

Plowman—I'm with you. Ho-hum Honing is miles above the best Dynamic Droning. Our first consideration when weighing preachers must be faithfulness to the Sacred Trust. When this is not the case, we leave the door wide open for compromise to set up camp in our hearts, homes, and churches.

Peregrinus—Nonetheless, I wish that some of our preaching and teaching had a little more fire and conviction in it.

THE GLORIOUS SALVATION MACHINE

Plowman—I'm with you. I wish we never had to suffer through a boring Honing. It shouldn't be that way. It doesn't have to be that way. But it is what it is.

The New Improved Minimization Configuration

Peregrinus—But there must be something else involved. It's hard to imagine that the Half-Havens are enjoying their present success merely because they have gotten rid of dry, boring preaching and introduced preaching that is easier on the ears.

Plowman—You got that right.

Peregrinus—So what am I trying to wrap my mind around?

Plowman—The New Improved Minimization Configuration.

Peregrinus—What's that?

Plowman—A modern ministry package aimed at giving men an up-to-date Glorious Salvation Machine experience.

Peregrinus—Dude, I think I need a little clarification.

Plowman—Men like to *feel* religious. They don't care if they really have a genuine relationship with the Crucified One. That is optional. But feeling religious is non-negotiable. They get this feeling and maintain it by doing the Weekly Duty.

There was a time when men were satisfied with the traditional Weekly Duty of the Glorious Salvation Machine. If they got organ music, stained glass, ceremony, and a preacher in special vestments who bored them with his Droning, they felt like they were properly religious.

During the past few decades, however, the religious values of the masses have shifted. A large percentage now want to do their Weekly Duty in a context that gives them contemporary churchiness. They want the Faith Form instead of the Sprinkle Form. They want preachers in suits or business casual instead of religious garments. They want Dynamic Droning instead of Dead Droning. They want more Wonderful Message preaching and more exposition of the Sacred Trust — fully compliant with the Innocuous Minimum, of course. They want up-to-date Big Here & Now music. And they want a full slate of Big Here & Now fun stuff — programs, activities, sports, and special events. They absolutely must do their Weekly Duty in this contemporary context, or they don't feel properly religious.

The Same Old Glorious Salvation Machine Religion

Peregrinus—So the Half-Havens are a modernized version of the same old Glorious Salvation Machine religion that has been around for centuries.

Plowman—That's right. Though we distinguish between the Half-Havens and the Glorious Salvation Machine, and though there is a higher percentage of real believers in the Half-Havens, yet the Half-Havens are Glorious Salvation Machine churches at heart. They utilize the same Innocuous Minimum, and they are just as entangled in the Big Here & Now.

Peregrinus—That explains why so many churchgoers in the Half-Havens don't follow the Crucified One any closer than the churchgoers in the Glorious Salvation Machine whom they disparage as *pew-warmers*.

Plowman—Yep. On the surface the Half-Havens look much better. The New Improved Minimization Configuration appears more faithful to the Sacred Trust and the Wonderful Message. But it *plies* the same old God Magic nonsense, *promotes* the same old Bible-trampling Minimizing, and *casts* the same old spell of Big Here & Now lukewarmness as the old version of the Innocuous Minimum.

Peregrinus—How does the spell of lukewarmness work?

Plowman—It works through the power of the Entanglement Llie — men have a God-given obligation to entangle themselves in the Big Here & Now: *maximizing* their own personal Big Here & Now and *sanitizing* this foul world, making it a better place to live. They gladly take this error to heart, which leaves them with insufficient heart and time for serious study of the Sacred Trust, which forces them to depend on the weekly spoonfeeding of Innocuous Minimum pablum, which makes it unlikely that they will ever see the predicament that they are in.

THE GLORIOUS SALVATION MACHINE

The Nasty-Bad Deception

Peregrinus—Dude! Talk about a scary scenario. When men began leaving the churches of the Glorious Salvation Machine by the droves, the guardians of stupification introduced a contemporary version of the Innocuous Minimum packaged in a Faith Form wrapping that appealed to modern taste buds. On the surface it looks like men are fleeing error, but in reality they are submitting to a more sinister form of the error.

Plowman—Scary is an understatement. The New Improved Minimization Configuration is a nasty-bad deception. It is the most potent sleep-inducing Minimization of all time. It is much harder to wake up folks rocked to sleep by modern Minimizing than folks rocked to sleep by traditional Minimizing.

When you wake someone in the Half-Havens, it is difficult to keep them awake. They sit up in bed half-awake, look around, see their Faith Form, see their lip service to the Wonderful Message and the Sacred Trust, breathe a sigh of relief, assure you that everything is okay, lay back down, and go back to sleep. When you wake men in the Glorious Salvation Machine, it is easier to keep them awake and persuade them to come to the Crucified One in real-relationship faith.

Peregrinus—I just wish that my friends like Luke W. Zeal could see that the fact that men are flocking to the Half-Havens is not a sign of good things happening, but a sign of bad things happening.

Plowman—There is no doubt that some are getting saved in the Half-Havens, but they are getting saved in spite of the Minimizing Message, not because of it. If we fairly weigh the situation — souls being saved and truth being lost — we are forced to conclude that the work of God is going forwards and backwards at the same time in the Half-Havens.

The fact is, the New Improved Minimization Configuration is the vanguard of the Great Murky Revival that shall smother the Evangelical church in the last days. When men embrace this Minimizing Message, they embrace a form of godliness that resists and rejects the heart-renewing, life-changing, Altarsmashing, disciple-molding power of godliness that we read about in the Gospels and epistles. They want to follow the Sweet One, not the Crucified One.

The Law of Attraction — You Get What You Draw

Peregrinus—I noticed that too. When preachers feed the flock with the Minimizing Message, a high percentage of their churchgoers manifest a form of godliness with little evidence of the power of godliness.

Plowman—That's right. The fact that the churchgoers in the Half-Havens manifest the same Big Here & Now indulging "form of godliness" seen in the Glorious Salvation Machine is a smoking gun that proves where their real loyalties lie. Their first love is the Big Here & Now. Their mantra is "Maximize your Big Here & Now." And they are fiercely committed to maximizing the tainted treasures and polluted pleasures of this present evil world.

Peregrinus—Is it overstating the case to say that preachers bear most of the blame for the poor spiritual state that reigns in the Half-Havens? It seems to me that the Half-Havens are filled with folks who practice Minimizing churchianity because the preachers attract them with a Minimizing Message.

Plowman—It is not overstating the case at all. The preachers do bear the bulk of the blame. They intentionally draw men with a Playground-promoting message, therefore they fill their churches with Playground-loving churchgoers.

Peregrinus—That reminds me of the verse, "Like the priest, so the people."

Plowman—Exactly. We call it the law of attraction. You get what you draw. If you draw men with the spirit of the Big Here & Now — tailoring the message to Big Here & Now taste buds — you attract men who have never broken up with the Big Here & Now and have no intention of doing so.

If you draw men with the Wonderful Message as it is found in the Sacred Trust — not watering it down or leaving out things that stumble carnal men — you will attract men who really have believed on the Crucified One and really have followed him outside the camp of the Big Here & Now.

The Two Big Here & Now Protocols

Peregrinus—The thought just struck me. Preachers can be divided into two camps: those who present the Big Here & Now as a playground and those who present it as a dangerous place to play.

Plowman—You got that right. The preachers in the Havens encourage men to engage the world according to Battleground Protocol. Half-Haven preachers discourage men from using Battleground Protocol — smearing it as fanaticism and legalism — and encourage them to engage the world according to Playground Protocol.

Peregrinus—How about a little clarification on this protocol stuff.

Plowman—A protocol lays down the guidelines for conduct in a given environment or the proper etiquette and procedure for particular occasions. Playground Protocol and Battleground Protocol lay down two very different guidelines on how believers are supposed to conduct themselves in the world during this present age.

Peregrinus—So what are the basic guidelines of Playground Protocol?

Plowman—Playground Protocol regards the Big Here & Now as a playground for the believer to play in: a playground intended by the Nice God to bring the believer fulfillment and happiness. This protocol requires men to maximize the Big Here & Now. For all practical purposes, it is a license for men to indulge Big Here & Now fun stuff: as much as they want, as often as they want, as long as they keep it clean.

Moreover, Playground Protocol requires only an insignificant amount of religion — the Innocuous Minimum — with the Passive Form as both the fact and the evidence of faith. Man does not have to worry about religion intruding into his life, demanding that he take his time and money out of valuable investments in Big Here & Now fun stuff and reallocate them in the mediocre investments of the things of the Crucified One.

Peregrinus—I'll bet religious folks love this protocol.

Plowman—How could they not? *First of all*, the genuineness of their faith is judged by the historical fact of the Form, not by the presence of obedience to the will of God revealed in the Sacred Trust. *Secondly*, they are free to pursue the Big Here & Now without challenge — unless they cross that hard-to-see line where dark grey shades into light black.

Peregrinus—What are the basic guidelines of Battleground Protocol?

Plowman—Battleground Protocol regards the Big Here & Now as a dangerous battlefield designed by the Mad Spirit to bring spiritual and moral harm to every man: stealing the heart away from God, promoting unbelief, filling the mind with Bible-undermining error, and corrupting the conscience.

Moreover, Battleground Protocol requires more than a weekly dose of insignificant religion from man. It requires men to turn to the Crucified One in real-relationship faith — as evidenced by tearing down the Altar of Worthy Self, surrendering entirely to his revealed will in the Sacred Trust, maximizing their time and opportunities down here for his purposes, and serving the captain of their faith as good soldiers. They are allowed to *use* the world for necessities, practicalities, and simple pleasures in moderation, but are strictly warned against *abusing* it for Big Here & Now purposes.

Peregrinus—That doesn't sound real appetizing if you love the Big Here & Now.

Plowman—Nope. But the real followers of the Crucified One love this protocol. They know only too well that the Big Here & Now is a dangerous battlefield that pollutes their hearts and plunders their time, money, and heart affections that should be devoted to things with eternal value. They want to have victory over this defilement and distraction. They don't want to be guilty of treasonous activity — as the Sacred Trust says, "He

THE GLORIOUS SALVATION MACHINE

that wants to be a friend of the Big Here & Now makes himself the enemy of God."

The Ultra-Vast, Mega-Variety Playground

Peregrinus—So when did man start treating the Big Here & Now as a playground?

Plowman—Right at the very beginning. In the fourth chapter of Genesis, we read that man went out from the presence of God and started the Playground, so he could find pleasure and fulfillment without God.

Peregrinus—So man is the founder of the Playground?

Plowman—Well, man is the builder. But the chief architect is the Mad Spirit, the prince and god of the Big Here & Now. He inspired man in the design of the world system.

Peregrinus—What was the Mad Spirit's purpose?

Plowman—The purpose of the Playground is to keep men so *full* they don't hunger for the things of God as they ought to, so *busy* they don't have time for the things of God as they ought to, and so *broke* they don't have money for the things of God as they ought to.

Peregrinus—Then he has done an outstanding job. Most of the professing Christians I know are full, busy, and broke.

Plowman—The Mad Spirit is definitely a master at robbing men of their time, money, and heart affections. He spreads out an incredibly vast array of fun stuff offerings that appeal to every man's taste buds — regardless of his religion, politics, personality, or morality. Does a man seek clean stuff, dirty stuff, or dishwater-grey stuff? The lust of the eyes, the lust of the flesh, or the pride of life? Education, career, or success? Possessions, experiences, or accomplishments? Worthy causes, noble aims, or humanitarian service? Games, amusements, or entertainment? Sports, recreation, or the outdoors? Excitement, adrenalin, or thrill-seeking? Hobbies, crafts, or art? Aesthetic gratification, sensuality, or carnality? Rebellion, wickedness, or perversion? Whatever a man seeks, he can find it in the Playground. This vast array of fun stuff is why the Big Here &

Now is called the Ultra-Vast, Mega-Variety Playground — or simply the Playground for short. And it is why the men of the Big Here & Now love the Mad Spirit and call him the Sweet One. He is all fun-stuff things to all fun-stuff-loving men.

History of the Innocuous Minimum

Peregrinus—How about the Innocuous Minimum? Where did it come from?

Plowman—Way, way back men grew tired of serving God because he kept meddling with their Big Here & Now. For a while they contemplated getting rid of religion altogether, but ultimately decided that it could be useful as long as it didn't interfere with maximizing the Big Here & Now. So they customized their own religion comprised of two main duties: the Passive Form and the Important Formality, commonly known as the Weekly Duty. The Weekly Duty, despite its name, only had to be attended occasionally. They called this whittled-down religion the Innocuous Minimum because it had minimal negative effect on their life.

Peregrinus—I'll bet it was well received.

Plowman—It was a smash hit overnight. Serving God was packaged in a convenient form that man could attend to with little trouble. Who wouldn't love that?

Peregrinus—And that turned things around for religion.

Plowman—No doubt about it. The Innocuous Minimum was a game-changer. It is widely regarded as the most important innovation in the history of the effort to keep God in the life and out of the way at the same time.

Prior to its introduction, churches were modest mustard-seed churches that were despised by worldly-minded men who had no interest in following the Crucified One according to the Sacred Trust. God was out of their way, but not in their life.

With the introduction of the Innocuous Minimum, everything changed. The message was engineered from a humble mustard seed that grew modest garden plants into a hellbred corruption that grew massive trees attractive to worldly-minded men. Now men could have God in their life and keep him out of their way at the same time. They could go to church and not fear that God would make a mess out of their life. This led to explosive growth in the church.

The Important Formality Keeps God Out of the Way

Peregrinus—Going to church and keeping God out of the way are two things I would have never associated. I thought men went to church to keep God in the picture, not take him out.

Plowman—It may seem counterintuitive to you, but it is true. According to Innocuous Minimum theory, if people give their piddling one hour per week, then the rest of the week is theirs to do whatever they please in the Big Here & Now. They have done their duty. Everything else they might do in the way of religion is above and beyond the call of duty. So people gladly do the Important Formality because it keeps God off their back and out of their hair.

Peregrinus—So doing the Weekly Duty is not serving God, but a substitute for serving God?

Plowman—Yep. People go to their preferred church and do their preferred version of the Innocuous Minimum, not because they have a heart to serve God, but because they do *not* have a heart to serve him.

Peregrinus—But if they don't have a heart to serve God, why even bother going to church at all? Why waste an hour doing the Innocuous Minimum?

Plowman—There are a couple reasons. For one thing, the Weekly Duty makes a good religious band-aid that men can put over their hurting conscience. For another thing, the Weekly Duty allows men to indulge the pride of being religious and moral, so they can feel good about themselves.

Important Formality Etiquette

Peregrinus—Dude! Confusing churchianity with faith in the living God is dangerous stuff.

Plowman—It sure is. God wants the whole heart for the whole week. Men give him half a heart for one hour and think this half-hearted service pleases him.

Peregrinus—I know all about the half-heartedness. For years I flattered myself that I was doing God some great service because I sat through the Important Formality. What a joke. My body was present, but my heart and mind were not. The Droning went in one ear and out the other. I couldn't tell you what the preacher said, much less whether what he said was right or wrong.

Plowman—That's the way it is everywhere in the Glorious Salvation Machine. The churchgoers do not trouble themselves with what was said in the Droning. While the most attentive might spend a minute or two discussing the Droning over a cup of coffee, this will be done in the same spirit as discussing the weather. To show more concern than that will raise red flags. You don't want to gain a reputation for being a criticizer who is always comparing what was said in the Droning with what the Sacred Trust says.

Peregrinus—How about the Half-Havens?

Plowman—Their practice is not significantly different. Half-Haven churchgoers are more likely to actually listen to the Droning and think about what was said. They are more likely to discuss the Droning with their family or friends. But they still abide by the three points of Important Formality etiquette. *One*, the churchgoer must not go very far or deep in critiquing the Droning. *Two*, it is irrelevant whether the Droning, in its content or conclusion, is true or false. *Three*, the only thing that really matters is being there and doing the Weekly Duty.

Solution to the Nasty-Bad Deception

Peregrinus—So what's the solution? How do we overcome the nasty-bad deception of the New Improved Minimization Configuration?

Plowman—The solution is the Sacred Trust. Every man who professes to be a follower of the Crucified One needs to be a diligent student of the Sacred Trust.

Peregrinus—In other words, a five-minute devotional once a day isn't going to fix the problem.

Plowman—That's highly unlikely. The man who only gives the Word of God five minutes a day, especially if he's letting some daily devotional guide hold his hand, is not likely to even recognize that there is a problem, much less make headway against the problem.

Peregrinus—How about a little elaboration.

Plowman—What must be understood is that Minimization, like all error, is advanced and maintained by the hosts of darkness through errors and lies. The only way to overcome these errors and lies is through the power of truth. And the only way to tap into the power of truth (making headway against deception and gains in sound doctrine) is to dig deep and often in the Sacred Trust. Indeed, every deception ever fostered upon the world is answered in the pages of this blessed book.

Peregrinus—That throws some very helpful light on spiritual warfare.

Plowman—I wish I could make every professing Christian see that the apprehension and application of the body of truth revealed in the Sacred Trust is the heart of spiritual warfare. Our main business is to set men free with the truth: free from unbelief, free from major errors, free from minor errors, free from sin, free from the Big Here & Now, and free from Worthy Self.

Peregrinus—And how does truth set men free?

Plowman—It opens the eyes of their understanding. They see the truth so clearly as the truth that every error and argument which contradicts it is exploded into smithereens. The pieces are scattered hither, thither, and yon with no force or weight left in any of them. They are exposed as the God-dishonoring fabrications that they are — they are no longer able to masquerade as truth. And once this work is done, it can't be undone. It is impossible to un-know the truth.

The Need for Honers in the Pulpits

Peregrinus—The environment in the Half-Havens doesn't promote that kind of digging in the Sacred Trust.

Plowman—No doubt about that. It promotes stupification. Whenever men get stirred and awakened over their misplaced confidence in the Faith Form, or their lack of discipleship, or their lukewarmness, or their Big Here & Now maximization, the Droners in the pulpits rock them back to sleep with their Lullaby Preaching and Lullaby Doctrine.

Peregrinus—Dude! We need Honers in the pulpits who will preach the Sacred Trust in its entirety, challenge men with its truths, and get them excited about knowing its contents.

Plowman—Amen to that. God give us fearless Honers who *refuse* to tickle ears with Innocuous Minimum death-rot and *choose*, in glorious contrarianism, to boldly preach that real-relationship faith is the only true faith and that the only true proof of faith is tearing down the Altar of Worthy Self and following the Crucified One.

True Balance

Peregrinus—I know you're right that if we're not careful, the clean stuff of the Big Here & Now will rob us of our time, our money, and our reward in Sweet Everlasting. But I don't want to be unbalanced. How do we find balance?

Plowman—True balance is not a 50-50 proposition. It is not balancing equal parts of fun stuff and service stuff.

Peregrinus—So what is it, then?

Plowman—True balance is being a faithful servant of the Crucified One who maximizes the time and money he was given to seek his Master's gain.

Peregrinus—That sounds like no balance. If we maximize our time and money for the cause of the Crucified One, then there's no time and money left for us.

Plowman—That's not the way things work. Soldiers, for example, need a little R & R from time to time, so they can continue to perform at a high level. If they don't get occasional rest and relaxation, their performance on the battlefield will decline. So a little downtime is a good investment.

Likewise, it is legitimate, indeed necessary, to use a little of our Master's money and time for R & R. We too will perform better on the battlefield in the long run if we have a little rest and relaxation in our life.

Peregrinus—So what we are trying to do is find the amount of R & R we need to maintain peak battlefield performance?

Plowman—That's right. We add and subtract R & R on the service side of the scale until the performance side reaches maximum height. If we add too little R & R, our performance drops. If we add too much R & R, our performance drops.

Peregrinus—That's an interesting thought. Both too much and too little R & R will drop performance.

Plowman—That's right. The Christian balance scale doesn't work in the same way as the common balance scale. When you put the proper mix of soldiership and R & R in the service pan, it raises the performance pan to its maximum height. From this ideal point, both adding and subtracting R & R lowers the performance pan.

Peregrinus—Dude! This is mega-helpful — like shining a floodlight down a dark alley. I sensed that something was wrong with the modern emphasis on fun stuff. I saw the bad effect it had on bearing fruit — my own included. I even toyed with the idea of giving up down-time activities altogether. But your balance solution is obviously the right way.

Plowman—Yep. We need to find our R & R sweet spot, the minimum amount of downtime that we need to stay razor sharp on the battlefield. Most of the professed soldiers of the Crucified One have been unsoldiered by their addiction to recreation, entertainment, and hobbies. Their downtime doesn't make them better soldiers; it makes them worse.

How can we wage the war before us as we ought if we waste the time that has been given to us? We can't. Obviously much of our time will be spent in necessary activities as sleeping, eating, working, and family time. But what do we do with the remainder of our time — our free time? How can we be good soldiers if we spend 90 percent of our time beyond necessities playing and only 10 percent training and fighting? We can't. Nor do we gain much if we adjust the ratio to 80/20 or 70/30 or 60/40. We need to break our addiction to playing. We have one short life to be a good soldier and one long eternity to be a fulfilled human being.

Peregrinus—We certainly don't have a problem today with too little R & R.

Plowman—That's for sure. While too little R & R has been a problem a few times in church history, causing missionaries, preachers, and evangelists to suffer the breakdown of their health, that is not a big problem in our day. The big problem in our day is too much R & R.

There Is No Clean Big Here & Now

Peregrinus—I wish believers could see how harmful their beloved fun stuff can be to their spiritual health.

Plowman—It is far more harmful than most believers think. But the harm doesn't begin and end with robbing believers of their time and money. It goes far beyond that. The clean stuff can get them dirty.

Peregrinus—How can the clean stuff can get men dirty?

Plowman—The clean stuff is so intertwined with the spirit of the Big Here & Now that it is almost impossible to engage in it without being influenced by this foul spirit. Indeed, the Mad Spirit, through millions of subordinate foul spirits, permeates every institution in the Big Here & Now, clean as well as dirty, energizing them with Big Here & Now pride, ideas, goals, and agendas. When believers get involved in these institutions, they get molded and motivated by pride, ideas, goals, and agendas that are not of the Father, but of the Big Here & Now. Make no mistake, these things dirty men.

Peregrinus—But if all the clean fun stuff is tainted with the Spirit of the Big Here & Now, then there is no fun stuff in the Big Here & Now that is truly clean.

Plowman—That's right. When we speak of clean stuff in the Big Here & Now, we are speaking relatively. There really is no clean stuff — absolutely speaking — in the Big Here & Now. The entire mass is *of* the Mad Spirit and *in* the Mad Spirit. He, as the god and ruler of the Big Here & Now, has his nasty hand in every fun-stuff institution. They are all tainted with the evil that taints him.

Peregrinus—Dude! That's a frightening thought. There is far more danger lurking in this world than I ever knew.

When It's Okay to Use the Clean Stuff

Peregrinus—But if everything in the Big Here & Now really is dirty and dangerous, shouldn't we just drop the distinction between clean and dirty and call everything dirty?

Plowman—Nope. There is a significant difference between clean stuff and dirty stuff. So distinguishing between the two is a helpful tool.

The dirty stuff is intrinsically dirty. It is dirty in and of itself. It is never right to use it. It is always wrong to use it.

The clean stuff is intrinsically neutral. It is not dirty in and of itself. It is a legitimate expression of human creativity that is dirtied by its context — by its deeply networked emplacement in the Big Here & Now system. These things can be used if we use them carefully and rightly.

Peregrinus—But how can we safely use the clean stuff if it can defile us?

Plowman—Everything hangs on whether or not our use is a matter of Sacred Trust based faith. When we take up clean stuff motivated by a *God-honoring purpose* that was quickened in us by the testimony of the Sacred Trust, we find the strength to use it profitably and not be defiled or distracted by it.

When we take up the same clean stuff motivated merely by *our own pleasure*, we put ourselves in a place where we cannot avoid defilement or distraction.

Peregrinus—That makes sense. We need a good reason. If we have a good reason, based on biblical precept or principle, we will walk in faith and thrive spiritually. If we have a bad reason, we will walk in pretension and wilt spiritually.

Plowman—You got it. And that is why the Sacred Trust says, "To the clean, all things are clean, and to the dirty, all things are dirty." If we walk in the Spirit, we can use the world and stay clean. If we walk in the flesh, we will abuse every thing we attempt to use, and we will further defile ourselves.

Yin and Yang in the Big Here & Now

Peregrinus—If the Mad Spirit has his hand in every part of the Big Here & Now, then the clean and the dirty, despite their differences, are two sides of the same coin.

Plowman—That's right. One of the most important points of spiritual discernment is to understand that the Big Here & Now operates on the principle of yin and yang. Black and white are intentionally and inseparably woven together in the tapestry of the Big Here & Now. All Big Here & Now black has white in it. And all Big Here & Now white has black in it.

Peregrinus—And the Mad Spirit runs the whole shebang as its god and ruler.

Plowman—That's right. He is the engineer and the director of the whole world system — clean as well as dirty.

Peregrinus—But if all the white has black in it, then it's really grey.

Plowman—That's right. What appears white to us, what we call white, is actually shades of grey, from nearly imperceptible grey to obvious grey. Sadly, much that men call white is so obviously grey that it can only be called white by pretending to not see what they really do see.

Peregrinus—Dude! This is revolutionary. It clarifies the teaching in the Sacred Trust that the Big Here & Now lies in the Wicked One and that everything in the Big Here & Now is not of the Father, but of the Big Here & Now.

Plowman—Yep. Men make a big mistake when they regard the clean stuff of the Big Here & Now as perfectly clean stuff from the hand of God given to men to indulge as much as they want, as often as they want, for any reason they want. Such thinking is discernment-challenged, spiritual immaturity.

Clean fun stuff is the Mad Spirit's plan B. If he can't get men to pollute themselves with defiling fun stuff, he gets them to waste their time and money on distracting fun stuff. And every clean distraction in the Big Here & Now is designed to bring men into circumstances and situations that are designed to lead them, through ever increasing compromise, back to defiling fun stuff. Many are the believers that have defiled themselves in matters of unspeakable shame because harmless fellowship in harmless fun stuff led to little compromises that led to medium compromises that led to big compromises.

The Sewer of Unbelief

Peregrinus—I know that I've been influenced by the line of thinking that says if we just avoid the dirty stuff, everything will be okay.

Plowman—It is a dangerous misconception that danger lies only in the dirty stuff. While dirty stuff is definitely dangerous, the ultimate danger, the source of all danger, is the unbelief that lies behind the pursuit of Big Here & Now stuff — whether dirty or clean. Men can give up dirty stuff and pursue clean stuff with undying passion — even religious stuff and noble stuff — and still be lost in profound unbelief.

Peregrinus—So unbelief is the real problem?

Plowman—You got it. Unbelief is behind every path in the Big Here & Now that does not lead to the Crucified One. It is behind every dirty path that seeks fulfillment in sin, rebellion, and perversion. And it is behind every clean path that seeks fulfillment in noble stuff, religious stuff, and fun stuff.

Peregrinus—Unbelief is some nasty stuff.

Plowman—You got that right. The entire Big Here & Now, clean paths and dirty paths alike, is energized by the motive of unbelief. And unbelief is as vile as the filthy heart that started the ball of unbelief rolling back in the garden.

Peregrinus—If unbelief is dirtiness, and every clean path is spawned by unbelief, then every clean path is actually dirty in its spirit.

Plowman—That's right. Unbelief often hides its dirtiness under a coat of white paint. As the Sacred Trust says, "If the light that is in you be darkness, how great is that darkness."

Peregrinus—That's downright scary. Men can pretend they are doing okay because they walk a path of religion, morality, or nobility, while in reality their religion, morality, or nobility is dyed with the same dirty unbelief as the vilest abominations.

Plowman—Yep. Unbelief is the Mad Spirit's aim. As long as he secures this, he does not care what path men take. Let them take a dirty path or a clean path. Let them take a low-life path or a sophisticated path. Let them take a counter-culture path or a main-stream path. Let them take a selfish path or a noble, sacrificial path. It's all the same when they walk in the dirtiness of unbelief.

Peregrinus—Dude! This is earthshaking. This turns the Half-Haven love affair with the clean paths of the Big Here & Now upside down. The clean paths are wrought by the same dirty unbelief as the dirty paths.

Plowman—That's right. When a believer looks upon the Big Here & Now with the eyes of God, he sees what God sees — one giant sewer of unbelief.

Peregrinus—A sewer of unbelief. Now that's what I call a potent illustration.

Plowman—Yep. The world in its entirety is a sewer of God-resisting unbelief. There is no part or corner that is not part of this sewer. This means that those who wade in the clean side of the Big Here & Now, wade in the same unbelief as those who wade in the dirty side. And this means that wading in the clean side can be just as fatal as wading in the dirty side. This is why the Sacred Trust says that even the plowing of the wicked is sin. No matter how clean the outward walk is, when a man does not walk in faith, his walk is sin.

Faith Is the Victory That Overcomes the Sewer

Peregrinus—If the Big Here & Now is a sewer of unbelief, how do we walk through it and not get defiled? It hardly seems possible.

Plowman—We can't walk in the sewer without getting our feet dirty. That's why we are exhorted to let our Master wash our feet. And that's why we have an obligation to wash each other's feet. We can, nonetheless, walk in the sewer without wading in it. This is the promise and power of faith. As we read in the Sacred Trust, "This is the victory that overcomes the sewer of unbelief, even our faith."

Peregrinus—How does faith find the strength and resolve to not wade in the sewer?

Plowman—Faith is a heart connection to God in the person of the Crucified One that taps into the power of God — even the power of the Word of God (the same Word that spoke the universe into existence) and the power of the Spirit of God (the same Spirit that raised the Crucified One from the dead).

This power transforms the believer's perspective. Although he is in the sewer, he is not of the sewer. His life is not to be found somewhere in the muck and yuck of the sewer, but is hid with the Crucified One in Sweet Everlasting. He has no heart for the sewer or the things of the sewer. He has nothing to gain or to lose in the sewer. This heavenly perspective energizes the believer, giving him the strength and resolve to conduct the time of his sojourn in the sewer in fear. It enables him to walk through the sewer without wading in it.

Peregrinus—You won't get this energizing perspective and overcoming power from cheap imitations of faith like the Faith Form or wimpy sentiment.

Plowman—You got that right. That is why I earnestly and constantly contend for the heart-faith once delivered unto the followers of the Crucified One. It never leads to an empty profession. It always leads to an energized practice.

What If My Faith-Turn Isn't Good Enough?

Peregrinus—Speaking of walking in victory over the world, I have a question that's been bothering me lately.

Plowman—Sure.

Peregrinus—How do I know that my faith really has been accepted by God? What if my faith-turn isn't good enough? What if my fruit is too sparse or too imperfect?

Plowman—Let me guess. You are bothered by the fact that your performance falls short of your ambitions.

Peregrinus—That's right. I don't do as well as I want to. I'm not swimming in the cesspool, but I'm definitely not what I could be and want to be. At times I find myself lazy in my prayer life and Sacred Trust reading. I get sloppy in guarding my heart and mind. I get zipper-lips in my testimony to others about what the Crucified One has done for me. These things cause me to wonder whether my faith-turn is good enough for me to be regarded as a believer.

Plowman—For what it's worth, my performance falls short of my ambition too. So does everybody's. None of us perform at the level of our intentions. Our attainments consistently fall short of our aspirations.

Peregrinus—But shouldn't continual shortfalls raise huge questions about one's relationship to God?

Plowman—If a man finds himself falling short of aspirations burning in his breast for biblical holiness and devotion — aspirations which only burn in the breast of true believers — that testifies that he is a true believer. So the only questions we ought to ask in such a case are questions that concern maturity and reward.

Peregrinus—But it's painful to fall short.

Plowman—It ought to be painful to fall short of such Bible-based aspirations. But we must bear in mind that no matter how high the heights of devotion and faithfulness we obtain, we will still fall short of the glory of God. Falling short of the glory of God is the universal experience of all men, even the very best that have ever lived. This we know from the testimony of the Sacred Trust and from many centuries of experience.

Peregrinus—So our shortfalls don't raise questions about the acceptability of our faith, they only raise questions about the rewardability of our faith.

Plowman—That's right. What we need to understand is that God does not accept us because he finds us praiseworthy. God finds us praiseworthy because he accepts us in his Son. And we are in his Son for one reason — God himself placed us there when we heart-believed on his Son as the *way* of salvation, the source and touchstone of *truth*, and the fountain of *life* eternal. This acceptance in the praiseworthy Son is one of the amazing truths that make grace so amazing.

Look for the Fact of the Turn, Not the Form of the Turn

Peregrinus—So when it comes to acceptance, it isn't a matter of how well we executed our faith-turn, but simply whether we actually executed one.

Plowman—That's right. It's the *fact* of the turn, not the *form* of the turn, that is the litmus test of reality. Did we turn or not? We can't look for a pretty turn, much less a perfect turn. They don't exist. All are beset by human weakness.

Our turn might be sloppy, choppy, or belly-floppy. We might wobble, hobble, or bobble. We might stumble, fumble, or tumble. We might be hampered with struggles, doubts, fears, hindering weights, or besetting sins. But such things don't matter as far as the genuineness and acceptability of our faith is concerned. Many a believer falls seven times and gets up again seven times before he obtains consistency in his walk.

Peregrinus—This is a breath of fresh air from heaven. I have been struggling with the idea that my acceptance depended on attaining the heights of exceptional performance.

Gracious Grace, Winking Grace, and Legal Grace

Peregrinus—So how do we make sure that we judge men the way that we ought to — not being too harsh or too soft?

Plowman—We need to walk in Gracious Grace. If we walk in this spirit, we will judge men in a gracious manner.

Peregrinus—Gracious Grace? What's that?

Plowman—Gracious Grace is the kind of grace we see God walking in when we trace his steps through the Sacred Trust. We walk in Gracious Grace when we walk in his steps — not straying to the left into Winking Grace or to the right into Legal Grace.

Peregrinus—I need a little illumination in my estimation. Start with Winking Grace.

Plowman—Winking Grace is a careless, marshmallow-soft, see-no-evil, judging-is-wrong spirit which pretends to be the grace of God and accuses true grace of being legalistic. It says everything is okay when the ship is sinking. It says the wishy-washy are doing fine. It says those wallowing in the Hog Pen are saved because they did the Faith Form. It says there is nothing to worry about when there is plenty to worry about.

Peregrinus—And what is Legal Grace?

Plowman—Legal Grace is what men tend to stray into when they figure out how wrong Winking Grace is. They overreact and wind up in the ditch on the other side of the road. This is a fault-finding, exacting, idealistic, quick-to-judge spirit which pretends to be the grace of God and accuses true grace of being wishy-washy. It undervalues the strengths and overvalues the failures of every hapless believer it meets. The weak believer is rejected as a non-believer for not being like Timothy. Timothy is scorned as a weak believer for not being more like Paul. Lazarus is reckoned yet dead because he still has some of his grave clothes on. John Mark is an apostate because he once left Paul and the work. Peter will never be trusted again because he once denied his Master. Elijah is just a whiny crybaby.

Peregrinus—And how about Gracious Grace?

Plowman—Gracious grace walks in love, patience, kindness, gentleness, and longsuffering — seasoned with salt. It has no stomach for the mindless displays of indifference to man's moral and eternal plight which pretend to be grace. It manifests true concern for men by exhorting them to flee the coming day of judgment by heart-believing the offer of mercy held out in the Wonderful Message. It speaks the truth in love — the truth in its entirety and purity — teaching men to live soberly, righteously, and godly in the present evil world. It longs to see mercy triumph over judgment, and gives legs to this longing by digging and dunging the roots of fruitless trees (that is, empty professions of faith).

Pointers on Judging Faith with Gracious Grace

Peregrinus—How about a few pointers on judging men with Gracious Grace?

Plowman—*First of all*, stop thinking degree or height and start thinking direction. Are they moving in the right direction? Are they submitting to the sanctifying influences of grace? Or are they resisting the sanctifying influences of grace? They may not be as far down the path as you think they should be. They may not be walking as fast as you think they should be. But these are questions of growth, not life.

Secondly, avoid assigning too much weight to any particular evidence or combination of evidences. People have different strengths and weaknesses. They fight the good fight of faith in different environments and circumstances. All we need to see is any combination of evidences that gives reasonable men reasonable assurance that someone is actually going forward in a faith relationship with the Crucified One.

Thirdly, keep your eyes on where men will be further down the road and what they will be when the Lord has finished the work that he has started in them. This is where the Lord's eyes are. This will help you keep things in proper perspective and help you to rightly appreciate where they are now.

Fourthly, be honest about your own weaknesses, failures, and shortcomings. Men are much more likely to judge with Legal Grace if they do not — daily — put their own life and heart under the searchlight of heaven. We need to realize how far short we fall of the praise of God and how dependent we are on grace, then we will walk in grace in our dealings with others.

There Really Is Grace in Grace

Peregrinus—I think I have failed to comprehend how much grace there really is in grace.

Plowman—You aren't the first. In the days of the apostles, many advocates of holy living falsely accused Paul of teaching a candy-coated message that gave men the freedom to live in compromise and sin. The grace he preached held out too much longsuffering, patience, and forgiveness. It held the bar too low. They thought they would obtain better results if they beefed up the message of grace with some lofty standards that men had to reach before they were worthy of salvation.

Peregrinus—But he wasn't overlooking sin or going easy on it, was he?

Plowman—Not by any stretch of the imagination. He was dispensing the only medicine that works — the incredible riches of the incredible grace of the incredible God lavished upon man the sinner and the sin of man. Only under the sweet influences of grace do we actually see men repent, believe the Wonderful Message, grow in faith and truth, attain the heights of devotion and holiness, and walk in consistency. As the Sacred Trust says, "There is forgiveness with God that he may be [profitably] feared."

Peregrinus—So we can lean on grace without the least harm to the cause of holy living.

Plowman—That's right. God did not harm the cause of holy living while he patiently waited for us to turn from darkness and believe on his dear Son. And he does not harm the cause of holy living while he patiently waits for us to grow in the image of his dear Son — watching us fall short of his praise again and again. "It is the Lord's mercies that we are not consumed. His compassions fail not. They are new every morning."

Search for Understanding As for Hid Treasure

Plowman—Well, it's getting late. We need to wrap things up.

Peregrinus—One more quick question.

Plowman—Sure.

Peregrinus—How did you get so much wisdom?

Plowman—Years ago I read in Proverbs, "Incline your ear unto wisdom. Apply your heart to understanding. Seek her as silver and search for her as for hid treasure. Then you shall understand the fear of the Lord and find the knowledge of God." I took this counsel to heart. The pursuit of wisdom and understanding became my chief passion, my life ambition. I committed my time and money to this goal. I spent the bulk of my spare time studying the Sacred Trust and books written by men who had committed their lives to studying it. I desired to learn all that I could about God, and his Word, will, and ways.

Peregrinus—It sounds like it's a lot of work to get wisdom.

Plowman—Yes, it is. But spiritual wealth is only found by the same kind of hard work and sacrifice that men use to find Big Here & Now wealth. The men of the Big Here & Now go to nearly unbelievable lengths to find the riches that shall perish. They toil night and day. They embrace hardship and sacrifice. They risk their health. Their risk all they own and all they can borrow besides. So we ought to spare no effort and no expense to gather the true riches of the knowledge of God and the Crucified One — riches that are worth a million-billion-trillion times more than all the wealth in the world.

Peregrinus—Wow! I never looked at the value and pursuit of wisdom quite like that before.

Nine Fine Rules for the Pursuit of Wisdom

Peregrinus—So what must I do to gain wisdom?

Plowman—Follow Plowman's nine fine rules for the pursuit of wisdom.

Peregrinus—So what are they?

Plowman—*One, read and study the Sacred Trust. Two, read and study the Sacred Trust. Three, read and study the Sacred Trust.*

Peregrinus—I like that. The Sacred Trust is the source of all wisdom and understanding.

Plowman—*Four, read the best books that have been written on every subject you study.* Take advantage of the great minds from the great Evangelical movements from the Reformation to the present. Every great movement was or is a torchbearer for the truth of God in at least one area of doctrine.

Peregrinus—That makes good sense. It reminds me of the verse that says, "He who walks with wise men will be wise."

Plowman—*Five, read both sides of every controversy you take up* which has Evangelicals on both sides. Reading only one side promotes error, imbalance, and ignorance.

Peregrinus—That makes sense too. As the Sacred Trust says, "He who states his case first seems to be in the right until the other comes and cross examines him."

Plowman—*Six, never hold any point of doctrine so sacred that it is exempt from Sacred Trust scrutiny.* Every point should be open for further illumination, or guarding, or balancing, or qualification, or broad modification, or even rejection.

Peregrinus—I can see the wisdom in that. The mind of God is the standard, not what man thinks is the mind of God.

Plowman—*Seven, test every doctrine that crosses your path of duty.* Never receive a teaching with superficial investigation. Never reject a teaching with superficial investigation. Be like the noble Bereans who went so far as to test Paul's teaching. Test all things, prove all things, hold fast to that which is good.

Peregrinus—I can see the wisdom in that too. Nothing is more common than men calling truth *error* and error *truth* because they are superficial in their studies.

Plowman—*Eight, walk in the light you have gained.* If you fail to apply what you have learned, you hinder further growth until you walk in the light God has already committed to you. As we read, "To him that has, more shall be given."

Peregrinus—That reminds me of the parable of the talents. If you invest what the Lord has given you, you keep it, and gain more. If you bury it, you lose not only the opportunity for gain, but even the little that you have.

Plowman—*Nine, walk in the humility of child-like faith in the Sacred Trust.* When men do this, their scholarship is an immense help to the work of God. When they don't, their scholarship is an immense detriment. The problem with pride is that it thinks too highly of its abilities and understanding. This overconfidence leads to superficial investigations which leave men susceptible to the wiles of error. This is why intellectual pride regularly falls prey to the wisdom of the Big Here & Now — both secular and religious — and winds up trampling on the Sacred Trust, on well-arrayed facts, and on the common-sense wisdom that cries aloud in the streets.

Peregrinus—Dude! That's some seriously good stuff. Can you imagine what the church would be like if every believer followed these rules?

Plowman—We would be in far better shape. There isn't a false doctrine ravaging the church today that wouldn't be nixed in short order if believers would apply these rules consistently in their pursuit of wisdom and sound doctrine.

The Sacred Trust No Longer Liver

Peregrinus—Speaking of the Sacred Trust, reading it used to seem like eating liver. I knew it was good for me, but I had to force myself to sit down and eat. Now I have such a hunger for the Sacred Trust that it doesn't seem like liver any more. I can't get enough. Now the battle is putting it down. I haven't watched the Mad Spirit Box for six weeks. And I often have to force myself to go to bed at a decent hour.

Plowman—You're on the right path. Don't let anything stand in the way. Keep that fire burning. Hunger for the Sacred Trust is the road to blessing. You cannot go wrong if you diligently read and study it. You cannot go right if you do not.

Peregrinus—I am still amazed by how powerfully the Sacred Trust began to work in my life once I started reading it and taking its teachings seriously.

Plowman—I've seen that many times. When men get serious about reading the Sacred Trust, their testimony goes from *mud* to *thud*. They go from slogging around in the quicksand, unable to free themselves from their besetting sins and compromises, to seeing the giant fall with a stone lodged in his forehead.

Peregrinus—Well, there is definitely plenty of smooth stones in the Sacred Trust. Hey, it looks like we better break camp and head for home. They're starting to lock up.

Plowman—Yep. The time goes by way too fast.

With that they picked up their Sacred Trusts and headed for the door.

Peregrinus—I'll see you Sunday morning, Brother.

Plowman—That you will, the Lord willing.

Peregrinus Muses on Wimps

That night Peregrinus sat in his favorite chair thinking and praying for a few minutes before he went to bed. He chuckled to himself. His life sure had changed — he had changed — in the past six months. He was a follower of the Crucified One and wanted to follow him with all of his heart. He didn't care what anyone said or thought.

There was a time when he would have been intimidated by scoffing friends, but no more. The other day one of his friends laughed at him for getting religious and dissed him with the snide comment, "Religion is for weak-minded wimps that want to play the rough-and-tumble game of life with touch-football rules." But it was really the other way around. The weak-minded wimps were those who avoided the Sacred Trust and refused to wrestle with the most important questions in life. They took the easy path — the broad road of rejecting truth and light — because they were afraid of the scoffing and reproach they would face if they took the narrow path of submitting to truth and light. They knew the right way, but the price was too high to pay.

CHAPTER SIX

QUACKSALVER RELOADED

Scorn and Ridicule

Peregrinus' family was rankled because he had left the family church — a well-respected fixture in the Glorious Salvation Machine — and had started attending a Haven. They spent hours trying to talk him out of this path. They reproached him for disrespecting his family. They heaped scorn upon him for rejecting the Sprinkle Form and the Big Cheese. They belittled his real-relationship faith as fanaticism. They ridiculed the hours he spent reading the Sacred Trust and accused him of pride for thinking he could understand it without professional help. But all their efforts came to nothing.

So they turned to stronger measures. They invited Reverend Quacksalver to show up at their house one Saturday morning when Peregrinus was visiting, thinking that he would be able to convince their son of his errors. To their disappointment the learned Reverend was no more able to move Peregrinus than they were. He was already solid in the Sacred Trust and in the faith of the Crucified One.

Quacksalver Beyond Worried

Rev. Quacksalver—I haven't seen you at the Important Formality for a long time. Your mother tells me you have gone down the Havenmonger path and started attending a Haven.

Peregrinus—I sure have. I like their freshbirth message, their emphasis on following the Crucified One, and their confidence in the Sacred Trust.

THE GLORIOUS SALVATION MACHINE

Rev. Quacksalver—Well, I appreciate your earnestness. The Nice God knows we could use a little more earnestness in religion around here. That would give us more money in the offering plate and a better softball team on the playing field. But people just don't take religion seriously anymore.

Peregrinus—Well, I don't want religion. I want the Sacred Trust and a real-relationship with the Crucified One.

Rev. Quacksalver—I can empathize with your aspirations. I went down that path myself as a young man. But it proved to be idealistic and impractical. Sooner or later you will figure out that taking the Sacred Trust in a strictly literal sense is not very practical. We live in the Big Here & Now and we need a practical religion that gets along with the Big Here & Now.

Peregrinus—It's working for me.

Rev. Quacksalver—That's a matter of opinion. My take on the matter is quite different. Quite frankly, I am worried. It was bad enough when you quit attending our wonderful Sprinkle Form church and began going to a Faith Form church. But now you are going to a Haven!

Peregrinus—What's wrong with the Havens?

The Goat Fix

Rev. Quacksalver—For starters, they deny the Goat Fix — the most important Dogma of the Glorious Salvation Machine.

Peregrinus—I know I've heard that term before, but I don't recall exactly what it means.

Rev. Quacksalver—Let me guess. You were daydreaming while I was Droning.

Peregrinus—Most likely.

Rev. Quacksalver—The Goat Fix infects the whole human race. It is *the* problem that stands between man and salvation. If a man's Goat Fix is not undone, he is lost regardless of any other considerations. If a man's Goat Fix is undone, he is saved regardless of any other considerations.

Peregrinus—The way I understand things, when men heart-believe on the Crucified One, the entire sin problem that separates them from God is addressed. God forgives their sin and freshbirths them, so they can walk in victory over sin.

Rev. Quacksalver—Well, I have a theological problem with that understanding. If we fix the sin problem on the shallow outside (sin in man's history and life) by some means like your vaunted heart-faith in the Crucified One, we still haven't fixed the sin problem on the Deep inside. And if we fix the sin problem on the Deep inside (the Goat Fix) by the Passive Form, then men are saved regardless of whether or not their sin problem on the shallow outside is ever fixed.

Peregrinus—So, whatever this Goat Fix is that you are trying to fix, it isn't the actual sin problem that shows up in our Daily Grind?

Rev. Quacksalver—Correct. The Goat Fix isn't a problem in the Daily Grind that can be fixed by Daily Grind efforts, such as the often touted heart-faith.

Peregrinus—What is this Goat Fix stuff, then?

Rev. Quacksalver—The Goat Fix is a mystical predicament on the Mystic Plane in which man bears the guilt and stain of a goat. The Nice God accounts man guilty for stuff he never did and reckons him dirty for stuff that isn't really in him. Because this guilt and dirtiness is on the Mystic Plane, there is no way for them to be removed by *real-relationship transactions* in the Daily Grind. They can't be undone — as Havenmongers claim — by heart-believing the Wonderful Message which results in real-relationship forgiveness of sin and real-relationship washing from sin. Even if the Nice God himself came down from heaven and preached the Wonderful Message to a sinner and he heart-believed, that would not result in the undoing of his Goat Fix.

Peregrinus—So how is the Goat Fix undone?

Rev. Quacksalver—Mystic Plane problems require Mystic Plane solutions. This means that Mystic Plane problems can only be fixed by *religious transactions* in the Daily Grind which enable men to tap into the mystery and power of the Mystic Plane. In the case under consideration, man's Goat Fix

THE GLORIOUS SALVATION MACHINE

on the Mystic Plane can only be fixed by Mystic Plane grace — which we call God Magic — which is administered in the Passive Form. When men do the Passive Form, the Nice God pours out his God Magic and washes away their Goat Fix.

Peregrinus—That's where the Sprinkle Form comes in.

Rev. Quacksalver—Exactly.

God Magic Is the True Grace of God

Peregrinus—Well, I don't believe that Passive Form junk. I believe that heart-faith in the Crucified One is God's way of salvation.

Rev. Quacksalver—The doctrine of salvation by heart-faith is bad, bad, nasty-bad heresy. It is a denial of salvation by God Magic.

Peregrinus—But I do believe in salvation by grace. We are all guilty sinners who deserve Awful Everlasting. We are all hopelessly lost. But God, in a demonstration of amazing grace, offered his own Son, the Crucified One, as the sacrifice for sin. On the merits of this sacrifice, God offers salvation to everyone who believes the Wonderful Message of salvation in his Son.

Rev. Quacksalver—Rubbish. Requiring men to heart-believe the Wonderful Message to obtain salvation is requiring them to save themselves by their own efforts. That is not salvation by grace, but salvation by Dead Works. If you really want to have salvation without Dead Works, you must turn to God Magic in the Sprinkle Form. Only there is the effort to obtain salvation without human effort actually untainted by human effort.

The Great Illumination

Rev. Quacksalver—This brings me to another serious error that infests the Havens — the denial of the Great Illumination.

Peregrinus—The Great Illumination? That sounds familiar.

Rev. Quacksalver—It ought to be familiar. It is one of the Invincible Dogmas of the Glorious Salvation Machine.

Peregrinus—So what does it say?

Rev. Quacksalver—The Great Illumination says, "All effort is sin." And all means all. Even the apparently noble effort to heart-believe is construed as sin by this teaching.

Peregrinus—So when a man really turns in his heart to God, that effort is a Dead Work — it is fatal sin?

Rev. Quacksalver—That's right. If we consistently apply the Great Illumination, then doing anything to obtain salvation — even heart-turning to God — is the bad, bad, nasty-bad heresy of Dead Works. And this absolutely overthrows the heart-faith error, for if we require men to heart-believe, we are requiring them to *do* something to be saved.

Peregrinus—Something doesn't sound right here.

Rev. Quacksalver—Whether it sounds right to you or not is beside the point. What matters is consistency with the Dogma that all effort is sin. When we offer men salvation through the Passive Form, we offer them salvation apart from human effort — apart from Dead Works. If you offer men salvation through heart-faith, you offer them salvation through human effort — through Dead Works.

And this gem of Mystic Plane Logic has Deep ramifications. The Havens, though they have a reputation for preaching against salvation by works, are actually guilty of Dead Works. And the Glorious Salvation Machine, though it has a reputation for preaching salvation by works, is actually not guilty of Dead Works.

Peregrinus—That is some seriously spooky logic.

Rev. Quacksalver—I admit that some points of the Glorious Salvation Machine system are spooky. But we take the whole thing in Deep Faith, Deep Trusting that the Deep One knows what he is Deep doing.

Effort Disengagement

Rev. Quacksalver—Now the heresy of human effort brings us to another important point of Invincible Dogma — Effort Disengagement.

Peregrinus—Effort Disengagement? I guess I'm a little rusty on Glorious Salvation Machine doctrine.

Rev. Quacksalver—This Dogma states that men cannot be saved by their own efforts, but must come to God disengaged from all effort. This is problematic, however, for men do not naturally disengage themselves. They are naturally inclined to come to God through carnal efforts like heart-faith. To help men come into the presence of God disengaged from all effort, the Glorious Salvation Machine has formalized the required moment of passivity into a convenient form — the Incredibly High and Exalted Passive Form.

Peregrinus—The Sprinkle Form.

Rev. Quacksalver—Exactly.

The Incredibly High and Exalted Passive Form

Peregrinus—I don't recall hearing the term The Incredibly High and Exalted Passive Form before.

Rev. Quacksalver—It is the full theological name for the Passive Form.

Peregrinus—So where does the term come from?

Rev. Quacksalver—It arose from our belief that the Sprinkle Form is not a mere form. When we Splash men, we are not merely going through religious motions. We are bringing them into contact with the Nice God on the Mystic Plane, who pours out his God Magic upon them, and — Shazam! — they lose their Goat Fix and pass from Mystic Plane death to Mystic Plane life. This is a momentous event, therefore we elevate it as the Incredibly High and Exalted Passive Form.

Defending the Integrity of Salvation by God Magic

Peregrinus—What about the inconsistency in your Passive Form system? It's obvious that infants who go through the Passive Form are not going to do anything that overthrows the desired passiveness. But what about adults who do the Passive Form? Doesn't their coming to faith prior to the Passive Form derail the attempt to have salvation untainted by human effort?

And how can they be truly passive when they go through the Passive Form? Won't they be standing there believing stuff and trusting stuff?

Rev. Quacksalver—While I can understand your concerns, there are two glaring deficiencies with your argument.

First of all, there are no rules when defending the integrity of salvation by God Magic against the fanaticism that requires heart-faith for salvation. Inconsistencies and absurdities are entirely beside the point. As the old adage says, "All is fair in love and war."

Secondly, the efforts manifested by a man on his way to or during the Passive Form do not detract from the efficacy of the Passive Form. How can efforts which support the truth oppose the truth?

The Incredible Deliverance

Peregrinus—I'm beginning to see the train of thought behind Glorious Salvation Machine religion.

According to the Dogma of the Goat Fix, salvation is the removal of man's mystical Goat Guilt and Goat Stain by God Magic in the Passive Form. Heart-faith is not necessary to this salvation. So why waste precious heart affections on heart-faith? Just do the Passive Form and keep your heart for the important things — the things of the Big Here & Now.

According to the Great Illumination, attempting to get right with God by heart-faith is the error of Dead Works. This not only discredits heart-faith as a condition of salvation, it puts its overall value in dubious light. For there are only two classes of valuable things: those required for salvation and those that promote happiness in the Big Here & Now. Heart-faith falls in neither of these classes. So why waste precious heart affections on something with no real value? Just do the Passive Form and focus on Big Here & Now things, which have real value.

These two Dogmas provide a theological rationale for the Glorious Salvation Machine insistence that true religion is not

THE GLORIOUS SALVATION MACHINE

founded on heart-faith and following the Crucified One, but on the Passive Form and Minimizing with the Sweet One.

Rev. Quacksalver—I'm glad you can follow the logic.

Peregrinus—The illogical is pretty logical when you catch on to the illogic.

Rev. Quacksalver—No doubt about that. But there is much more at stake here than an argument that is logical. Minimizing theology is a matter of freedom.

Long ago the inhabitants of the world groaned in religious bondage. Their obligation to God meant that they were not free to maximize the Big Here & Now. But everything changed with the invention of Innocuous Minimum religion. It delivered them from the Egypt of real-relationship faith and planted them in the Promised Land of freedom where they were allowed to maximize the Big Here & Now. Religion was no longer a ball and chain that hindered their happiness in the world, but an obliging servant that helped them find it. Men regarded the Innocuous Minimum so highly that they immortalized its arrival as the Incredible Deliverance.

Peregrinus—I can definitely see why men like it so much.

Rev. Quacksalver—Life is so much easier when there is no spiritual tension between God and the Big Here & Now. You can throw caution to the wind. You can turn your discernment mechanism off and set your pleasure mechanism on high.

Saved to Serve

Peregrinus—But Minimizing is one of the main problems we see in the Glorious Salvation Machine. Men don't have to lose their life and serve God. All they have to do is comply with the paltry requirements of the Innocuous Minimum.

Rev. Quacksalver—The use of the adjective *paltry* is a reprehensible misrepresentation of the Innocuous Minimum. We do not believe in fruitless salvation as some falsely accuse us of believing. We preach that men are saved to serve. We do not leave the service variable out of the churchianity equation.

Peregrinus—The service variable?

Rev. Quacksalver—The Innocuous Minimum is comprised of two parts — the salvation constant and the service variable. The salvation constant is comprised of the Passive Form and a few intangibles. The service variable is comprised of the Weekly Duty and other service stuff that ought to be seen in the life of every man committed to churchianity.

Peregrinus—So how much service are we talking about?

Rev. Quacksalver—However much men want to engage in, as long as it does not get in the way of their Big Here & Now.

Peregrinus—So how much do we actually see in the life of the typical churchgoer? I'm not talking about fun stuff like softball, bingo, bake sales, or concerts. I'm talking about discipleship stuff like reading the Word of God, evangelizing, prayer, and fellowshipping in the things of God.

Rev. Quacksalver—It usually hovers around miniscule, but can be as much as minimal, or as little as infinitesimal.

Peregrinus—And you're satisfied with that?

Rev. Quacksalver—The job of the preacher is to encourage the sheep, not discourage them. We discourage them when we saddle them with heavy discipleship duties. We encourage them when we give them liberty to pursue the service variable as little or much as they see fit, at their own pace.

Peregrinus—Why not exhort them to give up their Big Here & Now and serve God with all their heart? That's what the Crucified One did.

Rev. Quacksalver—That would be counterproductive. If we touch their Big Here & Now, we touch the apple of their eye. If we touch the apple of their eye, they get mad and leave the Glorious Salvation Machine. Then we don't have them in the church at all. Better to have them in the church with middling to piddling service, than to not have them at all.

Deep Faith

Peregrinus—How about the Deep Faith that you referred to a few minutes ago? How does it differ from real-relationship faith?

Rev. Quacksalver—Now we are getting to the marrow and mystery of real religion.

Peregrinus—Why do I get the feeling that another serving of mind-numbing, spooky stuff is on the way?

Rev. Quacksalver—Real-relationship faith is childish. Any twelve-year-old can come up with that kind of faith by simply reading the Gospels. Do you really want a kid leading you by the hand through the maze of religion? Of course not! But that's the kind of religion you get in the Havens.

Deep Faith, on the other hand, is a deep mystery. So deep, in fact, that the brightest minds can't plumb its depths — they can't prove or disprove its veracity. It alone deserves the name *faith*, for it alone gives us something to believe that transcends reason. This is not a minor quibble. True religion begins where reason ends. True religion begins where men take a leap of faith that goes beyond facts, evidence, and reason. So if we want true religion, we absolutely must maintain the distinction between *reason* and *religion*.

Peregrinus—I'm not sure that I understand.

Rev. Quacksalver—Do you need a leap of faith to believe that two plus two equals four?

Peregrinus—No.

Rev. Quacksalver—Do you need a leap of faith to believe the scores in the Sports section?

Peregrinus—No.

Rev. Quacksalver—Do you need a leap of faith to believe that the sky is blue?

Peregrinus—No.

Rev. Quacksalver—Do you need a leap of faith to believe that you are alive and really exist?

Peregrinus—No.

Rev. Quacksalver—Why don't you need a leap of faith for such things?

Peregrinus—I don't need a leap of faith to believe what is obviously true.

Rev. Quacksalver—Exactly. Everything in the Daily Grind is a matter of facts, information, and evidence that we process with reason. Nothing transcends reason. Nothing is irrational. Nothing requires a leap of faith to believe. There is no occasion for Deep Faith. When it comes to religion, however, things are different. We are asked to believe things beyond our normal capacity to believe — things that transcend the evidence, facts, and reason we use everyday in the Daily Grind. Therefore, we need Deep Faith.

An Unlimited Bible

Peregrinus—That explains a few things.

Rev. Quacksalver—Oh, more than a few things. When you go down the Deep Faith road, there is no limit to what you can find in the Sacred Trust, or what you can teach from the Sacred Trust, or what the Sacred Trust can mean.

Peregrinus—That sounds like a trainload of ugly to me.

Rev. Quacksalver—Ugly? *Au contraire*. That's the beauty of Deep Faith. Having an unlimited Bible gives us an unlimited religion and an unlimited God. Once we take our relationship with God out of the realm of reason and put it in the realm of religion, we are no longer bound by the constraints of the Sacred Trust determined by carnal exegesis that leans on carnal facts, carnal logic, and carnal reason. Our scholars are free to find whatever they want to find or need to find. And the rest of us are free to choose whatever we please from their scholarly smorgasbord, whether for convenience or pleasure.

Peregrinus—That's beyond spooky. That's like writing your own Bible.

Rev. Quacksalver—It is better than writing your own Bible. We get to take the words which everyone already owns as the words of God and make them mean whatever we want them to mean or need them to mean.

Peregrinus—Don't you think that our understanding of God and true religion ought to be limited to and constrained by what the Sacred Trust says on these subjects?

THE GLORIOUS SALVATION MACHINE

Rev. Quacksalver—A limited Bible gives you a limited God. Why would you want a limited God?

God Magic Cannot Be Judged

Peregrinus—Let's go back to God Magic. How do you know that someone really has experienced God Magic? What do you look for as evidence?

Rev. Quacksalver—There is no evidence to look for, so we don't look for it. We take it as a simple matter of Deep Faith that if a person has done the Passive Form, then he has been degoatified by God Magic.

Peregrinus—So we aren't supposed to look for anything in the Daily Grind except for the historical fact that a man was disengaged in the Passive Form?

Rev. Quacksalver—That is correct. There is no practical or necessary connection between God Magic and the Daily Grind. Chew on the ramifications of that for a moment. God Magic cannot be judged. It does not necessarily or normally manifest itself in the Daily Grind. In plain English — there is nothing to see because there is nothing to see. The entire transaction is a matter of Deep Faith.

Peregrinus—But the Sacred Trust says that we shall know believers by their fruits.

Rev. Quacksalver—We can know the recipients of God Magic by their fruits. God Magic does bear fruit: confidence in one's salvation, confidence in the Passive Form, confidence in God Magic, confidence in the Innocuous Minimum, confidence in the Big Cheese, and confidence in the Glorious Salvation Machine. That's a lot of fruit, don't you think?

Peregrinus—That's no fruit at all. The fruit we're supposed to look for is conformity to the revealed will of God, not superstitious confidence in God Magic, the Big Cheese, and the Glorious Salvation Machine.

Rev. Quacksalver—You are on very dangerous ground. If you are looking for fruit as the necessary proof of salvation, then you are judging God Magic. And if you judge God Magic, then you judge God. And if you judge God, then you are guilty of obnoxious unbelief. So draw the logical conclusion — you are guilty of obnoxious unbelief.

Unsplashed Holiness Iniquity

Peregrinus—I don't think you are dealing honestly with the statements of the Sacred Trust which say or imply that we shall know the followers of the Crucified One by the fruit they bear.

Rev. Quacksalver—The problem isn't looking for fruit. The problem is where you look for fruit. You folks in the Havens look on the shallow outside for proof that someone has been touched by the grace of God. We look on the Deep inside.

Peregrinus—But what about such verses as "Be holy, for I am holy" and "Holiness, apart from which no man shall see the Lord"? It seems to me that they refer to outward stuff.

Rev. Quacksalver—If you focus on the outward stuff, you will not be able to keep yourself from falling prey to the error of Unsplashed Holiness.

Peregrinus—Unsplashed Holiness? What's that?

Rev. Quacksalver—Unsplashed Holiness is obedience apart from God Magic. It is obedience in the lives of men who have not experienced God Magic and have no confidence in God Magic. Such obedience, no matter how wonderful it seems, is a serious problem. The Dogma of Unsplashed Holiness states, "If it is Unsplashed, it is Dead Works."

Peregrinus—How can obedience that was birthed by faith in the Word of God honestly be regarded as evil?

Rev. Quacksalver—A man can be heart-faith transformed into a paragon of Bible obedience — until he walks and talks like the apostles. But when this transformation occurs apart from experiencing and trusting God Magic, this transformation is deadly delusion. His faith is real in the sense that it really exists. But it is not real in the sense of being genuine. It is false, fake, foul, and fatal. It is the flesh. It is dead human effort. It is the error of Dead Works. It is a rejection of God Magic. Things may look rosy and wonderful in the Daily

THE GLORIOUS SALVATION MACHINE

Grind, but in the Mystic Plane he is still a wretch. His Goat Fix rises as a stench in the nostrils of God.

Peregrinus—So men can walk in real holiness, but not have genuine holiness?

Rev. Quacksalver—That's right. Just because we see men get out of the Hog Pen and walk in real holiness does not mean we see genuine holiness. Genuine holiness only comes through God Magic in the Passive Form — men experiencing it and trusting it. This holiness is pleasing to God even if it never manifests anything in the Daily Grind beyond a smidgeon of Innocuous Minimum and a little superstition.

Peregrinus—What about those who got Splashed when they were kids and later went the route of real-relationship faith in the Crucified One?

Rev. Quacksalver—Those who turn their back on the Splash are without the Splash. It is as if they had never been Splashed. As one of my favorite Ironclad Interpretations says, "Depart from me all you workers of Unsplashed Holiness iniquity, I never knew you." God does not put up with any nonsense in this matter, and neither should we.

The Hog Pen Is a Minor Problem

Peregrinus—So when men obey the call to leave the Hog Pen and follow the Crucified One, their efforts are in vain?

Rev. Quacksalver—That is correct. Their efforts are vain. But we need to define *vain*. I do not mean vain in the sense of *empty*. Their effort bucket is definitely full. They manifest a tremendous amount of change in the Daily Grind — very impressive from a purely scholarly perspective. Leaving the Hog Pen, in the face of the disapproval of society and in denial of one's own inner temptations, is no small feat.

What I do mean is that their efforts are vain in the sense of *meaningless*. They manifest change in the Daily Grind where change is optional, not on the Mystic Plane where change is mandatory. Their lives have been turned upside down, but they have not been degoatified by God Magic.

Peregrinus—How can leaving the Hog Pen be optional? The Sacred Trust, in at least a dozen different ways in at least a hundred different passages, commands all men everywhere to get out of the Hog Pen and come back home to the Father.

Rev. Quacksalver—The question is not what the Sacred Trust says. The question is how we ought to prioritize the many things it says. We need to prioritize its teachings according to God's perspective. When we do that, we are forced to conclude that the Hog Pen problem is minor compared to the Goat Fix problem. So, if you really cared about reconciling men to the Father, you would focus on the Goat Fix problem.

Peregrinus—How can man wallowing in the Hog Pen be a minor problem?

Rev. Quacksalver—The real question is, how can it be a major problem? If a man gets out of the Hog Pen in the Daily Grind, but is still Goat Fixed on the Mystic Plane, he is still at odds with God. On the other hand, if he gets his Goat Fix undone on the Mystic Plane, yet still pursues his slop-chomping and mud-romping in the Hog Pen in the Daily Grind, he is fully reconciled to God.

Therefore, wallowing in the Hog Pen is a minor problem that is neither here nor there in the big picture. Why would anyone get worked up over it? You need to let Invincible Dogma and Deep Logic get ahold of your heart. Salvation is merely and only a matter of resolving the Goat Fix through God Magic in the Passive Form. Forsaking the Hog Pen plays no part in the salvation equation. It is neither a condition nor an evidence of salvation.

All Wallow in the Hog Pen

Peregrinus—Well, I am worked up about forsaking the Hog Pen, and no amount of Innocuous Minimum nonsense is going to change my mind.

Rev. Quacksalver—You Havenmongers continually yammer and bluster about real-relationship faith in the Crucified One that delivers men from the Hog Pen. But you are propagating a dangerous deception that flies in the face of the Invincible Dogma that all men wallow in the Hog Pen in Talk, Think, and Walk every day.

Peregrinus—Where is the deception? The followers of the Crucified One are not pretending that they no longer wallow in the Hog Pen. They really have experienced the heart changing, life changing power of the gospel. Like the prodigal son, they have left the Hog Pen and gone back to their father's house. While they aren't perfect, they are definitely changed. They have experienced that wonderful freedom from the Hog Pen that the Sacred Trust holds out — they are washed, they are sanctified, they are justified.

Rev. Quacksalver—I don't deny that many Havenmongers forsake the Hog Pen. That is a real experience which they have really experienced. But experience is deceptive. It is dangerous to get your doctrine from your experience and foolhardy to use your experience to challenge Invincible Dogma.

Invincible Dogma states — and all the erudite scholars agree — that all men are stuck in the muck in the Hog Pen and wallow in it every day in Talk, Think, and Walk. We can't climb out or tunnel out. We can't be drawn out or dragged out. There is no escape from the mire. There is no deliverance from the trough.

We are forced to conclude, therefore, that when men heart-believe and forsake the Hog Pen, their experience is a delusion that does not really take them to the Father's house. Though they have a superficial departure from the Hog Pen in the irrelevant Daily Grind which appears to fulfill the letter of the Sacred Trust, yet on the all-important Mystic Plane, where true religion is found, they are still wallowing in the Hog Pen, gorging on vile unbelief, and trampling God Magic underfoot.

God's Alphabet

Peregrinus—Well, I am convinced that those who obey the Sacred Trust command to flee the Hog Pen and return to the Father, actually do flee the Hog Pen and return to the Father.

Their departure and journey home is neither a superficial nor a delusional experience. It is a life-changing reality which is wrought by the living and powerful Word of God.

Rev. Quacksalver—Listen carefully my works-mongering friend. You need to wash your hands of this Hog Pen nonsense. There is only one *G* in God's alphabet. And it is in the term *God Magic*. If men have to *Get up* from the trough, *Get out* of the Hog Pen, and *Go back* to the father's house, then you have added three more **G**'s to God's alphabet. You ought to be very afraid. It is a fearful thing to fall into the hands of the living God with four **G**'s in your alphabet.

Peregrinus—But what if the Havens are right? What if the Glorious Salvation Machine is wrong? What if men really-truly have to flee the Hog Pen and return to the Father in real-relationship faith?

Rev. Quacksalver—There is not one chance in a million that the Havens are right. If the insignificant Havens are right, then all the learned Innocuous Minimum preachers for the whole history of the Glorious Salvation Machine are wrong. How can so many well-taught and well-meaning people be wrong?

Extremism and Bare Feet

Rev. Quacksalver—Besides, actually fleeing the Hog Pen in the Daily Grind is just another instance of the fanatical extremism which characterizes the Havens.

Peregrinus—Fanatical extremism? Give me an example.

Rev. Quacksalver—You know as well as I do that they take all the hard sayings and all the holiness and devotion passages to ridiculous extremes. They all believe that the followers of the Crucified One should walk around with Bare Feet like the extremists of old.

Peregrinus—Bare Feet? Extremists? What are you talking about? I haven't seen anything like that in the Havens.

Rev. Quacksalver—Of course you haven't. You can't see it. Errorists are always blind to their own errors. But we can see

THE GLORIOUS SALVATION MACHINE

as plain as day that you are walking with Bare Feet down the path of extremism.

Peregrinus—Okay, so give me a few examples of Bare Feet that you have seen in the Havens.

Rev. Quacksalver—Where do you want me to start? How about teaching men to take up the cross of the Crucified One and follow him? How about teaching men to turn their backs on the Big Here & Now, with all its pleasures and pride, and live for Sweet Everlasting?

Peregrinus—I'm having a hard time seeing the Bare Feet.

Rev. Quacksalver—Oh, the Bare Feet are there. Trust me.

Peregrinus—Taking what the Sacred Trust says on the Big Here & Now seriously is not the same thing as walking in the ancient error of Barefoot extremism. We have withdrawn from the ungodly ways and defilements of the Big Here & Now. We have not withdrawn from concourse in the Big Here & Now. We are in the world, but not of the world.

Rev. Quacksalver—Every time I corner you, you split some hair to avoid the blunt force of the truth. Now you want to split a hair between taking the hard sayings literally and being a Barefoot heretic.

Peregrinus—Making a distinction between trembling at the plain teaching of the Sacred Trust and walking in the ancient error of Barefoot extremism is not splitting hairs.

Rev. Quacksalver—I pity you gullible, deluded, mind-bent Havenmongers who take the hard sayings in the Sacred Trust literally. Can't you see that even though you do not literally walk around barefooted as the Barefoot extremists of old did, you are guilty of the same Barefoot extremism they were?

Why go half-way with your Barefoot extremism? Why not go all the way? Why not live in a cave, wear rags, walk around barefooted, and eat stale bread? Or how about a contemporary version of this error? Perhaps we should all go live under a bridge, wear ratty clothes and worn-out boots, use a piece of cardboard for a blanket, and dumpster dive for our dinner?

Peregrinus—I don't think your observation is fair.

Rev. Quacksalver—Men plea for fairness when they don't want to face the facts. Why don't you just face the facts? You Havenmongers think men are obligated to follow the Crucified One according to the dictates of the Sacred Trust interpreted in a slavishly literal manner. Therefore, you hunker down in your little caves — which you call Havens — outside the camp of the Big Here & Now, cold, hungry, and miserable, counting all the Big Here & Now stuff that could warm, fill, and cheer you as garbage. What purpose or profit is there in such rigorous, excessive self-denial?

Following the Glorious Salvation Machine Is Following God

Peregrinus—Well, I know what the Sacred Trust says about following and serving the Crucified One. And I am determined to follow and serve him to the best of my ability according to the teachings I find in its pages.

Rev. Quacksalver—Right there is your whole problem. You think too much — way too much. The smartest thing you could do is stop thinking and start submitting. Lay down your pride, forsake your independent spirit, and submit to the authority and teaching of the Glorious Salvation Machine.

Peregrinus—You want me to follow men? I can't do that. It's not right to be a follower of men, no matter how wise and godly they are. We need to get our beliefs and practices from the Sacred Trust.

Rev. Quacksalver—I didn't say you ought to follow men. I said you ought to follow the Glorious Salvation Machine. There is a huge difference. Following the Glorious Salvation Machine is not following men. It is following God. God built the Glorious Salvation Machine. God ordained Big Cheese to keep the Glorious Salvation Machine running smoothly. God entrusted the Big Cheese with the Invincible Dogmas, which are the unquestionable truths of true religion. And God also entrusted the Big Cheese with the Ironclad Interpretations, so they could defend the Invincible Dogmas. From top to bottom the entire institution is from God. When men refuse to follow

God's provision — the Glorious Salvation Machine, the Invincible Dogmas, the Ironclad Interpretations, and the Big Cheese — they are refusing to follow God.

The Big Cheese

Peregrinus—So God wants us to let someone else interpret the Sacred Trust for us?

Rev. Quacksalver—No, God wants us to let him interpret the Sacred Trust for us. He knows how difficult it is for us to understand it, so he gave the correct interpretation to the Big Cheese, so they could give it to us.

Peregrinus—What if the Big Cheese are wrong?

Rev. Quacksalver—That is a preposterous notion. The only way they can be wrong is if God can make mistakes. But it is not even remotely possible that God could miscommunicate the truth to his shepherds or that they could miscommunicate the truth to us.

Think about the ramifications of what you are suggesting. If we can't trust his present chosen vessels, how can we trust his original chosen vessels — the apostles? And if we can't trust his apostles, how can we trust the Sacred Trust they penned? And if we can't trust the Sacred Trust, then we might as well make our own religion.

Peregrinus—But …

Rev. Quacksalver—The men whose expertise you question are *bona fide* scholars. They have earned degrees from honored Deep Signification Indoctrination Institutions. They are Deep men who have pursued Deep things for years. They know how to rightly Deep Significate the Sacred Trust and properly handle passages which require Ironclad Interpretations. They are adept at making the simple abstruse and the clear obtuse.

Peregrinus—But …

Rev. Quacksalver—Peregrinus, you have more buts than an ashtray. It is a lack of Deep Faith on your part not to trust the Big Cheese. You just need to "Let go and let God."

Peregrinus—I cannot do that. Not for any price. Not for any cause. Not for any reason. My trust is not in men, but in the Sacred Trust. Men can be wrong. The Sacred Trust cannot be wrong. Let God be true and every man a liar.

Rev. Quacksalver—I agree. We need to put our trust in the Sacred Trust, not in men. That is why I have labored for the past hour to convince you to stop trusting in yourself. When men trust their own interpretation of the Sacred Trust, they are trusting in themselves, and when they trust in themselves, they are trusting in men.

The only way to ensure that we are actually trusting the Sacred Trust, and not man's understanding of it, is to put our trust in the true understanding of the Sacred Trust. This is summed up in the Invincible Dogmas which God committed to his Big Cheese. This means that if we really trust the Sacred Trust, we will trust the Big Cheese and the Invincible Dogmas they were given to teach us.

Peregrinus—But what about testing all things? Doesn't the Sacred Trust lay upon us an obligation to test all things? If the Bereans were commended for testing Paul, how much more should we test our preachers?

Rev. Quacksalver—The man in the pew does indeed have an obligation to hold the Big Cheese accountable. But it is not his job to test their doctrine by what *he* thinks the Sacred Trust teaches. It is his job to test their doctrine by what the Sacred Trust really does teach, which is the body of truth handed down in the Invincible Dogmas.

Notice that we do not read that the noble Bereans tried Paul's preaching to see if it corresponded with their opinions of what the Sacred Trust taught. We read that they tried the apostle's preaching to see if it corresponded with what the Sacred Trust actually taught. This is a tremendous, stupendous fact. For the diligent Bible-reading types — the Bereans — no matter how diligent they are, are not the standard. Can you imagine what would happen if the entire Glorious Salvation Machine bowed

THE GLORIOUS SALVATION MACHINE

to the understanding of a zealous carpenter from Podunk Junction? I cringe just thinking about it.

Peregrinus—So the Big Cheese tell us what the truth is and we hold them accountable to that truth.

Rev. Quacksalver—Exactly.

Deep Trusting the Deep Significance

Peregrinus—I think your approach is backwards. We should use the Sacred Trust to judge the Invincible Dogmas and the Ironclad Interpretations, rather than use the Invincible Dogmas and Ironclad Interpretations to judge the Sacred Trust and dictate what it means.

Rev. Quacksalver—We don't judge the Sacred Trust by our Invincible Dogmas and Ironclad Interpretations. The Sacred Trust doesn't need to be judged and can't be judged. We only judge — and reject — false doctrine with them.

Peregrinus—How do you know for sure that your Invincible Dogmas and Ironclad Interpretations are true? What if they are wrong? What if they trample on the truth?

Rev. Quacksalver—You mean, what if the truth tramples on the truth? I don't see any likelihood of that ever happening.

Peregrinus—But it seems like you are begging the question. It seems like you are assuming what you need to prove. Don't you need to prove that the Invincible Dogmas and the Ironclad Interpretations are true?

Rev. Quacksalver—Proof!? Why would you ask for proof to prove what is obviously true? That is like asking for proof that the sky is blue or that water is wet.

Peregrinus—Invincible Dogma is not obviously true in the same way that the sky is obviously blue.

Rev. Quacksalver—Quibble all you want. We know that the Invincible Dogmas are true because everyone believes them. And everyone believes the Invincible Dogmas because they are true. Moreover, no one has ever raised a reputed Sacred Trust objection against an Invincible Dogma that isn't easily invalidated by one or more Ironclad Interpretations.

Peregrinus—That's pretty potent stuff. There is nothing like mixing circular reasoning and brute force.

Rev. Quacksalver—You have to love it. To be honest, this is one of the main reasons why I belong to the Glorious Salvation Machine. We don't have to think very much. We don't have to put any significant effort into the Sacred Trust. We just Deep Trust the Deep Significance handed down in the Invincible Dogmas and the Ironclad Interpretations, and this leaves us free to live our lives for ourselves, happily entangled in the Big Here & Now in whatever way we please.

Peregrinus—But we ought to tremble at the Sacred Trust.

Rev. Quacksalver—I do tremble at it. That's why I won't touch it except to dabble in it. I leave the interpretation to the experts. I do my job. They do their job. And I like it this way. I put enough effort into the Sacred Trust to give the churchgoers two DroNings every week, and then I call it quits.

The Sanitized Trust

Peregrinus—I get the feeling that you folks in the Glorious Salvation Machine don't really like the Sacred Trust.

Rev. Quacksalver—There is some truth in that observation. That's why we use the Sanitized Trust. It makes the Sacred Trust much more palatable to the average man.

Peregrinus—How convenient.

Rev. Quacksalver—Brilliant too. For centuries we labored uphill against the taste buds of mankind. An unacceptably high percentage of them found the Sacred Trust unpalatable. They didn't like what it said about how they were supposed to live their lives. Then brilliant men took it upon themselves to rectify this situation. Every distasteful passage was explained in a manner acceptable to men. What a godsend this has proved to be. Now the book behind religion promotes a religion that is tasteful to men who love the Big Here & Now.

Peregrinus—But there is one difficulty. If you have changed what the Sacred Trust means, how can your interpretation be true?

THE GLORIOUS SALVATION MACHINE

Rev. Quacksalver—You are just not getting it are you? The job of the Sacred Trust is to win the hearts of men to the Nice God. This means that any tweaking we can do to make it more successful at winning the hearts of men, makes it more faithful at doing its job.

Peregrinus—How do you figure that?

Rev. Quacksalver—Easy. When we consider the fact that *faithful* and *true* are synonyms — for example, a man that is faithful is a man that is true — and apply this distinction with a broad brush to the Sacred Trust, we are brought to the mind-boggling conclusion that whatever increases the heart winning *faithfulness* of the Sacred Trust also increases its *truthfulness*.

Peregrinus—That is using silly-putty logic to give men what they want.

Rev. Quacksalver—Absolutely not. We don't give men what they want, we give them what they need. But we just happen to be very adept at giving it to them in a way that they want it.

Peregrinus—But you are changing the Sacred Trust.

Rev. Quacksalver—We haven't changed anything. We still give men the entire Sacred Trust. They still get every verse in the Sacred Trust. Nothing has been deleted. The original Greek and Hebrew are the same. The English translation is the same. Nothing is changed. All we have done is give every offensive passage an inoffensive explanation.

Peregrinus—That is so wrong.

Rev. Quacksalver—How can it be wrong when the results are so wonderful? How can it be wrong to bring men to the place where they are able to believe every verse in the Sacred Trust? You do want men to believe the Sacred Trust don't you?

The Sanitized Trust Filled with Meaning and Medicine

Peregrinus—But the Sanitized Trust makes the Sacred Trust void. It empties passages of their real meaning.

Rev. Quacksalver—Empties the Sacred Trust? You have no idea what you are talking about. You Havenmongers are the ones who are guilty of emptying the Sacred Trust. The Sacred

QUACKSALVER RELOADED

Trust as interpreted by the Havens has no message or meaning for the modern man because it conflicts with the wisdom and desires of the Big Here & Now. For all practical purposes, it is an empty, meaningless book.

The Sanitized Trust, on the other hand, holds out a message and meaning that is up-to-date and relevant. It rings true and useful to the heart of modern man.

Peregrinus—But the Sanitized Trust isn't the medicine that God has prescribed.

Rev. Quacksalver—You want to talk about medicine? What good is medicine if men will not take it?

Peregrinus—Medicine is still valuable even if men refuse to take it. God's prescription for the heart is valuable whether or not men take it. We can't change men's hearts if we change the medicine that God has prescribed for them.

Rev. Quacksalver—I disagree entirely. The Sanitized Trust is filled with medicine. You have to understand the principle that the medicine is what we make it. There is no exact recipe in heaven that we are supposed to follow to the letter. We can concoct any formula or recipe we please as long as we include the three main ingredients — positive thoughts of the Nice God, positive encouragement to be play nice in God's sandbox, and positive encouragement in the Universal Quest to fill the Big Empty. And the last is the most important point. We have an obligation to help men keep their chin up through all of life's setbacks, owies, bumps, and bruises, so they can press on in the quest to find happiness and fulfillment in the Big Here & Now. This isn't easy, as you well know. The Big Here & Now is a rough and tumble place.

Deep Significance Calls unto Deep Hearts

Peregrinus—I'm going to stick with taking the statements of the Sacred Trust at face value. I don't think Deep Significance makes the Bible more relevant for modern man.

Rev. Quacksalver—That's because you have shallow on the brain. Shallow men with shallow minds are drawn to shallow things. When men get a little Deep on their heart, they can't be satisfied with the Shallow Fluff of the letter of the text. As a poet wrote in the Sanitized Trust, "Deep Significance calls unto Deep hearts."

Peregrinus—I guess I must be shallow. I don't hear the Deep Significance calling me.

Rev. Quacksalver—What a pity that you justify splashing around in the wading pool because you are too timid to learn to swim. Only when men turn to the Deep Significance do they find true religion. It brings them face to face with the Great Mysterious Unknowable One — the Inscrutable Other — and they are never the same. They have a mysterious, transcendent, existential encounter with him on the Mystic Plane which produces a mysterious, transcendent, existential change in their heart and life that no man can know or judge. Henceforth they are *not known* as he is *not known*.

Man's Supreme Duty

Peregrinus—Well, I have no interest in Deep Significance. I want an encounter with God that really-truly changes me in my Daily Grind with changes that are obvious to everyone — like leaving the broad road and walking on the narrow path.

Rev. Quacksalver—If you reject the Deep Significance, you are on a dangerous road. According to the Sanitized Trust, the Nice God hides his Deep Stuff from the wise who think they can understand the Sacred Trust on their own and trust its statements at face value as if they were reading the Sports page. He reveals his Deep Stuff to the simple who know they can't understand the Sacred Trust on their own and trust the Big Cheese to teach them the right understanding.

Peregrinus—That sounds like flushing your brain down the drain and letting someone else do the thinking for you.

Rev. Quacksalver—Well, that actually *is* what we want men to do. We want them to stop thinking for themselves. Thinking is dangerous. However, we don't like to come right out and tell men that we want them to flush. Men are proud, stubborn, and independent. If we require them to do the Flush, they simply refuse. If they refuse to flush, we are unable to teach them the Deep Stuff they must believe to be saved.

Peregrinus—So the end justifies the means?

Rev. Quacksalver—Oh, absolutely. It can't be wrong to tell men little white lies if that's what must be done to help them believe the truth. The church has got to do what the church has got to do.

Peregrinus—You really want men to quit thinking?

Rev. Quacksalver—No, I didn't say that. They can think all they want, as long as they only think authorized thoughts in an authorized manner inside the box that we give them.

Peregrinus—So you don't want independent thinking?

Rev. Quacksalver—That isn't really the case either. Men can think all the independent thoughts they want on dozens of meaningless subjects like sports, politics, business, education, music, and art. We are not trying to shackle the human mind. We just want men to leave the Glorious Salvation Machine and her Invincible Dogmas alone.

Peregrinus—So what you are trying to quash is independent men thinking independent thoughts on matters that could take them outside the God Magic box.

Rev. Quacksalver—Exactly. Man's Supreme Duty is to quit thinking for himself on matters of religion and let the venerable Glorious Salvation Machine think for him. That keeps him safe and sound inside the Innocuous Minimum box.

Peregrinus—So the use of the God-given brain gets in the way of God-given religion? That sounds pretty spooky to me.

Rev. Quacksalver—I know exactly how you feel. It is kind of spooky. I myself balked at the Flush for a while. But one day it dawned on me how much I stood to gain if I flushed. You gain the esteem of the Glorious Salvation Machine, which gives you a much bigger field in which to serve God. You gain acceptance with the Big Here & Now, which makes it much more likely they will want to be churchgoers. And you don't have to embrace a slavishly literal interpretation of the hard sayings in the Sacred Trust, which demand austere things like tearing down the Altar of Worthy Self and turning your back on seeking fulfillment in the things of the Big Here & Now.

Thinking and Asking Questions Is Unprofitable

Peregrinus—Well, I for one am not going to flush my brain down the drain for any consideration. Not to see gain. Not to flee pain. Flushing is just plain wrong. I don't see how anyone could submit to a ban on thinking and asking questions.

Rev. Quacksalver—Let me reiterate that there is no ban on thinking and asking questions *per se*. The ban covers the spirit of the investigation. If men think and ask questions in a spirit of idle curiosity, anemic scholarship, profound gullibility, or Deep Think Existentialization, we welcome their thoughts and questions. It is only when men think and ask questions in a spirit of serious investigation —challenging our authority and the veracity of Invincible Dogma — that they step out of bounds and fall out of favor.

Peregrinus—Why would anyone submit to a ban on thinking and asking questions in the arena of religion?

Rev. Quacksalver—Why would anyone not submit to such a ban? It is for their own good. Thinking and asking questions in this arena in a spirit of serious investigation is unprofitable.

Peregrinus—But how can thinking and asking questions in this arena be unprofitable?

Rev. Quacksalver—In two big ways. *First of all,* it damages relationships. Nobody enjoys being around a man who is on a relentless journey to know the teachings of the Sacred Trust. This restless spirit shares every new truth it finds with those around them, offending them with incessant chatter about the Sacred Trust, and driving wedges between the investigator and his family, friends, and associates.

Secondly, it damages reputations. When a man goes down the path of thinking thoughts that are banned and asking questions that are frowned upon, he soon falls out of favor. His integrity will be challenged. His scholarship will be questioned. His colleagues will distance themselves from him. Open doors will shut. No matter which way he looks, the ugly will be waist-deep and rising fast.

Peregrinus—But that isn't necessarily bad. The Sacred Trust does say, "Don't think that I came to bring peace on the earth. I came not to bring peace but a sword ... A man's enemies shall be they of his own house." The faithful follower may well have to face rejection by family, friends, colleagues, and church.

Rev. Quacksalver—Rubbish. We can do without that kind of faithfulness. We follow the Platinum Principle, "If you offend people, you can't do them any good." We avoid pricking the heart or the conscience at any cost. We are not interested in influencing little crowds. We want to influence big crowds.

Sucking the Life Out of the Big Here & Now

Peregrinus—I think the Glorious Salvation Machine is more concerned about its own temporal profit than man's eternal profit. It has turned religion into a business that gives men the religion they want, so it can make merchandise of them.

Rev. Quacksalver—Is it our fault if helping men to have an Innocuous relationship with the Nice God happens to be a profitable business?

Peregrinus—Preachers ought to bring men face to face with the God revealed in the pages of the Sacred Trust. They ought to charge them to love him with all of their heart, soul, mind, and strength. They ought to exhort them to heart-believe on the Crucified One. They have no business tickling men's ears with Innocuous Minimum nonsense.

Rev. Quacksalver—Love God with all of your heart, soul, mind, and strength? Ridiculous! Where would the Big Here & Now be if every man on the face of the earth determined to take the Sacred Trust at face value in a Daily Grind sense like they were reading the Sports page and actually loved God with all of his heart, soul, mind, and strength? I'll tell you what would happen! The life would get sucked right out of the Big Here & Now!

THE GLORIOUS SALVATION MACHINE

Thousands of glorious institutions of pleasure, profit, and the pride of life raised for our mesmerization and stupification, and sanctified by time and public opinion, would suffer from lack of attention and care. Is that what you want to happen? Do you think for a moment that the Nice God really intends for us to so callously and flippantly abominate things that are highly esteemed among men?

If you Havenmongers had your way, the entire Big Here & Now would come to a standstill. Men would quit laying up treasure for themselves. They would quit tearing down their barns and building bigger ones. They would quit pursuing fame, praise, honor, and riches. There would be nothing left to glory in or lust after. All would be emptiness. Can't you see? When you take away the Innocuous Minimum, you take away everything. May I remind you that it is the thief who robs mankind. The Sweet One came that men might enjoy life in the Big Here & Now more fun-stuff abundantly.

Big Here & Now First, Spiritual Matters Second

Peregrinus—You have minimized the Sacred Trust to such a degree that you might as well not waste your time.

Rev. Quacksalver—You underestimate the value we place on the Sacred Trust. We Deeply believe every line in it. We believe in such cherished Sacred Trust teachings as creation, the fall, the flood, Babel, the Exodus, and the Crucified One. But we believe in them for what they really are — a mixture of embellished historical accounts and religious fiction that is designed to communicate Deep Significance. And we believe in such teachings as the Second Coming, the Kingdom, Sweet Everlasting, and Awful Everlasting. But we believe in them for what they really are — a difficult to isolate germ of truth that is intermingled with mythologized aspirations after personal and societal rectitude. And while we don't pretend to understand the full significance of any of these teachings, we confess our Deeply felt need for whatever it is that they signify.

Peregrinus—Why don't you just come right out and say that indulging the Big Here & Now is more important to you than understanding the Sacred Trust?

Rev. Quacksalver—The Big Here & Now is more important to us, and we are not ashamed. We are realists not idealists. We accept things the way they are. Man's natural inclinations turn to Big Here & Now matters first and spiritual matters second. This is our nature. This is the way that God made us. So when we follow our natural inclinations, we honor the God who made us this way.

Peregrinus—So you think it is right to make the Big Here & Now our priority and let God have the leftovers?

Rev. Quacksalver—This isn't a moral issue. There is no right or wrong. There is no choice to be made. This is a matter of nature. Is gravity right or wrong? Are dogs right or wrong? Is eating right or wrong? We simply and humbly embrace the fact that we are Big Here & Now first and spiritual second.

Peregrinus—So Christians ought to be entangled in the Big Here & Now? They ought to find their life, their meaning, their purpose, and their happiness in the Big Here & Now?

Rev. Quacksalver—You speak as if entanglement in the Big Here & Now were a bad thing. It is a good thing. The Sanitized Trust says that every fun-stuff thing in the Big Here & Now is a good gift from the Father above. If we refuse to be entangled in the fun stuff of the Big Here & Now, we despise the Father's gifts. If we despise his gifts, we despise him.

You folks in the Havens overthrow the natural order of things with your fanatical efforts to be spiritual first. You set up an arbitrary standard of spirituality that you arbitrarily arrive at by taking the statements of the Sacred Trust in a slavishly literal sense like you were reading the Sports page in the newspaper.

We in the Glorious Salvation Machine have no interest in tinkering with the natural order. We are Big Here & Now first, and we are not ashamed. Underneath our creeds — as many and varied as they are — lies our true religion, the Big Here & Now Creed. While our religious creeds can be ignored, modified, or jettisoned if the need arises, the Big Here & Now Creed is inviolable. Nothing must be allowed to detract from it or take precedence over it. This creed, and this creed alone, has our whole heart.

The Big Here & Now Creed

Peregrinus—So what is the Big Here & Now Creed?

Rev. Quacksalver—"Let us enjoy as much Big Here & Now fun stuff as we can, while we can, for we shall soon pass from this pleasant scene and lay in a cold, cold grave."

Peregrinus—Why, that's just the Altar of Worthy Self.

Rev. Quacksalver—Of course it is. What else would it be or could it be? The true heart religion of the Glorious Salvation Machine is the true heart religion of every religion in the Big Here & Now — the Altar of Worthy Self.

Peregrinus—That is the broad road.

Rev. Quacksalver—Better a broad road than a narrow mind. You Havenmongers think that man ought to *lose* his life in the Big Here & Now, *pursue* the devotion of the apostles, and *look for* fulfillment in Sweet Everlasting.

We believe that a man ought to *find* his life in the Big Here & Now, *pursue* fun stuff as if there were no tomorrow, for there probably will not be a lot of fun stuff in Sweet Everlasting, and *look for* fulfillment in the things of this life.

Peregrinus—That's trashing man's present duty.

Rev. Quacksalver—Balderdash. The Nice God wants us to make Worthy Self as happy as we can. This means our duty is to dance passionately around the Altar of Worthy Self until our last breath. If we must have religion on the Altar to be happy, then let us go with the Innocuous Minimum, which is designed to be compatible with the Altar of Worthy Self.

The Big Troublemaker Put in His Place

Peregrinus—You have shoved God right out of the picture.

Rev. Quacksalver—Not me. This matter came to a head long ago. The men of the Big Here & Now grew tired of the Big

Troublemaker's meddling and decided to put him in his place. They called a meeting and informed him that they were too busy with important Big Here & Now matters to serve him according to the plain teaching of the Sacred Trust, that he was going to stay out of their affairs, and that they would come looking for him if and when they needed him.

Peregrinus—You mean they told God to buzz off?

Rev. Quacksalver—You make it sound so negative. What were they supposed to do? God just kept getting his hands into things that didn't pertain to him. They had to do something. So they confined him to the church building, and promised him a little freedom during the Weekly Duty if he promised to say only what they wanted to hear. Personally, I think it was the most brilliant innovation in religious history.

Peregrinus—But what does God think of it?

Rev. Quacksalver—The Nice God is a very understanding chap. He doesn't hold the confinement and limitations against us. He knows how busy we are and that we only did what we had to do. He graciously accepts the lesser role we have given him. He doesn't mind that we have put him on the shelf like a little Buddha, as long as we rub his belly from time to time.

For All Practical Purposes, Man Is God

Peregrinus—But how do you justify treating God this way?

Rev. Quacksalver—Justify this course of action? Oh my, aren't you behind the times. Power isn't worth anything if you can't manipulate it and control it. Electricity, for instance, has no value if we don't harness it and exploit it. Likewise, nuclear energy. And the same goes for our relationship with God. If we can't manipulate him and control him, he is of no use or value.

Peregrinus—That is way too spooky.

Rev. Quacksalver—We don't want anything in our life that we can't manipulate and control. This is the Ultimate Ultimate. Can't you see? Evolution is an advanced, secular version of the Innocuous Minimum. Evolution banishes God. The Innocuous Minimum says he can stay if he'll be a good boy. Both get God

THE GLORIOUS SALVATION MACHINE

out of the way and give the reins to man. We are the masters of our lives, our souls, our minds, our world, our fate, our destiny. We are the masters of the universe. We fashion and create as we will. We tear down and build as we please.

Peregrinus—What is the purpose of God, then? Why even have him in the picture at all?

Rev. Quacksalver—That is a very pressing and perplexing question. And the fact is, the brightest minds, in and out of the Glorious Salvation Machine, have been wrestling with it. After all, God doesn't actually have much of a say in what goes on down here. We do what we want, when we want, the way we want. And while we do ask his advice once in a while, we only follow it when we approve of it. So it does raise the question as to whether we actually need to have God around.

Peregrinus—For all practical purposes, then, man is God.

Rev. Quacksalver—If by *God* you mean the Inscrutable, Existential One behind all things, who may or may not be what our generalizations, lucubrations, and existentializations make him out to be, then *no*, man is not God.

But if by *God* you refer to that wonderful being who has the final say in all matters of history, reality, morality, religion, and ethics, then *yes*, for all practical purposes, man is God.

Peregrinus—Why would anyone want to squeeze God out of their life in the Big Here & Now?

Rev. Quacksalver—You misrepresent our position. We have not gotten rid of God. We carry him with us everyday, tucked away like a band-aid in a purse or a wallet, just in case we need him. It is good to know that he is there for us if we get an *owie* in the course of life.

Quacksalver Departs

Over the course of the conversation, Reverend Quacksalver's countenance changed from disturbed to disgusted. Peregrinus' steadfast insistence on the trustworthiness of the Sacred Trust, the knowability of God, the corruptness of the whole Big Here & Now, the waywardness of the Altar of Worthy Self, and the iniquity of the Innocuous Minimum had caused him to lose his composure. He was not going to waste one more minute of his precious time on an incorrigible fanatic. He brought the conversation to an abrupt close with a few curt words.

Rev. Quacksalver—Well, I have to cut this visit short. I am a busy man. I have to go prepare a message for the *Coddle Your Ego Society*, then socialize with a couple of big shots at the country club. If you want to be a big important somebody and go places in the Big Here & Now, you have to schmooze with the people that matter.

Reverend Quacksalver stood up, turned, started walking away, then wheeled back around, and spoke one last word.

Rev. Quacksalver—One last piece of advice. All men flush something. You can't avoid the painful choice. So choose your flush. Will you flush your brain down the drain with the normal people in the Glorious Salvation Machine, or will you flush the Big Here & Now down the drain with the fanatics in the Havens? Either way, the flush you choose will have a dramatic impact on your life.

With that Reverend Quacksalver stormed out the door and strode to his car.

CHAPTER SEVEN

LUKE W. ZEAL RETURNS

Faithfulness Often Leads down a Diverging Path

When followers of the Crucified One make faithfulness their number one priority, they often discover that their faithfulness leads them down a path which diverges widely from the path taken by friends who profess to be Christians. So Peregrinus discovered that his path diverged from the path Luke was traveling.

Their differences led to a dispute which they carried on through e-mails, chats, and phone calls. Luke impugned the teachings of the Havens as heresies. Peregrinus challenged the errors of the Half-Havens and attempted to demonstrate that they were contrary to the teaching of the Sacred Trust. The dispute strained their relationship. Luke became so frustrated that he determined to confront his friend and end the matter — for better or for worse.

He called Peregrinus and suggested they get together on the third Saturday of the month. Despite his pretense of wanting to spend some time together, Peregrinus knew that Luke's real purpose was to chide him for turning his back on the Sugar Kids Message and Half-Haven churchianity and convince him that the Havens were wrong. Peregrinus didn't want to rehash these issues again, and wasn't looking forward to a visit with Luke, but he reluctantly agreed.

When the time came, which happened to be a few hours after his unexpected visit with Rev. Quacksalver, Peregrinus drove, with a heavy heart, to the city park they had agreed upon. He parked, sighed, noticed Luke getting out of his car, and slowly got out of his own. He felt like he had an appointment with the executioner. They met, shook hands, made some small talk, and then the confrontation began.

Leaning on Your Own Understanding Is Dangerous

Luke W. Zeal—Peregrinus, you could be a spiritual giant if you would just humble yourself. You need to quit leaning on your own understanding.

Peregrinus—I don't lean on my own understanding.

Luke W. Zeal—Come on! Face the facts! You think that you know the Sacred Trust better than the Big Cheese. You think that you know sound doctrine better than the theologians in the Half-Havens. You regard the Invincible Dogmas and the Ironclad Interpretations as baloney.

Peregrinus—Well, I do have significant doctrinal differences with the Half-Havens. And there are passages where I think the sense of the Sacred Trust goes in a different direction than the interpretation that the Big Cheese want me to believe.

Luke W. Zeal—See what I'm saying! You lean on your own understanding.

Peregrinus—How can trusting what the Sacred Trust teaches be leaning on your own understanding?

Luke W. Zeal—Who do you think are better judges of what the Sacred Trust teaches? Little nobodies like yourself or the Big Cheese in the Half-Havens who have earned degrees from esteemed Deep Signification Indoctrination Institutions?

Peregrinus—But we don't need Big Cheese to understand the Sacred Trust. The Sacred Trust is its own interpreter.

Luke W. Zeal—That's what everyone says who leans on his own understanding and rejects the Invincible Dogmas.

Peregrinus, you are on a dangerous path. Truth is not what your little mind determines is the teaching of the Sacred Trust. That is subjective methodology that makes the mind of man the standard. Truth is the Invincible Dogmas that we are supposed to see in the Sacred Trust. This is objective methodology that makes the mind of God the standard. And the mind of God is

Deep. This means that superficial men who baby-crawl through the Sacred Trust with a superficial hermeneutic cannot uncover the mind of God. The Deep Significance is only uncovered when men use a robust Deep Signification Hermeneutic — like I'm learning at school.

Trusting Numbers Is Trusting God

Peregrinus—I think the Deep Significance is departure from the teaching of the Sacred Trust.

Luke W. Zeal—Departure? How about the Havenmongers going off by themselves to their own little caves, scorning the colossal craniums in the Half-Havens, trusting their own puny brains to find answers to the big questions of religion, and coming up with their own private interpretations? That's what I call departure from the teaching of the Sacred Trust. And in case you haven't noticed, private interpretations are contrary to the Sacred Trust.

Peregrinus—I know we are despised as an insignificant few and our meetings belittled as little caves, but our trust is not in numbers. Our trust is in the living God.

Luke W. Zeal—If you really trusted God, you would trust numbers, for God made this world we live in, and this world revolves around numbers. You can't succeed in life unless you trust numbers. We in the Half-Havens trust numbers. And the numbers have spoken. Very few folks think that the hardcore discipleship message heard from Haven pulpits is the truth. Tons of people think that the Innocuous Minimum heard from Half-Haven pulpits is the truth.

Peregrinus—Truth is not a popularity contest. In fact, the Sacred Trust plainly teaches that the way of truth is a narrow path and few are those that find it.

Luke W. Zeal—I agree one-hundred percent that truth is not a popularity contest, but a matter of finding the narrow path. And that raises an important question. Who should we trust to find the narrow path: ourselves or the experts? I trust the experts — the stupendous minds that teach the Sanitized Trust

THE GLORIOUS SALVATION MACHINE

in the Deep Signification Institutions. And when you look at the multitudes that follow them, it is obvious that they are doing an outstanding job of directing men to the narrow path.

Peregrinus—You can have the numbers. You can have the experts. I just want the truth you get when you take the Sacred Trust at face value.

Luke W. Zeal—If you stay on the path that you are on — despising the Half-Havens, the Big Cheese, the Sanitized Trust, the Deep Significance, and Invincible Dogma — you will find yourself lost in the wasteland of irrelevance and buried with the sands of insignificance.

Peregrinus—If that is the price that I must pay for trusting the unadorned Sacred Trust, then let me shrivel up and die.

Throwing Your Life Away

Luke W. Zeal—You are not the same Peregrinus that I once knew. You have changed. You have gone off the deep end.

Peregrinus—I have changed. But not all change is bad.

Luke W. Zeal—Change is bad when that change leads you to throw your life away.

Peregrinus—But I haven't thrown my life away. Following the Crucified One with all of your heart according to the plain teachings of the Sacred Trust is not throwing your life away.

Luke W. Zeal—Tell me, did you tear down the Altar of Worthy Self or sanctify it for the service of the Sweet One?

Peregrinus—No doubt about it. I tore it down.

Luke W. Zeal—Are you minimizing or maximizing your Big Here & Now?

Peregrinus—I am definitely minimizing it. I try to keep myself untangled in the affairs of life, so that I may please him who has called me to be a good soldier.

Luke W. Zeal—I rest my case. Face the facts like a man. You have thrown your life away.

Peregrinus—But I haven't thrown my life away. The Sacred Trust says that if a man loses his life in the Big Here & Now for the sake of the Crucified One and his Wonderful Message, he keeps it for Sweet Everlasting. I took this testimony at face value, and went forth in faith. I made an intelligent decision to set my life aside for the sake of the Crucified One and his Wonderful Message, and live my life in the Big Here & Now in a way that maximizes his interests down here, rather than my own. How can that be throwing my life away?

Luke W. Zeal—That has got to be the dumbest argument I have ever heard. You admit that you threw your life away, then turn around and ask how throwing your life away can possibly be regarded as throwing your life away. You are living in some kind of mind-bending denial.

Peregrinus—I did not throw my life away like it was a piece of trash to be despised. I invested it with the bank of heaven in an investment that pays returns a million-billion-trillion times bigger than any returns we can get from Wall Street. I gave the Crucified One my life for the short little time we have down here in this fallen Big Here & Now. Some sweet day I get my life back to enjoy the glorious riches of a royal inheritance as a child of God for a long, long eternity in Sweet Everlasting.

The Funstuffness of God

Luke W. Zeal—We need to leave Sweet Everlasting out of the discussion. We aren't talking about Sweet Everlasting. We are talking about right here, right now in the Big Here & Now. Yes, we are headed for Sweet Everlasting. But the question is not what we will do with the next life. The question is what we will do with this life. Why should the Sweet One trust you to maximize your Sweet Everlasting opportunity if you refuse to maximize your present opportunity in the Big Here & Now?

Peregrinus—But I am maximizing my present opportunity in the Big Here & Now. I am living my life for the Crucified One. As the Sacred Trust says, "I am crucified with the Crucified One, nevertheless I live, yet not I, but the Crucified One lives in me. And the life which I now live in the flesh, I live in the faith of the Son of God, who loved me and gave himself for me."

THE GLORIOUS SALVATION MACHINE

Luke W. Zeal—Well, that may sound like devotion, and it may pretend to be devotion, but it is just another expression of Barefoot legalism trampling on the Invincible Dogma of the Funstuffness of God. The Sanitized Trust plainly teaches that our Sugar Daddy in Heaven has given us all Big Here & Now fun stuff to enjoy and wants to have a fun-stuff relationship with us right here, right now in that fun stuff.

Peregrinus—The Funstuffness of God? That is twisting the Sacred Trust. If we trust the plain statements of Scripture, God does not want to have a fun-stuff relationship with us in this life. He wants to have a servant-soldier relationship with us. As my friend Plowman says, "We have one short life to be a good soldier and one long eternity to be fulfilled human beings."

Luke W. Zeal—Why are you so determined to live an empty life? The Crucified One did not die on the cross, so we could live an empty life.

Peregrinus—I am not living an empty life. I am walking in the truth of the verse that says, "A man's life does not consist in the abundance of the Big Here & Now fun stuff he enjoys." My life is filled with the Crucified One and his things. And this is the only abundant life I want down here. I don't want any abundance that takes me off the path of duty or distracts me while on it.

Havenmongers Live in Caves

Luke W. Zeal—Turning your backs on the Big Here & Now, like you Havenmongers do, is Barefoot heresy. It is going and living in a cave.

Peregrinus—But we don't live in caves. When a man makes an honest determination to obey the Sacred Trust teaching that believers should be *in* the Big Here & Now but not *of* it, he doesn't sell his house and move into a cave.

Luke W. Zeal—Where would the church be if every believer took the Havenmonger path and lived in a cave? Have you thought about that? Huh? Huh? Should the church live in the stone age while the Big Here & Now goes forward in the age of technology? Is that what God wants? God gave you a brain. Have you ever thought about plugging it in and turning it on?

Peregrinus—So where's the cave? We use technology like everyone else. We use cell phones, computers, and the Internet. We drive cars. We use ballpoint pens. We use plastic.

Luke W. Zeal—How can you communicate the Wonderful Message to the Big Here & Now if you live in a cave removed from society and don't mix with it? Have you thought about that? Huh? Huh? Don't you have a vision for souls?

Peregrinus—We don't live in a cave away from concourse with the Big Here & Now. We are *in* the Big Here & Now like everybody else. We get an education and get jobs like everyone else. We go shopping, and go places, and do stuff like everyone else. We rub shoulders with the folks of the Big Here & Now every day. We talk with them, listen to them, and share the Wonderful Message with them.

Luke W. Zeal—You can split hairs if you want, but if you are not *of* the Big Here & Now — if your heart roots are not sunk deep into the Big Here & Now, if you are not deeply integrated into the Big Here & Now, if you are not motivated and molded by one or more Big Here & Now institutions — then you are merely physically present in the Big Here & Now, and that is living in a cave.

You may not live in a *literal* cave outside the Big Here & Now, but you do live in a *spiritual* cave outside of it. And this is more odious than living in a literal cave. Living in a literal cave may have some legitimate Big Here & Now significance — religious, counter-cultural, or artistic. But living in a spiritual cave has zero Big Here & Now legitimacy.

No Lectures on the Rejected One

Peregrinus—Why would the followers of the Crucified One even want to be *of* the Big Here & Now? The Big Here & Now rejected the Crucified One. It did not want him to rule over them as the King of kings. It did not want his plan of salvation.

It did not want his religion or morality. It had such a low estimation of his worth that it crucified him.

Do you think the Rejected One crawled back to the Big Here & Now after the cross, begged for forgiveness, promised to play in their sand box according to their rules, and made peace with them on their terms? I don't think so. The Crucified One is still the Rejected One today. And there is no fellowship with him apart from joining him in his rejection. Those who would be his followers must take up his cross and follow him.

Luke W. Zeal—Enough already on the rejected stuff. I don't want to hear any lectures about serving the Rejected One. You Havenmongers take the rejection passages way out of context. Besides, there is a ton of hypocrisy in your stand. If you were really serious about the rejection of the Big Here & Now, you would build yourself a spaceship and fly to the moon.

Peregrinus—That's a misrepresentation of our position.

Luke W. Zeal—You want to talk about misrepresentation!? How about your misrepresentation of the Wonderful Message? The Sweet One came to save the Big Here & Now. Yet you say that he has rejected the Big Here & Now. How can you save what you reject? Isn't that a blatant contradiction? Did the Sweet One come to save the Big Here & Now or reject it?

Peregrinus—The Crucified One came to save the Big Here & Now in the sense of *mankind*. He died, so that everyone who believes on him will be saved. But he rejected and condemned the Big Here & Now in the sense of *the evil world system*. And he will judge the world system when he comes back in glory to reign in righteousness.

Luke W. Zeal—Now you want to get hung up on judgment. That's the problem with you Havenmongers. You go through the Sacred Trust looking for all the bitter parts: the evilness of the Big Here & Now, separation from the Big Here & Now, and the judgment of the Big Here & Now. This stuff fits your *cave* agenda. You need some balance. What about the passages that speak positively of the Big Here & Now?

Peregrinus—Positively? How can the Sacred Trust possibly speak positively about the Big Here & Now? Have you ever pondered what it has to say about the corruption of the Big Here & Now? It tells us that the god and ruler of the Big Here & Now is the Mad Spirit. This statement alone speaks volumes. It also tells us that the entire Big Here & Now — every square inch of it — lies in the Mad Spirit. And it tells us that all the stuff that is in the Big Here and Now is not of the Father, but of the Sewer of Unbelief.

Faith and Stuff

Luke W. Zeal—Stuff? Now you want to talk about stuff? Okay, let's talk about stuff. A proper perspective on stuff is critical to differentiate between true and false faith.

Peregrinus—I agree.

Luke W. Zeal—In Haven theology the essence of faith is *giving up* stuff. In Sugar Kids theology the essence of faith is *getting* stuff.

Peregrinus—We don't see faith merely as giving up stuff. We see faith as an exchange in which we give up the junk stuff of the Big Here & Now, which cannot be kept, to gain the good stuff of Sweet Everlasting, which cannot be lost.

Luke W. Zeal—I see several theological problems with your position on stuff.

Peregrinus—Enlighten me.

Luke W. Zeal—*First of all*, there is no scriptural basis for a blanket judgment of the stuff of the Big Here & Now, calling it all junk headed for the junkyard. This excessive view of the badness of the Big Here & Now is at odds with the teaching of the Sanitized Trust that God loves the Big Here & Now.

Secondly, God has more in store for men than merely fixing them, so they can go to Sweet Everlasting. He loves them and wants them to have a quality life here and now in the fun stuff of the Big Here & Now. This is axiomatic, for God is love, and love gives stuff to those it loves.

Thirdly, the Havenmonger view of stuff is fear-based, rather than faith-based. Nothing better characterizes the Haven view of the Big Here & Now than running from stuff. Everything in the Big Here & Now is polluted. Every worldly thing that sets the heart on fire with desire and every worldly accomplishment that kindles the pride of life in the heart is part of a conspiracy of unbelief headed up by the Mad Spirit. Don't touch anything. Don't savor life. Don't be a full-orbed human being. Go find a cave. Judgment is coming.

The Dead Letter vs. the Sweet Spirit

Peregrinus—But the Sacred Trust says …

Luke W. Zeal—That brings up another point that bugs me. Every time we talk about doctrinal matters, you harp on the Sacred Trust. Look this up. Look that up. Read this book. Read that chapter. Read. Read. Read. You act as if every question hangs on the letter of the Sacred Trust.

Peregrinus—Every question does hang on what the Sacred Trust says.

Luke W. Zeal—Don't get me wrong. We do need to know what the Sacred Trust teaches. But we need to know what the Sacred Trust *actually* teaches, not what it *you think* it teaches. And what the Sacred Trust actually teaches can't be learned through carnal human effort expended on the dead letter. It can only be learned by the illumination of the Sweet Spirit.

Peregrinus—So, how do we get this illumination of the Sweet Spirit?

Luke W. Zeal—By tuning in to the voice of the Sweet Spirit. For those who have a subjective ear to subjective hear, this is done by tuning in to the impressions, inclinations, feelings, and other subjective perception mechanisms that the Sweet Spirit uses to communicate his mind to his people.

Peregrinus—But aren't we supposed to labor in the Sacred Trust and test all things by what it says?

Luke W. Zeal—Spending long hours studying the dead letter of the Sacred Trust — and more long hours studying dead books written by men who devoted their lives to studying the dead letter of the Sacred Trust — is leaning on the flesh. That is how you turn off the spigot of the Spirit.

Peregrinus—But we ought to get our doctrine by diligently studying the Sacred Trust.

Luke W. Zeal—That is so misguided. The application of the human mind to the Sacred Trust is not the source of sound doctrine. The illumination of the Sweet Spirit shed upon the Sacred Trust is the source of sound doctrine.

Furthermore, while the Sweet Spirit typically illuminates the letter of the Sacred Trust to teach sound doctrine, he is not limited *by* the letter or *to* the letter. In fact, the Spirit's use of the Sacred Trust is inversely proportional to a man's faith. The stronger the faith, the less need for the dead letter. The weaker the faith, the more the need for the dead letter.

Peregrinus—But the words of the Sacred Trust are not dead letters. The Crucified One himself states that they are spirit and life. They are the living, life-giving, and powerful words of the living God.

Luke W. Zeal—There you go again. Exalting the dead letter over the Sweet Spirit. Why this fascination with dead things? Dead things can't give life. Only the Spirit gives life. Do you want life or death?

Circular Reasoning on the Sweet Spirit

Peregrinus—So why are you going to a Deep Signification Indoctrination Institution if believers don't need to put a lot of time into the study of the dead letter of the Sacred Trust, but only need the illumination of the Sweet Spirit? Why not stay home and dabble with the Sacred Trust, waiting on the Spirit for subjective illuminations, which you develop with subjective ruminations, so that you can feed the sheep with subjective elucidations — the true manna from heaven?

Luke W. Zeal—Because I want to be a Big Cheese and I can't become a Big Cheese unless I am properly qualified at a Deep Signification Indoctrination Institution.

Peregrinus—But why do you need the Deep Signification Indoctrination Institution to become a Big Cheese if you have the Sweet Spirit?

Luke W. Zeal—Because we need to study under Big Cheese who are taught of the Sweet Spirit to learn sound Sweet Spirit doctrine, so that we can discern the leading of the Sweet Spirit.

Peregrinus—But how do you know that your Sweet Spirit doctrine really is true?

Luke W. Zeal—The leading of the Sweet Spirit tells us that our Sweet Spirit doctrine is true.

Peregrinus—Your Sweet Spirit doctrine tells you that your Sweet Spirit leading is true. Your Sweet Spirit leading tells you that your Sweet Spirit doctrine is true. That sounds like circular reasoning to me.

Luke W. Zeal—It is. And I don't have a problem with that. God is a pretty well-rounded guy. He's definitely not a square.

Peregrinus—First you tell me that we don't need to study, but only need the Sweet Spirit's illumination. Now you tell me that study at a Deep Signification Indoctrination Institution is absolutely essential.

Luke W. Zeal—There is no contradiction here. Most men don't need to study. God hasn't given them that gift. You do believe in the gifts, don't you? God has given some the gift of Droning and others the gift of saying *Amen*. If God has given you the gift of Droning, then go study at a Deep Signification Indoctrination Institution and learn to rightly Deep Significate the Sacred Trust. But if God has given you the gift of saying *Amen*, then stop trying to interpret the Sacred Trust on your own and start cultivating the gift of saying *Amen*.

Quality Education

Peregrinus—So, if a man wants to be a properly qualified preacher, he has to go to school?

Luke W. Zeal—Merely going to school will not suffice. A man needs a quality education. There are many schools that go through the motions of education. They may grant degrees or certificates, but they don't give men a quality education. You need to go to a Deep Signification Indoctrination Institution to get a quality education.

Peregrinus—So what must schools give men to give them a quality education?

Luke W. Zeal—They must give them the two indispensable tools for the work of God. The *first* is a Deep theological education with a solid foundation in God Magic salvationology and Innocuous Minimization. The *second* is a robust, up-to-date Big Here & Now Toolbox featuring the newest and best Big Here & Now methodology. This powerful combination of tools enables preachers to attract the highest possible numbers of churchgoers.

Peregrinus—So what about men who get their education at a simple Sacred Trust school or in an informal setting?

Luke W. Zeal—No matter where men studied or how they studied, if they weren't given a Deep theological education and a Big Here & Now Toolbox, they didn't get an education. They may have gotten their heads packed with sand. But they didn't get an education.

Peregrinus—I guess we don't offer quality education in the Havens, then.

Luke W. Zeal—You can say that again.

Salvation Is by God Magic Alone

Peregrinus—Well, I don't like God Magic theology.

Luke W. Zeal—What you like and dislike is irrelevant. The only thing that matters is theological integrity. And upholding a consistent God Magic testimony is the essence of theological integrity.

Peregrinus—So show me the proof that men are supposed to be saved by the Passive Form.

Luke W. Zeal—The proof is staring you in the face. Men are stuck in the muck in the Hog Pen. This is a desperate situation. They can't extricate themselves. They can't obey the call to repent and heart-believe, not even if God himself came down

THE GLORIOUS SALVATION MACHINE

and preached to them. They need God Magic in the Passive Form or they are doomed.

Peregrinus—That Passive Form stuff is nonsense. Besides, if you were serious about men being passive, you would use the Sprinkle Form like the Glorious Salvation Machine does. It is the only consistent Passive Form. Infants can't possibly do or think anything toward their own salvation. Adults can't stop doing stuff or thinking stuff.

Luke W. Zeal—You are being hypertechnical about the passiveness of the Passive Form. In the Sanitized Trust we see an active component in man's passive salvation — we see men leaving their nets and coming to the Sweet One to be a passive lump of clay in his hands. This means that the Faith Form is the most Scriptural expression of the Passive Form. For it alone emulates the Passive Form picture that we see in the Sanitized Trust — men making an active effort to come into the presence of the Saviour to experience a special moment of passiveness where they are disengaged from all effort.

Peregrinus—So men don't have to heart-believe to be saved?

Luke W. Zeal—That's right. Salvation is by God Magic alone through the Faith Form alone, not by Dead Works lest any man should boast. Even noble efforts like heart-faith are Filthy Rags if they don't cooperate with and support God Magic.

Peregrinus—So we can't know believers by their fruits?

Luke W. Zeal—That's right. Men are not only *initially* saved by God Magic without works, they are *continually* saved under the umbrella of God Magic without works. This draws the line in the sand as far as evidence of salvation is concerned. This means that it is wrong — it is serious error — to look for the fruits of heart-faith as the evidence of salvation. Whether six days, six weeks, six months, six years, or six decades after the reception of God Magic in the Faith Form, such looking is a blatant denial of salvation by God Magic alone.

Peregrinus—So we can't tell a believer by how he lives?

Luke W. Zeal—That's right. Believers often walk for years in sin and unbelief before their God Magic works its way to the outside. Sometimes it never shows its face. But this doesn't mean that the God Magic isn't there. It just means it hasn't worked its way to the outside yet. This is why we shouldn't get nitpicky about looking for fruit. Men make fools of themselves when they nitpick someone about their lack of evidence, and then six months, or two years, or twenty years later that person has a God Magic breakout. Talk about eating humble pie.

The Big Here & Now Toolbox Works Better

Peregrinus—Now I understand why the Half-Havens are so excited about Big Here & Now Toolboxes. You rejected real-relationship faith in the Crucified One as your drawing card. This left you without a drawing card. You realized that you would have a difficult time drawing men without a significant drawing card. So you went and got yourselves Big Here & Now Toolboxes, so you could draw men with Big Here & Now wisdom and Big Here & Now fun stuff.

Luke W. Zeal—Typical Havenmonger response. Why do you have to be so impractical? How hard is it to simply accept the fact that the Big Here & Now Toolbox works better, and go get one? You remind me of a crazy do-it-yourselfer who bangs away with a crescent wrench trying to drive a nail because he is too lazy to go get a hammer.

Peregrinus—What about preaching the Wonderful Message in its pristine purity, just as we see it in the Sacred Trust — in the Gospels as well as the Epistles — without subtraction or addition?

Luke W. Zeal—Many bright minds toiled for years, looking high and low, leaving no stone unturned, painstakingly testing thousands of Big Here & Now methods, and selecting only the best, so that Half-Haven preachers could present a Sanitized Message that draws the greatest numbers from the widest range of classes. And you find fault with that? Was their hard work for nothing? Do you really want to present a Wonderful Message that offends the Big Here & Now? How dumb is that?

Peregrinus—But we should draw men to the Crucified One with the truth, not with their taste buds.

Luke W. Zeal—You want to teach me about drawing men? What could you possibly know about drawing men that I would have any interest in? Our high-powered churches draw far bigger crowds than your sputtering little Havens. And you want to teach me about drawing men?

Peregrinus—Just because something appears to work does not mean that it is profitable.

Luke W. Zeal—Profitable? What could you possibly know about being profitable? Profit is something you can count. We have countable stuff coming out of our ears. We have piles of people in our meetings and mounds of money in our offerings. What do you have that you can count? Next to nothing!

Peregrinus—But we should be concerned about quality and not just quantity. The Great Commission not only exhorts us to make followers in every nation, it also exhorts us to teach these followers to obey "all things whatsoever" that the Crucified One has commanded.

Luke W. Zeal—Why do you insist on quibbling over minor details? The fields are white for harvest. There are jillions of men that would easily be persuaded to embrace the Innocuous Minimum if we would just tickle their ears. They are willing to do the Passive Form and sit, at least occasionally, through the Weekly Formality. All we need to do is preach the message they want to hear, packaged in the way they want it packaged, and the work of God will go forth in God Magic power. The Mad Spirit will get a tremendous whipping, and droves of men will flee the camp of madness for the camp of gladness.

The Deep Presentation Adjustifier

Peregrinus—But the Sacred Trust says we shouldn't tickle the ears of men when we preach.

LUKE W. ZEAL RETURNS

Luke W. Zeal—You would see things way differently if you had a vision for the work. Then you would care far more about the tools you use. Slipshod carpenters carry around old, beat-up junk that doesn't get the job done. Professional carpenters carry new toolboxes full of up-to-date, high-quality tools.

Peregrinus—So what kind of tools are found in a Big Here & Now Toolbox?

Luke W. Zeal—That can vary significantly depending on a preacher's preferences and circumstances. The most important tool that pertains to the subject we are talking about, however, is a Deep Presentation Adjustifier.

Peregrinus—What does that do?

Luke W. Zeal—It helps preachers and pastors get their cool-bean rating up.

Peregrinus—Because if the Big Here & Now doesn't think you are cool beans, you can't influence them.

Luke W. Zeal—That's right.

Peregrinus—So how does this Adjustifier thing work?

Luke W. Zeal—You start by pushing the *Quantifier* button. This brings up a list of questions about your present message and method. You answer each question by entering a number between 1 and 10. Low scores are bad. High scores are good.

Next you push the *Comparifier* button, and it compares your answers to the latest information on what the Big Here & Now wants in terms of message and method. (This information is updated weekly.) After a few moments it spits out a cool-bean rating to the nearest cool bean. You can optionally set it, so that it will give you a thumbs up, a question mark, or a thumbs down along with the cool-bean reading.

Lastly, you push the *Adjustifier* button, and it runs your data through a nifty Innocuous Minimum algorithm and spits out an appropriate, up-to-date Innocuous Minimum, custom designed for your situation. It is guaranteed to put far more bodies in your meetings than you ever thought was possible.

THE GLORIOUS SALVATION MACHINE

Everything That Produces Numbers Is Faithfulness

Peregrinus—Bodies in the meetings and butts in the pews. Why are you so concerned about numbers? Isn't faithfulness to the Sacred Trust our first responsibility? Shouldn't we get our message and method from its pages and then stick with them, regardless of how few or how many they bring into the church?

Luke W. Zeal—Why do you Havenmongers insist on forcing a contrast between numbers and faithfulness? What is your big problem with numbers? Every time we bring up numbers, you bring up faithfulness. You need to understand that numbers are crazy-important. That's why number-crunching scientists win Nobel Prizes, number-crunching businessmen make fortunes, and number-crunching Half-Haven pastors grow big churches.

Peregrinus—Because we should sort men out with truth, not with the spirit of the world. When we mix the spirit of the world with the message of the Crucified One, it sorts out men differently than God wants us to sort them out. It removes the wall that once divided the *religious* Pharisees from the *real-relationship* disciples.

Luke W. Zeal—You just don't get it, Peregrinus. We have been given a commission to persuade as many men as possible to do the Faith Form. This means numbers is our job. And if numbers is our job, then everything that produces numbers is faithfulness.

This approach to the great commission is paradigm changing. We are free to *utilize* any Big Here & Now methods we please, as long as they are not dark grey, *manipulize* the message, so it resonates with current Big Here & Now trends, and *harmonize* the mind of God with the mind of man.

Negativity Must Be Your Spiritual Gift

Peregrinus—The Crucified One counts hearts, not heads.

Luke W. Zeal—Why do you always have to be so negative? Negativity must be your spiritual gift. You are always bringing up observations from the Sacred Trust that put a negative spin on something that should be the most positive thing on earth.

Count hearts not heads. Take the strait gate and narrow path. Take up the cross. Offer yourself a living sacrifice. Be a good soldier. Be a faithful steward. Love not the world. Blah. Blah. Blah. There's a whole realm of positiveness in the Sanitized Trust that you have never tasted.

Peregrinus—How can the plain statements of the Sacred Trust be negative? Is God negative?

Luke W. Zeal—The negativism of the Havens is sour grapes. You don't have the tools, skills, or vision for a big harvest. So you hunt around in the Sacred Trust for negative stuff, so you can fault our success and justify your laziness and ineptitude.

Peregrinus—When we stand in review before our Redeemer at the judgment seat, it will be seen that a harvest undertaken with our eyes on heart-faith and faithfulness will gather more abiding fruit than a harvest undertaken with our eyes on the Faith Form and numbers.

Luke W. Zeal—You need to chill out on your negativity and get some Big Here & Now appeal. Seriously.

Stop Thinking So Much

Peregrinus—But I think, based on what I read in the Sacred Trust …

Luke W. Zeal—That's the whole problem right there. You think too much. You can't take everything in the Sacred Trust in a Daily Grind sense like you were reading the ingredients on a cereal box. The Deep Significance often runs tangentially or countercurrently to what the letter appears to say. There is stuff that doesn't mean what it appears to mean and stuff that means what it doesn't appear to mean. Even the most erudite Deep Significating experts find some portions hopelessly confusing.

Peregrinus—Are you saying that men of average intelligence are incapable of figuring out what they are supposed to believe and how they are supposed to live by reading the Sacred Trust?

Luke W. Zeal—Of course not. Men of average intelligence can figure such things out if they let the Big Cheese hold their

THE GLORIOUS SALVATION MACHINE

hands and walk them through the ins and outs of the Deep Significance once delivered unto the Minimizers.

Peregrinus—But don't believers have an obligation to test and prove all things — teachers and doctrines — comparing what they say to the Sacred Trust?

Luke W. Zeal—Yes, provided we test them by the actual teaching of the Sacred Trust, not by our personal interpretation of the Sacred Trust. The Sacred Trust states very plainly that no prophecy is to be given a personal interpretation.

Peregrinus—Let me guess, the actual teaching is summed up in the Invincible Dogmas.

Luke W. Zeal—That's right.

Peregrinus—So we are supposed to blindly follow the Big Cheese?

Luke W. Zeal—Of course not. We follow them with eyes that have been illuminated by the Deep Significance.

Peregrinus—Now it all makes perfect sense. The Big Cheese teach men the Invincible Dogmas. Then men judge the ministry of the Big Cheese by the Invincible Dogmas and follow them only insofar as they are faithful to these Dogmas. And because men are following the Invincible Dogmas, nobody can accuse them of blindly following the Big Cheese.

Luke W. Zeal—You really need to stop thinking so much. Bad things happen when people think too much.

The Need for Deep Humility

Peregrinus—But we are supposed to think. From Genesis to Revelation the Sacred Trust assumes and requires the use of our God-given reason. It calls the faithful Christian life our "reasonable service." If men candidly think about the holiness and devotion that numerous passages ask of them, they will conclude that this request is reasonable. It makes sense. It rings true to man's moral nature. It rings true to his innate propensity to find meaning and purpose. It rings true to his situation in this corrupt, God-rejecting, Bible-rejecting Big Here & Now.

Luke W. Zeal—Will you never stop? Where does humility come into the picture? Or is humility optional?

Peregrinus—But I do try to walk in humility before God.

Luke W. Zeal—Well, you are going to have to try harder. When men walk in Deep Humility, which is the only kind of humility that is truly humble, they don't bash and trash the Invincible Dogmas, toot their own horn, and pretend that they understand the Sacred Trust better than all the learned men in the Half-Havens.

Peregrinus—But true humility trembles at the Word of God. It bows to the revealed will and truth of God in the pages of the Sacred Trust.

Luke W. Zeal—Here we go again. Everything comes down to little nobodies favoring their own private interpretations and faulting the collective wisdom of the schools and pulpits of the Half-Havens. What a blot on Churchianity. Doesn't it seem like pride to go off by yourself to your own little cave and interpret the Sacred Trust for yourself? No preacher that I respect believes that we are supposed to handle the Sacred Trust with that kind of proud humility.

Peregrinus—You can ridicule my confidence in the Sacred Trust as pride if you like. But you cannot shame me into giving up my simple trust in the Sacred Trust.

Luke W. Zeal—Peregrinus, I am mega-concerned and mega-perplexed. Why are you so unwilling to chain your brain to the Big Cheese? Is your brain bigger than those that repose in the craniums of the wisest men in the Half-Havens?

Peregrinus—I don't claim to possess a colossal intellect. I simply want the Sacred Trust to have its proper place and voice in the work of God. I think that a return to the authority of the Sacred Trust is the biggest need in the Church today.

Luke W. Zeal—Don't put the cart before the horse. We must secure Deep Humility before we focus on the authority of the Sanitized Trust. Think about it. Christians do not naturally submit to the authority of the Sanitized Trust and embrace the Deep Truth taught in its pages. They must first experience a

Deep work in their heart, bringing them to the holy ground of Deep Humility, then they will readily and gladly submit to the authority of the Sanitized Trust.

When the cart goes before the horse — as it does in the Havens — and men handle the Sacred Trust without Deep Humility, they come up with their own doctrines, toss the Invincible Dogmas in the trash, and trample the authority of the Sanitized Trust underfoot in the mire of their own pride.

Deep Humility Is Like a Man Made of Silly Putty

Peregrinus—Well, I am not going to let any man or group of men dictate to me what I am supposed to believe. The Sacred Trust is the ultimate judge of doctrine and practice. It judges all. It answers to none.

Luke W. Zeal—A stubborn spirit that is unwilling to budge is the whole problem. God only has one sandbox down here — the salvation machine sandbox. You need to Deeply Humble yourself and get in this sandbox. Once you are in his sandbox, you can choose whether you play on the classic-machinery side or the Half-Haven-machinery side, but you don't get to choose the rules you play by. You are obligated to play by salvation machine rules. Things go much better when God's kids play nicely in the sandbox. God wants us to play in Deep Humility.

Peregrinus—So what is this Deep Humility that you keep insisting on?

Luke W. Zeal—Imagine a man made of silly putty.

Peregrinus—A man made of silly putty? Why do I have the feeling this is headed nowhere real fast?

Luke W. Zeal—Trust me. This is good stuff. It will knock your socks off.

Peregrinus—I can feel them sliding off already.

Luke W. Zeal—Deep Humility will bend over backwards to conform to the *status quo* of legitimate Minimizing churches. This promotes harmony. Refusing to bend is Deep carnality. It leads to bad things like friction, disagreement, and division.

Deep Humility can stretch its jaws to a mind-boggling degree, allowing it to swallow anything necessary to maintain God Magic salvationology and Minimizing churchianity. It can believe that the obvious is not obvious. It can believe that the not-obvious is obvious. It can believe that facts are fiction. It can believe that fiction is fact. It can believe that the illogical is logical. It can believe that the logical is illogical.

Peregrinus—Well, you can keep your Deep Humility. That reminds me of the Flush.

Luke W. Zeal—It should. Deep Humility and the Flush are two sides of the same coin. If you see Deep Humility, that proves that a man has done the Flush. If you can see the Flush, that proves that a man is walking in Deep Humility.

Peregrinus—I will never flush my brain down the drain. Not for any man. Not for any church. Not for any doctrine. Not for any reason. No way. No how. I will die before I flush.

Luke W. Zeal—Pride goes before a fall. Don't be surprised if you fall off the blessing train. The Sanitized Trust warns us that Sugar Daddy resists the Inflexibly Proud and gives grace to the Deeply Humble. The path of Deep Humility is the path of blessing. As one of my favorite choruses goes:

Flush your brain down the drain,
Ride the Minimum train,
And be fulfilled with fun stuff,
Flush your brain down the drain.

Anywhere Is Better Than a Haven

Peregrinus—Nonsense like that is why I go to a Haven.

Luke W. Zeal—You really need to get out of the Havens. They are a nasty brood of pride vipers.

Peregrinus—The Sacred Trust says that when churches are what they are supposed to be, they are the pillar and ground of truth. They stand on the truth. They uphold the truth. I find this in the Havens. I don't find this outside of the Havens.

Luke W. Zeal—Come on! If you can stand on your truth and walk all over it, then you obviously don't value it very much.

And if your truth needs you to hold it up, then it isn't worth holding up. You have to give me a better answer than that.

Peregrinus—Doesn't it bother you to twistify a passage of the Sacred Trust like that?

Luke W. Zeal—That isn't twistification. That is Nice God honoring Deep Signification.

Listen, Peregrinus. Get out of that Haven. Go find yourself a Half-Haven that you like. Anywhere is better than a Haven.

Peregrinus—My experience with the Half-Havens has been pretty disappointing.

Luke W. Zeal—Your experience is based on your limited exposure. God has given us an amazing variety of churches in the Half-Havens that satisfy the entire spectrum of religious taste and inclination. They range from old-fashioned churches with stained glass and ritual to modern churches with stirring music and entertainment. No matter what your preferred setting for doing the Weekly Duty, there is something that will meet your needs. If you are unsatisfied with one Half-Haven, try another. Keep looking. Eventually you will find something that tickles your fancy.

Peregrinus—Where does the Sacred Trust fit in your church selection equation?

Luke W. Zeal—We are not talking about the Sacred Trust. We are talking about atmosphere. That is the focus of the Half-Havens. Whatever atmosphere a man craves, the Half-Havens can satisfy his soul. Whether he craves a solemn atmosphere, an intellectual atmosphere, an electric atmosphere, or a laid-back atmosphere, he can feel what he wants to feel. And when men attend the Important Formality in an environment that gives them the feelings they want to feel, they go home with the feeling that they have done their Weekly Duty in the presence of the Sweet One.

Listen to Some Conservative Half-Haven Preachers

Peregrinus—I am not into atmosphere. I am into truth.

Luke W. Zeal—I know you think that the Half-Havens don't have anything to offer you. But what can it hurt you if you listen to some conservative Half-Haven preachers? You may be pleasantly surprised at how good their preaching is and how solid their doctrine is.

Peregrinus—Yea, right. Deceptively good like junk food and deceptively solid like jello.

Luke W. Zeal—Do yourself a favor. Give the Half-Havens another chance. Go hear a couple of their best preachers.

Peregrinus—Whatever. Give me a couple names.

Luke W. Zeal—Why don't you try Strawberry Nostrum and Willy Rush Forward. I think you will like them. They remind me of you. Both teach that repentance is part of the Wonderful Message. Rush preaches against the easy-believe message that men don't have to do anything to be saved. Strawberry teaches a strong message on the necessity of reality in our Christianity.

Peregrinus and Luke W. Zeal Say Good-Bye

The two young men wound their conversation down and said their good-byes. But their parting was painful, not sweet. Both felt heaviness over the error his friend held. One felt heaviness over error that really was error. The other felt heaviness over error that really was the truth. Both felt a sense of honor in their defense of the truth. One felt honor over his defense of truth that really was the truth. The other felt honor over his defense of truth that really was error.

This illustrates the fact that feelings have no intrinsic value. The same feelings can be attached to truth or error. Happy is the man whose sense of honor is attached to truth that shall be vindicated as truth on that day when our life, our heart, our work, and our doctrine shall be tried by fire.

CHAPTER EIGHT
MORE STEAMING JOE

In Need of Spiritual Refreshment

Peregrinus was spiritually and emotionally exhausted. For several months he had endured opposition from family and friends regarding his faith in the Crucified One and his confidence in the Sacred Trust. The past weekend had been especially brutal, for he had tangled with both his friend Luke and Reverend Quacksalver. Their attacks had taxed him to his limits. He felt as heavy as lead, had a hard time eating and sleeping, and could barely drag himself through each day. Friday evening could not come fast enough. He really needed some spiritual refreshment.

At long last Friday evening arrived, and Peregrinus hastened to the Steaming Joe. He was drinking his second cup of coffee and flipping through the Psalms when Plowman arrived at five-minutes-to-seven. Peregrinus jumped up, pulled out a chair for him, and greeted him warmly. Visit forty-three was under way.

Consider Yourself in Good Company

Plowman—How's the battle been going Peregrinus?

Peregrinus—It has been going pretty rough. On Saturday my family invited Reverend Quacksalver over to convince me of the error of my Haven ways. He hammered on me for turning my back on the Glorious Salvation Machine and the Sprinkle Form. Then a few hours later my friend Luke worked me over for rejecting the Half-Havens and the Faith Form.

Plowman—I'm sorry to hear that. But I know what you're going through. There was a firestorm in my family when I left the Glorious Salvation Machine. They said I had gone off the deep end. A couple years later when I left the Half-Havens and their Faith Form, my best friend was incensed with me. To this day our friendship is strained.

Peregrinus—I can't believe how my family and friends are acting. You would think that they would be pleased with my newfound interest in reading the Sacred Trust and following the Crucified One. But no, they dislike the path that I'm on.

Plowman—That, in varying degrees, is the experience of all who follow the Crucified One according to the plain dictates of the Sacred Trust. As the Crucified One said, "Don't think that I have come to bring peace on the earth. I haven't come to bring peace, but a sword. From now on a man's enemies shall be those of his own household." Those who love God Magic and Innocuous Minimum religion get upset with anyone, especially family members and friends, who preach real-relationship faith in the Crucified One. They may sheath the sword in an uneasy truce, but they will never bury it.

Peregrinus—The worst part of it is, they accuse me of things that I'm not guilty of.

Plowman—Consider yourself in good company. The Sacred Trust says, "Count yourself blessed when men falsely accuse you of evil for my sake. Rejoice and be glad, for great is your reward in heaven, for so they persecuted the prophets before you."

Living Right Is a Reproof

Peregrinus—Their main accusation is that I continually ride them for being wicked sinners. But I don't ride them for being sinners. On a few occasions — most of them occasioned by their own demands to know why I left the Glorious Salvation Machine — I have shared the Wonderful Message with them in a generic sense: all men have gone astray, and therefore all men need to heart-turn and heart-believe on the Crucified One.

Plowman—Even though you haven't been riding them, their conscience has been because of light you have shed on their darkness. When we preach the necessity of heart-faith, we level the accusation of heart-unbelief — the chief crime against God and the root sin behind all sin. So when you shared the gospel with them, you — in essence — informed them that they were ungodly sinners guilty of the ungodly crime of unbelief. They knew you were right, and now they are mad at you because their conscience bothers them.

Peregrinus—That is exactly what is going on.

Plowman—Moreover, the fact that you *dismantled* the Altar of Worthy Self, *rejected* the Innocuous Minimum, *renounced* the camp of faith in God Magic, and *joined* the camp of real-relationship faith in the Crucified One is a plain accusation, written in bold letters on the wall of life, that they are guilty of rejecting God's way of salvation.

Peregrinus—I never thought about it like that before. We are preaching a lot of truth even when we don't say a lot.

Plowman—That's right. Living right in a wrong living world is itself a reproof. Even if we rarely open our mouth, our life — with its choices and priorities — says enough to prick a man's conscience with reminders of our testimony. Those who don't want a heart relationship with the Crucified One get agitated with those who manifest one. Those who reject the authority of the Sacred Trust get aggravated with those who submit to it. Men don't want anyone telling them how to live or serve God. And when believers transgress on this point, whether in talk or in walk, they find themselves out of favor or even hated.

Peregrinus—I've sure tasted a lot of that lately.

Plowman—This hatred is what moved Cain to murder his brother Abel. The issue wasn't that Abel was too talkative and reproved his brother one too many times. Nor was it that Abel was using the wrong methods in his ministry efforts. The issue was, as the Sacred Trust clearly states, that Abel's works were righteous. Abel was going in the right direction — heart-faith. And his obedience and righteousness bore witness to his faith and testified against his brother's unbelief. This always causes friction even if the party going in the right direction is as meek as Moses and as wise as Solomon.

A Dose of Reality

Peregrinus—I had no idea when I began seeking God that I was going to face such opposition. I was caught off guard by the acrimony that was manifested when I left St. Lethargic's Sprinkle Form Church to walk in the light. And I was unprepared for the flak I received when I left Jumping Jack's Faith Form church to walk in yet clearer light.

Plowman—Got a dose of reality, did you? You found out the hard way that pursuing God with any kind of seriousness is treated as a crime against churchianity.

Peregrinus—Big time. The truth is beginning to sink in. The world is opposed to real-relationship faith.

Plowman—Yep. Men want religion, not a real-relationship with God. And they don't take it lightly when you touch their religion — whether exciting religion, bland religion, esoteric religion, rigorous religion, ecumenical religion, pagan religion, or atheistic-evolutionistic religion. And you don't even need to speak against their false ways to stir up their opposition. All you have to do is insist upon the need for heart-faith in the Crucified One.

The Trial of Faith

Peregrinus—Hey, I have a question about trials. Some of the stuff I have been reading in the Sacred Trust seems to indicate that both the Adversary and God have their hands in our trials.

Plowman—That's right.

Peregrinus—This is definitely a clarification situation.

Plowman—When the Mad Spirit sees believers seeking or enjoying higher ground, he is furious. He seeks permission from God to sift them as he did Job and Peter. Then he pursues them with all the malice of his dirty heart, aiming to make them fall, or worse, break their faith.

But God has his own purposes in such trials, and his purposes always prevail. He uses the same events, circumstances, and people to purify and strengthen the faith of his dear ones. He uses the *heat* of the trial to bring their dross to the top, like the refining of gold, so it can be skimmed off. He uses the *exercise* of the trial to increase their spiritual strength, so they can gain victory over things like self-seeking, poor priorities, laziness, and worthless baggage.

Peregrinus—So the Mad Spirit — despite his evil intentions — is ultimately an unwitting tool in the hand of God to forward God's purposes in the lives of his dear believers.

Plowman—That's right. While the Mad Spirit intends evil with our trials, our Father in heaven intends good with them. He is behind the scenes managing every one of them. He does not allow the Mad Spirit to try us beyond what we are able to bear. And in every trial he provides a way of escape that we may be able to bear it — not a way to escape from having to face the trial, but a way to bear up in the trial.

The Narrow Path Is Yucky

Peregrinus—This leads to something that's bugging me. I've been on the narrow path for months now and parts of it still seem yucky no matter how much I seek God and read the Sacred Trust. For instance, I still find it yucky when I displease others with my beliefs. I know the narrow path shouldn't seem yucky, but I'm just being honest. How can I fix that?

Plowman—You can't, and that's okay. Many parts of the narrow path are yucky.

Peregrinus—Really? You think the narrow path is yucky too?

Plowman—Of course I do. All believers do. Who likes stuff like the sword in the household, friendships cooling off, false accusations, tribulation, opposition, suffering, and hardship?

Peregrinus—Dude, I'm all ears.

Plowman—When we put our faith in the Crucified One and follow him, we choose a path that gives us a mixture of yucky and pleasant. It takes no effort to like the pleasant stuff. And we are not required to like the yucky stuff — indeed, we can't like it. Nor are we required to pretend that we like it.

Peregrinus—Pretending. That's what I've been doing lately. I've been trying to pretend that the yucky stuff really isn't yucky. But it hasn't been working.

Plowman—You're not the first to try that and you won't be the last.

Peregrinus—So what do we do with the yucky stuff?

Plowman—We follow the example of our Saviour "who for the joy that was set before him endured the cross, despising the shame." In other words, he recognized the shame of the cross as yuckiness that must be endured, and despised this yuckiness as a small price to pay for the glory that was set before him.

The Cost Pile and the Gain Pile

Peregrinus—So the secret to dealing with the yucky stuff is to regard it as a small price to pay for Sweet Everlasting.

Plowman—That's right. Everyone who follows the Crucified One soon realizes that there is a cost — a lot of yucky stuff. This cost starts piling up at the time of salvation and continues piling up throughout the course of life. There is no avoiding it. Every believer gets a big pile of cost: some a barely big pile, some a very big pile, and some a scary big pile. But believers are able to look at this pile and laugh at it as an insignificant price to pay for the blessings of Sweet Everlasting.

Peregrinus—That's what I find confusing. We are supposed to count the cost pile as a small price to pay. Yet the pile is not small. It's a big pile of yucky stuff that just keeps getting bigger and bigger. It can get pretty discouraging watching that ugly pile grow. How do we keep from getting discouraged?

Plowman—When you count the cost of something, you need to know more than what it costs. You also need to know how that cost compares to an accepted standard, so you can figure out the actual meaning of the cost. Otherwise the cost is just a meaningless number. For example, if I told you that something cost ten gazillion wookydingles, that would mean nothing to you, though it would sound like a substantial amount. But if I added that one gazillion wookydingles is worth three grains of sand, now the price would mean something to you. It has been quantified as having the same value as thirty grains of sand.

In the same way, you can't just look at the pile of cost that is piling up in your life in the Big Here & Now. If you do, you will conclude that the cost of following the Crucified One is too high. You also need to compare that pile to the fixed standard — the pile of gain that awaits in Sweet Everlasting. When you look at both piles side by side, you see things in very different light. For putting the cost pile next to the gain pile is like putting an anthill next to Mt. Everest.

Peregrinus—I see where this is going! The cost pile looks like a huge price to pay until you compare it to eternity. Then you see how little it is actually worth — a few grains of sand.

Plowman—That's right. As the Sacred Trust says, "Our light affliction, which is but for a moment, works for us a far more exceeding and eternal weight of glory." What this is saying is that God has a much bigger shovel than the Mad Spirit. Every *lightweight* shovel load of yucky that the Mad Spirit shovels onto us and we shovel into our cost pile is matched by an *eternal-weight* shovel load of glory that God shovels onto our gain pile. This means that our gain pile is growing infinitely faster and infinitely larger than our cost pile.

Peregrinus—I'm totally liking this! This puts trials in a very different perspective.

Plowman—Yep. Putting the cost pile next to the gain pile is why the old hymn-writer could write, "Tell me not of heavy crosses, nor of burdens hard to bear." Those who have this eternal mindset toss every piece of yucky that comes their way onto their cost pile like they were throwing trash in the garbage can. They don't fret any more over the stuff going in their cost pile than they do over the empty catsup bottles that they throw out. For they know that some sweet day they shall trade their little cost pile for an infinite pile of gain in Sweet Everlasting.

THE GLORIOUS SALVATION MACHINE

The Wild Beasts Don't Die

Peregrinus—Here's another question. Do we ever cease to be tempted by sin?

Plowman—Let me guess. You are struggling with the fact that you still have a pack of wild beasts raging in your heart, trying to get out of their cage, so they can run wild.

Peregrinus—Dude! I feel like a heathen at times.

Plowman—Well, the godly still have the same wild beasts in their hearts that the ungodly have.

Peregrinus—So how do we tell the difference between the godly and the ungodly in this matter?

Plowman—The difference lies in how they handle their wild beasts. The ungodly leave the cage door open, let their wild beasts run wild, and feed them when they howl. The godly lock their wild beasts in the cage and refuse to feed them or let them out no matter how much they howl. They are trying to starve them.

Peregrinus—Somewhere I got the idea that believers should come to the place where they no longer desire sin or struggle with temptation — where they no longer have wild beasts.

Plowman—No. We all have to fight temptation — the wild beasts that dwell in our hearts — until our last breath.

Peregrinus—So the wild beasts don't die?

Plowman—Nope. They don't die until that Wonderful Day when we are glorified and God debeastifies our hearts.

Peregrinus—Is it possible for some of our wild beasts to die in this life?

Plowman—Sometimes men appear to experience the death of one or more of their wild beasts. This tranquility, however, is usually interrupted by the beasts unexpectedly rising again from their supposed grave, catching those men completely unprepared. They weren't really dead. They had merely buried themselves in the muck of the man's heart, conserving their strength for an opportune day. On the rare occasions when the apparent demise continues to the end of a man's life, the inactivity is better explained by hibernation than death.

The Wild Beasts Are Sin

Peregrinus—Are the wild beasts sin?

Plowman—Having wild beasts in the heart is not sin in the sense of the *commission* of sin. It is not walking in darkness. It does not break our fellowship with God. It is not an act of sin that gets recorded in the account of all that believers do in the body, both good and bad, which account is tried by fire at the judgment seat of the Redeemer.

But the wild beasts are definitely sin in the sense of the *indwelling* of sin. They are sinful desires that live in the heart, forever stirring up a sinful ruckus, and begging to be set free, so they can go on a sinful rampage.

Peregrinus—When does our relationship to the wild beasts become sin in the sense of committing an act of sin?

Plowman—We commit an act of sin when we reach our hand through the bars of the cage, scratch them between their ugly ears, and say, "Sorry I'm not allowed to feed you or free you, old boy. I sure wish things could be different."

Peregrinus—Dude! That's long before most folks would start regarding their actions as acts of sin.

Plowman—You know it. But if we don't label ear-scratching as sin and tremble at it as sin, the consequences are disastrous. Soon we will be slipping our wild beasts a few scraps here and there. Then we will be back to buying them Wild Beast Chow. Then we will start letting them out for a little exercise from time to time. Before long we will be saddling them up when no one else is around. Ultimately, if we don't quit our madness, we will be riding them in public without shame.

Struggling with the Wild Beasts

Peregrinus—I hate to admit it, but sometimes I find myself looking longingly at my wild beasts like they were imprisoned friends and wishing I could let them out.

Plowman—That's why one of our foremost duties in the good fight of faith is to guard our hearts and keep the wild beasts locked in their cage. They are an inner fifth column aligned with the Mad Spirit, waging a relentless war against our soul, trying to retake it for the cause of darkness.

Peregrinus—So what does my struggle with temptation say about my spiritual state?

Plowman—That depends upon what you mean by *struggle*. If you mean that you sometimes struggle with the temptation to feed your wild beasts or let them out, but don't give in to the temptation, that is a sign of spiritual strength, not weakness. But don't let your guard down. Continue watching and praying.

If, however, you mean that you are feeding the wild beasts, you are in a bad spiritual state. That is not struggling with temptation. That is watching out for the welfare of your wild beasts. And if you have unlocked the cage and let them out, hugged your favorite, combed his mane, saddled him up, and once again ride him from gratification to gratification, you are in grave danger. That is a mad-passionate love affair with wickedness.

Peregrinus—That sure puts things into perspective.

Plowman—Good illustrations have a way of doing that.

Backriding the Wild Beasts

Peregrinus—What about professing Christians who let their wild beasts out of their cage and go back to riding them again? Are they saved or lost?

Plowman—The fate of so-called backriders is a complicated question, so let me give you a complicated answer.

Believers have been given tremendous weapons to fight their battles — faith, the Holy Spirit, and the Word of God. Faith is able to quench every fiery dart that the Wicked One can throw at us. The Holy Spirit provides us with such overwhelming protective power that if we walk in the Spirit, we are unable to fulfill the lusts of the flesh. The Word of God is powerful, able to wash us from every defilement and character flaw. These three weapons are more than able to give a believer victory.

So when we see a professing Christian who is continuously falling prey to besetting sins, this indicates that he is not using the weapons that have been given to believers. And there are only two reasons why men don't use them as they ought — lack of proficiency and lack of possession. In other words, immature life and imitation life.

In the case of immature believers who lack proficiency in the use of their weapons, the struggle with besetting sin is a bump in the road that will be soon and successfully negotiated.

In the case of imitation believers who lack possession of the weapons, the struggle with sin is a farce. There is no genuine struggle. What we see is a hypocrite dancing with the enemy in his foxhole while pretending to fight the battles of the Lord.

All Wallow in the Hog Pen in Talk, Think, and Walk

Peregrinus—Quacksalver claimed that all believers wallow in the Hog Pen every day in Talk, Think, and Walk. I argued against that view, because it didn't seem right. Yet I felt like I was arguing against the truth because I know my own heart and experience — I'm not perfect.

Plowman—I'm glad you feel that tension. It indicates that you are on the right path. We must make a distinction between the Sacred Trust doctrine that believers *sin* in Talk, Think, and Walk every day and the Dogma that believers *wallow* in the Hog Pen in Talk, Think, and Walk every day.

Peregrinus—I'm all ears.

Plowman—The Sacred Trust teaches that believers are not perfect. James wrote, "We all offend in many ways." This indicates that even mature believers on the heights of holiness still manifest imperfection. And Peter wrote, "Above all have fervent love among yourselves, for love covers a multitude of sins." This indicates that even in the camp of the truly holy there is a need for fervent love, for there is an abundance of shortcomings and failures. Such passages establish the doctrine that all believers *sin* in Talk, Think, and Walk every day.

But the Sacred Trust also teaches that believers walk in real purity and holiness. In First John we read, "He that is freshborn of God cannot continue in sin." This is a plain declaration that the power of wallowing in the Hog Pen has been broken for believers. They may have a little mud remaining on themselves that needs to be washed off, but they have fled the Hog Pen.

We also read in John, "He that has bathed his whole body does not need to wash any part of his body except his feet. He is completely clean." In other words, believers walk in real personal holiness, but they still need to wash their feet because they walk in a dirty, defiling world.

Such passages overthrow the Dogma that all believers *wallow* in the Hog Pen in Talk, Think, and Walk every day.

Peregrinus—So the Glorious Salvation Machine is guilty of twistifying a Sacred Trust truth.

Plowman—That's right. They twistify the *sobering* truth that believers fall short of the glory of God every day into the *besotting* error that they wallow in filth, depravity, wickedness, and rebellion every day.

Scoop and Goop

Peregrinus—Is it fair to say that sinister motives are behind every twistification of Sacred Trust truth?

Plowman—Absolutely. For example, people don't take up the Dogma that believers wallow in the Hog Pen every day because they desire to prevent the weeds of perfectionism from growing in the heart. They take it up because it allows them to indulge the Big Here & Now as far and as dirty as they dare.

Peregrinus—So they use the letter of Scripture and the form of sound doctrine to defend Bible undermining error.

Plowman—That's right. They use the *form* of truth to teach the *essence* of error. That's why we call it Scoop and Goop. They take the doctrines of the Christian faith, *scoop* out the God-given content that is in keeping with real-relationship faith, then fill these empty shells with *goop* that is in keeping with faith in the Passive Form and Innocuous Minimizing.

Peregrinus—That's scary.

Plowman—It's beyond scary. When you mix man's desire to indulge the Big Here & Now with sneaky Innocuous Minimum error dressed in the sheepskins of truth, you have an extremely dangerous combination. That's why the Half-Havens have become so popular, influential, and widespread.

The Universal Truth Filter

Peregrinus—I don't understand how men can believe such nonsense. How can a doctrine so obviously wrong be so widely received as right?

Plowman—In the Big Here & Now profit is everything. As an old maxim says, "Profit drives the world." This passion for profit has changed the dynamics of how men determine and define truth. It gave rise to the Universal Truth Filter, which states, "Everything that is personally profitable is pragmatically good. Everything that is pragmatically good is existentially true. And existential truth is the only truth that matters."

This has potent ramifications. As one leading advocate of the Filter wrote, "There is no absolute truth. And even if there were absolute truth, we would still prefer existential truth. We prefer truth that lets us interpret reality the way we want, lets us believe what we want, and lets us do what we want. For us, truth is an egotistical exercise, a fact which is reflected in the definition of truth that frequently appears in our literature — Self Gratification Authentication."

Peregrinus—In other words, men believe what they want to believe.

Plowman—Exactly.

Saved from the Wonderful Message

Peregrinus—So the folks in the Glorious Salvation Machine and the Half-Havens believe God Magic salvationology and the Minimizing Message because it is profitable to believe it.

Plowman—You got it. With them as with all men, the pursuit of happiness in the fun stuff of the Big Here & Now is non-negotiable. They are willing to adapt or change in most aspects of their life, even in their religious and political views, but they will not budge an inch on this matter.

But their happiness is threatened by the Wonderful Message recorded in the Sacred Trust, which they profess to believe, for it exhorts them to turn their backs on fulfillment in the things of the Big Here & Now and seek their fulfillment in the things of the Crucified One.

This conflict of interest brings them to an impasse. They are unwilling to go forwards in their relationship with the Sacred Trust, taking everything it says in dead earnest, for that would require them to give up the pursuit of happiness in the stuff of the Big Here & Now. And they are unwilling to go backwards in their relationship with the Sacred Trust, giving up their profession of confidence in it, for then they wouldn't be able to indulge the feeling of being religious, which is an important part of their pursuit of happiness.

Thankfully, the Innocuous Minimum saves them from the Wonderful Message recorded in the Sacred Trust. They don't have to choose between God and the world. They can follow the Sweet One and wallow in the world. They don't have to choose between the Sacred Trust and the Big Here & Now. They can dabble with the Sanitized Trust and canoodle with the Big Here & Now.

Peregrinus—No wonder men love the Innocuous Minimum.

Plowman—Yep. It is held in the highest regard by those who want religion to be an important part of their pursuit of happiness in the Big Here & Now.

Man's True Religion Is Worthy Self

Peregrinus—It always comes back to the Altar of Worthy Self, doesn't it? As I have heard you say a hundred times, man's true religion is Worthy Self.

Plowman—That's right. Religious religion is just a thin coat of paint on the outside. On the inside all men are the same. All men dance around the Altar of Worthy Self. When you bang the drum of Worthy Self, they dance and bow down. When you threaten the Altar, they go on the warpath. Worthy Self is the only real object of their devotion and service.

Peregrinus—And they serve Worthy Self with all of their heart, soul, mind and strength.

Plowman—Every moment of every day. When Worthy Self makes its will known, every effort is made and no expense spared to gratify, as soon as possible, that worthy being whom their souls love supremely. They exhibit the greatest industry and ingenuity in pursuing whatever their eyes desire, whatever their soul hankers after, and whatever gives them the pride of attainment in the Big Here & Now.

Peregrinus—I wish we believers were even half that diligent in the things of God.

Plowman—So does God. As the Sacred Trust states, "The children of the Big Here & Now are wiser in their generation than the children of light." They are more adept at working for Big Here & Now profit than we are at working for profit in Sweet Everlasting. They exhibit more sacrifice, more diligence, more effort, more gumption, more perseverance, more wisdom, more ingenuity, more savvy. They exhibit more of everything that is needed to get the job done and get it done right.

Fig Leaves and the Central Integrity Processor

Peregrinus—It seems like men use religion to cover up and ignore the fact that they have strayed from the known will of God.

Plowman—That's right. Men put on fig leaves, like Adam and Eve once did, to hide their nakedness. But there is one vital difference between our ancestors in Eden and men today.

Peregrinus—What's that?

Plowman—Adam and Eve were willing to own their mistake and trade their fig leaves for God's redemption when it was offered. Most men are not. They want to keep their fig leaves because man-made religion allows them to pretend that they are right with God though they are going their own way.

Peregrinus—Doesn't their conscience bother them?

Plowman—Deep inside they know better. But they trample on their conscience, ignore their better judgment, keep the fig leaves, and rush headlong down the path of pretending because they are committed to maximizing their Big Here & Now. This creates an integrity crisis — their Central Integrity Processor is torn between serving God and serving Worthy Self.

But this crisis cannot continue long, for man cannot serve two masters. Eventually he gives his heart to one and despises the other. A few give their heart to God and pursue his things with abandon. Most give their heart to Worthy Self and pursue their own things with abandon. When men do this, they are forced to redouble their delusional efforts — they must pretend that they aren't pretending — which overloads their Central Integrity Processor, causing it to overheat and burn out. From that point, men are no longer able to discern right and wrong, pretending and not pretending, which makes the path of deception an easy downhill coast.

Sophisticated Idolatry

Peregrinus—So when men follow religion, like the Glorious Salvation Machine, they are pretending.

Plowman—That's right. They pretend that the God revealed in the pages of the Sacred Trust taken at face value does not exist. They serve, instead, a pretend god who winks at their sin, gives his blessing to the Innocuous Minimum, smiles upon the Altar of Worthy Self, and helps them maximize their Big Here & Now. This pretend god is a reflection of Worthy Self shining on the wall of their imagination with a little glitter and tinsel added — it is a god made in man's image.

Peregrinus—Dude! They are doing the same thing as the so-called heathen who fashion idols out of gold, or stone, or wood.

Plowman—You have hit the nail on the head. Minimizing is idolatry. The only difference between it and classic idolatry is that the gods fashioned by the Minimizers are much more sophisticated and subtle.

Peregrinus—Then all who reject the Crucified One and serve the Sweet One in Innocuous Minimum religion are idolaters!

Plowman—That's right. They are no less idolaters than those who engage in classic idolatry.

More Effective Than Burning the Sacred Trust

Peregrinus—I get goose bumps when I think about the deceit that is behind the Sanitized Trust. This bold and potent effort to make the Sacred Trust teach Innocuous Minimum churchianity robs men of the Sacred Trust without actually taking it away.

Plowman—You got that right. When preachers use ingenious arguments to empty passages of meaning they don't like and fill them with meaning they do like, they deprive men of those passages and the truth God intended to communicate with them just as effectively as if they were actually removed from the Sacred Trust.

Peregrinus—That is bone-chilling scary.

Plowman—That it is, indeed. The Sanitized Trust is far more effective at robbing men of truth than burning the Sacred Trust ever was. When the Minimizers burned the Sacred Trust in centuries past, the loss was obvious. Men knew that the Sacred Trust had been taken from them. But when the Minimizers sanitize the Sacred Trust, men don't realize that vast portions and vital truths of the Sacred Trust have been taken from them. They read through passages that have been heisted from the Sacred Trust and don't even notice that they are missing.

Muddifying the Sacred Trust

Peregrinus—It seems to me that we have a similar problem in the Havens.

Plowman—We sure do. Haven preachers sometimes mistreat the Word of God in the same way, though in a lesser degree and on lesser matters. For various reasons, they embrace error as the truth of God — which erroneous truth we call Mud. This Mud necessitates that various passages of Scripture be given false interpretations which darken the counsel of God — a practice we call Muddifying the Sacred Trust.

Peregrinus—How does error find any place to make camp in the churches of the living God?

Plowman—Error pitches its tents in ignorance and prejudice, but prejudice is its favorite haunt. When men are influenced by error because they are babes — who are innocently ignorant — there is not much to worry about. Their errors tend to slough off as they grow in understanding. But when men defend error because they are inflamed with doctrinal prejudice, they are difficult to win. And when error is nurtured by a culture of prejudice and ignorance, those who are convinced are nearly impervious to the truth.

Peregrinus—When you look at how widespread, varied, and shrewd error is and how it constantly assails the church from the outside and the inside, you realize the awful responsibility that preachers bear.

Plowman—That's why the Sacred Trust says, "Be not many teachers, for we shall receive greater judgment." Teachers are going to give account to God for what they taught. If they labor deeply enough and candidly enough in the Sacred Trust and in doctrine, their ministry will be purged of Mud. But depth and candor do not come easily or cheaply. Loyalty to churches, creeds, and doctrines often makes their price so *steep* that preachers put their Mud-discernment to *sleep*, embrace Mud as truth to *keep*, and feed this worthy Mud to the *sheep*.

The Dark Light Juggernaut

Peregrinus—Speaking of the proper handling of the Sacred Trust, Quacksalver said that men are not supposed to interpret it for themselves, but ought to let the Big Cheese interpret it for them. When I replied that such an approach to the Word of God was flushing your brain down the drain, he agreed, but insisted that flushing was a good thing, not a bad thing. I can't imagine flushing. How do the Big Cheese persuade men to submit to such domination?

Plowman—Most men need very little persuasion. They are happy to submit to religion that allows them to maximize the

Big Here & Now, even if that religion makes a few minor impositions upon them, like discouraging them from the study of the Sacred Trust for themselves. But for the few that need more persuasion, they resort to Head Pounding. They bring out their battering rams and pound away.

Peregrinus—Oh yeah, Head Pounding. Of course. Now it all makes sense.

Plowman—When men start uncovering the true gospel in the pages of the Sacred Trust, they are hounded and pounded with Mystic Plane charges like interpreting the Sacred Trust on their own, trusting Dead Works, or denying salvation by God Magic. These Mystic Plane sophistries overwhelm them, nipping their heart-faith in the bud, withering their confidence in the Word of God, and bringing them back into the fold of lukewarmness.

Peregrinus—Where is the spirituality in that?

Plowman—There isn't any. When men cave in to Head Pounding and flush their brain down the drain, they overthrow spirituality. God gave us a brain and expects us to use it. Spirituality is when men use their God-given reason to apprehend the mind of God revealed in the Word of God and then submit to this revealed truth with their God-given heart.

Peregrinus—Watching men get crushed by the Minimizing Machine and their Head Pounding reminds me of the ancient juggernaut.

Plowman—No doubt about that. The Minimizing Machine — as a modern day Dark Light juggernaut — rolls over all who would think for themselves, using Invincible Dogmas and Ironclad Interpretations to smush truth and discernment out of men and squish the mind of God out of the Word of God.

Peregrinus—So how do we deliver men from the Dark Light juggernaut?

Plowman—Men can only be delivered from the power of the Dark Light juggernaut by the power of the Sacred Trust. This power manifests itself on the behalf of all who submit, without reservation, to the authority of the Sacred Trust as the Word of God. And those who thus submit to its authority are known by two traits. *One*, they exalt the Sacred Trust above every human pretension to divine authority — including Invincible Dogmas and Ironclad Interpretations. *Two*, they allow the Sacred Trust to be its own interpreter — in other words, they allow God to give them his own interpretation of what he wrote.

When men study the Sacred Trust with such a heart, willing to believe whatever it teaches regardless of the cost, then the Dark Light juggernaut loses both its terror and its power. Then it will be seen for what it really is — a raft of flimsy arguments held together by ignorance and prejudice and manned by hacks who promote Minimizing religion for temporal gain.

The Pride Charge Is a Mega-Leverage Arm Bar

Peregrinus—It bugs me when people accuse me of pride just because I refuse to submit to Invincible Dogma.

Plowman—We all go through it. It comes with the territory. It is impossible to be in humble submission to God's revealed mind in the Sacred Trust and not be charged with pride.

Peregrinus—Why is that?

Plowman—The pride charge is a result of Dark Light logic. The Invincible Dogmas are the truth. Rejecting the truth is proof of pride. Therefore, everyone who rejects the Invincible Dogmas is guilty of pride.

Peregrinus—That explains a few things. It seems like the real purpose behind the charge of pride is not to address real character deficiencies in me, but to persuade me to flush my brain down the drain.

Plowman—You're right. The pride charge in the mouths of Minimizers is not about concern for the spiritual welfare of the sheep. It's about controlling the sheep. It's like a wrestling move designed to force an opponent into submission. And few tactics are as successful at forcing men to submit to the Brain Flush as using the pride charge like a mega-leverage arm bar.

Peregrinus—So it's really about their pride?

Plowman—That's right. When men refuse to submit to their Dark Light, that wounds their pride. When men submit to their Dark Light, that scratches their pride between the ears.

Peregrinus—It's interesting to observe that those who level the charge of pride are usually more guilty of pride than those whom they accuse.

Plowman—We call that the Moral Inverse Principle. When Dark Light advocates level charges of sin or error against those who question or oppose them, the accusers are generally more guilty of the supposed shortcoming than the accused.

True Humility Submits to the Sacred Trust First

Peregrinus—So what is true humility? It obviously involves submission. But submitting to men who want you to submit to Dark Light can't possibly be the humility that God seeks.

Plowman—You're right. Submitting to men, in and of itself, is neither the path nor the proof of humility. The world is filled with men who submit to religious institutions, not because they are humble, but because they are proud. The institutions offer them an occasion to indulge their pride and flatter themselves.

Peregrinus—So how can we recognize true humility? What kind of submission should we be looking for?

Plowman—True humility submits first and foremost to the Sacred Trust. It trembles at the entire book, from the first line of Genesis to the last line of Revelation, as the very words of the living God. It embraces without qualification its authority, its inspiration, its sufficiency, and its perspicuity. It seeks, in its pages, to know the mind, heart, will, ways, and salvation of the God who has revealed himself in those very pages.

True humility submits secondly and subordinately to servant-shepherds, who watch over the spiritual welfare of the sheep according to the Sacred Trust. These servant-shepherds are vetted by Sacred Trust loving men, using the qualifications for the pastoral post mentioned in the Sacred Trust.

We Have the Anointing and Don't Need Any Man

Peregrinus—So no man and no human institution is allowed to intrude upon the preeminence of the Sacred Trust.

Plowman—That's right. The Sacred Trust says that we have the anointing (the indwelling Spirit of truth) and don't need any man to teach us. In this same vein the Crucified One said, "Call no man teacher, for one is your teacher."

Peregrinus—In the light of such strong statements, why do we even have teachers in the church?

Plowman—Because such passages don't mean that there is no need at all for teachers in the church — they can't mean that. Such an interpretation contradicts other portions of the Sacred Trust which teach that God has given us teachers for the edification of the church. And if God gave us teachers, we can rest assured that we need teachers.

Peregrinus—Then what does it mean that we don't need any man to teach us?

Plowman—It means there is no *absolute* need for teachers. If a young believer were in a desperate situation, with no human means for instruction, and nothing but a copy of the Bible, he would have everything he needs to gain an intimate knowledge of the Crucified One, learn the foundational doctrines of the faith, and discover how he should walk in this evil world.

This sense harmonizes with the many passages which teach that there is a *relative* need for teachers. Teachers expedite the process of learning God's Word, will, and ways. And if we have the mind of God in the matter, we will show double honor to teachers that labor in the Word and in doctrine.

True Humility Takes the Narrow Path

Peregrinus—Let's go back to humility for a minute. If true humility submits to the authority of the Sacred Trust without reservation or exception, then true humility will be found on the narrow path following the Sacred Trust, not on the broad path following the Sanitized Trust.

Plowman—You're absolutely right. True humility chooses the lonely road with the despised carpenter from Nazareth, not the road of popularity with the Pharisees. It aligns itself with David in the wilderness, not with Saul in Jerusalem. It votes with Joshua and Caleb to fight the giants, not with the scouts who "humbly" regarded themselves as grasshoppers. It stands on Mount Carmel with Elijah against error, not with the four hundred and fifty prophets of Baal for error. It takes up the unpopular message of coming judgment with the true prophets of God, not the popular message of ease in Zion with the self-appointed, self-anointed prophets of the Sweet One.

The Counterfeit Principle

Peregrinus—Dude! It just struck me, in every one of these instances, real humility was regarded as pride by the religious ringleaders and the general populace.

Plowman—Yep. There is a constant struggle between *true humility*, which seeks the path of faithfulness, and *pretend humility*, which defends the status quo: whether compromise, error, or lukewarmness. But this conflict between true and false isn't limited to humility. It extends across the entire range of Christian character — every fruit of the Spirit has a subtle counterfeit. We call this the Counterfeit Principle.

Peregrinus—Can you give me a few examples?

Plowman—Sure. Pretend faith is confidence in the Passive Form. True faith is heart-faith in the Crucified One.

Pretend love for man winks at iniquity and error. True love cannot wink because it rejoices in straight paths and truth.

Pretend love for God honors the Sweet One and observes the Weekly Duty. True love for God follows the Crucified One and keeps his commands.

Pretend grace teaches churchgoers that they should overlook ungodliness and Big Here & Now desires in each other. True grace teaches believers that they should discourage ungodliness and Big Here & Now desires in each other.

The Big Cheese and the Servant-Shepherds

Peregrinus—And this distinction between true and pretend extends to preachers too.

Plowman—Absolutely. Throughout history there have been preachers who *taught* the truth and preachers who *fought* the truth — as the true prophets and the false prophets in the OT and the disciples and the Pharisees in the NT. This distinction endures today with the servant-shepherds and the Big Cheese.

Peregrinus—How can we tell them apart?

Plowman—Big Cheese and servant-shepherds differ in three main ways: how they want men to follow them, what they feed the sheep, and where the focus of their ministry lies.

Peregrinus—How do they differ in the way they want men to follow them?

Plowman—Big Cheese want men to be blind Minimizing followers of blind Minimizing preachers. They don't want men to dig too much or too deep into the Sacred Trust lest they discover that their Minimization of the Christian faith and their maximization of the Big Here & Now is contrary to the Word of God.

Servant-shepherds want men to be discerning followers of discerning preachers. They are in dead earnest about following the Sacred Trust and they want men to follow them only as far as they follow the Sacred Trust. To this end they encourage men to dig deep and daily in the Sacred Trust, comparing the ministry they are getting with the Sacred Trust to ensure that what they are being taught is the truth of the Sacred Trust.

Peregrinus—How do they differ in what they feed men?

Plowman—Big Cheese give men what they want — a hybrid message that combines a watered-down version of Christianity palatable to the Big Here & Now with lots of practical advice on being their Big Here & Now best.

Servant-shepherds give men what they need — the Sacred Trust in its entirety, unmingled with the Bible-undermining, truth-denying wisdom of the Big Here & Now.

Peregrinus—How do they differ in their ministry focus?

Plowman—Big Cheese are focused on their own personal gain: praise, prestige, and mammon.

Servant-shepherds are focused on the Crucified One. They fill the Lowly Post for his sake, longing to hear his "Well done thou good and faithful servant." There is no Big Here & Now gain for them that anyone in the Big Here & Now would covet. They bear a double portion of the world's reproach of the followers of the Crucified One as "The scum on the bottom of society and the scapegoats for every problem."

Peregrinus—The Big Cheese path seems self-serving to me.

Plowman—No doubt about that. The Big Cheese in the Half-Havens sound the Minimizing trumpet to gather crowds around themselves as Minimizing gurus. The spirit of their ministry is, "I must increase and become a big, important somebody." The servant-shepherds, on the contrary, sound the Calvary trumpet to rally men around the only person worth rallying around — the Crucified One. They know that they are just another soldier doing his job. The spirit of their ministry is, "He must increase and I must decrease."

The Lofty Office and the Lowly Post

Peregrinus—So the Lofty Office isn't merely something that can be abused, it is an abuse.

Plowman—That's right. Man invented the Lofty Office to give himself a religious option in the pursuit of being a big, important somebody. For centuries he had to choose between being a preacher and being a somebody. Now he can be both. He can be a big, important, religious somebody.

Peregrinus—That means that the Lowly Post is the only God-given, God-honoring pastoral position.

Plowman—That's right. The Crucified One gave the Lowly Post to his church, so he could have shepherds after his own heart watching over his sheep. These servant-shepherds *seek* their Master's things, not their own; *lay* down their lives for the sake of the flock, not reign over a flock to find their life; *feed* the flock in the pastures of the Sacred Trust, not the pastures of worldly wisdom; and *conduct* their shepherdship in the spirit of a servant, rather than in the spirit of a big, important somebody.

Peregrinus—Is there any lofty in the Lowly Post?

Plowman—Nope. The Lowly Post is not a coveted seat in the Sanhedrin. It is a difficult post on the battlefield. And while the sheep respect their servant-shepherds and honor them greatly for their work's sake, yet they do not regard them as holding any lofty office or sitting in any lofty seat. There isn't much in the Lowly Post that looks attractive to men who hanker to be big, important religious somebodies in the Big Here & Now.

The Path of Weakness

Peregrinus—What about the reproach that the Half-Havens are strong and the Havens weak? I know that the Half-Havens are going in the wrong direction. Yet I still feel a little sting in this reproach because we are kind of wimpy compared to the successful churches in the Half-Haven circles.

Plowman—Yep. We are weak and wimpy compared to them.

Peregrinus—So what do we do about it?

Plowman—Nothing. We stay on the path of weakness. We don't want strength based on worldly influence and power. When we are strong in the Big Here & Now, we cannot be strong in the Lord. Only when we are weak in the Big Here & Now, can we be strong in the Lord.

Peregrinus—So their strength is a bad thing because they get it from the Big Here & Now, and our weakness is a good thing because it means we are looking to God for strength.

Plowman—That's right. The strength we want is the strength men find when they reject the strength of the Big Here & Now and look to God that they might be strong in him and the power of his might. As a prophet once cried out, "Not by Big Here & Now might, nor by Big Here & Now power, but by my Spirit says the Lord."

This way of weakness is the Lord's way. Over and over again in the Sacred Trust, we observe the Lord taking up weakness to advance his cause here on earth: a despised tribe of slaves in

Egypt, a nobody named Gideon, a single soldier and his armor bearer, the jawbone of an ass, an oxgoad, an old woman with broken millstone, and a handful of fisherman. The Lord wants the glory of the victory to be all his own. He will not give his glory to another. So if we want showers of blessing, we must follow this pattern. We must learn with Paul to glory in weakness and scorn Big Here & Now strength.

Peregrinus—In other words, it's his way or the dry way.

Plowman—You got it. We offend God when we lean on the broken reed of the Big Here & Now, for that is leaning on the god of the Big Here & Now, the Mad Spirit.

Peregrinus—Dude! That is pure spookiness.

Plowman—You know it. And this spooky truth is the dark lining to the silver cloud of blessing that many churches seem to be enjoying today. The work of God is going forward more by machinery, minimizing, and worldly momentum than by the Spirit and Word of God. Come the day of trial, this strength shall be manifest as the weakness that it really is, and the Great Murky Revival shall be exposed as the Great Murky Reversal.

The Crucified One's Toolbox

Peregrinus—What about the argument that we must have a Big Here & Now Toolbox if we would have credibility with the men of the Big Here & Now?

Plowman—Credibility? Toolbox? Did any man ever have more credibility than the Rejected One? Did any man ever have better tools in his toolbox than the Rejected One? Yet he had no credibility with the Pharisees or the Sadducees, or the Jews at large, or the Romans, or anyone else for that matter, except for the remnant that followed him. And nothing in his toolbox could fix the situation. Nothing could give him one ounce more credibility or success.

Peregrinus—Dude! I never looked at credibility from that perspective before.

Plowman—It's the only way to look at credibility. The only way to be credible in the eyes of the Big Here & Now is to be unfaithful. I don't want any more credibility than the Crucified One had. I don't want any tools that weren't in his toolbox. A toolbox that gives me a better reception from the Big Here & Now than he received is not on my shopping list.

Peregrinus—When you put the toolbox question in that light, it answers itself.

Plowman—Darkness does have a habit of evaporating when you shine a little light on it.

Peregrinus—So what do we want in our toolbox?

Plowman—The same things that were in the Lord's toolbox: absolute confidence in the Word of God; pursuing faithfulness to the Word of God, rather than credibility in the eyes of the worldly church; shooting straight regardless of the cost; giving men the whole counsel of God, even if it offends them; drawing men with truth, rather than vanity; and preaching the Wonderful Message in its entirety — hard sayings included.

The Big Here & Now Has Not Changed

Peregrinus—Judging by their indulgence and defense of it, the Half-Havens seem to think that the Big Here & Now isn't as bad as it used to be — that it is less dirty and less harmful.

Plowman—Yep. If you want proof that men turn their brains off, you don't need to look any further.

Peregrinus—But the Big Here & Now really hasn't changed in any significant way has it?

Plowman—Not in the least. Whether we talk about its moral compass (which is broken), its essential heart character (which is unbelief), its morality (which is relative), its center of gravity (which is the Altar of Worthy Self), or its relationship to God (which is rebellion), the world is as wicked as it ever was.

It is the same festering mass of rebellion and sin that it was in the days of Noah, in the days of Sodom, in the days of the Crucified One's earthly pilgrimage, in the dark centuries when the Babylonish church slew millions of believers, and in the awful decades when rivers of believing blood were shed behind the Iron Curtain and the Bamboo Curtain.

It still hates, harries, and hounds the prophets of God. It still saws Isaiah asunder. It still leaves Jeremiah up to his armpits in a miry pit. It still throws the apostles into prison. It still beats Paul with rods and bruises him with stones. It still boils John the Beloved in oil. It still offers John the Baptist's head on a platter for a little sensual pleasure. It still hates all who speak for God without compromise. It still hates the Crucified One and his faithful followers with the same passion it ever did.

Let no man be deceived. Where the world's hatred is not manifest in persecution, it is present, nonetheless, simmering away on the back burner, waiting for favorable circumstances that allow it to boil over with impunity.

The Church's Duty in the Big Here & Now

Peregrinus—There is no way that we can clean up or fix up the Big Here & Now, is there?

Plowman—Nope. The Mad Spirit is the god and ruler of the Big Here & Now. He controls, dominates, directs, manipulates, and exploits the entire world system — every institution in every society on the entire planet — with powerful, perverse, seductive wisdom.

The only way to remove the influence of the Mad Spirit in the Big Here & Now is to actually remove the Mad Spirit from the Big Here & Now. As we read in one of the Gospels, "The strong man's goods cannot be spoiled until the strong man is bound." This binding and removing does not take place until the Lord himself descends from heaven to clean this mess up.

Peregrinus—What about those who think it is the church's duty to clean up this sewer of unbelief?

Plowman—They are wasting their time, money, and energy trying to change what cannot be changed. The best they can do is change dirty unbelief into clean unbelief. Not only are such efforts a profitless venture, they are a foolhardy venture. For all who would transform this world for the better must necessarily entangle themselves with the movers and shakers of the world — a situation which influences them for the worse. As we read in First Corinthians, "Bad company corrupts good morals." My own paraphrase says, "Non-narrow-path fellowship, for cause or for pleasure, undermines narrow-path values and virtues."

Peregrinus—So what is the church's duty in the Big Here & Now?

Plowman—Our duty is to give our lives to changing the only two things we can — the hearts of unbelievers from unbelief to faith and the hearts of believers from weak faith to strong.

Our duty is the great commission — to make disciples in every nation, baptizing them in the name of the Father and the Son and the Holy Spirit, and teaching them to obey everything that the Lord has commanded.

Our duty is to call men out of the Big Here & Now, leaving this vile world in its corruption, waiting for that day when the Lord shall descend in glory, seize the reins of the nations, bind the Mad Spirit, and transform the Big Here & Now into God Here & Now.

Two Kinds of Negative

Peregrinus—Luke says the message we preach in the Havens — like talking about the world's wickedness and judgment — is too negative. People don't like it. He says we unnecessarily offend multitudes of people who wouldn't be offended if we were more positive. Is there anything in this? Should we be more positive?

Plowman—To answer the question, we need to make a clear distinction between a negative *attitude* and a negative *message*.

Having a negative attitude is a matter of right and wrong. We hinder the Wonderful Message if we present it with a negative attitude. And we make it more attractive if we present it with a warm, friendly, positive attitude. So if we have any shortfalls in this regard, we should make every effort to correct them.

Having a negative message, however, is not a matter of right and wrong. Some right messages are negative. Telling a man that cancer surgery is necessary, for instance, is just as negative as it is right. He may not like to hear it, but he definitely needs to hear it.

Likewise, many parts of our message are negative. Men don't want to hear that the Big Here & Now is rotten to the core, that the Glorious Salvation Machine is rotten to the core, that they are ungodly sinners walking in ungodly unbelief, that an awful judgment of fire from heaven is coming that will wipe out the present Big Here & Now, and that all unbelievers will spend eternity in the eternal hell-fire of Awful Everlasting. But they need to hear and believe these negative things. And they can only hear them from us — God's ambassadors. We cannot quit preaching them, no matter who complains.

Peregrinus—So we must positively present truth that the Big Here & Now regards as negative.

Plowman—Until our last breath.

The Wonderful Message Really Is Positive

Peregrinus—I know that the accusations of negativity come from men walking in the footsteps of Demas — men who want more softness and less hardship, more playground and less battleground. But I still sometimes find myself wishing that the message we were given to preach was a little more positive in the eyes of man.

Plowman—How can a message get any more positive than the Wonderful Message we preach?

First of all, God offers pardon to the entire camp of ungodly rebels, who have taken up arms in rebellion against him.

Secondly, this offer of pardon is based on the fact that God's Son has already borne the penalty of death for their rebellion. There is no earning or paying or qualifying involved. There is nothing for them to do but believe and receive — just lay down their arms, cross the lines, embrace the Son, and be pardoned.

Thirdly, the rebels are not merely pardoned, they are adopted into the royal family as heirs of God and coheirs with his Son, in which position they shall enjoy an eternal weight of glory and blessing at the Father's right hand.

Peregrinus—That does put our message in a positive light.

Plowman—It sure does. A story with a happy ending is not negative just because the heroes pass through some negative experiences. Likewise, the Wonderful Message is not negative just because believers must endure some negative things before the positive ending.

Peregrinus—So the Christian life is like a feel-good movie in which the heroes go from bad times to good times, from negative stuff to positive stuff, only better.

Plowman—Infinitely better. For one short season we endure negative things like taking up the cross, enduring hardship as a good soldier, suffering reproach and persecution, and bringing an unwanted message to a complacent if not hostile world. For one long eternity we shall enjoy infinite, eternal blessings in Sweet Everlasting.

How to Deal with the Negative Stuff

Peregrinus—Is it possible to present the negative stuff in a more positive manner?

Plowman—If someone can show me how I can present the negative stuff in a more positive presentation, I will be all over it like kids on ice cream. But typically, that which is called a "more positive presentation" is a more unfaithful presentation. The negative parts — whatever ungodly men dislike — are white-washed, watered-down, or removed as far as preachers dare. Men are given Minimizing cotton candy instead of a faithful, manly message that a prophet or an apostle would not be ashamed to preach.

Peregrinus—In other words, the negative stuff is negative, so we just have to man-up and deal with it.

Plowman—That's right.

Peregrinus—So how do we deal with the negative stuff?

Plowman—We overcome it by faith. Faith looks at the big picture and weighs the things of time in the scale of eternity. Faith counts false accusations and persecution as pure joy, for it knows that it has a great reward in heaven. Faith counts the reproach of the Crucified One greater riches than the treasures and pleasures of the Big Here & Now, for it has respect unto the recompense of reward. Faith counts it a small thing to lose its life for the sake of the Crucified One, for it knows that God will not forget our labor of love.

Peregrinus—That almost makes the negative look positive.

Plowman—Absolutely. When believers walk through the Big Here & Now in triumphant faith, the negatives begin to take on a glory of their own. They regard the good fight of faith as glorious, because there is no glorious victory without a glorious fight. They see the arduous race as glorious, because it leads to glorious reward. They view their trials — which leave their heads hanging and heart flagging — as glorious, for refining in Man's Day brings honor in God's Day.

God's Math vs. Man's Math

Peregrinus—It amazes me how the Half-Havenists read the same Sacred Trust we do, yet come up with a different path — following the Sweet One instead of the Crucified One.

Plowman—They come up with wrong answers because they use the wrong math. They use the same math the world uses — man's math. The school of God throws man's math in the trash and does its figuring with God's math. These two systems are very different.

Peregrinus—I'm all ears.

Plowman—They *value* things differently. *God's math* values things like the widow's mite, a patch of lentils, a young lad's sling, the jawbone of an ass, a cup of cold water in the name of a prophet, twelve simple laborers, and mustard seed faith. *Man's math* assigns little value to such things. It values things that are highly esteemed in the eyes of the Big Here & Now like worldly greatness, worldly wisdom, unrighteous mammon, and the pride of life.

They *order* things differently. *God's math* seeks the things of the Crucified One first. *Man's math* inserts the handy-dandy Lip-Service Constant in the equation, so they can seek the Big

THE GLORIOUS SALVATION MACHINE

Here & Now first yet be credited with seeking the things of God first. As they love to say, Innocuous Minimizing is Sweet One prioritizing.

They **count** stuff differently. *God's math* counts hearts that have turned in real-relationship faith. *Man's math* counts tongues that have wagged in the Faith Form.

They **add** things differently. When *man's math* adds up the cost of following the Crucified One — reproach, suffering, sacrificing, and hardship — it seems too high a price to pay, so it opts for the Innocuous Minimum instead. When *God's math* adds up such costs, it seems like an insignificant price to pay for a relationship with the Crucified One, so it trades all that it has for the pearl of great price.

They **subtract** things differently. When *man's math* subtracts the Altar of Worthy self from its life in the Big Here & Now, it comes up with a big, ugly zero, so it keeps the Altar, rejects the Crucified One, and serves the Sweet One. When *God's math* subtracts the Altar it comes up with infinity — for it sees an incredible opportunity that leads to Sweet Everlasting where men shall enjoy an infinite and eternal reward as the children of the infinite and eternal God.

Peregrinus—Dude! Man's math is terrible.

Plowman—That's the understatement of the day.

Sincerity and Insincerity

Peregrinus—But what about sincerity? Doesn't that count for anything? What about those who sincerely use man's math because that is what they have been taught?

Plowman—No amount of sincerity can save men from the consequences of using bad math. Some men flatter themselves that God will not let them get the wrong answer, even if they use the wrong math, because their hearts are right. But this is insanity. Math is math and math is inexorable. If you use the wrong math, you get the wrong answer — without exception.

Moreover, the longer a person walks down a bad-math path, the lower the odds that he travels that path sincerely. For there is a strong correlation between length of time on a bad-math path and insincerity. When men are sincere, they deal honestly with light and submit to it. This takes them off bad-math paths, usually sooner rather than later. When men are insincere, they deal dishonestly with light. They pretend that light is darkness and darkness light. This keeps them on bad-math paths.

The Quality of Life Roadblock

Peregrinus—What about the quality of our life? The Half-Havenists claim that tearing down the Altar of Worthy Self is contrary to the truth that God cares about the quality of our life.

Plowman—Yep, I hear that one all the time. I call this piece of fiction the Quality of Life Roadblock. It is the same old plea for happiness in the stuff of the Big Here & Now that men have made since the dawn of time. It just has a fresh coat of modern, intellectual-sounding whitewash painted over it.

Peregrinus—But doesn't God care about the quality of our life?

Plowman—Of course he does. That is axiomatic. But the question isn't whether God cares about the quality of our life.

Peregrinus—So what is the right question?

Plowman—We must answer the question of the *context* of our life before we can answer the question of the *quality* of our life. For the context in which we live determines what kind of life is legitimately regarded as a quality life. For instance, what would be regarded as a quality life in time of peace would be regarded as out of place were it lived in time of war on the frontlines. And what would be regarded as a quality life in time of war would be looked upon as spartan or even eccentric were it lived in time of peace.

Peregrinus—I can see where this is going. Are we trying to lead a quality life in the stuff of the Crucified One as a good soldier in the time of war. Or are we trying to lead a quality life in the stuff of the Big Here & Now as if we were not on a battlefield in the middle of a raging war.

Plowman—Exactly. This is not the time of rest. This is the time of war. We are not in Sweet Everlasting in some idyllic post-war setting. We are in a world corrupted by unbelief and spiritual iniquity. The only life in this scene that merits the adjective *quality* is the life of a faithful, valiant soldier of the Crucified One ardently fighting the good fight of faith: holding forth light in the darkness, turning rebels from their unbelief, and instructing believers in the truth of God. And it is entirely out of place for believers to fill their foxholes with fun stuff and indulge a life of softness while the war rages around them. That is not quality soldiership. That is quality lukewarmness.

Peregrinus—Dude, this clears a lot of things up.

Plowman—Truth has a way of doing that.

The Abundant Life

Peregrinus—I suppose the abundant life teaching should be seen in the same light as the quality of life teaching?

Plowman—Absolutely. The believer's abundant life does not consist of the abundance of his Big Here & Now possessions or experiences. It consists of an abundance of spiritual and eternal wealth that the Big Here & Now cannot give or take away.

What *riches* a man has if he is filled with the Spirit of God — enjoying peace that passes understanding, joy the world cannot know, and songs in the heart come thick or thin!

What *treasure* he has if he is filled with the hope of a royal inheritance in Sweet Everlasting — possessions which can't be lost, stolen, or taxed and which can't rust, wear out or break!

What *resources* he has if he is filled with faith — trusting God to provide for every need, contingency, and God-ordained project, on time and in full, according to his glorious riches!

Peregrinus—That means that any believer in any century, in any part of the world, under any circumstances, no matter how yucky, can enjoy an abundant life.

Plowman—That's right. A believer can enjoy the abundant life that the Sacred Trust promises in prison, in the hospital, in poverty, in suffering, in adversity, in persecution, in flight, in bitter loss, and under the oppression of unjust government. No matter the circumstances, faith can rise triumphant in our heart, filling us with the joy of our true riches.

The Errors of the Sugar Kids Message

Peregrinus—That's a far cry from the popular view of the abundant life that the Sugar Kids preach.

Plowman—The Sugar Kids Message is a monstrous lie that is wrong on three vital points.

First of all, it is wrong in *theory*. It advocates an abundant life that is beyond the grasp of the vast majority of men that have ever lived. Most who embrace this teaching fail to enjoy any advantage from it. And this lack is not due to lack of faith in their heart, but lack of truth in the teaching.

The entire world system is in moral upheaval and under the curse of God. Wars, catastrophes, health problems, financial problems, capitalistic injustice and socialistic injustice, gangs and thugs, wear and tear, rot and rust, and numerous other evils turn this world into a giant vacuum that sucks up men's efforts and goods. Only by a combination of Big Here & Now savvy and luck do a few rise above the circumstances and live a life that belies the moral upheaval and curse.

While the believer does enjoy a promise, expressed in various ways in various verses, that God will prevent the curse and the moral upheaval from touching him in a way that prevents him from using his God-given gifts to accomplish his God-given work, yet there is not one line in the Sacred Trust that promises the believer freedom from the curse or the moral upheaval prior to the resurrection. These troubles belong to the whole human race until the end of the age, when the King of kings descends from heaven to establish his kingdom: when he shall bind the Mad Spirit, remove the ungodly, and take away the curse.

Secondly, it is wrong in its *abundance*. The abundance that the Sugar Kids pursue is garbage and useless junk that shall be burned up as wood, hay and stubble when their life is tried by fire at the judgment seat of the Crucified One.

Thirdly, it is wrong in its *essence*. The Sugar Kids life is just baptized hedonism sporting a Sweet One bumper sticker. And hedonism is just paganism stripped of every idol but the idol of idols, the Altar of Worthy Self.

Peregrinus—Dude! You sure have a way of laying the ugly facts bare.

Plowman—Truth is in the business of exposing the ugliness of error. And make no mistake, every error is ugly. For every error tramples on either the character of God (as his goodness or holiness or sovereignty) or the revealed truth of God (things that are known or ought to be known).

Three Kinds of Stuff

Peregrinus—I don't want to over-react against praying for stuff just because the Sugar Kids Message is wrong. What kind of stuff is it okay to pray for?

Plowman—Well, there are three kinds of stuff: necessary stuff, commission stuff, and frivolous stuff.

Peregrinus—I think I can see where this is going.

Plowman—Yep. The theory isn't difficult. Believers ought to boldly pray for necessary stuff and commission stuff, but it is an abuse of our stewardship to pray for frivolous stuff.

Peregrinus—Can you give me a little elucidation on this classification?

Plowman—Sure. *Necessary stuff* is what we need to meet life's necessities and responsibilities: as food, water, clothing, housing, transportation, tools, maintenance, health, practical furniture, time-saving conveniences, and even simple pleasures pursued in steward-soldier moderation.

Commission stuff is what we need to carry out our obligations in the work of God through evangelism, discipleship, teaching, and church planting: as funds, meeting places, printing presses, computers, books, literature, musical instruments, broadcasting equipment, buildings, grounds, and training.

Frivolous stuff is what we need to satisfy our sensual desires when we pursue paths that are not based on the revealed will of

God in the Sacred Trust: as majoring in R & R, rather than the work of God; squandering time, money, and heart affections on sensual pleasure; pursuing goals with no Sweet Everlasting rewardability; and indulging in extravagance and the pride of life. May we ever bear in mind that whatsoever is not based on the word of God is not of faith.

Peregrinus—So the question really boils down to whether or not our request is based on the Word of God. If our request is based on the Word of God — whether precept, principle, or pattern — then it is a legitimate request.

Plowman—That's right. God never promised anywhere in the Sacred Trust to fill our foxholes with Big Here & Now fun stuff. He promised to meet all of our needs according to his glorious riches. And by this we are to understand not what we think our needs are, but what our needs really are according to his gifting, his calling, and his plans for our life.

Taking Up the Cross Is Not Bare Feet

Peregrinus—Here's another issue that has been bugging me. The Half-Havens say that interpreting the "take up your cross" passages in a literal sense is Barefoot extremism.

Plowman—There is not one drop of Barefoot extremism in taking up the cross. When men take up the cross, they are not taking up an arduous course of religious duty, or an austere religious lifestyle, or a yoke of religious works. They are not engaging in will-worship or the religious deprivation of human nature. Such practices are flesh-gratifying, man-pleasing, man-impressing religion that is contrary to the cross. The cross does not gratify the flesh. It crucifies it.

Peregrinus—So, is there any danger at all of men taking the Bible so literally and seriously that they stray into the error of Bare Feet?

Plowman—Not in the least. The fact is, the more diligently that men pursue and obey the teachings of the New Testament, the less likely they are to fall into the error of Bare Feet. Men only fall into this error when they depart from the Sacred Trust and the real-relationship faith it teaches.

Peregrinus—Why the accusations of extremism, then?

Plowman—The Innocuous Minimizers must protect their turf if they want to keep their machinery running. They do this with Head Pounding arguments that make real-relationship faith look bad and confidence in the Passive Form look good. One of the key components of a full-orbed Head Pounding platform is raising a ruckus over the "take up the cross" passages, insisting that taking them literally is Barefoot extremism.

The Cross Is Simply the Cross

Peregrinus—So what does it mean to take up the cross?

Plowman—You can't answer that question unless you first determine what the cross is.

Peregrinus—Okay. So what is the cross?

Plowman—The cross is simply the cross. It is the old rugged cross on which the Son of God was hung and killed nearly two thousand years ago — where God's mercy and God's justice embraced, where God's amazing love for man was displayed in amazing fashion, where God manifest in flesh paid the infinite debt for all sin, so that men don't have to pay the infinite debt for their sin — so that all who believe may have eternal life.

Peregrinus—If the cross is simply the cross, then what does it mean to take up the cross and die to self?

Plowman—Taking up the cross means nothing more, nothing less, and nothing other than believing on the Crucified One.

Peregrinus—Just simple heart-faith in the Crucified One? Nothing added? Nothing extra?

Plowman—That's right.

The Hard Sayings Guard Against Emptification

Peregrinus—What is the purpose, then, of the "take up your cross" passages and the other hard sayings if they demand of man nothing more and nothing other than what is demanded of him by the simple command to believe on the Crucified One?

Plowman—God put this class of passages in the Sacred Trust to guard faith against emptification.

Peregrinus—Emptification?

Plowman—Emptification is the transmogrification of faith from heart-faith in the Crucified One into superstitious faith in the Passive Form. Since the days of the apostles, treacherous men of Glorious Salvation Machine stamp have Hounded and Pounded men with Minimizing arguments that empty faith of its intrinsic vitality — working, obeying, and overcoming — and convince men that faith is confidence in the virtue and efficacy of the Passive Form.

Peregrinus—So the hard sayings guard against emptification because they associate faith with stuff like obedience and fruit, making it nearly impossible to confound biblical faith with the emptified faith of the Passive Form system.

Plowman—Yep. But if men want to believe that Minimizing slop, there is no passage in the Bible that can make them stop.

Peregrinus—In other words, the hard sayings only benefit those that tremble at the Sacred Trust.

Plowman—Exactly.

Peregrinus—Can you delineate a few of the ways in which the hard sayings illuminate faith?

Plowman—The hard sayings portray faith as choosing God's way when faced with the choice between his way and man's way. This choice is expressed in various ways: taking up the cross or rejecting it, losing your life or finding it, following the narrow path or the broad road, and selling the field (to buy the pearl of great price) or keeping the field.

The hard sayings portray faith as a point and a path that are inseparably associated. For example, faith is a point (the strait gate) and a path (the narrow path), a point (taking up the cross) and a path (following the Crucified One), a point (Abraham believing the promise) and a path (Abraham leaving Ur of the Chaldees). Make no mistake, if Abraham had stayed in Ur, that would have proved that he didn't believe the promise, even if he had started a religion that professed to believe it.

The hard sayings present the fruits of faith as necessary in the salvation equation — not as a condition of salvation, but as the evidence of salvation. For example, "My sheep hear my voice and follow me, and I give unto them eternal life." I like to paraphrase this, "Do you want to know who has eternal life? Look for those who tremble at my sayings in the Sacred Trust and follow them, for following them is following me."

The hard sayings embody and echo the Sacred Trust teaching, "By their fruits you shall know them," which we sum up in the principle, "No fruit means no faith means no salvation."

Peregrinus—I don't understand the blindness that reigns in the Half-Havens. Men come into regular contact with the Word of God, yet their noggins are filled with Innocuous Minimum notions that leave them just as much on the road to hell as the atheist who pretends that God doesn't exist. How do they miss such basic Sacred Trust truths as the necessity, vitality, and visibility of real-relationship faith in the Crucified One?

Plowman—I don't even try to understand. I just shudder.

Tip-Toeing Around the Hard Sayings

Peregrinus—If the hard sayings in the Gospels are so easily harmonized with heart-faith, why do so many good preachers tiptoe around them? They seem afraid of them. Even Mr. Radio Preacher, who preaches against the errors of the Glorious Salvation Machine, does a little tip-toe dance when he comes to them.

Plowman—The tip-toe dance is partly due to *confusing* the error of legalism (works as a condition of salvation) with the truth of evangelicalism (works as the evidence of salvation) and partly due to *fear* of fellow preachers who draw a line in the sand and stigmatize the hard sayings as Dead Works.

Peregrinus—Nothing that a little light and a good dose of man-up and gumption can't fix.

Plowman—That's right. They just need a little clarification on the distinction between legalism and evangelicalism. How can the hard sayings be legalism? How can it be legalism when a man joyfully heart-turns in heart-faith to accept an amazing invitation to follow an amazing Saviour in an amazing cause down an amazing path in an amazing faith-adventure that leads to an amazing Sweet Everlasting?

The Power of the Cross

Peregrinus—Where does faith find the power to walk in the victory that the Sacred Trust claims for it?

Plowman—Through the cross.

Peregrinus—How can the cross be the power of faith?

Plowman—Through that awful event which the cross was designed to promote — death. When we believe upon the Crucified One, we are joined to him in spiritual union in his death. We are crucified with him. From that moment we are, *in principle*, dead to the Big Here & Now. This death is our power over it. It can no longer touch us — not with its pains or with its pleasures — because we are outside of its realm.

Peregrinus—So for all practical purposes, our relationship to the Big Here & Now is like a man lying in a grave.

Plowman—Not quite. The cross of the Crucified One is not like the death of a man. When a man dies, that's the end of the story. He never sets foot in the Big Here & Now again. But when the Crucified One died, the grave couldn't hold him. He rose from the dead and walked on earth again. And just as he was raised from the dead, so we too are raised by the Spirit of God that we may walk in newness of life. Though dead to the Big Here & Now, we do lay not in a grave, but walk yet in it — albeit as dead to it as if we did lay in a grave. Dead men have nothing to gain or to lose in the Big Here & Now.

Peregrinus—Wow! Looking at it from that perspective, the question isn't how believers find the power to walk in victory over the temptations and trials of the world, but how they fail to find it. They have the power of death and the power of the resurrection working in them.

Plowman—You're absolutely right. As Paul wrote, "I am crucified with the Crucified One. Nevertheless I live, yet not I, but the Crucified One lives in me." This *crucified life* gives believers power over all that the Big Here & Now offers them or throws at them, making them other-worldly. It is why they cease pursuing the sins indulged by the Big Here & Now, why they cease running after the things highly esteemed by the Big Here & Now, and why they are impervious to threats, abuse, prosecution, and persecution.

Peregrinus—If believers would walk in the full potential of the power that is theirs in principle, that would mess their Daily Grind up pretty good.

Plowman—No doubt about that. The world takes notice when men die. As Paul wrote, "We are unto God a sweet savor of the Crucified One in them that are saved and in them that are lost. To the one we are the stench of death and to the other we are the fragrance of life unto life." When the Big Here & Now sees men who are dead to their causes, passions, and pursuits, they smell death. Now they forgive those who smell like death if they are physically dead and destined for a cold grave. But it is an unforgiveable crime in their books when men smell like death while they are yet physically alive.

The Mutual Rejection of the Cross

Peregrinus—So what's behind the world's rejection of the Crucified One?

Plowman—The world rejected the Crucified One because he rejected the glory of the world — its coveted power, prestige, positions, institutions, and riches — as worthless and vain. He chose not to be born into them. He didn't seek them at any time in his life. He refused them when they were offered. The world he lived for was not the present world, but the world to come. Therefore, the world rejected him and conspired to get rid of him. They said, "We will not have this man to reign over us."

Peregrinus—But why such animosity and aversion? Why not just indifference? They could have just ignored him instead of hanging him on the cross.

Plowman—Because men tend to be resentful and vindictive when anyone touches their ego. So when the Crucified One rejected the glories of the world that the egos of the movers and shakers were attached to, he wounded their pride.

Peregrinus—And we get the same treatment don't we?

Plowman—Yep. There is mutual rejection in the cross. When we follow the Crucified One in his rejection of the Big Here & Now, rejecting the vain things that men glory in, the Big Here & Now takes notice, takes offense, and returns the rejection with a vengeance — giving us the same spiteful rejection it gave the Crucified One.

The Cross Symbolizes the World's Rejection of God

Peregrinus—I was just thinking how the cross isn't merely an isolated instance of nastiness, but the nastiest instance in a long string of nastiness perpetrated by the Big Here & Now.

Plowman—You got that right. The God-defying spirit which hung the Son of God on the cross first reared its ugly head in the garden. Since that awful day, it has manifested itself in a long and ugly history of God-defying iniquity.

It was at work when Cain rejected the revealed will of God on true worship, offered the fruits of the earth, and murdered his brother. It was at work when Pharaoh king of Egypt hardened his heart against the revealed will of God, refused to let the children of Israel go, and chased them across the Sinai. It was at work when the children of Israel themselves refused the revealed will of God, turned to broken cisterns, and killed their own prophets. And it was at work on that fateful day when the Jews and the Romans hung Jesus the Nazarene on the cross.

But though the cross is just one more link in the long chain of iniquity that the world is fashioning on the anvil of unbelief, yet because it was the Son of God that they crucified, this foul deed stands out as the zenith of iniquity. No greater act of iniquity is possible.

Peregrinus—It's the Mt. Everest of ungodliness.

Plowman—That's right. And because the killing of the Son of God on the cross is the preeminent instance of the world's rejection of God, the cross has come to symbolize — indeed epitomize — the world's rejection of God.

Blind-Sided by the Cross

Peregrinus—It never dawned on me when I gave my heart to the Crucified One that following him would cost so much ugly stuff. I feel like I got more ugly than I bargained for.

Plowman—Got blind-sided by the cross, did you?

Peregrinus—I sure did — not that I'm having any thoughts of turning back or throwing in the towel. But am I an odd duck, or do others have this experience too?

Plowman—You're not an odd duck. New believers typically get blind-sided by the cross. It's part of the learning curve. They don't understand how much they turned their backs on the Big Here & Now when they believed on the Crucified One and how much the Big Here & Now would find their behavior unacceptable.

Peregrinus—But believers always come through okay, right?

Plowman—Absolutely. The Crucified One watches over his lambs with a tender eye: keeping them from trials they cannot bear and strengthening them in the trials he allows. And no matter how awful or painful the trial, they can trust that all their trials work together for their own good — they are being refined and purified on the path that leads through sanctified to glorified.

Emotional Zeal Is Over-Rated

Peregrinus—Hey, I have a couple questions about zeal.

Plowman—Go ahead.

Peregrinus—I have a difficult time understanding how my friend Luke W. Zeal can be so zealous, yet be so departed from the truth and so committed to error.

Plowman—One of the most important principles of spiritual discernment is that emotional zeal has no intrinsic moral value.

Men can be zealous for error as well as for truth. The fact is, zeal is more often found advocating error than truth.

Peregrinus—Maybe I'm astray here, but I thought that zeal would eventually lead people out of error and into the truth.

Plowman—Nope. Emotional zeal is over-rated. If it actually led men out of error, there would be a stream of zealous men flowing out of the Half-Havens and into the Havens. But this is not the case. More often than not, those that are zealous depart for churches that are more compromised, not less.

Peregrinus—You're right. So where am I getting hung up?

Plowman—Men tend to focus on the zeal of the *soul* with its natural fervency and enthusiasm. This is a mistake. This zeal is highly subjective in its associations and commitments, and it often appears in high degree without any true spirituality.

Peregrinus—So what kind of zeal should we be looking for?

Plowman—The zeal of the *spirit*. This is a controlled fire in the combustion chamber of the heart that serves the living God in intelligent worship. Its first act of worship is a determination to pursue and defend the entire body of revealed truth in the Sacred Trust. Its second act of worship is a determination to live a life whose beliefs, purposes, plans, commitments, and directions are crafted and circumscribed by the body of revealed truth in the Sacred Trust.

Peregrinus—Dude! This puts zeal in totally different light.

Plowman—It sure does. We will not go astray if we cast a *little eye* on soulish zeal and a *big eye* on the zeal of the spirit. We need warm hearts guided by concrete principles based on the Sacred Trust, not hot hearts guided by enthusiasm adrift from the Sacred Trust.

Luke W. Zeal Exposed

Peregrinus—This explains why Luke is so committed to his path of Sugar Kids error. He has truckloads of soulish zeal, but he is lukewarm when it comes to spiritual zeal.

Plowman—Yep. His worship is in soul and error, not in spirit and truth. He has an eye for religion that is compatible with the

Altar of Worthy Self, not an eye for truth. This leaves him vulnerable to every wind of Minimizing doctrine that tickles his ears — as the Sugar Kids Message.

Peregrinus—By the way, what is Luke's middle name? He refuses to tell me.

Plowman—I'm not surprised. The Sugar Kids camp tries to avoid every fact that would expose their Minimizing fantasy. His middle name is *Warm*.

Peregrinus—Dude! That means his full name is Luke Warm Zeal. No wonder he wouldn't tell me.

Plowman—Yep. And it certainly fits him, for he weighs tepid on the spiritual-worship scale.

Peregrinus—The spiritual-worship scale?

Plowman—The spiritual-worship scale weighs the only zeal that matters — the zeal of the heart. It does this by weighing a believer's pursuit and implementation of the truth revealed in the Sacred Trust. The scale ranges from tepid on the low end to intrepid on the high end.

Peregrinus—Intrepid? Now that's an interesting adjective to use with zeal.

Plowman—But it is an excellent choice, for spiritual zeal is a matter of character, vigor, and God-honoring purpose, not of emotion, feelings, and enthusiasm. It is a matter of embracing and implementing the revealed truth of God, no matter how many or how great the difficulties that stand in the way.

Plowman's Counsel on Visiting the Half-Havens

Peregrinus—Luke hounded me to visit a couple Half-Havens and hear some conservative Half-Haven preaching. He thinks I should go hear Strawberry Nostrum and Willy Rush Forward.

Plowman—Well, I'm not particularly excited about the idea.

Peregrinus—I'm not excited about the idea either, though I am inclined to go, so I can hear them myself. They probably are just as unsound as you say they are, but I don't want my estimate of their Half-Havenism to be based on hearsay. I want to get my evidence from the horse's mouth.

Plowman—I can appreciate your concern for fact-gathering. I myself have read a few books and heard a few preachers where the only purpose and profit was fact-gathering to gain a better understanding of errors devastating the church.

But if you are going to go hear Strawberry and Rush, make sure that you don't miss any of the meetings of the local church just to hear them.

Peregrinus—I'm with you. There is no way under the sun that I would skip out on the fellowship of Sacred Trust loving pilgrims to investigate the errors of the Laodiceans.

Parting Comments

Peregrinus—Hey, it's getting late. I need to scoot.

Plowman—Yep, me too.

Peregrinus—I really appreciate our evenings together.

Plowman—I'm glad to hear that. Your excitement brings back memories of the days when I was a babe — when I was beginning to see the difference between the Faith Form errors and the plain teachings of the Sacred Trust.

Peregrinus—Well, I am excited about growing in the Sacred Trust, in the truth, and in discernment. I want to know God. I want to know his Word, his will, and his ways.

Plowman—God will bless and honor that desire.

Peregrinus—He already has. The Sacred Trust used to seem so difficult. I couldn't understand most of it. The preachers in the Glorious Salvation Machine and the Half-Havens made it worse when they opened up the Deep Significance. No matter how hard I tried, no matter how hard I studied, I could not see the Deep Significance. I used to think the problem was with me and that I had some kind of perverted blindness. But now I realize that the problem was with them. I was trying to take the hard sayings of the Sacred Trust at face value. They were trying to conform them to the Passive Form and the demands of the Innocuous Minimum.

Plowman—I myself once struggled with fears of perverted blindness. But trusting and clinging to the plain teaching of the

THE GLORIOUS SALVATION MACHINE

Sacred Trust enabled me to work through those fears and undo them forever. But speaking of working through things, I need to work my way home.

With that Plowman stood up, downed the last few swallows of coffee in his cup, put his tip under the saucer, grabbed his Sacred Trust, shook Peregrinus' hand, said good-bye, and headed for the door.

CHAPTER NINE
STRAWBERRY NOSTRUM

A Fact-Checking, Fact-Gathering Mission

Peregrinus searched on the Internet and found Strawberry's church, the Big Here & Now Friendly Sweet One Center. They were holding special meetings the last full week of the month, every evening at seven. He penciled in a visit on his calendar to hear Strawberry preach on Tuesday of that week.

On the designated evening he found himself getting ready at a lackluster pace. For a while he contemplated not going. An evening at a Sweet Once Center seemed about as inviting as a hot tub full of frog slime. But he decided that the evening was supposed to be a fact-checking, fact-gathering mission, not a good time. So he picked up the pace, finished his supper, got in his car, and headed off to do what he had to do.

The Big Here & Now Friendly Sweet One Center

As he pulled into the parking lot, he said "wow!" under his breath. The Big Here & Now Friendly Sweet One Center was a massive building with Wall Street flair. It touched a nerve with him. Believers were supposed to practice stewardship, not squandership. Even in the Havens there was a need for a little more modesty, practicality, and functionality in their buildings. They were supposed to be utilitarian battlefield headquarters, not examples of high-end architecture.

He entered through an immense door on a wall of glass and found himself in a lavish entryway. Then he made his way into the auditorium where a sea of plush seats spread out before an enormous stage festooned with a vast array of stage lights. On

THE GLORIOUS SALVATION MACHINE

the stage a troupe of talented musicians were warming up. He mused to himself, "If only such gift was devoted to the narrow way, instead of the Minimizing way."

He made his way to some empty seating about halfway down the upper section and settled in. Within a few minutes the song leader promenaded himself across the stage to the microphone, shared a few sappy thoughts on serving yourself with the help of the Sweet One, then signaled the worship team to crank up the first song. It sounded more like a head-banger concert than a time of pilgrim worship. The words were no better — they were as shallow as the music was sensual. After five songs the song leader gestured for Strawberry, who appeared from behind the curtain and sauntered to the microphone.

Strawberry Flatters Himself

Strawberry Nostrum—Thank you for coming out tonight to hear my wonderful ministry. I have a tremendous amount of insight into the Deep Significance of the Sanitized Trust. You can trust what I have to say. I am not your typical, average-nobody preacher. I have three advanced degrees from highly respected Deep Signification Indoctrination Institutions. I have shared the platform with some of the biggest names in the ranks of the Big Cheese. I shook hands with the President once. And I won the egg toss three years ago at the *How to be a Spiritual Giant in Three Easy Steps* conference.

We Don't Do Shallow Drivel Here

Strawberry Nostrum—Now for those who are newcomers or visitors, one thing you need to know about this church is that we don't do shallow drivel here.

First of all, we refuse to manipulate men with emotionally-charged meetings designed to give them the warm-fuzzies and make them think that they are freshborn. Men are saved by believing facts, not by experiencing feelings.

Secondly, we don't scratch around on the surface like a bunch of chickens. No sir. Not on my watch. None of that chicken scratching shallowness for us. We go Deep here, real Deep. I hope you brought your scuba gear tonight because you are going to need it.

Before I get into my message, let me share with you a Deep nugget that I discovered several years back. I call it the Five Minute Miracle. If the followers of the Sweet One will do a five-minute devotional every day — two minutes in prayer and three minutes reading the Sanitized Trust — they will find victory. "Five minutes a day keeps the Mad Spirit away." Give this amazing weapon a chance to revolutionize your life.

But enough dallying. I won't keep you waiting any longer for the reason we are here tonight — precious Deepness from the Sanitized Trust.

Salvation Is a Free Gift

Strawberry Nostrum—My text is Romans 6:23, "The Free Gift of the Nice God is Sweet Everlasting." This is one of the Deepest verses in the entire Sanitized Trust.

Now there are many things we could pursue in this verse. We could delve into the ways of the *Nice God*. We could take up the term *gift* and investigate its nuances and complexities. We could look into *Sweet Everlasting*, although we wouldn't see much, for there really isn't much to see. The Sacred Trust tells us, "Eye has not seen, nor ear heard." N*othing* is revealed about it and *nobody* knows anything about it. We know that it exists and that's about it.

What I want to stress tonight is the word *free*. This word is pivotal. Salvation is not merely a gift. Salvation is a *Free* Gift.

Now what does it mean that salvation is a Free Gift? It means that salvation is free in the same way that all free gifts are free. Men don't do anything at all to receive free gifts. They just receive them. This means that men don't have to do anything to obtain the Free Gift of salvation except to receive it. They just have to say *yes* to the offer. This also means that if we tell men they have to do anything other than say *yes* to the offer of free salvation, we are guilty of preaching a Dead Works message that overthrows the freeness of the Free Gift.

Stuck in the Muck in the Hog Pen

Strawberry Nostrum—Now some have raised a controversy over the Dogma of free salvation. They deny that Romans 6:23 teaches that salvation is a Free Gift. They want men to work for salvation through the carnal effort of heart-faith. So who is right? Those who say that salvation is free or those who insist that men must work for it? Thankfully, you don't have to take my word for it or theirs. You can test the matter for yourself and see who is right.

Now the best test for whether a doctrine is true or false is how it relates to sound theology. If it clashes with sound theology, it is false. If it harmonizes with sound theology, it is true.

Let's take up one of the central pillars of sound theology — the Invincible Dogma of the Hog Pen. This doctrine says that all men are totally Hog. They are stuck in the muck in the Hog Pen and unable to save themselves. They are so stuck, in fact, that even if God himself came down from heaven and preached to them face to face and demanded that they flee the Hog Pen, they would still be unable to do so.

Does *working* for salvation harmonize with this Dogma? No. It fits like a square peg in a round hole. If men are stuck in the muck, they are unable to move. And if they are unable to move, they are unable to work — they are unable to flee the Hog Pen — no matter what the heart-faith jibber-jabber says.

Does the *Free Gift* of salvation harmonize with this Dogma? Yes, it does — like a hand in a glove. Even if men are stuck in the muck, they can still say *yes* to the Free Gift of salvation.

We conclude, therefore, that it is not unsound exegesis to see *free* salvation in Romans 6:23. It is sound exegesis that agrees with Invincible Dogma. Therefore, we say, "Let the Nice God be true and every Havenmonger a liar." Therefore, we shout it from the housetops — SALVATION IS FREE! FREE! FREE! ABSOLUTELY FREE!

STRAWBERRY NOSTRUM

The Gospels in the Deep Signification Adjustifier

Strawberry Nostrum—Now what are we supposed to do with the troublesome passages in the Gospels that lay upon us such stupendous moral imperatives that they take our breath away — as take up your cross, strive to enter the strait gate, and lose your life? How do we reconcile their testimony that man must do something to be saved with the Invincible Dogma that man must do nothing? How do we reconcile their apparent validation of real-relationship faith with the Faith Form faith that we preach in our Minimizing Message?

Simple. We put them in the Deep Signification Adjustifier, turn the handle a few times, and — Presto! — the troublesome passages in the Gospels are turned into law, which means they don't have anything to say on the faith question. This makes it much easier for us to adjustify faith down to almost nothing — merely saying *yes* to the Free Gift in the Faith Form. And this almost nothing faith allows us to maintain salvation by faith without undermining the integrity of the Dogma that man must do nothing. For while *almost nothing* is not *absolutely nothing*, it still falls well within the pale of *nothing*.

The Teensy-Weensy Window

Strawberry Nostrum—Now it is absolutely essential that we keep ourselves on the road of almost nothing faith — avoiding the ditch of the Sprinkle Form error of absolutely nothing faith on the left and the ditch of the Haven error of real-relationship faith on the right — that we might save both ourselves and them that hear us from the perils of ditch theology.

To ensure that men follow us down the Minimizing road of almost-nothing faith in the Faith Form, we use teensy-weensy theology. This theology says that although man is muck-stuck in the Hog Pen, he still has, nonetheless, a teensy-weensy bit of free will that allows him to respond to the message of free salvation with a teensy-weensy Faith Form *yes*. As one of my professors succinctly put it, "Despite his Hog Pen predicament, man yet has a teensy-weensy ability to open the teensy-weensy window of his heart and ask the Sweet One to come in."

Make no mistake, guiding men into a teensy-weensy Faith Form is not a convenience, but a necessity. If men attempt to lay hold of the Free Gift of salvation with even the faintest stirrings of real-relationship faith in their breast, they have left the road of almost nothing faith and driven into the muddy ditch of Dead Works.

The Hog Pen Prayer

Strawberry Nostrum—Now my favorite method to guide men into a teensy-weensy Faith Form is the Hog Pen Prayer.

What are the ingredients of the Hog Pen Prayer? Not much. Just confess that you are stuck in the muck in the Hog Pen, that the Sweet One died for muck-stuck men, that muck-stuck men can't be saved by Dead Works like real-relationship faith or fleeing the Hog Pen, that muck-stuck men can only be saved by God Magic, and that you are now trusting in God Magic alone for your salvation.

The moment a man utters the words of this prayer, the Sweet One rides down from the Mystic Plane on the gossamer wings of God Magic and takes up residence in his heart.

The Sweet Presence of the Sweet One

Strawberry Nostrum—Make no mistake, the presence of the Sweet One in the heart, which we call the Sweet Presence, is salvation — eternal salvation.

All who have the Sweet Presence are saved — *regardless* of the motives and intents of their heart, *regardless* of the muck and slop they are indulging, *regardless* of how they live in the Daily Grind, *regardless* of anything, even if they continue in unbelief and rebellion against God for the rest of their life.

Can you say *AMEN!* with me? What a blessing to know that our salvation is a self-authenticating Deep Fact that cannot be questioned, proven false, or invalidated. It is a matter of Mystic Plane truth, not objective discernment in the Daily Grind.

This brings up one of my biggest theological conundrums. I cannot fathom the opposition of the Havens on this point. How anyone could have a problem with the Sweet Presence of the Sweet One is a colossal, mind-bending mystery. But it just goes to show that when men run after real-relationship faith, they cease to have a proper focus. They take their eyes off the Sweet One — they look for the presence of fruit rather than his Sweet Presence as the evidence of salvation.

The Sweet Presence Is Not a Form

Strawberry Nostrum—Now those that find fault with our Minimizing ways love to bash the Faith Form as a dead form and the Sweet Presence as religious pretension. But there are two problems with this ignorant accusation.

First of all, this is a misrepresentation of the Half-Havens. We don't believe in dead forms. It is a plain fact of church history that we walked away from churchy ceremonies and formalism long ago. Formalism is not in our DNA. We are all about reality, not dead religion. And the epitome of reality in religion is the Sweet Presence of the Sweet One in the heart.

Secondly, this is a travesty of discernment. How can men be so naive that they confuse a sinner *praying* the Hog Pen Prayer with a Pharisee *pretending* with dead forms? How can they be so incompetent that they confuse the *reception* of the Sweet Presence with the *deception* of dead religion?

The Dry Splash More Faithful to the Sanitized Trust

Strawberry Nostrum—As long as we are on the subject of the Half-Havens' rejection of dead religion, I should take a moment to defend our position in the Splash controversy. Why do we use the Dry Splash (the Faith Form), rather than the Wet Splash (the Sprinkle Form)? There are two reasons.

One, the Faith Form is much more faithful to the theology of salvation taught in the Sanitized Trust. While the Sprinkle Form meets the *without works* requirement, it fails to meet the *almost-nothing faith* requirement. The Faith Form, however, meets both as it gives us "almost-nothing faith without works."

Two, the Faith Form is more faithful to the experience of salvation we see in the Sanitized Trust — man answering the call of the Sweet One by doing some teensy-weensy salvific form as touching the hem of a garment, standing up from a table, or dropping his nets. The Sprinkle Form bears no resemblance to this experience of salvation. An infant can't consciously and intelligently answer the call of the Sweet One to come to him through a salvific form. But the Faith Form bears a marked resemblance to it in both the *general concept* of a salvific form (ceasing to work), which we see in various passages where men walked away from their jobs, and in the *various expressions* of a salvific form as reaching out the hand in prayer, or standing up, or going forward to meet the Saviour.

Most Believers Are Wishy-Washy Disciples

Strawberry Nostrum—Returning to our train of thought, the faultfinding Havenmongers love to point out that most of those who do the Faith Form never show any evidence in their Daily Grind that they are followers of the Crucified One: the Altar of Worthy Self is not torn down, besetting sins are not forsaken, the Word of God is not continued in, and the narrow path is not taken. They throw a conniption fit over these wishy-washy believers, as if their wishy-washiness were a serious problem.

Well, I have news for them. Their wishy-washiness is not an issue. That is just the way that salvation by God Magic works. Most believers are wishy-washy. And I'm perfectly cool with that because the Nice God is cool with that.

I don't, however, expect you to take my word for it. So I am going to give you six potent theological arguments which prove that wishy-washiness is a non-issue. I want your faith to be built on the Sweet truth, not the opinions of men.

Slowgressive Sanctification

Strawberry Nostrum—My *first* argument in proof of the fact that wishy-washiness is a non-issue is that believers do not get sanctified all at once when they get saved. Their cleansing, conversion, and growth in devotion occurs over time through a process of Slowgressive Sanctification.

This process begins at the time of the Faith Form with an initial burst of sanctification that registers somewhere between hypothetical and paltry. After this the process settles into a more sustainable rate — usually around the speed of an inkspot on a workshirt, but occasionally closer to the speed of molasses in January in North Dakota.

So if you have a problem with believers who bear really slow fruit, you have a problem with Slowgressive Sanctification. And if you have a problem with Slowgressive Sanctification, you have a problem with the Sanitized Trust, for that is the only doctrine of sanctification that can be found in its pages.

Not a Hog Pen Question, But a Sweet One Question

Strawberry Nostrum—My *second* argument in proof of the fact that wishy-washiness is a non-issue is that we live in the age of God Magic. The soteriological significance of this fact is summed up in the well-known maxim, "In the age of God Magic, salvation is not a Hog Pen question, but a Sweet One question." This maxim has two tremendous implications for sound doctrine.

One, forsaking the Hog Pen is not a *condition* of salvation. The only condition of salvation is the Faith Form. If a man has done the Faith Form, he is saved.

Two, forsaking the Hog Pen is not an *evidence* of salvation. The only legitimate evidence of salvation is the historical fact of the Faith Form.

Now don't get me wrong. Don't peg me for someone who is indifferent to the Hog Pen. I don't like the Hog Pen. And I could wish that we saw a lot less slop-swallowing and muck-wallowing among those who have done the Faith Form. But as

THE GLORIOUS SALVATION MACHINE

far as salvation is concerned, it is entirely beside the point if a man continues to swallow and wallow in the Hog Pen after he has said the Hog Pen Prayer. Let me read you a quote from a well known Big Cheese, Dr. Max Imumblight, who teaches at the Swollen Head Institute of Dark Light Studies and has a Ph.D. in Subterfuge.

"When a man is saved, he is saved on the Mystic Plane from the *penalty* of wallowing in the Hog Pen. He is not saved in the Daily Grind from the *power* of wallowing in the Hog Pen, except as a theoretical abstract, which may or may not some day possibly manifest itself in victory. All we need to see in a man to know that he is saved is that sweet, and often invisible, impress of the Sweet Presence, whose only infallible evidence is the Faith Form."

You Can't Know Believers by Their Turning and Doing

Strawberry Nostrum—My *third* argument in proof of the fact that wishy-washiness is a non-issue is that believers cannot be known by their turning and doing. Now some balk at this, but their skepticism leaves me dumbfounded. Do men need proof that the day has arrived? Of course not. And why not? Because the daylight around them is so obvious that nobody needs proof. If a man, despite the daylight, denied that the day had arrived, those around him would suspect him of either levity or insanity. This is the way it is with all obvious facts. They just don't need proof. So why should we have to prove the obvious fact that believers cannot be known by their turning and doing?

Is it not true that everyone who does the Faith Form is saved? Yes! Is it not obvious that the vast majority of those that have done the Faith Form are still in the Hog Pen and not walking the path of discipleship? Yes! Therefore, it is obvious that believers cannot be known by *turning* from the Hog Pen and *doing* discipleship stuff. This is why the Sanitized Trust says, "Never, ever judge anyone under any circumstances, for everyone who even thinks about judging is a hypocrite."

Being a Believer and Being a Disciple Not the Same

Strawberry Nostrum—My *fourth* argument in proof of the fact that wishy-washiness is a non-issue is the Deep Distinction between being a believer and being a disciple. It may come as a surprise to you, but they are not the same thing.

And where do we get this Deep Distinction? It is a simple matter of consistency with Innocuous Minimum Dogma. Is it not true that everyone who does the Faith Form is saved? Yes! Is it not obvious that most who have done the Faith Form are not disciples? Yes! Therefore, we are forced to conclude that being a disciple and being a believer are not the same thing.

Now the importance of this distinction cannot be emphasized enough. When men equate believers and disciples, it invariably leads them into false doctrine. This is why, for example, the Havenmongers deny salvation through the Faith Form alone. If you start with the *assumption* that every believer is a disciple and add the *observation* that most who do the Faith Form are not disciples, you will be forced to draw the *conclusion* that the Faith Form is just a piece of empty superstition.

Further, when men make the mistake of equating believers and disciples, it causes them to have a wrong focus. They take their eyes off the Sweet One and focus on things other than his Sweet Presence. They focus on the presence or absence of Hog Pen mud. Why would anyone want to focus on mud? They focus on human effort: running the race, wrestling, fighting the good fight. Do! Do! Do! Why would anyone want to focus on Dead Works?

Now I could wish that everyone who has done the Faith Form would get radical and pursue discipleship, yet we must walk in reality. Men are saved by God Magic not works. This means that discipleship has absolutely nothing to do with salvation — neither as a condition nor as an evidence. And this means that it is entirely out of place to judge whether or not a person is a believer by whether or not we see discipleship in their Daily Grind. We may *encourage* men to be disciples, but we must not *require* them to be disciples.

THE GLORIOUS SALVATION MACHINE

James in the Deep Signification Adjustifier

Strawberry Nostrum—Now I can hear the Havenmongers hollering that James says, "Faith without works is dead." Well, they can holler all they want. I will not give in one inch to the legalizing ways of those who want to trample on salvation by God Magic. This is a matter of honor. This is a matter of sound doctrine and a sound hermeneutic. The fact is, the only reason anyone finds unsound doctrine like real-relationship faith in the book of James is the lack of a sound hermeneutic.

So how does a man get a sound hermeneutic? By obtaining and using a Deep Signification Adjustifier. And where can you get one of these wonderful tools? Every preacher who studied at an institution that affirms the Minimizing Imperative has one in his Big Here & Now Toolbox. And what does this wonderful tool do? It takes passages that seem as unpleasant as mold to men and alchemizes them into Minimizing gold.

Let's take, for instance, the well-known problematic passage in Hebrews which says, "Holiness, without which no man shall see the Lord." Now the hermeneutic of the Havens gives us an interpretation as unappealing as mold, "Without holiness in his life, a man shall never see God." In other words, the freshbirth infuses holiness into the heart of the believer, so if a man doesn't have holiness in his life, he is not freshborn, he is not a believer, and he is not going to Sweet Everlasting.

The hermeneutic of the Half-Havens, on the other hand, gives us Minimizing gold, "Without holiness, no man shall see the Sweet One in your life." In other words, the freshbirth is the Sweet Presence of the Sweet One, which does not necessarily manifest itself in the Daily Grind, so if you don't have holiness in your life, there is nothing to worry about. This does not mean that you are not a freshborn believer and that you are not going to Sweet Everlasting. It only means that no man can see outward evidence that you are freshborn.

Likewise, when we run James through our Deep Signification Adjustifier, we derive a hermeneutically sound interpretation that upholds the Sweet Dogma of salvation by God Magic alone through the Faith Form alone. The phrase "faith without works is dead" does not mean that your *faith* is dead if men cannot see obedience in your life. It simply means that your *testimony* is dead. Can you see the difference? The fact that those who have done the Faith Form are not *showing* works does not mean they are not *going* to Sweet Everlasting. It only means that others are incapable of *knowing* that they are going. Back in my Deep Signification Indoctrination Institution days, I learned a handy aphorism from one of my professors — "No show means no know, not no go."

Sweet Position Theology

Strawberry Nostrum—My *fifth* argument in proof of the fact that wishy-washiness is a non-issue is the Dogma of Sweet Position. When a man does the Faith Form — the Eternally Efficacious Evangelical Event for those who love theological terminology — he enjoys a Sweet Position in the Sweet One. When God looks down from heaven, he doesn't see him, he sees the Sweet One in his perfect righteousness. This means that there is no danger — ever — that a man who has done the Faith Form might be exposed as an unsaved hypocrite with an empty profession of faith, no matter what he does or is.

But what about professing Christians who have no intention of forsaking their sin? Not a problem. What about professing Christians wallowing in some of the nastiest mud in the Hog Pen? Not a problem. What about professing Christians who are as wicked as the Mad Spirit himself? Not a problem.

My friends, if you only learn one thing tonight, let it be this. Salvation has nothing to do with what a man does or how he lives — it has nothing to do with his *state*. Salvation is entirely a matter of his *standing* on the Mystic Plane. And his standing is based on the Faith Form alone. There is zero relationship between state and standing. Isn't this the Sweetest piece of Sweet theology you have ever had tickle your ears?

THE GLORIOUS SALVATION MACHINE

The Believer Is Two Persons

Strawberry Nostrum—My *sixth* argument in proof of the fact that wishy-washiness is a non-issue is the Dogma of Two Persons. Salvation doesn't change a man; it makes him two persons. This is my absolute favorite argument.

Prior to the Faith Form a man is only one person, the Old Man. The Old Man lives in the Hog Pen. When a man does the Faith Form, God puts a second man inside him, the New Man. Now he is two persons: the Old Man and the New Man. These two must not be confused. They are entirely different persons.

The Old Man cannot be cleaned up, changed, or converted. He can't escape the Hog Pen, nor can he be delivered from it. All he can do is wallow and swallow in its filthy confines every day in Talk, Think, and Walk.

The New Man, on the other hand, is perfectly clean and can't get dirty. There is no need, nor shall there ever be a need, for him to undergo change or conversion. He is stuck outside the Hog Pen and can't get in it.

This has incredible, ear-tickling ramifications for those who love the sweet song of salvation by God Magic alone through the Faith Form alone. We can wallow in the Hog Pen all we please, and it doesn't affect our Sweet Everlasting one bit, because what the Old Man does is entirely irrelevant. We have Sweet Everlasting because the New Man — in all his Mystic Plane glory — lives in us.

Are you following me! **We can be carnal! We can be lazy! We can turn our backs on following the Crucified One! And we still have a ticket to Sweet Everlasting! Can you shout *Amen*! Isn't this good stuff!**

The New Man Is Not a Daily Grind Reality

Strawberry Nostrum—Now a right understanding of the New Man is necessary if we would enjoy the blessed assurance of free salvation.

The New Man is not a Daily Grind reality. It has nothing to do with an actual washing and renewing of the heart by the

Word of God and the Spirit of God. It has nothing to do with changes on the outside that testify to all that the inside has been changed. Requiring real heart change that brings real change in the Daily Grind is the horrible, deplorable heresy of Dead Works.

The New Man is a Mystic Plane reality. This means that the New Man is under no obligation to change anything in a man's heart or Daily Grind. In most believers he does little more than sit in his lawn chair, watching and waiting — watching the Old Man frolic in the Hog Pen and waiting for the blessings of Sweet Everlasting. Occasionally he gets motivated and makes a few half-hearted changes, but nothing significant enough to challenge the integrity of the Dogma of the Hog Pen — all men, even believers, wallow in the Hog Pen ever day in Talk, Think, and Walk.

The Deep Challenged

Strawberry Nostrum—Now Havenmongers point out that we don't have this wishy-washiness problem if we preach real-relationship faith instead of the Faith Form. Maybe not. But then we have a worse problem — trampling on sound doctrine. What good are things like repentance, obedience, holiness, and serving God if we must trample on the Invincible Dogma of salvation by God Magic alone through the Faith Form alone to see them in the lives of men?

And why do Havenmongers trample on sound doctrine? For one reason: they are Deep Challenged. They have no doctrinal depth. They read the Sacred Trust with superficial glasses that keep them from seeing the Deep truths that captivate the lovers of God Magic.

My friends, Depth is the greatest need of our day. The church is filled with shallow men who focus on superficial things that look good in the Daily Grind — like heart-faith with its turning and doing. What we need are Deep men who focus on Deeply Significant things which truly are good — like God Magic in the Faith Form.

Don't underestimate the gravity of the crisis that is brewing around us. Spiritual Depth is not a matter of preference, like whether you prefer coffee or tea. It is a matter of faithfulness to sound doctrine. If we don't take a Deep stand and build a Deep sea-wall of Deep doctrine in the hearts and minds of faithful churchgoers everywhere, the tsunami of shallowness welling up on the horizon will wash away all the glorious salvation machinery in the land.

Real-Relationship Faith Is Heresy

Strawberry Nostrum—Now the first step to taking a Deep stand is learning to recognize and reject real-relationship faith for what it is — heresy. While dozens of arguments could be forwarded that prove its heretical nature, I am only going to give you four. If you familiarize yourself with them, you will never be blown and tossed — much less shipwrecked — by the winds of Haven doctrine.

First of all, it tramples on the Invincible Dogma that salvation is by God Magic alone through the Faith Form alone, not through the Dead Works of real-relationship faith, lest any man should boast of real-relationship faith.

Secondly, it tramples on the Invincible Dogma of the Hog Pen, which states that man cannot believe on the Crucified One with real-relationship faith — he cannot forsake the trough and the mire, climb out of the Hog Pen, and return to the Father — not even if the Crucified One himself came down and preached to him face to face.

Thirdly, it tramples on the Great Illumination, which states that all effort is sin. Folks, man is at war with God and human effort is part of this war. If he attempts to end the war with the human effort of heart faith — actually drawing near to the Crucified One, surrendering, and laying down the weapons of unbelief (his sins) — he continues the war. Make no mistake, this human effort to end the war is tantamount to shaking one's fist in God's face. It is no surrender at all. It is continuing in rebellion.

The only way to actually end this war is to submit to the Faith Form. When a man makes this effort at effortlessness, the Nice God graciously accepts it as the end of human effort and declares him a non-rebel on the Mystic Plane.

Fourthly, it tramples on the Invincible Dogma of Unsplashed Holiness, which says that whatsoever is not of participation and confidence in the Faith Form is sin. No matter how much you see and how good it looks, the apparently noble stuff in the Daily Grind of a Havenmonger is only the illusion of holiness. It is Unsplashed Holiness. It is dead human effort.

Faith Is Believing Facts

Strawberry Nostrum—So what is faith, then, if it isn't real-relationship faith? It is simply believing facts. Nothing more, nothing less, and nothing else. And by faith I mean head-faith. Faith is a function of the brain cells, not the heart cells.

And what facts are we supposed to believe? The Four Muck-Stuck Facts:

One, all men are helpless Hog Pen wallowers. They are stuck in the muck in the Hog Pen without remedy or recourse.

Two, salvation was purchased for Hog Pen wallowers by the blood of the Sweet One.

Three, God ministers his salvation to Hog Pen wallowers by God Magic through the Faith Form.

Four, all who give lip-service to the first three points in the Faith Form are saved with eternal salvation.

Isn't this wonderful? Faith boils down to *simply trusting* in God Magic in the Faith Form. This is so simple. Why do men want to make faith so complicated? Faith just relaxes in God Magic like frogs floating in a pond.

Repentance Means "Change Your Mind"

Strawberry Nostrum—Now what does repentance mean if faith is simply mental assent to a few Innocuous doctrines in the Faith Form? Have I got some Sweet ear-tickling music for your ears! If we run repentance through the Deep Signification

THE GLORIOUS SALVATION MACHINE

Adjustifier, we discover that it does not mean forsaking sin. It does not mean turning one's back on slop-swallowing and mire-wallowing in the Hog Pen. It simply means "to change one's mind." That's it. And the only change of mind we need is to admit that we are Hog Pen wallowers who need God Magic salvation. If this sounds familiar, if this sounds like the Faith Form, that's because it is the Faith Form. Repentance and the Faith Form are Sweet synonyms.

Salvation Is a Nothing, Nothing Proposition

Strawberry Nostrum—Well, it is time to start winding this message down. Tonight we took a good, close look at what the Sanitized Trust really says about salvation. And what must we conclude? For all who have an ear that can be tickled, "Salvation is a nothing, nothing proposition." There is nothing that must be done as a *condition* of salvation — not even something as apparently noble as real-relationship faith. And there is nothing that must be seen as *evidence* of salvation — not repentance, not obedience, not holiness, not purity, and not devotion. Absolutely nothing is required. Not one ounce of heart-faith to *be* saved. Not one piece of fruit to *see* saved.

Flush Your Carnal Understanding

Strawberry Nostrum—In the light of such clear testimony, why do the Havens reject Faith Form salvation? Why do they hammer away at simple Faith Form believers, challenging them to go back to the Sacred Trust and study, study, study to see whether the Faith Form and the Invincible Dogmas that support it are true?

There is only one reason — lack of humility. In their pride they lean on their own carnal understanding and refuse to do the one thing that is absolutely essential to see and appreciate sound doctrine — they refuse to flush. If they could only, somehow, be persuaded to flush, their eyes would be opened, and they would see that the error they oppose is really the truth.

Now don't misunderstand me. I am not asking men to flush their brains down the drain. The Nice God gave us a brain and he expects us to use it. I am asking men to flush their carnal confidence in their own carnal understanding down the drain. I am asking them to put off the carnal mind and put on the spiritual mind. I am asking them to use their God-given brains the way the Nice God intended — looking up a few Ironclad Interpretations given as proof texts, saying *Amen*!, and trusting the Invincible Dogmas.

This brings up a wonderful side benefit of the Flush. Men don't have to study, study, study. They don't have to figure out for themselves what the Sacred Trust teaches. They don't have to waste their precious time investigating the context or the testimony of the rest of the Sacred Trust looking for light. If they lean on the Big Cheese, they can get by with a superficial knowledge of the Sacred Trust. They don't have to continue in the Word, or labor in the Word and in doctrine, or study to show themselves approved.

Tickling Ears Saves Souls

Strawberry Nostrum—Now fault-finding men will not be moved by arguments like those I have given you tonight. They will still complain about the lack of fruit in the lives of those who do the Faith Form. You know what I say? Let them run their mouths. If they want to worry about secondary matters like fruit and discipleship, that's fine. That's their business. I have made primary matters like evangelism and outreach my business. I aim to be as productive as possible in these matters. I want results. And why do men of God like myself make such a big deal about results? Because God cares about results. He wants to see the biggest numbers possible.

That's why we mix Minimizing theology and Big Here & Now methodology in our outreach. Nothing produces big numbers better than this combination. It is *the* cutting edge of evangelism. This combination intentionally capitalizes on the fact that men prefer to do the Weekly Duty in a Big Here &

Now environment that conforms to their Big Here & Now tastes. It intentionally exploits the fact that men prefer to sit through Droning that reinforces the ear-tickling message that they don't have to choose between filling their Big Empty with the Big Here & Now and fulfilling their duty to God.

God Wants Men to Be Happy.

Strawberry Nostrum—Speaking of filling the Big Empty, it is an Innocuous Minimum axiom that God wants men to be happy. Not merely happy despite our Big Here & Now because we have a happy Sweet Everlasting coming, but happy right here, right now in the stuff of the Big Here & Now. Of course, we don't want to go to Sugar Kid extremes and focus on *quantity*. Man's happiness does not consist of the abundance of his possessions. We want to focus on a *quality* life. That is the life that truly honors the Sweet One.

So how do we live a quality life? By living life to its fullest. Make no mistake. This isn't about us. This isn't a hedonistic, man-centered pleasure trip. This is about honoring the Sweet One. The Sanitized Trust says that the Sweet One came that we might have a more abundant life — a life lived to its fullest — in the Big Here & Now. So if we would honor the Sweet One, we must make a concerted effort to live life to its fullest.

And how do we live life to its fullest? Simple. We determine that from this day forth we are number two, not number one. This means that we quit maximizing the Big Here & Now in a self-centered way and start maximizing it in a Sweet-One-centered way.

And how do we do this? By doing three simple things. *One*, we give glory to the Sweet One in everything we place on the Altar of Worthy Self: whether coveted pleasures, coveted possessions, or the pride of life. *Two*, we only place stuff on the Altar that the Sweet One approves of according to a fully-legitimate Minimization of the Sanitized Trust. And *three*, in our pursuit of fun stuff, we don't forget noble stuff. Adding a little noble stuff to the mix makes us complete Big Here & Now persons.

When we do these three things, we can actually fit more stuff on the Altar of Worthy Self, and we are actually more likely to fill the Altar of Worthy Self to overflowing. In other words, there is Big Here & Now gain, not Big Here & Now loss, when we make ourselves number two.

So if you haven't yet done it, make yourself number two, make the Sweet One number one, fill the Altar of Worthy Self to overflowing, and live life to its fullest.

Tearing Down the Altar Is Bare Feet

Strawberry Nostrum—My friends, turn a deaf ear to anyone who tries to tell you that God wants you to tear down the Altar of Worthy Self and turn your back on pursuing a quality life in the fun stuff of the Big Here & Now. This path is wrong on three accounts.

One, it rejects God's way of happiness — which we just went over — which is living life to its fullest in the fun stuff of the Big Here & Now.

Two, it rejects God's design for man. God created us to be human beings here on earth. If we tear down the Altar and turn our backs on the Big Here & Now, we deny our humanity.

Three, it rejects God himself. Rejecting God's way and God's design is rejecting God.

Those that take this happiness-rejecting, humanity-denying path might as well throw their shoes away and go live barefoot in a cave, far from civilization. For turning one's back on the Big Here & Now is the same error, in spirit, as the ancient error of Bare Feet extremism — whether ascetics in cold caves or monks in cold monasteries.

Strawberry Leads in the Hog Pen Prayer

Strawberry Nostrum—Now what about you? Do you want to enjoy the quality life that the Sweet One came to give man?

THE GLORIOUS SALVATION MACHINE

It all starts with accepting his Free Gift of salvation. And the only way to accept this Free Gift is to do the Faith Form.

I am going to give everyone here tonight the opportunity to do the Faith Form in the comfort of your own seat. Will everyone please bow your heads and close your eyes. Thank you. Now, if you want to get right with the Sweet One, just repeat the following prayer after me.

"Dear Sweet One ... I confess that I am hopelessly stuck in the muck in the Hog Pen ... And helplessly devoted to eating the swill in the trough ... I believe that you died for all Hog Pen wallowers ... So that we can be saved no matter what ... Even if we never forsake the Hog Pen ... Please come and live in my Hog-swill heart ... And save me from the penalty of my sins regardless of the state of my heart ... And give me Sweet Everlasting without condition or evidence in my Daily Grind ... I thank you for giving me your Sweet Presence ... Amen."

Once in God Magic, Always in God Magic

Strawberry Nostrum—Congratulations to those who prayed this prayer. You are now saved with *eternal* salvation. This means that your salvation is a settled matter. It can never be legitimately called into question or exposed as a sham.

Never fear that you might be pretending to be a Christian — no matter how much carnality, lukewarmness, or filth you see in your heart and Daily Grind. Don't let anyone bully you into questioning your salvation because you are still in the Hog Pen — no matter how deep your wallow or nasty your slop.

The Sanitized Trust says, "He that does the Faith Form shall be saved by God Magic." That means that if you said the Hog Pen Prayer, you are saved by God Magic. And God Magic is as definite and permanent as a moment in history — it can never be taken back or undone. As the Deep maxim says, "Once in God Magic, always in God Magic."

Peregrinus Hears Enough

Peregrinus could bear no more. Though the meeting was not finished, he stood up and made his way to the exit. He paused at the front door, sighed, pushed it open, and headed for his car. He was grieved and unnerved. The God Magic error was deeply entrenched in the Half-Havens — far worse than he had suspected. It reminded him of a verse he had read that morning, "The whole head is sick, and the whole heart faint. From the sole of the foot to the head, there is no soundness."

He climbed into his car, stared into space for a moment, then turned to God in prayer. He asked him to raise up leaders that would take the work forwards and not backwards, to higher ground, not lower ground. Then he started his car, backed out of his parking spot, and headed for home — to the comfort of his favorite chair and his favorite book, the Bible.

CHAPTER TEN
WILLY RUSH FORWARD

Peregrinus Hesitant

After listening to Strawberry Nostrum preach, Peregrinus was hesitant to go hear Willy Rush Forward. It seemed like a waste of time to endure another message that would almost certainly be another God Magic corruption of the Wonderful Message. Why waste an evening that could be spent reading the Sacred Trust and a good book, like the classic book on prayer he had recently purchased?

Yet his conscience — based on the passage which said that he ought to judge matters on the basis of two or three witnesses — prodded him for three witnesses. Strawberry and Jumping Jack made two. If he heard Rush, he would have three. Then his estimation of the God Magic error in the Half-Havens would be founded upon sufficient observation.

In the end principle prevailed against preference. He checked Southside Decision Elicitation Station's calendar of events on the Internet and discovered that they were having a series of special evangelistic meetings starting that very Thursday night. He sighed and made plans to go.

Southside Decision Elicitation Station

On Thursday Peregrinus found himself fighting heaviness the whole day at work. He wasn't looking forward to the evening. On the drive home his heaviness intensified. By the time he got home, it felt like his pants were filled with sand. He shuffled slowly around the house getting ready to go. He compared his predicament to that of a man getting ready to go out to a nice

THE GLORIOUS SALVATION MACHINE

restaurant for dinner — to enjoy a steaming plate of nasty pond algae. Yet somehow he managed to get ready, get behind the wheel, and get going down the road.

When he arrived, he discovered that the parking lot was full. He drove around for several minutes trying to find an empty spot. He was just starting to entertain the idea of giving up and going home — a prospect he was only too happy to indulge — when he spotted an empty place. He parked, dragged himself out of his car, and trudged to the main entrance.

When he entered the building, he noticed the main auditorium doors directly in front of him and headed for them, weaving his way through milling groups of churchgoers. As he passed through the doors, he spotted several empty aisle seats off to his far left, made his way to one, and settled in.

The piano player was playing a rousing hymn in a pepped up manner to help induce a high-powered atmosphere. Spotlights highlighted the microphone at center stage where the star of the show would soon stand. He sighed as he contemplated the contrast between the showmanship prevalent in many churches and the earnest spiritual warfare of those attempting to pursue the same path which the great men and movements in church history pursued — faithfulness to the Wonderful Message, the Sacred Trust, the Crucified One, and the foundational doctrines of the faith no matter what the cost.

The Song Leader Flatters Willy

A few minutes later the song leader stepped up to the front, announced the first hymn, and led the audience in old-time worship — randomly picking two verses from each selection. At the close of the fifth and final hymn — another rousing piece — he gave a little testimony.

Song Leader—I absolutely love it here at Southside Decision Elicitation Station. We see people make decisions in every meeting. I thank the Nice God a hundred times a day that he gave us such a mighty preacher. Our Willy is a born salesman. He could sell sand to camel ranchers in the Sahara Desert. You know, if it wasn't for Willy, I wouldn't be in a church building this evening doing the Weekly Duty. But when he showed me how easy it was to get right with the Nice God and how I didn't have to leave the Hog Pen or give up anything in the Hog Pen, I just knew getting saved was the right thing for me. So here I am today.

Well, let me turn it over to Willy …

Welcome to Our World Class Operation

With that introduction Willy stepped up to the microphone with all the swagger of a well-oiled politician and began to work the audience.

Willy Rush Forward—Welcome to the Southside Decision Elicitation Station. Not only do we have one of the premier decision elicitation operations in the country, we have the best church softball team in the state and a shelf full of trophies to prove it. This is a world-class operation.

Everything is geared to persuade as many people as possible to make a decision to accept salvation. We aim at precision decision elicitation. Nobody does it better. We have this down to a science. We do whatever it takes to bring men in and get them to do the Faith Form. Our motto is "As many as possible, as fast as possible."

However, despite our great burden to win souls, we won't compromise in our evangelistic endeavors. We don't believe in that Mega Growth stuff, which brings men in with fun stuff. No way, not on my watch. We bring them in with truth. If men aren't drawn by the truth, they aren't drawn at all. And what truth do we draw men with? Two glorious truths: the truth of free salvation by God Magic through the Faith Form and the truth of serious Innocuous Minimizing.

But just because we refuse to draw men with fun stuff doesn't mean that we don't offer fun stuff. We have fun stuff galore for men after they have been drawn by the truth. Those that have been coming here for a while know exactly what I am talking

THE GLORIOUS SALVATION MACHINE

about. We are not afraid to go head-to-head with any church in the country in fun stuff opportunity comparison.

We Practice Exsnoozitory Teaching

Willy Rush Forward—Now although we emphasize free salvation and serious Minimizing, they are not the only truths we teach and preach. We give people the whole counsel of God. We practice exsnoozitory teaching. Every four years we preach through the entire Sacred Trust: every book, every chapter, every verse, and every word.

Now there are passages that we don't say much on because we don't have much to say on them, because we don't understand them, because we don't study them, because they aren't important enough to us to study them. But we do give them the obligatory lip service, because they are in the Sacred Trust.

I hope no one thinks that this superficial treatment reflects negatively on us. It actually reflects negatively on the passages themselves. They don't have anything important to say to us. They cover subjects that are irrelevant as far as our Minimizing testimony is concerned.

But despite their irrelevance, despite the fact that they don't offer anything for the edification of Minimizing churches, they still deserve to be heard. Like a row of grinning, squirming four-year olds up in front of the church trying to recite a memory verse, they are a necessary piece of protocol.

Bugaloojistan and Bible Prophecy

Willy Rush Forward—Speaking of protocol, that reminds me of politics, which brings to mind current events, which leads me to ask: have you heard about the amazing things that are happening in Bugaloojistan? I have spent a lot of time the past few days trying to get to the bottom of this story. The real truth is nothing like the carefully crafted propaganda we are fed by the major news outlets. This isn't surprising of course. You can't believe one iota of what you hear or read in the media.

Major media is just a pile of propaganda rags that take their cues from the shadow barons behind the scenes. They filter, manipulate, and doctor the news to make agenda-promoting fodder for the masses. If you don't already know, you will soon figure out that one of my favorite themes is exposing the collusion, the cover-ups, and the crafty conditioning — the surreptitious brainwashing — of the media.

But cutting to the chase, let me give you the real inside scoop. In my not so humble opinion, I think these events are alluded to in the Bible in an obscure prophecy in the book of Isaiah …

Willy then regaled the audience for more than fifteen minutes with his perspective on current events, his insight into global affairs and world politics, and his own speculations on how the current events in the news could possibly lead to scenarios that could possibly degenerate into the circumstances that will — according to the Bible — lead to the rise of the antichrist. After this long-winded perambulation down the path of prophetic speculation, interspersed with several puffs of his expertise in such matters, Willy worked his way back to his message.

Three Easy Steps

Willy Rush Forward—Now that I got that out of my blood, let's turn our focus to the reason we are here. My proof text this evening is the story of the prodigal son. This passage is often misunderstood. Preachers put way too much emphasis on external, irrelevant details like the prodigal actually leaving the Hog Pen. If we run this passage through the Deep Signification Adjustifier we remove the external, irrelevant details and focus on three vital things that the prodigal son did. One, he *rose* up. Two, he *rushed* to his father. Three, he *recited* a preplanned prayer of repentance.

This is a simple message of salvation. And this is why we preach a simple message here at Southside Decision Elicitation Station. Just like we see in our text this evening our message has three easy steps: RISE, RUSH, and RECITE. All a man needs to do is *rise* up off his seat, *rush* down to the altar, and

THE GLORIOUS SALVATION MACHINE

recite the Hog Pen Prayer. We call these steps the three R's of Decision Elicitation. They get men down to the altar in droves to lay hold of free salvation. We have experienced explosive growth since we started using them.

Men Must Do Something

Willy Rush Forward—Speaking of salvation, I am tired of hearing people say that men don't need to do anything to be saved — like surrender or repent. Where do they come up with such nonsense? Don't they read the Sacred Trust anymore? Does it just sit around the house collecting dust?

Where do people come up with silly notions like the teensy-weensy window? Seriously! — all men have to do is open the teensy-weensy window of their heart and ask the Sweet One to come in!? I don't see that in my Sacred Trust!

Where do people come up with ideas like having everyone bow their head, and then asking those who want to be saved to raise their hand. Raise your hand!? Where's that in the Bible!

What similarity do such methods bear to the surrender and repentance that the Sweet One preached? None! That's why we don't use such shallow techniques around here. No sir.

In my Sacred Trust I read that when the Sweet One called his disciples they did something — they got up from what they were doing and went to him. They surrendered and repented. That is why we do things differently around here. That is why we are neither ashamed nor afraid to preach that men must *do* something. They must surrender and repent without delay. Today is the accepted time.

Surrender and Repentance Mean the Altar Call

Willy Rush Forward—Now don't confuse a sound view of surrender and repentance — that is, a Sanitized view — with a Dead Works view of the same. Surrender is not submitting to the will of the Crucified One. And repentance is not fleeing the Hog Pen. Even if God himself descended from heaven in all his glory, stood eyeball to eyeball with a trembling sinner, and demanded that he surrender and repent in the legalistic sense, he couldn't. Man is stuck in his Hog Pen ways. He can't come to his senses and walk away from his trough and his mire. He is doomed to Hog swallow and Hog wallow every day in Talk, Think, and Walk.

My friends, not even God Magic is able to fix this Hog Pen problem to any great extent in most instances. The majority of those who are saved by God Magic never produce significant changes in their Daily Grind like Hog Pen departure. But this does not mean that they aren't saved by God Magic. It just means that they haven't been changed by God Magic.

So what do I mean by surrender and repentance? I mean the good old-fashioned Altar Call — coming down to the front and publicly acknowledging that you are powerless and can't do anything, that you are done with carnal human effort, and that you are putting your confidence in salvation by God Magic alone through the Faith Form alone. This is the only surrender and repentance that means one hoot to God.

Repentance Means "Change the Behind"

Willy Rush Forward—While we are on the topic, I should point out that many preachers wrongly teach that repentance merely means "change the mind." This is shallow theology. While it is true that repentance means "change the mind," that is not all that it means. Repentance is not merely a mental exercise. It is a mental exercise that leads men to get up and walk away from their old way of life to embrace a new way of life — like we see in the pages of the New Testament.

Now the Altar Call streamlines scriptural repentance into a simple form that makes it easy for men to walk away from their old way of life (saying *no* to the Sweet One) and embrace a new way of life (where they *know* the Sweet One). In fact, the Altar Call is — hands down — the best choice in Faith Form methodology if you want to emphasize going through the motions of repentance. All men have to do is get off their behind, get their behind down to the front, and get right with

God. This is why you sometimes hear me say that repentance means "change the behind."

The Altar Call Is Not an Empty Religious Form

Willy Rush Forward—Now some preachers are determined to discredit the Altar Call. They insist that it is just an empty religious form which has no more value than the state of the man's heart. In their estimation, if a man answers an Altar Call moved by heart-faith, he is saved. If, however, he answers it moved by mere religious inclinations or considerations, he is not saved. But this thinking is fatally flawed. It fails to take into consideration three strong arguments why the Altar Call is not an empty religious form.

One, we in the Half-Havens do not believe in salvation by empty religious forms. Our rejection of empty religious forms is a fact of church history. We are death on empty religious forms. Yet we utilize the Altar Call. Chew on the ramifications of this for a few minutes. Would we be using the Altar Call if it were an empty religious form? No! Therefore, the Altar Call cannot possibly be an empty religious form.

Two, God's chosen means to communicate salvation to man is the Faith Form. God invites man to receive the Free Gift of salvation, and man says *yes* to the offer in the Faith Form. Now it is beyond dispute that the particular practice of the Altar Call belongs to the general category of Faith Forms — indeed, it is the grand daddy and gold standard of Faith Forms. But if the Altar Call belongs to the category of Faith Forms, how can it rightly be regarded as an empty religious form?

Three, all who do the Faith Form are indwelt with the Sweet Presence of the Sweet One. Now, as I just mentioned, the Altar Call is indisputably a Faith Form. This means that all who do the Altar Call receive the Sweet Presence. And this means that the Altar Call cannot possibly be an empty religious form. For it is unthinkable that God would impart the Sweet Presence of the Sweet One just because men did an empty religious form.

Your Hog Pen Doesn't Matter

Willy Rush Forward—Now for those of you who have done the Altar Call, don't get too worked up if you don't see much change in your life and heart. It may take a while for God Magic to get traction in your life and the inside change to show up on the outside. It may take a long while. It may take a long, long while. It may take never. That's okay. Just trust the Nice God. Man looks on the outside. The Nice God looks on the inside. Don't let anyone call your salvation into question just because they can't see repentance or obedience or fruit in your Daily Grind. Insisting on such things is the horrible, deplorable heresy of Dead Works.

Bear in mind that we live in the age of God Magic. Salvation is not a Hog Pen question, but a Sweet One question. No matter how deep you are in the wallow, no matter how nasty the swill in your trough, if you have done the Faith Form, the Sweet One lives in your heart. And if the Sweet One lives in your heart, then your salvation is a settled matter. Neither its validity nor its reality can ever be called into question.

But I don't want you to lean on my opinion. I want you to be strong in the Sweetness of sound Minimizing doctrine. So let me give you three theological reasons why your Hog Pen doesn't matter if you have done the Faith Form.

The Old Man Is Irrelevant

Willy Rush Forward—The *first* reason why your Hog Pen doesn't matter is the Invincible Dogma that the saved person is two persons. This Dogma states that the man who has not done the Faith Form is just one person, the Old Man, while the man who has done the Faith Form is two persons, the Old Man and the New Man. You heard me right — two different persons. When a man does the Faith Form, God puts a New Man inside him and he becomes two persons.

Now getting this twoness right is critical. The believer must not confuse himself with the New Man. The believer is not the New Man. The believer has a New Man. The believer is the

THE GLORIOUS SALVATION MACHINE

Old Man. The Old Man is stuck in the muck in the Hog Pen, can't be cleaned up easily, is rarely cleaned up in any serious degree, and doesn't need to be cleaned up — not as a condition of salvation and not as an evidence of salvation.

So what is the New Man? The New Man is the God Magic person which the Nice God puts inside the believer — right next to the Sweet Presence of the Sweet One — when he does the Faith Form. The New Man is not there to clean up the Old Man. The New Man is there as a co-testimony with the Sweet Presence that the person is saved by God Magic.

Now this Sweet Dogma has some Sweet ramifications. The first is the irrelevance of the Old Man. Don't worry about him. What he does or does not do in your Daily Grind has nothing to do with your salvation.

The second is the irrelevance of sin. If the Old Man does not matter, then neither does the sin that he commits. This is good news. Sin can make you feel bad. Sin can mess up your life. Sin can hurt you or kill you. But sin cannot take you to Awful Everlasting no matter how deeply or wickedly or rebelliously you wallow in it.

If men look at your life and see a sow returned to her wallow, or a dog returned to its vomit, or a white-washed sepulcher, that's beside the point. If you refuse to take up the cross, or walk the narrow path, or turn from your idols, that's beside the point. Such things are foul, but not fatal.

Now don't get me wrong. I'm not saying you *should* live this way. I'm just saying you *could* live this way, and it wouldn't matter one bit. It wouldn't keep you out of Sweet Everlasting. Salvation is a matter of God Magic in your heart, not you out of the Hog Pen.

Two Kinds of Faith

Willy Rush Forward—The *second* reason why your Hog Pen doesn't matter if you have done the Faith Form is the Invincible Dogma that there are two different kinds of faith — *saving* faith and *serving* faith.

Saving faith is one-hundred percent Faith Form focused. The only thing it does is bring a man to do the Faith Form and trust in it. Attempting to get it to do anything else is about as dumb as trying to get mustard out of a ketchup bottle. It wasn't designed to do anything else.

Serving faith does stuff like flee the Hog Pen, take up the cross, follow the Crucified One, fight the good fight of faith, and endure hardness as a good soldier. This faith, contrary to popular superstition, is not an expression, manifestation, or extension of saving faith. It is an entirely distinct exercise of an entirely distinct faith that is entirely optional. Men regularly manifest saving faith without manifesting any serving faith whatsoever in their Daily Grind.

Finished Salvation

Willy Rush Forward—The *third* reason why your Hog Pen doesn't matter if you have done the Faith Form is the Dogma of Finished Salvation. If you have done the Faith Form, your salvation is a Finished work. There is nothing left for you to do. Everything that needs to be done is done.

Sadly, many today don't believe in Finished Salvation. They believe that men need to finish their salvation with their own carnal efforts. So they exhort men to whip up some heart-faith in the Crucified One that really follows him in the Daily Grind. Then they pull out their Hog Pen litmus paper and test those who have done the Faith Form, looking for Hog Pen departure. If they don't see it in a man's life, they deny that he is saved. They say that his faith is just an empty profession based on a dead form. This fixation on Hog Pen departure makes my blood boil. It is a denial of the Finished Salvation of those that have been Dry Splashed with God Magic in the Faith Form. It is a denial of the eternal security of the believer. As the Sweet axiom says, "Once in God Magic, always in God Magic."

My friends, when the Sweet One was hanging on the cross, he cried, "It is finished." This means that if a man has done the Faith Form, then he has already done everything — and I mean

THE GLORIOUS SALVATION MACHINE

ABSOLUTELY EVERYTHING — that he needs to do to be saved or to be seen as saved. He doesn't need to heart-believe. He doesn't need to serve, follow, or obey the Crucified One. He lacks nothing. He stands perfect in the Sweet One.

Discipleship Is Not Optional

Willy Rush Forward—Now I hope nobody misunderstands the Invincible Dogma of Finished Salvation. This Dogma does not make discipleship optional as many falsely claim.

Discipleship is not optional. The Sweet One never gave us the option to either take discipleship or leave it. He never said, "If you are interested, there is an optional discipleship option." He gave us the astounding moral imperative — "Leave your stuff and follow me." And so we see Peter in the Sacred Trust leave his nets and follow the Saviour. And so we see Matthew get up from his desk in the tax office and follow the Saviour.

Now, I grant that most believers don't take this discipleship mandate seriously. There is little or nothing in their life that resembles the discipleship that we read about in the pages of the New Testament. This is tragic. I wish I could wave a magic wand and make all who have done the Faith Form live a life of serious discipleship. But their lack of discipleship doesn't call their salvation into question. It only calls their discipleship into question. It only says that they have treated their non-optional discipleship as if it were optional.

Zero to Mediocre in However Long It Takes

Willy Rush Forward—We want to be careful, however, that we don't make too much out of the lack of discipleship that we see in most of those that have done the Faith Form. Just because we don't see any discipleship, doesn't mean that there isn't any. It just means that we don't see any.

Interestingly enough, our own *practical* distinction between believers and disciples has contributed to the problem of being too concerned about the lack of discipleship. We use the term *believer* to refer to all who have done the Faith Form and the term *disciple* to refer to believers who manifest discipleship. While this distinction is legitimate, for it helps us guard against the real-relationship faith error, which says that all believers manifest discipleship, there is, strictly speaking, no *theological* distinction between believers and disciples. Believers and disciples refer to the same group of people.

"How can this be?" you ask. Because the Sanitized Truth is, all who have done the Faith Form have some discipleship, even if infinitesimal. They are on the Sweet path of Slowgressive Sanctification, and the Sweet One will bring them from zero to mediocre in however long it takes. Sometimes progress is slow in coming. Sometimes it moves at a snail's pace. Sometimes no progress is made at all during an entire lifetime.

But whether slowgressive or nogressive, the lack of progress is not a problem. It is, rather, an occasion for praise. The Sweet One is at work in his people — in all the glorious working of his Innocuous sovereignty — and he will, in his Sweet time, Slowgressively complete the work that he has Slowgressively started.

There Is No Such Thing As an Empty Profession

Willy Rush Forward—Now faultfinders often ask me what I do with all the empty professions we make in the Half-Havens by running men through the Faith Form like salvation was some kind of mass manufacturing process. You know what I say? "Not my business." What men do after their decision, after their Faith Form, is between them and God. My business is to get as many men as possible saved. And that means my business is to get as many as possible to do the Faith Form.

But if this *practical* answer doesn't deter the faultfinder, then I turn to the high-powered *theological* argument. THERE IS NO SUCH THING AS AN EMPTY PROFESSION! How can there be? Everyone who has done the Faith Form has an infinite manifestation of God Magic residing in his heart in the person of the Sweet One. And it is the height of folly to regard this fullness as emptiness.

THE GLORIOUS SALVATION MACHINE

So don't be bothered by Hog Pen fanaticism. No man who has the Sweet One in his heart has an empty profession, no matter how dark his heart or immoral his life. And therefore, we have no business claiming that a profession is empty based on things we see or don't see. We need to quit looking at irrelevant stuff on the outside, like fruit, and start looking at the relevant stuff on the inside, like God Magic. Would you look for an orange on an apple tree? No! Then why would you look for evidence of God Magic in the Daily Grind? Making an issue out of the Hog Pen is trampling on salvation by God Magic and dishonoring the indwelling Sweet One.

So Great DO NOTHING Salvation

Willy Rush Forward—Now the arguments we have looked at this evening — as the fact that the believer's Hog Pen is a non-issue and the fact that there is no such thing as an empty profession — all point to one wonderful truth. The salvation held out to man in the Sanitized Trust is a "so great DO NOTHING salvation." Man need not and must not do anything to obtain salvation. And we refuse to compromise this truth for any consideration. That is why we reject real-relationship faith as a condition of salvation and why we utilize the Faith Form.

Now nitpickers love to point out that doing the Faith Form is doing something and that doing something is inconsistent with DO NOTHING salvation. But is such nit-picking legitimate? No! When a man does the Faith Form, he makes a sincere effort at Effort Disengagement — he comes to God doing nothing for salvation except trusting in God Magic. And it is inconceivable to think that God would fault this sincere effort to be effortless. So we — as "imitators of God" — turn a deaf ear to those who fault the Faith Form as inconsistent with "so great DO NOTHING salvation."

Too Much Concern for Holiness Tramples on God Magic

Willy Rush Forward—If anything I said tonight sinks into your noggin, may it be this: don't worry if DO NOTHING salvation does nothing in your life. One of the fastest ways to fall into error is to start worrying about obedience and holy living. When men get concerned over the slowness of their Slowgressive Sanctification, when they grow tired of waiting for God Magic to clean up their life, they take matters into their own hands and flee the Hog Pen in their own carnal strength.

Don't be deceived by the apparently wonderful results you see in the lives of those who undertake this self-manufactured holiness. While their Hog Pen departure and their following of the Crucified One look good at first glance, a closer look reveals that underneath the thin coat of apparent holiness there is a thick layer of Unsplashed Holiness — a holiness which is completely unacceptable to God because it despises the Faith Form, tramples on God Magic, and obeys the commands of God with human strength and effort.

Real-Relationship Faith Shuts Down the Machinery

Willy Rush Forward—Now I have already pointed out this evening a few reasons why I don't like real-relationship faith. But let me give you the two biggest reasons why I reject it.

The *first* really big reason is that if the Half-Havens took up the message of real-relationship faith, our salvation machinery would be brought to a standstill.

How so? Through lack of interest. Nobody wants to hear that they must turn to the Crucified One in heart-faith, tear down the Altar of Worthy Self, and actually follow the Crucified One. Men find this message discouraging. If we discouraged them with it, they would quit doing the Weekly Duty. If they quit doing the Weekly Duty, we would have fewer butts in the pews on Sunday morning. If we had fewer butts in the pews, there would be fewer bucks in the offering plate. If there were fewer bucks in the plate, our butt collection centers would run out of money. If they ran out of money, our glorious salvation machinery would grind to a halt. That would be tragic! That would be a stunning blow to the message of salvation by God Magic alone through the Faith Form alone.

THE GLORIOUS SALVATION MACHINE

The Proper Use of the Altar of Worthy Self

Willy Rush Forward—The *second* really big reason I reject real-relationship faith is that it requires men to tear down the Altar of Worthy Self, supposedly for the glory of the Crucified One. I emphatically deny that tearing down the Altar glorifies the Sweet One. How can it? Tearing down the Altar is horrible, deplorable extremism. And extremism cannot glorify him. One of the most important Minimizing lessons that any churchgoer can learn is the virtue and value of avoiding extremes.

Now I won't labor the point that tearing down the Altar of Worthy Self is an extreme, for the odds are that none of you need any convincing in this regard. But I do want to spend a few minutes on the extreme position of the Strawberry camp.

The Strawberry error makes the Sweet One number one in your life and you number two. This sounds good in theory, but it falls far short of true discipleship. The Sweet One does not want you to be number two; he wants you to be number zero. If you are number two, then you are still important and still have authority to put stuff on the Altar. If you are still putting stuff on the Altar, then you are stacking stuff all around the Sweet One, crowding his space with stuff. Do you really think that he is pleased that you force him to share the Altar with stuff?

Friends, the Sweet One must be the only thing on the Altar of Worthy Self. He must be our whole life. We must quit serving ourselves and let the Sweet One serve us. We must stop putting stuff on the Altar and only indulge fun stuff that he holds out to us with his own hand. If it doesn't come from his hand, we don't want it.

And don't fear that this course will lead to boring, for it leads to blessing. We can trust the Sweet One. He knows far better than we do what fun stuff we need to be fulfilled human beings. So what will it be? Will you continue piling fun stuff on the Altar? Or will you shovel the fun stuff off the Altar and put the Sweet One alone on it?

WILLY RUSH FORWARD

Willy Gives an Altar Call

At this point Willy quickly moved the message into Altar Call mode while the intensity of the moment still lingered in the air. He dropped his voice and began to speak in hushed tones. At the same time the piano player began to softly play appropriate Altar Call music.

Willy Rush Forward—Religion is not a mere matter of the head. Head religion is dead religion. Real religion involves the will. That's why we use the Altar Call. The Altar Call requires an exercise of the will. You must choose to get up from your seat and come down to the front.

Now I know how difficult it is to get up and come down in front of hundreds of people. But that is precisely why we use the Altar Call. Through an act of the will in a difficult situation, we weed out the serious seekers from the half-hearted seekers. So if you really want to get saved, just decide to stand up and come on down to the front. Everybody who comes down to this altar for salvation gets saved.

There was a short pause here as Willy waited for men to get up and come down to the altar. When it became obvious that the response was somewhere between piddling and middling and not the mad rush he desired, he took further measures to get the desired effect.

Willy Rush Forward—You know, we really need to fill this altar tonight. The Nice God loves to see an altar full of seeking, hungry, thirsty souls. If you would like to rededicate your life to the service of the Sweet One, you too are invited to come down to the altar. If you have felt spiritually dry this past week, come on down. If you need direction for your life, come on down. If you have a special prayer request, come on down. If you have a head-ache or a tummy-ache, come on down. If your dog died or your washing machine quit this week, come on down.

PRAISE THE SWEET ONE, AT LEAST THREE-QUARTERS OF THOSE HERE TONIGHT HAVE LEFT THEIR SEATS AND ARE HEADED FOR

THE GLORIOUS SALVATION MACHINE

THE FRONT! WE ARE HAVING A REVIVAL! My dear friends, I beg you, if you desire to be saved, now is the time to come down. Don't worry. You won't be alone. You're not going to stick out like a sore thumb. Hundreds have already come down to find blessing from the Nice God and hundreds more are on their way as I speak. If you want to be saved, just stand up and come down. You will find the Sweet One and eternal salvation.

Encouragement for the Newly Faith-Formed

After the flow to the front had slowed to a trickle, Willy and numerous counselors joined the crowd that had come forward. For the next ten minutes, they mingled with them and prayed for their needs. Then Willy returned to the pulpit and dismissed the seekers back to their seats. When everyone was settled back in, he shared a few closing thoughts with the audience.

Willy Rush Forward—Congratulations to every one of you who came forward this evening and did the Faith Form. You have begun a fulfilling new chapter in your life — life with the Sweet One living in your heart. Let me give you a few words of encouragement to help you in your new-found religion. If you take these words to heart, you will grow strong in the Minimizing once delivered unto the churchgoers.

One, with regard to salvation, don't let any doubts or doubters try and take your salvation away from you. The Sanitized Trust says, "For the Nice God so loved the world that whosoever does the Faith Form shall not see Awful Everlasting but have Sweet Everlasting." You **did** the Faith Form. Therefore, you **have** Sweet Everlasting.

Two, with regard to sanctification, learn to let go and let the Nice God. Don't try too hard. Just trust him. Remember that bearing fruit is passive. It is the work of the Nice God, not the carnal work of your own obedience and choices.

Three, give up serving yourself. Determine that you will stop piling stuff on the Altar, that only the Sweet One will be on the Altar, and that you will only indulge fun stuff that comes from his hand. You can trust the Sweet One in this. He cares about your happiness and knows far better than you do what Big Here & Now fun stuff will fill your Big Empty.

Four, with regard to the Weekly Duty, don't miss it any more than you really have to. I understand that things like sports, hobbies, vacations, and recreation get in the way sometimes. I understand that we may not see you on Sunday evenings during football season. That's okay. Just don't let it get out of hand.

Peregrinus Walks Away

Peregrinus couldn't bear to stay for the last few minutes. He rose from his seat — indignation burning in his breast — and headed for the exit. But he was not merely leaving the building and the meeting. He was walking away from Half-Havenism with a doctrinal clarity and a finality that he didn't have when he left Jumping Jack's church. At that time he had merely been uneasy with teachings and practices that didn't seem to square with the Sacred Trust. Now he saw clearly that the well-oiled salvation machinery was an intentional perversion of the Wonderful Message, that the Sanitized Trust was a willful corruption of the Sacred Trust, and that Innocuous Minimizing was an intentional debasement of Christianity.

Now he didn't, of course, flatter himself that the Havens were perfect and had no faults. But one thing was certain: they were serious. They were serious about understanding and applying the entire Sacred Trust. They were serious about heart-faith that really followed the Crucified One. And they were serious about keeping themselves undefiled from the Big Here & Now and from the Great Murky Revival.

CHAPTER ELEVEN
THE GOD MAGIC MENACE

A Bazillion Questions

The next day Peregrinus found it hard to concentrate at work. All day long his mind was occupied with questions that the ministry of Strawberry Nostrum and Willy Rush Forward had raised. He could hardly wait for evening to come, so he could discuss these questions with his preacher friend.

When his shift ended, he ran to his car, raced home, hurried through his wash-up ritual, devoured a bowl of ramen noodles, and sped to the Steaming Joe.

He arrived a half an hour early. When Plowman walked in, Peregrinus was sipping his third cup of coffee, reading the Sacred Trust, and jotting thoughts in his notebook. Peregrinus jumped up and greeted him.

Peregrinus—Hey Brother, am I glad to see you. I have a bazillion questions to ask you after listening to Strawberry and Willy preach their Faith Form nonsense.

Plowman—Fire away.

The Obedience Fuss

Peregrinus—I know we have been over this ground several times already, but how do you answer the charge that looking for turning and doing is Dead Works? The Half-Haven preachers throw a huge fuss over looking for fruit as evidence of faith. They say that requiring men to turn from bad stuff and do discipleship stuff is requiring them to trust in their own carnal efforts and righteousness.

THE GLORIOUS SALVATION MACHINE

Plowman—Keep in mind that Half-Haven preachers make their living by marketing Passive Form salvation. This means that they will protect their living by opposing everything that threatens it. Nothing poses a greater threat to their Passive Form merchandising than real-relationship faith. Therefore, Half-Haven preachers must throw a fuss when men teach and require real-relationship faith.

Peregrinus—So their fussing is just Head Pounding.

Plowman—Yep. And when their Head Pounding is focused on obedience as the evidence of faith, we call their efforts the Obedience Fuss.

Peregrinus—Even Mr. Radio Preacher, though he generally stands against the compromises of the Half-Havens, seems to waver on this point. He argues that the freshbirth is a genuine work of God that bears real fruit. Then he turns around and warns against Dead Works in an unguarded way that *makes* no clear distinction between the dead works of unbelief and the obedient works of faith. This, sad to say, *undermines* works as the evidence of salvation.

Plowman—Yep. Many good preachers have that problem. They try to address the problems caused when men preach a Minimizing gospel, yet they are so intimidated by the Dogma of salvation by God Magic alone through the Faith Form alone that they end up with a half-way solution that never fully frees them or their hearers from the Faith Form quagmire.

Peregrinus—So the Half-Haven nonsense is making inroads in the Havens.

Plowman—There is no doubt about that. The sophistries of Half-Havenism have wormed their way into influential schools, pulpits, and presses, corrupting the Havens and conditioning many preachers to respond in ways that are inconsistent with the real-relationship faith they profess to believe and defend. They think of the Faith Form every time they hear the word *faith*. They water down passages that uphold obedience as the evidence of faith. And they regard every profession of faith as a possession of salvation, even when fruitless and faithless.

Peregrinus—But how do they square such nonsense with the real-relationship faith that they profess to believe?

Plowman—Their solution is to believe (hope for a miracle) that Faith Form professions will metamorphose sooner or later into real-relationship faith in the Crucified One. But this is just as silly as waiting for a stone to metamorphose into a butterfly. You need real-relationship life on the inside in order for real-relationship life to show up on the outside.

The Passive Harangue

Peregrinus—I don't understand how people can people can believe that Passive Form slop.

Plowman—You must remember that the dominant message today is the Faith Form gospel. Day in and day out believers are bombarded from the pulpit, the printed page, and the radio with Faith Form doctrines and mantras until they can't think straight — until they are thoroughly Head Pounded. Every time the issue comes up, they hear the Faith Form earworm whisper the Deep Truth in their ear, "Salvation is by God Magic alone through the Faith Form alone."

Peregrinus—I remember being pounded and hounded when I was in the Half-Havens — man is incapable of doing anything but the Passive Form; man is stuck in the muck in the Hog Pen so bad that not even the life-changing power of the Word of God preached by the Almighty himself can bring him to heart-faith in the Wonderful Message; all who look for evidence of faith in the Daily Grind are putting carnal trust in the bad, bad, nasty-bad heresy of Dead Works; true faith is doing and trusting the Faith Form. Pound. Pound. Pound. Blah. Blah. Blah.

Plowman—That's why we call it the Passive Harangue.

You Can't Argue with Invincible Dogma

Peregrinus—One thing I have noticed about Half-Havenists is that they have no ear for correction. You can't show them from the Sacred Trust that their Invincible Dogmas are wrong.

Plowman—Yep. You can quote the Sacred Trust until you are blue in the face and not get anywhere because the Sacred Trust is not the infallible authority; Invincible Dogma is. The Sacred Trust is merely its handmaiden.

Peregrinus—That is so wrong.

Plowman—Yep. They have things totally backwards. The Invincible Dogmas are not the result of sound exegesis; they are the touchstone of Deep exegesis. The Sacred Trust is not used to determine sound doctrine; it is used, rather, to defend Invincible Dogma.

Peregrinus—It seems crazy to have such confidence in your doctrine that you can't hear a well-framed argument from the Sacred Trust that challenges or overthrows it.

Plowman—It sure does. But their doctrines, in their mind, are not potentially wrong concepts that man has come up with. They are the truth of the living God that cannot be challenged or questioned. To challenge them is to challenge God.

Peregrinus—In other words, you can't argue with Invincible Dogma.

Plowman—That's right. As their Sanitized Trust says, "Man shall not live by bread alone, but by every Invincible Dogma that has proceeded from the mouth of the Nice God."

Putting Band-Aids on Optional Discipleship

Peregrinus—I wish preachers could see that the Faith Form makes discipleship optional. Don't they care about how people live?

Plowman—Sadly, how the sheep live is a secondary issue for many preachers. They rarely teach on topics as discipleship, soldiership, the cross, or obedience. When they do, they bring out their Deep Signification Adjustifier and adjustify them, so they agree with serious Innocuous Minimizing. Their primary focus — what they really care about — is operating a big piece of smooth-running, fast-growing, fun-loving church machinery.

Peregrinus—It's all about numbers. Lots of butts in the pews and lots of bucks in the plate.

Plowman—Most of them would never admit that, but that is what it really boils down to.

Peregrinus—How about preachers that really do care about how their flock lives? Preachers like Mr. Radio Preacher? How do they deal with the problems that are caused by the optional obedience of the Faith Form?

Plowman—They suffer many heartaches and headaches over the frustrating fact that discipleship doesn't naturally follow the Faith Form. They don't know what to do. They have a problem with the missing discipleship. They believe in discipleship and want to see it. But they have a bigger problem with letting go of the Dogma of salvation by the Faith Form alone.

Peregrinus—So when push comes to shove, trust in the Faith Form comes out on top, and the obedient, devoted living that is the result of heart-faith in the Crucified One gets trampled on.

Plowman—That's right. Rather than fixing the problem by letting go of the Faith Form error and replacing it with the truth of real-relationship faith, they resort to dubious messages and methods designed to encourage men to add discipleship to the Faith Form.

Peregrinus—They're just putting band-aids on their optional discipleship problem when major surgery is what is needed.

Plowman—Yep. And their efforts work about as good as sticky notes with dried up sticky. It's hard to get them to stick, and when they stick, they don't stick long.

Peregrinus—You can't add discipleship to a heart that isn't truly freshborn.

Plowman—Amen to that. You can teach churchgoers all day long from the Word of God, but unless they have been truly freshborn, unless they have a new heart from above that thirsts for righteousness and truth, such teaching will not take root and bear fruit.

Shirking Faith and Working Faith

Peregrinus—What do you think of the teaching that there are two kinds of faith — saving faith and serving faith?

THE GLORIOUS SALVATION MACHINE

Plowman—It's a wonderful piece of fiction that allows men to continue living in the Hog Pen, yet flatter themselves that they are on the road to the Father's house.

Peregrinus—How can men believe something so obviously wrong?

Plowman—An old proverb warns us, "Fire in the heart sends smoke in the head." When men commit themselves to a false doctrine, they lose the ability to think clearly about that subject and gain the ability to believe any nonsense that is necessary to maintain the error.

So when men embrace the fiction of salvation by the Faith Form, they are enabled to believe the fiction that there are two kinds of faith — Shirking Faith and Working Faith. They are able to believe that they are saved by Shirking Faith, which boils down to a superstitious confidence in the Faith Form that doesn't change them in any way except for a little Innocuous Minimizing. And they are able to believe that Working Faith, which really follows the Crucified One, is optional. Things like forsaking the Hog Pen and obeying God can be gotten around to whenever they get around to them, if they get around to them. And it really doesn't matter if they get around to them.

Believers and Disciples Refer to the Same Group

Peregrinus—It seems like the distinction which many make between believers and disciples is pretty much the same error as the distinction between saving faith and serving faith.

Plowman—You're right. They are essentially the same error. According to the Faith Form gospel, men exercise saving faith — and become believers — when they do the Faith Form. A small percentage later become disciples when they begin to exercise serving faith.

Peregrinus—I thought I was on the right track.

Plowman—Yep. The Half-Havenists make a mistake when they make a distinction of *reference* between disciples and believers. The disciples are not a small subset of the believers. If we let the Sacred Trust speak, it everywhere assumes that *believers*, *Christians*, and *disciples* are interchangeable terms that refer to the same group of people. For instance, in Acts we read that the believers were originally referred to as *disciples* and later received the name *Christians*.

Peregrinus—So is there any distinction in meaning between disciple and believer?

Plowman—Yes, there is. But the proper distinction is one of *emphasis*. *Disciple* refers to the outward aspect of follower or student that all men can see in our Daily Grind. *Believer* refers to the inner aspect of heart confidence that men can only infer indirectly by what they see in our Daily Grind.

The Great Faith Divide

Peregrinus—Speaking of believers, in the past few months it has become clear to me that the nature of faith is one of the watershed issues that divide the Havens and the Half-Havens.

Plowman—No doubt about that. The Half-Havens and the Havens teach very different conceptions of faith. If one is right, the other is wrong.

If faith is confidence in a religious form — the Faith Form — which does not necessarily produce any changes in the heart or the life, then the Havens are wrong. If faith is confidence in a person — the Crucified One — who changes men on the inside in such a powerful way that their outside changes too, then the Half-Havens are wrong.

These two different concepts of faith are formally known in the theological arena as the Great Faith Divide. Believers must choose one or the other. There is no middle ground. There is no straddling the fence.

Peregrinus—I suppose which side of the fence you stand on makes a big difference in how you understand such verses as "Without faith, it is impossible to please God."

Plowman—Absolutely. Does that verse mean, "Apart from the Faith Form, it is impossible to please God"? Or does it mean, "Apart from real-relationship faith in the Crucified One, it is impossible to please God"?

Or how about the latter half of the verse? Are we supposed to understand, "He that comes to God must give lip service to his existence and must suppose that he fun stuff blesses those that diligently Minimize"? Or are we supposed to understand, "He that comes to God must believe not only that he exists, but that he is a rewarder of them that diligently seek him"?

Obeying the Sacred Trust Is Not Disobeying the Sacred Trust

Peregrinus—I know we have covered this a few times, but how do you answer the argument that requiring repentance is requiring Dead Works? For instance, men quote the Sanitized Trust, "To him that does not work, but simply does the Faith Form, his Faith Form is accounted to him for righteousness," and think they have overthrown the necessity of repentance.

Plowman—That argument is just Head Pounding designed to intimidate men into rejecting heart-faith and embracing the Faith Form.

Peregrinus—That's what I thought. But I can't put my finger on how to answer it.

Plowman—As in all controversies, we must start by standing on the ground of the *congruity* of Scripture. It is impossible for one part of the Sacred Trust to contradict another part. This means that obeying the Bible command to get right with God by repenting cannot possibly be disobeying the Bible warning against trying to get right with works.

It is downright laughable when you watch the Half-Havenists engage in exegetical alchemy trying to change gospel passages that present repentance as a condition of salvation into gospel passages that don't require repentance. Where is their trust in the Sacred Trust? Was God so careless — so sloppy — when he wrote the Sacred Trust that he misrepresented the gospel response that he seeks from men? I don't think so!

Peregrinus—So how do things like repentance fit into the faith picture?

Plowman—The gospel command to believe is presented in the Sacred Trust from several perspectives.

Sometimes the command stands unadorned in its *simple* form: "believe."

Sometimes it appears in its *complex* form, that is, combined with subordinate commands. For example, "believe and be baptized" and "repent and believe." These complex forms say nothing different, in essence, than the simple form "believe." For such things as repentance and baptism, rightly understood, are the fruits of faith and implied in faith.

Sometimes it appears in its *proxy* form, being couched in commands to bring forth the fruits of faith without mentioning faith itself. For example, "repent and be converted" and "repent and be baptized."

Peregrinus—But why the variety of expression?

Plowman—This variety ensures that candid men, who resist Head Pounding and refuse to flush their brain down the drain, will see that the faith advocated by the Sacred Trust is real-relationship faith. They won't confuse the Faith Form with faith. They won't be hornswoggled by the ridiculous notion that a man can have faith without "the obedience of faith."

Peregrinus—This puts the passages which warn against works in far different light than the Half-Haven camp puts them in.

Plowman—That it does. The warnings against works in the New Testament were never intended by God to be warnings against real-relationship faith and its fruits. They were intended to be warnings against the religious works, the self-righteous good works, and the superficial morality which worldly men pursue in the dead faith of form-based religion.

Peregrinus—So rather than forcing what the Sacred Trust says on faith and works to conform to Invincible Dogma, men should conform their doctrinal understanding to what the Sacred Trust says on faith and works.

Plowman—Yep. Far better to let the Sacred Trust shine its light on man's thinking than let man's thinking throw its pall of Dark Light on the Sacred Trust.

THE GLORIOUS SALVATION MACHINE

Faith — Man's Heart in God's Hand

Peregrinus—How about the Dogma of So Great Do Nothing salvation? This teaching seems to take a kernel of truth (we don't work for salvation) and distorts it into error (men can be saved without actually heart-believing on the Crucified One). Sometimes I feel like responding to this error by insisting on So Great Do Something salvation.

Plowman—I empathize entirely. But we must be careful that we respond to error, not react. If we react, we increase the odds that we will embrace an unbalanced position. If we respond, we are far more likely to find a healthy balance. And because faith is a foundational matter, an unbalanced understanding of it will throw the whole of our Christianity out of kilter.

Peregrinus—So how do we balance the doctrine of faith?

Plowman—By bearing in mind that even though man is commanded to believe, his faith is not something he can take a lot of credit for. God is the author and finisher of faith. Its origin and vigor are traced to his hand, not our own. Faith is kindled in the heart of man by the empowering Word of God, the life-giving Spirit of God, the conquering love of God, and the superintending providence of God. And God's hand in faith doesn't stop the moment of salvation. The same Word, the same Spirit, the same love, and the same providence which kindled faith, continue to strengthen and sustain it. From start to finish, faith is man's heart in God's hand.

Faith Is Believing a Person

Peregrinus—What about the teaching that faith is believing facts? I can't bring myself to say that it isn't true, because faith does believe facts, but something seems dreadfully wrong with the Half-Haven handling of this subject.

Plowman—The Half-Haven treatment of faith falls down on two regards.

First of all, the *focus* is wrong. Faith is not merely believing a few doctrinal propositions about salvation. Faith is first and foremost believing a person. It is trusting Jesus the Nazarene,

God manifest in flesh, who was crucified for our salvation. Faith is trusting his integrity, his goodness, his love, his Word, his will, his ways, his promises, his sovereignty, his deity, and his salvation. It is trusting all that he is, all that he says, all that he does, and all that he gives.

Secondly, the *facts* are wrong. What the Half-Havens give us is a discombobulation of true facts and false facts — the truth of salvation by grace is hopelessly entangled with the errors of salvation by God Magic.

Peregrinus—It's the same old problem. Men are getting their doctrine from Innocuous Minimizers, rather than the Bible.

Plowman—That's right. But it doesn't have to be this way. The unadulterated facts of God's salvation can be readily found and readily ascertained by anyone who will study the Sacred Trust with a little honesty and elbow grease.

Look for the Fact of Faith, Not the Act of Faith

Peregrinus—Once you understand that faith boils down to a *relationship* with a person and not *confidence* in a form, it puts things in a whole new perspective.

Plowman—It sure does. Faith is not superstitious trust in some Magic Moment. It is a powerful moral force in the heart, invigorated by the Word of God and energized by the Spirit of God, that is bursting with virtue, valor, and vigor. Its definitive proof is not a moment in the past (the moment of the Form), but a life in the present ("the obedience of faith"). Its proof is *going* the right direction, *gaining* spiritual understanding, and *growing* in grace, faith, hope, and love.

Peregrinus—That reminds me of the passage in James that says, "Faith without works is dead."

Plowman—Yep. If we take the testimony of James at face value, faith is so readily known by what it manifests in the Daily Grind that men may say, "Show me your faith without works, and I will show you my faith by my works." As I like to paraphrase it, "See my Daily Grind? That proves I believe. See your Daily Grind? That proves your Faith Form isn't worth a handful of sand."

Peregrinus—As I have heard you say many times, we need to look for the *fact* of faith, not an *act* of faith.

Plowman—That's right. Men make a costly mistake when they rip the heart out of faith and turn it into a lifeless Faith Form. This easy-believe message bloats many churches with multitudes of decisions who are supposedly sheep, but are, in fact, Hogs. They are committed to their swill and their wallow. They will not forsake their beloved Hog Pen, no matter what the Sacred Trust says, and no matter how many times they are exhorted by those who care about their spiritual welfare.

Saved by the Point, Evidenced by the Line

Peregrinus—I know that the Faith Form teaching isn't true, but men are saved at a definite point in time, right? They are saved the moment they believe, right?

Plowman—Absolutely. A man is saved the moment he turns to the Crucified One in his heart and believes on him. Salvation is by faith alone, not by works.

Peregrinus—The reason I ask is that I am having trouble reconciling the fact that salvation happens in a moment with the fact that we discern salvation by looking for a pattern of obedience over a period of time.

Plowman—When God looks down from heaven upon a man going through the motions of faith, he sees something we can't see — the state of his heart. He knows immediately whether a man has actually heart-believed on the Crucified One or merely engaged in the religious pretension of the Faith Form. He knows immediately whether or not the point of profession will be followed by a line of possession. And in that very moment he seals all who really have believed with his Holy Spirit for the day of redemption.

We have no such ability to peer into the inner recesses of the heart. Therefore, we cannot know a man's state with any degree of certainty until we have seen sufficient evidence in his

Daily Grind. We need to see the presence of the line to know that the point we saw was a real-relationship point and not merely a Faith Form point.

Peregrinus—So man is saved by the point, which is the first moment of faith, but his salvation is evidenced by the line, which is the obedience of faith that follows.

Plowman—That's right. The Sacred Trust does not teach that we can know believers by their point. It teaches, rather, that we can know them by their line. Those who regard the point as the only necessary evidence of faith are religious legalists who are defending salvation by God Magic in the Faith Form.

Peregrinus—But we seem to give people the benefit of the doubt.

Plowman—That we do. As a matter of practice, we give the benefit of the doubt to all who profess faith in the Crucified One until we see conclusive evidence to the contrary. But this isn't normally a long, drawn-out process. Either they start to follow the Crucified One, or they don't.

What Does Faith Look Like?

Peregrinus—Strawberry said another thing that I wasn't sure how to answer. He said we shouldn't look for faith because it can't be seen, and then he ridiculed — with sarcastic questions — those who were stupid enough to look for faith. "What does faith look like? What color is it? How big is it?"

Plowman—When we look for faith, we are not looking to see faith itself. We are looking for the evidence of faith. We cannot see faith any more than we can see the wind. But just as we can know the presence of wind by observing its effects, so we can know the presence of faith. Just as there is no such thing as wind that doesn't cause the pine trees to whisper and the oak leaves to rustle, so there is no such thing as faith that does not make a stir in the Daily Grind. We know that faith is present because of what we see and hear in a man's life.

THE GLORIOUS SALVATION MACHINE

Peregrinus—Dude, that's helpful. So what kind of things will we see in the Daily Grind that indicate that someone really does heart-believe?

Plowman—We will see men *hear the voice of the Crucified One and follow him*. This is not subjective — it is not feelings and impressions. This is objective — it is obeying all things whatsoever that are commanded in the Sacred Trust.

We will see them *make decisions* which indicate that they are on the narrow path of faith in this ungodly Big Here & Now. We will see them *forsake* the lust of the eyes, the lust of the flesh, and the pride of life. We will see them *depart* from heart citizenship in the Big Here & Now and *embark* on a pilgrim journey even as Abraham left Ur of the Chaldees to seek a better land. We will see them *choose* the people of God over the pleasures of sin for a season. We will see them *rise* to the occasion with Gideon, Samson, David, Samuel, Jephthae, and all the great men of God in obtaining promises, being made strong in weakness, waxing valiant in fight, and overcoming in every tribulation and trial.

Most of the "Judge Not" Stuff Is Garbage

Peregrinus—If heart-faith always produces obvious fruit in the Daily Grind, and believers can always be known by their fruits, then most of the "judge not" stuff we hear is garbage.

Plowman—You're absolutely right. The "judge not" passage in Matthew, for instance, does not ban discerning the spiritual state of men. It bans judging them with a hypocritical spirit. It does not ban attempting to remove crud from the eyes of our brethren. It bans attempting to remove crud from their eyes when we have not first removed the crud from our own.

This is obvious to all who pay attention to the context. Early in the passage we are admonished, "First get the crud out of your eye, then you can see clearly to take the crud out of your brother's eye." Later we are exhorted to discern between true prophets and false prophets, faithful teachers and unfaithful teachers. Finally, we are advised not to cast our pearls before swine or give that which is holy to dogs. Now the plain truth is, we cannot obey these solemn charges unless we — contrary to the Half-Haven taboo — judge men and compartmentalize them according to their spiritual state and character.

Peregrinus—So the essence of the "judge not" passage in Matthew isn't a *ban* on judging, but a *tutorial* on judging.

Plowman—That's right. The essence of the passage is that believers must be right, so they can see right, must get right, so they can set right. There is plenty of testimony-marring crud in the church that ought to be dealt with. But we are unable to deal with it profitably unless we have first dealt with our own crud. God wants us to make things better not worse — he wants us to remove crud, not add to it.

Peregrinus—It seems like very few use this passage right.

Plowman—Yep. Most of the time this passage gets turned on its head. Men use "judge not" as an excuse to not deal with the unbelief, sin, error, and compromise that mars the testimonies of those they fellowship with. And they level "judge not" against faithful men who challenge churchgoers to pursue the real-relationship faith that we see in the Sacred Trust.

Peregrinus—It seems to me that the Sacred Trust actually requires us to judge.

Plowman—It sure does. The Sacred Trust lays upon every believer the solemn obligation to "prove all things." Those that are spiritual take this obligation to heart and "judge (discern) all things." They compare all things with the Word of God, weigh all things in the scale of the Word of God, and try all things in the crucible of the Word of God.

The Necessity of Crud Removal

Peregrinus—So what is judging with a hypocritical spirit?

Plowman—It is judging when you have a piece of crud in the eye of your heart — as some sensual pleasure, or some sin, or some error, or some compromise, or some point of pride, or some point of agitation, or some point of bitterness. This skews how you view and weigh things. It throws your judgment out of whack. You will call darkness light and light darkness. You will judge men unjustly — either too lightly or too harshly. You will defend what you ought to oppose and oppose what you ought to defend. You will justify what you ought to confess and confess what you ought to justify.

Peregrinus—In other words, we need to get dead serious about crud removal — starting with our own eye — so that we can judge righteous judgment.

Plowman—Absolutely. The crud needs to come out — all of it. It is impossible to see right when we have crud in our eyes. And if our spiritual vision is hindered, it is impossible to make the right decisions and take the right directions when we face the issues of the day.

Therefore, let it be taken to heart that mutual crud removal is a vital part of the work of God — a crucial aspect of spiritual warfare — that promotes the spiritual health of the church. And if we go forth with the Lord in spirit and in truth, we will give ourselves, with fear and trembling, to this uncomfortable task. We will *sharpen each other* as iron sharpens iron, *wash each other's feet*, which get dirty just passing through this vile Big Here & Now, and *spur one another on* to love and good works.

Peregrinus—Thanks for the light. It gives me a much better grasp on what the "judge not" passages actually teach. And it came at a good time too. I was getting so tired of hearing folks quote "judge not" to defend wickedness that I found myself wishing that such verses weren't even in the Sacred Trust.

Plowman—Been there, done that. But many passages in the Sacred Trust have been placed on the anvil of unbelief and hammered into senses that God never intended for purposes that God never intended. The "judge not" passage in Matthew has been hammered into one of the main defenses of God Magic salvation and the Innocuous Minimum. Everyone who knows a verse or two from the Sanitized Trust can quote "judge not." Try to find a Dry Sprinkled Hog that can't quote this verse when you talk to him about his Hog Pen.

We Are What We Manifest

Peregrinus—I know the Sacred Trust teaches that we ought to discern the spiritual state of those around us, so we can help them — either to embark upon or prosper in a pilgrim journey. But I still get nervous about judging since we can't know what is on their inside.

Plowman—If we make a proper use of the outside, we don't have to fear judging by what we see. Man is true to his heart. What is in his inside will show up on his outside — usually today, sometimes in the near future. As the Sacred Trust says, that which comes out of a man's mouth is the overflow of his heart. In other words, what comes out of a man's mouth tells us what his heart is filled with — be it anger, bitterness, hatred, lust, unbelief, or what have you. In the same way, what comes out in a man's Daily Grind is the overflow of his heart. It tells us what his heart is filled with — whether anger, bitterness, hatred, lust, unbelief, or what have you. The life and the tongue don't lie. They accurately reflect a man's heart. This is why the Sacred Trust says that we can know men by their fruits.

Peregrinus—The life and the tongue don't lie. I like that.

Plowman—Though we might try to paint our inside better than what our outside looks like, what men see in our Daily Grind is what we are. As we often say in Haven pulpits, "We are what we manifest." If we manifest weak faith, we are weak believers. If we manifest strong faith, we are strong believers. If we manifest immature faith, we are babes in the faith. If we manifest progress in laying aside weights and besetting sins, we are growing in the faith. If we manifest compromise, we are compromisers. If we manifest hypocrisy, we are hypocrites. If we manifest wickedness, we are wicked. And if we manifest rebellion, we are rebellious.

Peregrinus—How about an example from the Sacred Trust on properly discerning men by their outside?

Plowman—In the book of Acts, Peter received Simon Magus on his profession and even baptized him, but he later rejected him at the first clear evidence of empty profession. He did not let it drag on for days, weeks, or months, much less years. He called him on the spot over his unbelief. Simon Magus had made a profession of following the Crucified One and was, therefore, obligated to do so. When he did not follow the Crucified One out of his iniquity and into the light, Peter called him out, and when he did not repent, Peter ushered him out.

Man Looks on the Outside, God Looks on the Inside

Peregrinus—What about the verse that says, "Man looks on the outside, but God looks on the inside"? The Half-Haven folks claim this verse means that nothing on man's outside has value. They claim it bans the discernment of a man's state by any test other than the presence or absence of the historic fact of doing the Faith Form.

Plowman—Yep. I've heard that one a million times myself. That is a false application of Sacred Trust truth. It is true that man looks on the outside and God looks on the inside. This is indisputable. But this verse was never intended to advise us of the *wrongness* of judging men by their outside. It was intended to advise us of the *weakness* of judging men by their outside.

Because we are humans and not God, the only way we can figure out what is on a man's inside is by what we see on his outside. This means that the discernment of a man's state is a *difficult* responsibility. It does not mean that it is *impossible*. We can do a fair job of discerning a man's inward state if we weigh his outward stuff with gracious grace in the scale of the Sacred Trust. But if we indulge Dark Light in the eye of our heart as the Pharisees did, we will be muddled in our judgment.

Peregrinus—So how do we go about judging fairly?

Plowman—The most important thing is that we must train ourselves to look at a man's life and character in general and not focus on a moment of weakness.

If we look at David's life at the wrong moment, we might think he was an ungodly man. But if we look at his life as a whole, we see a man of God with a little weakness and one bad fall. And if we look at Saul's life at the wrong moment, we might think he was a godly man. But if we look at his life as a whole, we see an unbelieving man with some worldly virtue.

Paul's Contrast Between Believing and Working

Peregrinus—Can we go back to the Sanitized verse, "To him that doesn't work, but simply does the Faith Form, his Faith Form is accounted to him for righteousness"? I know this view isn't true, but perhaps you can throw a little light on Paul's contrast between believing and working.

Plowman—The Glorious Salvation Machine and her stepchildren in the Half-Havens have taken Paul's contrast between believing and working and turned it backwards. They teach that *believing* is trusting in the Passive Form and that turning to the Crucified One in real-relationship faith is *working*. This is doctrinal iniquity. In Paul's understanding — or rather God's understanding — *believing* is heart-faith in the Crucified One and *working* is attempting to be saved by things like religious forms, self-righteous good works, and the superficial morality of the Big Here & Now.

Peregrinus—I know I haven't ironed out every wrinkle in my understanding of the faith and works issue, but it has sure become obvious to me that there is no excuse for confusing the requirement of heart-faith in the Crucified One with teaching works salvation.

Plowman—You got that right. Any teaching that regards real-relationship faith in the Crucified One as a Dead Work is so far removed from the plain teaching of the Sacred Trust that it must be regarded as an iniquitous misrepresentation of the truth. While ignorant babes can be blown and tossed by every wind of doctrine, no man of stature can continue in error of this kind unless he is in a committed relationship with Dark Light. And no man of stature indulges a committed relationship with Dark Light unless there is dubious gain in it for him. The gain may stroke his pride (as a larger following or intellectual credibility or acceptance with some group) or it may stroke his lust (as a license to indulge a pet sin). But there is always a motive involved. Such doctrinal departure is never accidental.

Men Unwittingly Surrender the Ability to Think Independently

Peregrinus—This Faith Form stuff is way messed up. How can anyone believe it? You would think that people would just read the Sacred Trust and see that it's complete nonsense.

Plowman—The primary reason that any error gains an upper hand is that men unwittingly surrender their ability to think independently. Through some ignoble motive — as the desire to be intellectually superior, or the desire to belong to some spiritually superior group, or the desire to have Deep insight — men are convinced that spurious doctrine is important "truth" and henceforth give special deference to its teachers as Bible teachers *par excellence.*

The ignoble motive gives the error special immunity in their heart, which hinders their ability to candidly weigh any issue that touches on the error, which hinders the Bible's ability to mold their views. They may gain a good knowledge of the letter of Scripture, but their understanding of what the Bible means is limited to the understanding of the teachers they trust.

This is a dangerous practice. While it gives favorable results to those lucky enough to sit under the ministry of sound Bible teachers; it gives less than favorable results to those who sit under the ministry of men that are unsound in one or two areas of doctrine; it gives disastrous results to those who trust the Big Cheese in the Half-Havens; and it gives fatal results to those who trust the ministry of the false prophets in the cults.

All Error Works the Same Way

Peregrinus—So the Faith Form error deceives men the same way any other error does?

Plowman—Yep. All error works the same way. Men are taught that some Invincible Dogma is the unchallengeable truth of God, they are instructed in the Ironclad Interpretations used to teach that Dogma, and this systematic twistification becomes central to their handling of the Sacred Trust.

Peregrinus—That is magnum bogus.

Plowman—No doubt about that. Invincible Dogma tramples on the proper place of the Sacred Trust as the *only* rule of faith and practice.

The only way to give the Sacred Trust its proper place is to *rigorously test* the doctrines you are being taught to determine if they really are the truth of God and *summarily reject* those that fail the test — no matter how spiritual, how devoted, how godly, or how beloved the men who teach them.

Peregrinus—What steps should we take to ensure that we really do test the doctrines we are taught and don't merely rubber stamp them after a cursory investigation?

Plowman—There are three crucial steps in the investigation of any doctrinal subject. *One*, search the Scriptures diligently, so you gain a familiarity with the entire body of passages that touch on the subject. *Two*, compare Scripture with Scripture, so you understand the subject the way that God intends for you to understand it. And *three*, mercilessly compare your teachers' treatment of the subject with the Bible's treatment of it.

Peregrinus—That sounds like a lot of work.

Plowman—It is a lot of work. It is far more work to uphold the Sacred Trust as the touchstone of truth than it is to uphold some testimony or doctrinal position as the touchstone of truth. But the effort, though often costly and painful, is well worth while. Truth is the most valuable commodity we have. Apart from truth we have no idea what to believe or how to live.

Peregrinus—One thing I have observed is that those who hold Invincible Dogma disdain serious investigation of their Dogma as an unhealthy exercise that leads to disastrous results.

Plowman—That is just more Head Pounding. The truth has nothing to fear from the most rigorous examination — it can only be proved and clarified. Error, on the other hand, has everything to lose in a rigorous examination. Its survival depends on men *indulging* a fog of confusion that would evaporate with a little honest reflection and *presuming* the truth of one or more points that would readily be disproved by candid investigation.

Error must, therefore, dissuade its adherents from rigorous examination that actually subjects the touted "truth" to the crucible of Scripture. One of the most successful ways to do this is to accuse those who question Invincible Dogma of a carnal mind, a lack of spirituality, an independent spirit, pride, unbelief, or some such accusation.

Peregrinus—The more I learn, the more I see how important it is for men to think — to use their brain to apprehend the truth that God has revealed to them in the Sacred Trust.

Plowman—Yep. No brain, no gain. If you don't think, you will sink — into the abyss of Invincible Dogma.

Surrender Is Giving Up the Root Sin of Unbelief

Peregrinus—What about the claim that surrendering to God to get right with him is a Dead Work that must be rejected?

Plowman—Doesn't it sound silly to teach that laying down our weapons and surrendering is maintaining the war because it is trusting in our own dead efforts to end the war?

Peregrinus—It does sound silly.

Plowman—Any argument against the necessity of surrender is an attack on heart-faith.

Peregrinus—I know you're right, but I could use a little elaboration on the proper explanation.

Plowman—Man's war with God is first and foremost a war of unbelief. Unbelief is the root sin behind all other sins. When unbelief rebels against the living God, it takes up weapons (sins) and brandishes them in rebellion. Therefore, the primary focus of the call to surrender is not the *result* (the sins), but the *cause* (the unbelief). When men answer this call and believe, the evil motive of unbelief that incited them to take up arms is melted away by the goodness of God, and they gladly lay down the sins of their rebellion.

Peregrinus—That makes sense. The call to surrender is not a call to some religious path of austerity and self-abnegation. It is a call to forsake the root sin of unbelief and trust God.

Plowman—That's right. And when men forsake the root sin of unbelief, they forsake — in essence — the sins that unbelief spawns.

Peregrinus—Can men lay down their sins apart from faith?

Plowman—Nope. It is impossible for men to lay down their sins apart from faith. Unbelief never has and never will give up its sins. Just as it is impossible to have sunlight without the sun, so it is impossible for men to manifest the beauties of faith while they are yet in the uglies of unbelief. Human religion may persuade a man to exchange his dirty sins for cleaner ones, but it will never persuade him to lay down his sins across the board — big and small, trashy and refined. Only faith can bring a man to do that. Therefore, it is a monument of stupidity when preachers decry surrender as a Dead Work.

Peregrinus—Is there any merit in surrendering?

Plowman—None whatsoever. What merit is there in being forced by the sword-point of truth to confess that we are guilty of departing from God in wicked unbelief? What merit is there in being persuaded by the messengers of heaven to lay down our sins and iniquities and make peace with God, lest we face his overwhelming power and overwhelming wrath? The fact is, when we surrender to God, there is nothing to glory in. There is only cause for shame over our unbelief and sin.

This is why Haven preachers often say that the sinner must come to God with both hands empty — not clutching his sin in his left hand nor claims of merit in his right. He must not only forsake his sins, he must own his moral bankruptcy. He must come clinging to nothing but the grace that God holds out to man in the Crucified One.

Such Hog Pen Wallowers Were Some of You

Peregrinus—I know we talked about this before, but how do you answer the Dogma that believers wallow in the Hog Pen

THE GLORIOUS SALVATION MACHINE

every day? I know this teaching is wrong, but I don't quite know how to answer it.

Plowman—The plain testimony of the Sacred Trust answers this error. Paul wrote, for instance, "Such Hog Pen wallowers were some of you, but you are washed, you are sanctified, you are justified." He also wrote, "They that are the Crucified One's have crucified the flesh with its Hog Pen affections and lusts." And again he wrote, "You were once Hog Pen darkness, but now you are light." This portrayal of separation between the believer and his Hog Pen is not Mystic Plane pretend. It is Daily Grind reality. Believers really do leave the Hog Pen in a way that all men around them can see.

Peregrinus—I understand the part that believers really can and do flee the Hog Pen. The part I have trouble with is how to defend the truth of Hog Pen departure without offending the truth that believers sin in Talk, Think, and Walk every day.

Plowman—When men who tremble at the Sacred Trust use the phrase "believers *sin* in Talk, Think, and Walk every day," they are lamenting the painful fact that, despite their flight from the Hog Pen and their fight with sin, they still fall short of the glory of God. They aren't defending or excusing the relatively minor shortcomings that still stick to them. They are expressing, rather, sincere brokenness over them and an ardent desire to walk in yet greater degrees of victory and holiness.

On the other hand, when men who tremble at God Magic use the phrase "believers *wallow* in Talk, Think, and Walk every day," they are defending and excusing the fact that they yet wallow in the Hog Pen. They show no remorse or fear over their sin, only an ardent desire to continue slopping at the trough and wallowing in the mire.

Peregrinus—Wow! We sure need caution in this matter. The two camps use the same language for two entirely different purposes. One uses it to promote departure from the Hog Pen. The other to promote indulgence of the Hog Pen.

Plowman—Yep. This is why believers need discernment that goes beyond the letter of Scripture and the letter of doctrine.

Error often dresses itself in the language of truth to pass itself off as sound doctrine. The Scriptures refer to this practice when they warn us of false teachers who cover their wolfness with sheep's clothing.

The Wonderful Message Breaks the Power of Hogness

Peregrinus—Can a man get himself out of the Hog Pen?

Plowman—Absolutely not. Man left to himself cannot depart the Hog Pen. He does not have nor can he find the strength and determination to depart. No human motive is strong enough to draw him out or scare him out. He loves his wallow and swill and does not want to give them up. While he may forsake a few dirty Hog Pen pleasures for Big Here & Now profit, he has no interest in giving up the Hog Pen itself. To further complicate things, he is lost. He wouldn't know the way to the Father's house even if he did somehow manage to get out.

Peregrinus—But the Wonderful Message holds out to man the help that he needs.

Plowman—That's right. The Wonderful Message, which is the power of God unto salvation, breaks the power of Hogness. It *breaks through* the unbelief, darkness, and lies that keep men in the Hog Pen and *inspires faith* in their hearts, giving them the motivation, determination, and strength to flee the Hog Pen.

Peregrinus—What a huge difference there is between the real power of the Wonderful Message and the pretend power of the Sanitized Message.

Plowman—No doubt about that. The Wonderful Message brings a man into contact with grace, which delivers him from the Hog Pen (in both power and penalty), so he can be right with God. The Sanitized Message brings a man into contact with God Magic, which delivers him from God, so he can party without fear in the Hog Pen.

Peregrinus—The Sanitized Message almost seems to justify the sin, rather than the sinner.

Plowman—You're right, it does. When a sinner believes the Wonderful Message, God justifies him (declares him okay).

THE GLORIOUS SALVATION MACHINE

When a sinner believes the Sanitized Message, the Nice God justifies the Hog Pen (declares it okay).

The Righteousnesses of the Believer Not Filthy Rags

Peregrinus—What about the claim that the righteousnesses of the believer are Filthy Rags? It seems like every time the subject of devoted Christian living comes up, some God Magic zealot goes off on a rant about how the righteousnesses of the believer are Filthy Rags in the eyes of God.

Plowman—Yep. The way they run off at the mouth, you would think that no sin under the sun is as dirty as the sin of being serious about obedience. But this rant is just one more ploy to trample on heart-faith and promote the Faith Form.

Peregrinus—Is there any truth at all in this charge?

Plowman—None. It is pure, unadulterated bogus. The Sacred Trust does not teach that the righteousnesses of the believer are Filthy Rags. It teaches that the righteousnesses of the unbeliever are filthy rags. There is a huge difference.

Peregrinus—I'm all ears.

Plowman—The "filthy rags" passage in Romans 3, which the God Magic advocates love to quote, ends with the statement, "Whatever the law says, it says to those under the law, that the whole world may be guilty before God." Notice the phrase "under the law." These three words are crucial to the right understanding of the entire passage. And what do they mean? Romans 6 tells us what they mean — believers are *not* "under the law." We are forced to conclude, therefore, if we let the Sacred Trust be its own interpreter, that the charge of filthy rags does not apply to the righteousnesses of believers, but only the righteousnesses of unbelievers.

The Fine Linen Is the Believer's Righteousnesses

Peregrinus—So what are the believer's righteousnesses if they are not Filthy Rags?

Plowman—They are a God-honoring testimonial robe. In Revelation 19 we read, "To the church it was granted that she should be arrayed in fine linen, clean and white, for the fine linen is the righteousnesses of the saints."

Peregrinus—But how do we know that the fine linen robe is the believer's testimony? It seems like everybody believes and teaches that the fine linen robe is the believer's justification — his imputed righteousness.

Plowman—We know from the context itself. *First of all*, the word translated "righteousness" here is not the word used when God declares men righteous (justification), but the one used for the righteous deeds and works of believers as they walk in the obedience of faith (sanctification).

Secondly, the word is actually "righteousnesses" (the plural form), not "righteousness" (the singular form). This use of the plural fits with the believer bringing forth a chain of God-wrought righteousnesses in his testimony (sanctification), but not with God's one-time act of imputing righteousness to the believer (justification).

So if we let the Sacred Trust say what it appears to say and mean what it appears to mean, then the fine linen robe is the believer's testimonial robe — his walking in the righteous ways of God — not his justification.

Peregrinus—But how can the believer's righteousnesses be regarded as fine linen? How can they comprise a God-honoring testimonial robe?

Plowman—Because they are not mere human righteousness wrought by mere human effort. Such righteousness would be filthy rags. They are the *imparted* righteousness of God which he works in every believer by the washing of the Word and the renewing of the Holy Spirit.

Peregrinus—But even with the help of the Word of God and the Spirit of God, we fall short of the glory of God.

Plowman—That's true. But bear in mind three things. *One*, though our righteousness is marred, it is, nonetheless, genuine righteousness wrought in us by God. We are his workmanship, created in the Redeemer unto a testimony of good deeds and noble efforts that are acceptable in his sight.

Two, God, in his unfathomable grace, accepts the obedience of faith, no matter how feeble or marred, as praiseworthy and rewardable. He does not contemn it as junk or filthy rags.

Three, if our faith is acceptable, then so is the obedience of our faith. If the obedience of our faith is filthy rags, then so is the faith that produces it. To deny this is theological inconsistency of a jaw-dropping magnitude.

Peregrinus—Dude! This has mega-ramifications for the God Magic camp! If the believer's righteousnesses are wrought by God himself and he himself regards them as fine linen, then those who call them Filthy Rags are calling holy things unholy and — far worse — labeling God a bungling workman!

Plowman—That's right. It is one thing to confess that the believer's righteousnesses fall short of the glory of God. For the imperfection of our testimony is just as obvious as its genuineness. But it is another thing altogether to reckon the believer's righteousnesses as Filthy Rags. That is a reckless charge that imputes evil to the handiwork of God.

The Testimonial Robe Is Washed in the Blood of the Lamb

Peregrinus—Doesn't the Sacred Trust speak somewhere of the believers washing their robes in the blood of the Lamb and making them white?

Plowman—It sure does. In Revelation 7 we read, "The saints washed their robes and made them white in the blood of the Lamb."

Peregrinus—That's what I thought. It just dawned on me, if the robes must themselves be washed in the blood of the Lamb, then they cannot possibly represent, in and of themselves, the washing in the blood of the Lamb.

Plowman—That's right. The robes cannot possibly be, in and of themselves, the imputed righteousness of the Redeemer, for they can get defiled, and must then be made white again by the imputed righteousness of the Redeemer. The robe and the whiteness are two distinct things.

Peregrinus—Dude! Your explanation makes so much sense — the white robe portrays the believer's testimonial cleansing by the Word of God, and the spotless whiteness portrays his judicial washing in the blood of the Lamb.

Plowman—That's right. The believer's testimonial robe of Spirit-wrought sanctification, though obviously white, is yet stained with the sins and shortcomings that have sullied the testimonies of the very best men. But the obviously white robe is made perfectly white in the blood of the Lamb. His record is expunged and he is declared righteous — as if he had never sinned.

Laziness and Prejudice

Peregrinus—I like being free from the pretending that is part of the Faith Form package. We don't have to pretend that clean testimonial robes are Filthy Rags. And we don't have to pretend that the invisible cleaning of God Magic in the Faith Form takes the filthy ragness out of man's real filthy rags.

Plowman—That's a big Amen.

Peregrinus—Tell me, how do Invincible Dogmas like Filthy Rags maintain their dominance in the church?

Plowman—They maintain their place of dominance for two main reasons — *laziness* and *prejudice*. These evil twins are the death knell for advancement in truth.

When men embrace the Half-Haven message, they become spiritual couch potatoes addicted to *laziness*, which keeps them from serious study of the Sacred Trust, which saddles them with a lack of knowledge regarding the Word of God and sound doctrine.

Rather than take measures to correct their laziness and lack of knowledge, they lean on authorities (Big Cheese) who tell them what to believe (Invincible Dogmas) and how to interpret the Sacred Trust (Ironclad Interpretations). This nurtures them in *prejudice* (judging without sufficient information) instead of *spiritual discernment* (judging with a sufficient breadth and depth of information). It teaches them to handle passages and

THE GLORIOUS SALVATION MACHINE

subjects in a manner that is superficial and reckless, oblivious to every indication that they might be wrong.

Peregrinus—But many folks in the Half-Havens, especially preachers, put a lot of time into study. They don't appear to be lazy. Don't their efforts count for serious study?

Plowman—Nope. It is not serious study to show diligence in shallow, prejudiced studies that further God Magic salvation or any other significant error — whether it panders to baptized hedonism or caters to religious pride. Such diligence is not spiritual diligence, but spiritual laziness.

It is only serious study when men show diligence in using the Sacred Trust as it was designed to be used — a merciless crucible. When men walk in this path, they *consciously elevate* the body of truth contained in the Sacred Trust above every human effort to formulate these truths, *rigorously try* every man-framed doctrine to determine whether or not it be true, and *rigorously refine* those that stand the test.

Slowgressive Sanctification Is Not Progressive Sanctification

Peregrinus—Strawberry also insisted that real-relationship faith can't be the faith that God seeks because it tramples on the Dogma of Slowgressive Sanctification. But something is wrong in this line of thinking, for Slowgressive Sanctification seems to overthrow sanctification, not promote it.

Plowman—You're right. Slowgressive Sanctification does overthrow sanctification. Sadly, many believers today cannot discern the difference between the Slowgressive Sanctification of the God Magic system and the progressive sanctification of the Sacred Trust.

Peregrinus—So what's the difference?

Plowman—Progressive sanctification is the outflow of real-relationship faith. Everyone who really turns to the Crucified One manifests progress in their Daily Grind — right from the very start. While they don't go from zero to maturity overnight, they definitely and continually change, grow, and bear fruit.

On the other hand, Slowgressive Sanctification is, for all practical purposes, nogressive sanctification. Most who do the Faith Form never make any progress at all in sanctification. They start at zero and stay at zero. They manifest no change, no growth, and no fruit. And the few that do show a little progress don't show anything that isn't fully in keeping with the mediocrity of the Innocuous Minimum.

Progressive Sanctification Starts with a Bang

Peregrinus—So the difference boils down to whether or not sanctification starts progressing at the point of salvation.

Plowman—That's right. Slowgressive Sanctification doesn't give us much progress to observe or measure. Quite often it doesn't even get out of the starting block. And when it does, it takes a few half-hearted steps down the track, then drops out of the race.

Progressive sanctification, on the other hand, starts with a bang — an initial burst of change — for it steps from unbelief to faith. This is no insignificant step, for it transfers a man from darkness to light, from death to life, from the broad road to the narrow path, from insurrection to surrender, from following the Mad Spirit to following the Crucified One. No man can take this step and not change his Big Here & Now — immediately, significantly, and irreparably.

Peregrinus—And this initial step of faith, which significantly sanctifies the believer, is followed by a succession of steps that progressively sanctify the believer.

Plowman—That's right. After the initial crisis, when a man's life explodes with the evidences of his new life, he continues down the narrow path — going from faith to faith, being ever the more conformed to the will of God, and having his mind ever the more renewed by the Word of God. Sometimes this progress comes faster, sometimes slower, but it never comes at Slowgressive speeds, like the speed of a half-dead snail.

Peregrinus—So the proper view of progressive sanctification is that it starts with a flurry of change at the time of salvation and continues throughout the believer's life.

Plowman—In the main, yes. I would add one further detail, however. Believers sometimes experience *seasons* where they experience accelerated growth or *crisis experiences* where they make substantial gains almost overnight. For this reason I like to say that progressive sanctification begins with a flurry of change, continues with measurable growth in any reasonable timeframe, and may evidence seasons or crisis experiences of rapid advancement.

Repentance Means "Change the Mind"

Peregrinus—What do you think about the Half-Haven claim that the definition of repentance is "change the mind"?

Plowman—Repentance does mean "change the mind." But the pivotal question isn't whether repentance means "change the mind." The pivotal question is, what does "change the mind" mean? As is their usual practice, the Faith Form camp has framed a controversial question in a way that obscures the truth and gives credibility to their error.

They start by asserting the obvious fact that repentance means "change the mind." Then they trot out the observation — self-serving and unsubstantiated — that because repentance means "change the mind," it can't mean "depart from sin" and can't necessitate departure from sin. The only thing it can mean or necessitate is men changing their minds about sin. Then they dumb down this changing of the mind about sin until it means nothing more than giving lip service in the Faith Form to the Invincible Dogmas.

Peregrinus—So what does "change the mind" really mean?

Plowman—*Mind* is used in a broad array of senses in both English and Greek. It can bear the sense of *thought* as in "bear in mind." It can bear the sense of *concern* as in "never mind." And it can bear the sense of the *will* or *purpose* as in "I have a mind to do such a thing."

Peregrinus—Two of those senses involve the *heart* and not merely the *head*.

Plowman—That's exactly right, and that's exactly where I'm going with my argument. The *moral sense* (change of purpose) is the usual sense of "change the mind" in the Sacred Trust and in extra-biblical Greek literature of moral or religious stamp. But the Faith Form camp hates this sense, for it poses a huge threat to their salvation machinery. Instead, they cling to the *mental sense* (mere change of sentiment) — like frantic men clinging to a life preserver — because it allows them to regard men as having repented, though they yet wallow in the Hog Pen and have no intention of leaving it.

The Brain-Mind and the Heart-Mind

Peregrinus—I never noticed before that *mind* is used of both the head and the heart.

Plowman—Yep. *Mind* can be used of either the brain-mind or the heart-mind. The *brain-mind* is the living hard drive that God has placed in us for the storage of information. The *heart-mind* is the living processor that God has equipped us with for processing, organizing, and utilizing this information.

The living hard drive of the *brain-mind* is just a tool for the heart to use. Having the right information in the brain — and knowing that it is right — doesn't do anything except provide opportunity. And opportunity alone will not put a man on the right path or put him in right relationship with God.

The living processor of the *heart-mind* is the true workhorse. It must search for good information as for hid treasure, sort and organize this information with the utmost care, weigh it with fear and trembling, draw legitimate conclusions, and determine how best to put these conclusions into practice. This is why the Sacred Trust exhorts us to guard the heart-mind, for "Out of the heart-mind come the issues of life."

Peregrinus—That brings to mind the passage in Romans that illuminates the struggle between the mind of the Spirit and the mind of the flesh.

Plowman—That is one of the key passages on the subject. It proves that *mind* is used of the heart. For there we read that the mind set on the flesh pursues the things of the flesh and the mind set on the Spirit pursues the things of the Spirit. And it is the heart that sets its mind on things good or bad, not the brain.

Repentance Means "Change the Grind"

Peregrinus—Is it legitimate, then, to say that repentance is a change of the heart?

Plowman—Absolutely. Repentance is a change of the heart-mind, not the mere acknowledgment of a few facts in the brain-mind. It is the heart forsaking wrong ways that the head knows are wrong. Many a man is unwilling to forsake wrong things that he knows are wrong. This is the great failure of the devils. They are unwilling to abandon a course they know is wrong and submit to the truth they know is the truth.

This, too, was the error of the Pharisees. They knew the letter of the Sacred Trust. They were intimate with the messianic prophecies. When the day of visitation came, they saw Jesus of Nazareth fulfill the messianic prophecies before their very eyes. But they were unwilling to let go of their errors and pride, therefore they refused to embrace their Messiah. Instead they sought high and low for flimsy arguments why Jesus couldn't be the Messiah.

Peregrinus—So repentance is a change of the heart-mind, a transfer of loyalty from some false way to the true way. And this transfer of loyalty always shows up in the Daily Grind.

Plowman—That's right.

Peregrinus—And that's why we often hear Haven preachers say that repentance means "change the Grind."

Plowman—You got it. When we say that repentance means "change the Grind," we are presenting repentance from the perspective of its *result*, rather than its *process*. This result focus — with reference to forsaking sin, error, and wrong ways — is the most common use of repentance in the Sacred Trust. Faithful preachers follow this biblical pattern and preach repentance with its result focus. This is both necessary and profitable, for it indicates to their hearers that God is not looking for empty Faith Form repentance, but heart repentance that manifests itself in the Daily Grind.

Peregrinus—And the repentance message that you preach makes a big difference in the results that you get.

Plowman—That's right. The Big Cheese in the Half-Havens have committed themselves to preach the Faith Form version of "change the mind." Therefore, the Half-Havens are filled with men who "changed their mind" in the Faith Form. These churchgoers have a few innocuous notions rattling around in their head, but they have no more repentance than the devils or the Pharisees.

Sweet Position Is Not Positional Truth

Peregrinus—Strawberry also taught that everyone who does the Faith Form has a Sweet Position in the Sweet One. He is guaranteed Sweet Everlasting even if he is still wallowing in the Hog Pen. I know that the Sacred Trust teaches the security of the believer, but this Sweet Position stuff makes me feel uncomfortable.

Plowman—It should make you feel uncomfortable because it is a twistification of the truth. The Half-Haven preachers are right in the *theory* of positional truth. The blessings we receive through our position in the Crucified One are infinitely better than what our practice deserves. We all fall short — far short — of the glory of God. Were we to be given what our practice deserves, we would all spend eternity in Awful Everlasting.

But they are far astray in the *application* of positional truth. They hold out the positional blessing as the possession of all who do the Faith Form. And they malign as legalists those who teach that the positional blessing belongs only to those who heart-believe on the Crucified One.

Peregrinus—That's way messed up.

Plowman—No doubt about that. The Invincible Dogma of Sweet Position is a travesty of positional truth. When men insist that every profession of faith cranked out by the salvation machinery has Sweet Everlasting, they stand the Sacred Trust on its head, confuse a religious form with faith, call ungodly men godly, and give ungodly men false hope of salvation.

Finished Salvation Means Diminished Salvation

Peregrinus—How do you answer the claim that the Sweet One has done everything for us and that if we add anything to the Wonderful Message that man must do, like heart-believe or repent, we are not trusting in Finished Salvation?

Plowman—There are several problems with the Invincible Dogma of Finished Salvation.

First of all, we can't add real-relationship faith or repentance to the Wonderful Message. They are already a part of it. God, in his infinite wisdom, made them a part of it. This is obvious to all who read the Sacred Trust free of Faith Form prejudice.

Peregrinus—I thought you would say something like that.

Plowman—*Secondly*, it is sloppy theology to talk about the work of salvation being finished. While the work of atonement is finished, the work of redemption as a whole is not finished.

Peregrinus—This is definitely an elaboration situation.

Plowman—The atonement was completed when the Saviour shed his blood on the cross. Not partly accomplished. Finished. It is a historical fact. Sin was paid for. One payment for all sin for all men for all time. But the atonement is only one part of our three-fold redemption.

We were saved from the *penalty* of sin through justification — on the basis of the atonement — when we believed.

We are being saved from the *practice* of sin through the sanctification of the Spirit and the Word of God.

We shall be saved, some wonderful day, from the *presence* and the *results* of sin through glorification. Our souls shall be delivered from indwelling sin and our bodies redeemed from corruption (the curse for sin).

Peregrinus—I can hardly wait for that day.

Plowman—Amen! And those that truly long for that day are strengthened by the hope of that day, and those that are thus strengthened purify themselves from the defilements of the Big Here & Now, even as their Master is pure from the defilements of the Big Here & Now.

Peregrinus—Now you said, "several points," so you must have at least one more.

Plowman—Yep. I have one more. My *third* and last point is this, it is a serious blunder to treat redemption like a cafeteria lunch. Men don't go through the redemption line with the option of saying *yes* to justification and *no* to sanctification. This view of salvation is doctrinal iniquity. We don't get to choose which parts of salvation we will take and which we will pass on. We either take all of the Redeemer and his redemption, or we take none of him and his redemption.

Peregrinus—And sanctification is the litmus paper of faith.

Plowman—That's right. Where sanctification is not soon and obviously forthcoming, the supposed faith is just pretension, the freshbirth never transpired, justification never occurred, and indulging the hope of glorification and Sweet Everlasting is indulging fantasy.

Peregrinus—How about good men, like Mr. Radio Preacher, who talk about finished salvation in a sloppy way?

Plowman—We can bear with a little theological sloppiness in good men. When they talk about finished salvation, they don't mean that men don't have to heart-believe. They aren't undermining real-relationship faith and establishing the Faith Form. They merely mean that the Redeemer will finish the good work that he has started, that he has sealed the believer with the Holy Spirit of redemption (the down payment or promise money of redemption) for the day of redemption, and that the salvation of the believer is as good as finished — it is, as men say, a done deal.

But we have no patience when Half-Haven preachers hammer and harangue on the Invincible Dogma of Finished Salvation. This makes our blood boil. They intentionally muddle things

THE GLORIOUS SALVATION MACHINE

with their warped doctrine which takes heart-faith out of the picture and puts the Faith Form in its place.

Peregrinus—Dude! They are peddling some serious error.

Plowman—No doubt about that. The Dogma of Finished Salvation is a diminished salvation. It rips the fight out of faith and turns it into a wimpy religious form. It rips the cross out of the gospel call and turns it into a chintzy sales pitch. It rips the obedience out of discipleship and turns it into the Innocuous Minimum.

Supernal Security and Infernal Security

Peregrinus—How about the security of the believer? I am so sick and tired of hearing Faith Form preachers hold out security to everyone who does the Faith Form, that just hearing folks talk about security makes me uncomfortable.

Plowman—I hear you. I've been there. But we must not let unsound notions about the security of the believer dissuade us from believing what the Sacred Trust says about it. The Sacred Trust plainly states that the Crucified One will not cast out anyone who comes to him in faith, that he will finish the work that he has started in every believer, that believers are kept by the power of God through faith, that believers (those born of God) cannot continue in the way of sin, and that believers (known by their heeding and following) will never perish.

Peregrinus—So the question isn't *whether* the Sacred Trust holds out a promise of security, but rather *who* enjoys the promised security.

Plowman—That's right. We must discern between the true doctrine (*supernal* security), which holds out the promise of security to all who heart-believe on the Crucified One, and the false doctrine (*infernal* security), which holds out the promise of security to all who do the Faith Form.

Peregrinus—How about a little expansion on the distinction?

Plowman—Those who enjoy *supernal* security are known by the fact that they hear the voice of their Shepherd and follow him down the narrow path of faith — which hearing and following, as you have often heard me say, is not a condition of salvation, but an evidence of salvation.

Those who indulge *infernal* security are known by the fact that they have nothing to point to as proof of their salvation aside from the Faith Form and a piddling pile of Innocuous Minimum. If anyone questions their salvation because the obedience of faith is missing, the questioner is castigated for his doctrinal ignorance and hammered with Faith Form clichés like "Once in God Magic, always in God Magic."

Peregrinus—How about the phrase *settled matter*? Is that a shallow Faith Form cliché too?

Plowman—Not necessarily. Salvation can be and ought to be a settled matter. As First John says, we can *know* that we have eternal life.

But, sadly, most men don't use the phrase *settled matter* to promote assurance of salvation among those who heart-believe, but rather to promote the pretension of salvation among those who have done the Faith Form. As they often say, "If you have done the Faith Form, your salvation is a settled matter."

Salvation Is a Gift

Peregrinus—What about the Dogma that salvation is a Free Gift? The Half-Haven preachers say that if we do anything other than the Faith Form to be saved, then salvation is no longer a Free Gift, but something we must work for.

Plowman—There is no question that salvation is a gift. We can't earn salvation. The very thought is preposterous. We are morally and spiritually bankrupt sinners with an infinite debt that we cannot repay. The most and the best we can give is a paltry handful of worthless junk — feeble morality tainted with sin, paltry goodness tainted with badness, religion tainted with unbelief, and a few good deeds tainted with self-promotion. That does not go very far towards an infinite debt.

Peregrinus—But if salvation truly is a gift, then there must be no contradiction between God offering the gift of salvation to the sinner and the sinner reaching out the hand of his heart in faith to receive it, just like there is no contradiction between a rich man offering alms to a beggar and the beggar reaching out his hand to receive it.

Plowman—That's right. There is no contradiction.

Peregrinus—Then the Invincible Dogma of the Free Gift is just one more effort to badger and cajole men into trusting the Faith Form.

Plowman—You got it.

Peregrinus—Another thing that bothers me about the Half-Haven handling of this subject is that they are inconsistent in a huge way. How can it be okay to reach out the hand of the heart to the Sweet One in superstitious faith and not okay to reach out the hand of the heart to the Crucified One in a fact- and reality-based faith?

Plowman—Yep. That laughable piece of inconsistency well illustrates the principle that error is always inconsistent.

If it is Dead Works for the destitute sinner to reach out the hand of his heart to the Crucified One for a cup of living water, how much more is it Dead Works for him to reach out the hand of his heart to the Sweet One for a cup of stagnant water?

Sincere Effort to Lead a Devoted Life Not Bare Feet

Peregrinus—Do you mind going over the Bare Feet stuff one more time? Strawberry hammered pretty hard on this point and shook me a little bit.

Plowman—The only reason that the Half-Havenists level the charge of Bare Feet against those who make a sincere effort to lead a devoted life is that they love the Big Here & Now and want to pile as much of it as they can on the Altar of Worthy Self. They are justifying themselves and their compromise.

Peregrinus—That is certainly what it looks like to me.

Plowman—The fact is, it is ridiculous to equate tearing down the Altar and losing your life for the sake of the Crucified One with the ancient error of Bare Feet. If anyone would candidly compare the discipleship seen in the New Testament with the ancient error of Bare Feet, he would see that there is no comparison. They aren't even close.

Moreover, if we are guilty of being Pharisees caught up in the dead works of dead religion because we follow the teaching of the Crucified One literally and diligently, then the apostles were guilty of being Pharisees caught up in the dead works of dead religion because they too followed the teaching of the Crucified One literally and diligently.

Peregrinus—So a believer can earnestly follow the Crucified One — offering himself a living sacrifice, laying aside every weight, indeed conforming his life to the whole body of strong exhortations in the New Testament — and not have to worry about falling into the error of Bare Feet.

Plowman—That's right. Following the Crucified One with your whole heart is not Bare Feet and doesn't lead to Bare Feet. This slander reeks of the serpent in the garden. It comes from men who hate the pilgrim path in the wilderness and love the leeks and onions in Egypt. It comes from men who hate being on the plains of Mamre with Abraham and love being in the gates of Sodom with Lot. It comes from men who hate following the Saviour with real-relationship faith and love the Faith Form.

No Danger of Real Righteousness That God Must Reject

Peregrinus—What about the supposed danger of men making themselves righteous in their own strength?

Plowman—There is no such danger. There is no such thing as real righteousness that God must reject because it was done in human strength. It is absolutely impossible to obtain real righteousness — that is, to have a heart, mind, and life pleasing to God — by human strength.

A man walking in his own strength can be a whitewashed Pharisee, a wolf in sheep's clothing, or a pretender like Simon Magus. He can be with the people of God, while grumbling against Moses. He can teach, cast out devils, and do miracles in the Sweet One's name, while indulging iniquity. But he cannot

THE GLORIOUS SALVATION MACHINE

walk in real righteousness with the patriarchs, judges, prophets, and apostles. That can only be accomplished by the strength of the living God. And men can only tap into the strength of God by walking with him in real-relationship faith.

Peregrinus—So there are not two kinds of real righteousness — real righteousness wrought by human strength, which God must reject, and real righteousness wrought by divine strength, which God can accept.

Plowman—Nope. There is only one kind.

Peregrinus—Dude! Then the discernment of right-living is a straightforward matter. If we see righteousness, then it is God-wrought and God-honoring.

Plowman—That's right. That's why the Sacred Trust says, "Let no man deceive you, he that does righteousness (he that lives right) is righteous, even as he is righteous."

Peregrinus—Okay, so there is no danger of men obtaining righteousness in human strength. What about the danger of men pursuing righteousness in their own strength?

Plowman—When it comes to young believers and immature believers, it is a given that they will lean on their own strength in the pursuit of righteousness. This is why they frequently find themselves lacking the strength to do the God-honoring things they want to do. But there is no significant danger in this. Their failures are simply part of the learning curve. Because they are the children of God, God teaches them how to walk in faith, and they learn their lessons. As time rolls by, they lean less on their own strength and more on his, they find victory where they once met defeat, and they ever press on to higher ground, attaining both more and purer righteousness.

The Unsplashed Holiness Rant

Peregrinus—Then what is the danger that the Sacred Trust refers to when it warns men against rejecting the righteousness of God and establishing their own?

Plowman—God's righteousness is a two-fold administration of his grace that revolves around heart-faith. When men heart-believe in the Crucified One, they are both justified (declared righteous) and sanctified (made righteous). Men reject God's righteousness when they reject real-relationship faith and the sanctification that goes with it. And they establish their own righteousness when they put their trust in the Faith Form.

Peregrinus—So the danger actually lies on the path that the Half-Havens are on, not the path that the Havens are on.

Plowman—That's right. The danger lies on the path that the Half-Havens are on, which is the same path that the Glorious Salvation Machine is on and the Pharisees were on. This path turns from God's righteousness and leads men to the quagmire of righteousness on the basis of works — religious forms, superficial morality, and Innocuous sentiment.

Peregrinus—So when the Half-Havens charge those walking in the real righteousness of heart-faith with making themselves righteous, they are just slinging ugly.

Plowman—Yep. They are taking up the time-honored rant of Unsplashed Holiness. All who refuse to bow to the golden calf of God Magic in the Faith Form will have their right living slandered as Unsplashed Holiness wrought by human strength and effort.

Peregrinus—And the Half-Havens got this argument from the Glorious Salvation Machine.

Plowman—That's right. For centuries the Glorious Salvation Machine used Unsplashed Holiness as a favorite argument to undermine the credibility of heart-faith and uphold God Magic in the Wet Splash (the Sprinkle Form). When the Half-Havens arose with their distinctive God Magic system that revolved around the Dry Splash (the Faith Form), they adopted the argument of Unsplashed Holiness as their method of choice to denounce heart-faith and defend the Dry Splash.

The Little Ball of God Magic

Peregrinus—What do you think about the Sweet Presence? How can this doctrine be right when those who teach it use it to trample on heart-faith and uphold the Faith Form?

Plowman—The Sweet Presence is not the actual presence of the Crucified One in the heart, but an iniquitous fabrication.

Peregrinus—So what is it, then?

Plowman—The Sweet Presence is a little ball of God Magic that the Nice God places inside a man when he does the Faith Form.

Peregrinus—So what is the proof that a man has this little ball of God Magic in him?

Plowman—There really isn't any objective proof. While it often brings forth Minimizing religiosity that bears a haunting resemblance to the superficial morality and form-based religion that prevails in all the religions of the Big Here & Now, it doesn't have to bring forth any evidence at all. It is a matter of Deep Faith for all who do the Faith Form.

Peregrinus—So man is saved by the presence of a little ball of God Magic whose presence can't be proved or disproved?

Plowman—Yep. The Sweet Presence is a Mystic Plane truth that must be taken as a matter of Deep Faith. If a man has done the Faith Form, he has the Sweet Presence and is saved, no matter how ugly, how immoral, or how unbelieving his life looks in the Daily Grind.

There Are Not Two of You

Peregrinus—What about the Dogma that the believer is Two Persons? Both Strawberry and Rush said that when a man gets saved he is no longer one person, but two — an Old Man and a New Man. If he continues to wallow in the Hog Pen after he has done the Faith Form, there is no need to worry, for that is just the Old Man, who has nothing to do with salvation. Salvation is based on the presence of the New Man.

Plowman—That is just another piece of Hog-Pen-defending nonsense. It is contrary to common sense and sound theology to believe that a man who has done the Faith Form can indulge the Hog Pen with impunity because his salvation is entirely a matter of the New Man — a little ball of God Magic created in the Sweet One unto Innocuous Minimizing.

Peregrinus—Are the Dogmatizers wrong that believers are two persons? Or do they misunderstand the two persons?

Plowman—They are wrong. The believer is not two persons. There are not two of you. There is only one of you.

Peregrinus—So what are we supposed to do with what the Sacred Trust teaches on the old man and the new man? I mean, it does teach that we have an old man and a new man, right?

Plowman—The Sacred Trust does teach that believers have an old man and a new man. But this teaching must not be misconstrued into the Two Persons Dogma. The believer is not two distinct persons in one body. The believer is one person, who has both an old man and a new man.

Peregrinus—So what are the old man and the new man?

Plowman—The old man and the new man are two opposing principles working in the believer, vying for supremacy of the heart.

The old man is who you were in your old way of life — indulging in unbelief, wallowing in the Hog Pen, and loving the Big Here & Now with its worldly passions and pride.

The new man is who you are created in the Crucified One to be and become. It is a new way of living — loving God with all your heart, soul, mind, and strength; and being conformed to the mind, character, and will of the Crucified One recorded in the pages of the Sacred Trust.

Peregrinus—Dude! The lights just came on. Because I am one person who has an old man and a new man, I can obey the exhortation to "Put off the old man and put on the new." But the Two Person Dogma gets stuck in an awfully deep quandary if it tries to traverse this verse. For if I am the Old Man, I can't put off the old man and put on the new man. And if I am the New Man, I can't put off the old man and put on the new man.

Plowman—That's right. Error always runs aground on the contrary testimony of the Sacred Trust — unless you run the troublesome passages through a Deep Signification Adjustifier.

THE GLORIOUS SALVATION MACHINE

The Sinner Isn't Converted, He Is Replaced

Peregrinus—The Two Person Dogma — with its little ball of God Magic — is the infinity of stupidity.

Plowman—It is definitely reckless theology. Nobody that trembles at the Sacred Trust and lives in reality can believe that he is two persons — that he is free to wallow in the Hog Pen without fear because he can blame it on his irrelevant Old Man and that his salvation is based on the New Man, a little ball of God Magic whose presence is a matter of Deep Faith. This is just as ridiculous as blaming your sin on your pretend evil twin and pinning your hope of salvation on Santa Claus living in your heart.

Peregrinus—What about conversion? If a man can stay in the Hog Pen, then he doesn't have to be converted.

Plowman—That's right. The sinner doesn't get converted in the Two Person theology. He gets replaced. The sinner says a Hog Pen Prayer and gets a New Man put inside him. The Old Man (the sinner) continues in his Hog Pen ways. The New Man sits in his lazy chair watching the Old Man frolic in the filth. When death arrives on his doorstep, the two are separated. The Old Man ceases to exist. The New Man goes to heaven.

Peregrinus—But they don't actually believe that. They don't believe that the real person frolicking in the Hog Pen ceases to exist and the pretend God Magic person goes to heaven.

Plowman—You're right. They don't. What they believe and what they teach are inconsistent, and they are utterly oblivious to their inconsistency. What they really believe is that the Old Man and the New Man exchange identities at death.

Throughout life the real person frolics in the Hog Pen under the guise of the Old Man while the pretend God Magic person carries on as the New Man. At death they trade identities. The real person assumes the identity of the New Man and goes to heaven while the pretend God Magic person assumes the identity of the Old Man and ceases to exist.

Peregrinus—It's hard to believe that anyone can hold such inconsistent, far-fetched nonsense.

Plowman—I agree. But there is sinister power at work in error, for those who hold it are somehow able to overlook the brain-dead inconsistencies that cling to it like stink on a skunk.

Peregrinus—So where did the Two Persons Dogma come from?

Plowman—The Dogma of Two Persons taught by men like Strawberry and Rush is just a modern version of the ancient error of gnostic dualism, which taught that men were saved by the supposed presence of the Spirit on the inside, no matter how immoral and ungodly they were on the outside.

Peregrinus—I don't know much about Church history and the history of doctrine, but it does seem like the same errors keep popping up over and over again.

Plowman—You're right, they do. Once an error rears its ugly head, it never goes away. When you think you have defeated an error in battle and that it has retreated to die in some hole, it has really just slinked away to its foul den to lick its wounds and transmogrify itself into a new form.

Error Has a Racy Edge

Peregrinus—You would think that such inconsistency would make error less attractive.

Plowman—Nope. The disconnect between error and reality gives error a raciness that makes it attractive.

Peregrinus—How's that?

Plowman—Many people find life less than fulfilling unless they gratify themselves with edgy excitement that seems risky, against-the-grain, ill-advised, irrational, or even stupid.

For example, they indulge the excitement of *illicit activities* (as drugs or sexual immorality) that transgress legal or moral boundaries, *dangerous recreation* that throws caution to the wind and risks life and limb for a shot of adrenalin, and *risqué subcultures* whose dress, adornment, demeanor, values, and lifestyle toss common sense and practicality in the dumpster.

They see their love for excitement — for living on the edge — as a positive strength that sets them apart from average men and their average stuff. But wise men reject their sources of excitement because they are either wrong or imprudent.

Peregrinus—It's hard to imagine that religious error belongs in the same class as illicit activity, dangerous recreation, and risqué subcultures.

Plowman—This is one of those counterintuitive observations that no longer seems counterintuitive once you understand the principles that are at work.

Those who indulge significant error manifest the same self-will and the same line-defying, wrong-fork-in-the-road-taking spirit that we see in those who indulge edgy excitement. They can't be reproved or reasoned with. They are wiser than seven men who can render a reason. When men show them that they have crossed a line or taken a wrong fork in the road, they fault common sense and levelheaded reason as weakness — or even wrongness — and snarkily give their half-baked reasons why they don't have to heed the signs in the Sacred Trust that mark the line or the fork in the road.

Peregrinus—That does seem to be the spirit of the cults and many men in the Half-Havens.

Plowman—Yep. There are many men who — whether due to a sense of morality, a bent for religion, a streak of timidity, or some such thing — don't want dirty and dangerous excitement, so they indulge their wild side in doctrinal excitement.

Deny the Obvious and Embrace the Deep

Peregrinus—So how does error offer edgy excitement?

Plowman—It gives men an exciting motive (as we are the ones who have the truth, or true Christianity, or the Holy Spirit, or sound doctrine). And it gives them this excitement in an edgy context, for a man must trample on caution, candor, and sensibility to *embrace* the erroneous teaching as the teaching of the Bible and *reconcile* the glorious sounding claims of its profession with the less-than-glorious facts of its experience.

Peregrinus—So the edginess comes from going against the grain of what naturally or normally seems right?

Plowman—That's right. For a man to believe doctrinal error, he must *deny* the commonplace understanding — the obvious understanding — that men invariably arrive at when they let common sense harmonize every pertinent passage in the Bible. And he must, instead, *embrace* a Deep Signification testimony comprised of a Deep key (based on a twisted proof-text or two) that unlocks the Deepness of the Bible, a Deep rationale that justifies the doctrine, and Ironclad Interpretations that empty opposing testimony with their Deep understanding.

Peregrinus—So men really can't commit themselves to error unless they are at least a little wayward in their heart?

Plowman—Well, I dare not blame young believers, for they are always ignorant and often trusting to a fault — even to the point of carelessness. But the origin and lifeblood of error is the tang of sensual excitement in the heart — as indulging the carnal desire to stand out, or be different, or be better, or be more spiritual, or have intellectual credibility with the world — which leads men to see, find, and embrace Deep insights. This Deepness makes error exciting. It fuels the errorists with the pride that they alone are standing for Deep Truth that most Christians are not spiritual enough to see and not brave enough to embrace if they did.

When men walk in this spirit, they handle the Sacred Trust in a provocative manner, similar to the way worldly folks dress in a provocative manner. They pass through doctrinal subjects in a fast and loose manner, even as many folks pass through life in a fast and loose lifestyle.

Peregrinus—But excitement in and of itself isn't a problem, is it?

Plowman—Absolutely not. The truth of God revealed in the Sacred Trust is exciting and fulfilling. Edgy excitement is the problem. If we don't crucify the flesh with its latent hankering for sensual excitement, we will become animated with some Deep Truth and trample on the Bible we profess to uphold.

THE GLORIOUS SALVATION MACHINE

The Mystery of Iniquity Is Tightening Its Grip

Peregrinus—There is one thing that I don't quite understand. I am used to thinking of those that indulge edgy excitement — whether dangerous, dirty, or doctrinal — as the minority, not the majority. But in our day it seems that edgy excitement is going mainstream in the world. And worse yet, it seems that it is spreading rapidly in Evangelical churches — in a watered-down form — leading them down paths that are contrary to the revealed mind of God in the Sacred Trust.

Plowman—As the mystery of iniquity tightens its grip on the Big Here & Now, extending its vile tentacles more deeply and broadly into society, increasing numbers of men are stepping over long-drawn lines. Indeed, stepping over lines has become the new norm. And when the mystery of iniquity has run its course, the world will have stepped over every line they could find. It will have defied and defiled every institution of God. And churchianity — including the Half-Havens — won't be far behind them.

Peregrinus—That will be a sad day.

Plowman—No doubt about that. There once was a time when Evangelicalism was on the Reformation path of departure from error and darkness. As the decades and centuries went by, her various churches collectively gained more light and forsook more darkness. What a glorious work of God! But in our day Evangelicalism has lost her spiritual momentum and the glory of her legacy. In many quarters she is happily rushing headlong down the path of the Great Murky Revival — worm-eaten with error and compromise.

The Freshbirth Is a Real Renewing of the Heart

Peregrinus—You know, it seems like the difference between the Haven view of the freshbirth and the Half-Haven view is that the Havens insist on a real heart work and the Half-Havens insist on a pretend heart work.

Plowman—No doubt about that. The Havens teach that the freshbirth is a real renewing of the heart wrought by grace through the *washing* of the Word of God and the *renewing* of the Spirit of God. And the heart thus changed is taught to deny ungodliness and Big Here & Now desires, and to live soberly, righteously, and godly in the Big Here & Now. All things are made new in both the heart and the Daily Grind.

The freshbirth of the God Magic system is a pretend renewing that leaves the heart unchanged — it is the same dance-around-the-Altar-of-Worthy-Self heart that it was before. And this unchanged heart introduces no changes in a man's Daily Grind except for the two components of Glorious Salvation Machine deception — *superstitious faith* in things like God Magic, the Passive Form, and the Sweet Presence and *superficial religion*, which can be either a classic or a contemporary version of the Innocuous Minimum.

Peregrinus—I find it amusing that the God Magic advocates defend their bankrupt system with the claim that requiring the freshbirth to change a man's heart and outside is requiring the impossible.

Plowman—They have it exactly backwards. A freshbirth that doesn't change a man's heart in a way that changes his outside is what is impossible. The freshbirth is wrought by two very powerful forces — the *same powerful Word* that spoke the universe into existence and the *same powerful Spirit* that raised the Crucified One from the dead. These two forces infuse a man's heart with new life, enabling him to both will and do the will of God.

Peregrinus—No wonder the Sacred Trust paints the life and walk of the freshborn man in such victorious light.

Plowman—You got that right. The infused power of God is why the Sacred Trust makes such bold statements as, "He that is freshborn overcomes the Big Here & Now," "He that is freshborn cannot continue in sin," and "He that has this hope in himself purifies himself even as he is pure."

THE GLORIOUS SALVATION MACHINE

We Cannot Freshbirth Ourselves

Peregrinus—Strawberry says that preaching heart-faith as a condition of the freshbirth is encouraging men to freshbirth themselves with their own carnal efforts.

Plowman—That is just more ugly-slinging. Believing is not carnal effort, for we are not the authors of our faith. God is the author and finisher of our faith. We did not give ourselves faith. He worked faith in our hearts. As the Sacred Trust says, faith comes by hearing and hearing by the Word of God. How can faith be carnal if it is wrought by the hand of God through the Word of God?

Peregrinus—But believing is an effort, right? It is something that we do, right?

Plowman—Absolutely. Faith is something that we do. But we must not confuse apples and oranges. Let faith be active. Let faith involve human effort. There is still no ground for the accusation that heart-faith is man trying to freshbirth himself.

Peregrinus—And how is that?

Plowman—Because man can't freshbirth himself. The feat is absolutely impossible. The idea is ludicrous. The freshbirth far transcends man's moral ability, even that of the strongest faith. It is far beyond the moral renovation of the heart (which is itself humanly impossible). The freshbirth is the regeneration and invigoration of the heart by the indwelling Holy Spirit, which God places in those who believe.

Peregrinus—I see your point. We can no more freshbirth ourselves than we can raise ourselves from the dead. The only thing we can do is obey the Sacred Trust's command to believe the Wonderful Message.

Plowman—That's right. But even in the matter of our faith, where we are obviously active, we cannot take a lot of credit for our faith. For we know from the testimony of the Sacred Trust and from our own experience that our faith is drawn out of us in a way that leaves us amazed at the grace of God. Our faith is not the result of our paltry seeking of God, but his seeking of us. It is not the result of our dauntless pilgrimage for light, but his glorious light shining in our darkness.

Peregrinus—That reminds me of the medicine illustration that Mr. Radio Preacher uses. We are on our deathbed with a fatal illness. God comes alongside and prescribes medicine which will restore our health. We take the medicine. It works. We get well. But we can't take credit for healing ourselves. It was the medicine that healed us. Nor can we take credit for making the medicine. God made it. Nor can we take credit for prescribing the medicine. God prescribed it. Nor can we take credit for convincing ourselves to take the medicine. God convinced us. The only thing we can take credit for is taking the medicine, which we only did after lots of prodding. God gets the credit for healing us.

Plowman—Amen to that. That's a good illustration.

The Same Hocus-Pocus Religion

Peregrinus—Another thing I have been thinking about is that Half-Haven preachers seem to have the same confidence in the Faith Form that the Glorious Salvation Machine preachers have in the Sprinkle Form.

Plowman—You nailed it. The Half-Havens have the same hocus-pocus religion that has prevailed in the Sprinkle Form churches for many long centuries, except that they have taken the hocus-pocus out of the classic *ceremony form* package and put into a modern, more evangelical *conversion form* package.

Peregrinus—So it is not merely a striking resemblance. It is the same religion.

Plowman—Absolutely. Both maintain the two golden calves of Innocuous Minimum religion — *God Magic* and the *Passive Form*. Both reject heart-faith as a condition of salvation and the "obedience of heart-faith" as the evidence of salvation. And both regard requiring them as the error of Dead Works.

Peregrinus—So the main difference between them is that the Half-Havens employ the Dry Sprinkle to dispense God Magic on adults while the Glorious Salvation Machine uses the Wet Sprinkle to dispense God Magic on children.

Plowman—Yep.

Peregrinus—It amazes me that the Half-Havens profess to reject the error of salvation through religious forms, which the Glorious Salvation Machine practices, yet they have their own version of salvation through religious forms.

Plowman—That's right. The Half-Havens pretend that the Faith Form is not a religious form like the Sprinkle Form, but a moment when men come face to face with the Nice God and get saved. In this spirit they refer to the Faith Form — with industrial strength hair-splitting — as the Eternally Efficacious Evangelical Event to distinguish it from religious forms like the Sprinkle Form. But regardless of what they call the Faith Form, it is still the God Magic error.

The God Magic Menace

Peregrinus—The Faith Form is one of the most deceitful and destructive errors of our day.

Plowman—No doubt about that. Wherever it goes, it leaves behind a trail of calamitous damage. It *woos* preachers with sweet promises of fruitfulness, *wows* them when it appears to be working, and *wounds* them when they discover that their Faith Form converts can't internalize Sacred Trust truth, don't want Sacred Trust discipleship, and clamor to roil the flock with murky churchianity.

The Havens need to wake up to the ominous threat they face in the God Magic salvation system — I call it the God Magic Menace. This system is an adulterated gospel that threatens the spiritual health of every church in the land. Its hocus-pocus nonsense will make every preacher in the land pay, one way or the other, sooner or later. So they can either pay now and pay the price of being a faithful man of God who stands against this threat, or they can pay later and pay the price of being a moral coward in the hour of need.

THE GOD MAGIC MENACE

Moral Reference Shift

Peregrinus—How did the hocus-pocus salvation system ever gain ascendancy in the church? It is so obviously wrong that it is hard to imagine anyone being duped by it.

Plowman—Hocus-pocus salvation came into power a couple centuries after the apostles when cunning innovators fabricated and implemented one of the most daring and successful *moral reference switches* in church history.

Peregrinus—Uh, dude, can you explain that?

Plowman—A moral reference shift is when preachers hijack doctrinal concepts, empty them of the content God gave them in the Sacred Trust, fill them with their own content, and make them mean something very different than God intended. This is precisely what the hocus-pocus innovators did. They took vital salvation concepts, emptied them of their Sacred Trust content, and filled them with God Magic nonsense. When they were done, they had turned theology upside down. Heart-faith and its fruits were smeared as Dead Works. Confidence in the Sprinkle Form was regarded as faith.

Peregrinus—So the innovators established a perversion of the Wonderful Message that called faith works and works faith.

Plowman—That's right.

The Passive Harangue and Persecution

Peregrinus—You would think that the innovators would need more than a switcheroo to overthrow the truth.

Plowman—They did need more than that, and they had more than that.

First of all, they held out the benefits of Innocuous Minimum religion. For the most part, men jumped at this opportunity. It allowed them to maintain the Altar of Worthy Self and still entertain hope of Sweet Everlasting. It allowed them to be ungodly and godly at the same time. It allowed them to walk in unbelief and yet be deemed a believer. It allowed them to serve the Sweet One, rather than the Crucified One. Who wouldn't want such religion?

Secondly, they employed a potent Passive Harangue. Those who dared to question Sprinkle Form salvation, or challenge the legitimacy of the Innocuous Minimum, or insist that the freshbirth came by heart-faith, or opine that the freshbirth made significant differences in a man's Daily Grind faced a horrible onslaught. They were accused of denying God Magic, charged with trusting in Dead Works, and threatened with falling out of the favor of the Glorious Salvation Machine.

Peregrinus—Were there many folks that didn't cave in under the pressure of the Passive Harangue?

Plowman—There were always a scattered few.

Peregrinus—What did the Big Cheese do to convince them?

Plowman—Those who could not be persuaded by the Passive Harangue were subjected to the stronger persuasive powers of persecution. First they would be threatened. If that didn't work, they would be put on the rack or in the fire. This, of course, didn't always convince the incorrigible parties themselves, but it went a long ways toward convincing friends and family.

Religion Is Big Business

Peregrinus—How about the preachers? I suppose they were in favor of the change to the hocus-pocus religion.

Plowman—They jumped at the opportunity. They were tired of the Sacred Trust principle, "Where there is *motion*, there is life." This required them to ascribe life only to those they could see moving down the narrow path that leads to eternal life — a practice which produced little flocks, not big machinery.

They were glad to adopt the Mystic Plane principle, "Where there is *Potion*, there is life." This allowed them to ascribe life to anyone who did the Passive Form — a practice that enabled them to super-sized their churches. For when you institute the God Magic system, you validate the Altar of Worthy Self and incorporate the Innocuous Minimum.

Peregrinus—Why did they want big churches?

Plowman—It's all about money and power. If you draw large crowds, you will have money and power.

Peregrinus—So religion is big business?

Plowman—That's right. In one stroke the church went from being a little flock of faithful followers of the Crucified One to a big business. Well, big business for the men at the helm of the machine. For the men in the pew, it was a social club.

Peregrinus—So what are they selling?

Plowman—They are selling lies that tickle men's ears. They are enabling men to indulge a fantasy that they are right with God and will go to Sweet Everlasting though faith is far from their heart.

Peregrinus—So they're fleecing the people.

Plowman—It's an ancient profession. Making a living by giving people the kind of religion they want has been around for thousands of years. Very few are the preachers who won't change the message for financial gain.

Peregrinus—So preachers adopt the Splash for the cash.

Plowman—That's a blunt way to put it, but apt.

Peregrinus—Don't the people care that they are being taken advantage of?

Plowman—No. As the Sacred Trust says, "My people love to have it so." The man in the pew is more than happy to pay the preacher a few dollars to tickle his ears, stroke his ego, and give him that good old painless religion.

Peregrinus—So it was a win-win situation.

Plowman—Yep. It was a no-brainer. The people got to keep the Altar of Worthy Self. The Glorious Salvation Machine got to fill her coffers with gold. Everyone got what he wanted, and everyone was happy.

Peregrinus—It's way too easy to deceive a man that wants to be deceived.

Plowman—You know it.

Immune to the Wonderful Message

Peregrinus—It's scary to observe that those who trust in the Faith Form can't be persuaded — not even by the strongest arguments from the Sacred Trust — that they must heart-believe in the Crucified One.

Plowman—Why should they be moved? They have nothing to gain, nothing to fear, and much to lose. They have nothing to gain, for they think they already possess a guaranteed entrance to Sweet Everlasting. They have nothing to fear, for they think they are guaranteed that they will never see Awful Everlasting. And they have much to lose, for their life is piling up Big Here & Now pleasures and treasures on the Altar of Worthy Self.

Peregrinus—It's like they have some powerful resistance to the Wonderful Message.

Plowman—They do have a resistance to it. They have been inoculated with the Sanitized Message. Now they are immune to the Wonderful Message.

Peregrinus—Inoculated against the truth. That makes perfect sense. That explains exactly what's going on. They had a shot of dead, form-based, Sweet One religion injected into their spiritual veins, and it keeps them from coming down with a case of real-relationship faith in the Crucified One.

Plowman—That's right. The Mad Spirit does more damage to the church by watering down the truth and mixing it with religion than he does when he out-and-out opposes it.

Revival Depends on a Faithful Wonderful Message

Peregrinus—What do you think about seeing revival in our day? Is it possible?

Plowman—There is a lot of talk about revival in our day and a lot of prayer for revival, but so long as the church preaches a message that *transmogrifies* faith into the Faith Form and grace into God Magic, so men can *maintain* the Altar of Worthy Self and *maximize* the Big Here & Now for their own Big Here & Now purposes, we will talk and pray until the end of the age without seeing the results we claim we want to see.

Peregrinus—So we need to forsake the sham and scam of the Faith Form message if we want to see revival.

Plowman—That's right. Revival is categorically ruled out until preachers start preaching the Wonderful Message as it is found in the Sacred Trust. We need preachers that tremble at the Bible, not preachers that know better than the Bible.

Peregrinus—I know one thing, it sure bothers me when men devote their time, energy, and money to worthless Big Here & Now things, and then pray as if it was God's responsibility to set them free from their lukewarmness and compromise.

Plowman—I see it all the time. Men disobediently stack their foxhole to the brim with the fun stuff of the Big Here & Now, and then have the audacity to pray that God would send some special God Magic blessing to revive them and make them good soldiers. They don't need some special magic to fall out of heaven. They need to heed the plain statements of the Sacred Trust, repent, thin out the junk in their foxholes, and start being good soldiers.

Peregrinus—I know that a fire has been kindled in my heart to follow the Crucified One with all my heart, soul, mind, and strength as a good soldier, no matter what it does to my Big Here & Now.

Plowman—Good for you. In our day discipleship has been turned on its head. Most of what is called "following the Sweet One" is a travesty of the truth. The typical believer today does not walk from faith to faith; he walks from fun to fun. The typical church today does not major in pilgrims; it majors in programs. The typical message today does not make disciples; it makes religious soap-bubble stackers. This needs to come to a screeching halt.

Peregrinus—Everyone is so afraid they are going to miss out on happiness.

Plowman—They just need to trust the Crucified One and his promises in the Wonderful Message. He knows better than we do what we need to make us truly and eternally happy. True happiness is found with our Redeemer in Sweet Everlasting. If we lay hold of his happiness, we can have "joy unspeakable and full of glory" right here and now while we walk in the Big

Here & Now — happiness which the Big Here & Now cannot give, cannot take away, and cannot understand. All other happiness is soap-bubble happiness.

Peregrinus—So what do we need to do if we want to go forward as we ought in our growth and in the work of God?

Plowman—We need to take it to heart that we have one long Sweet Everlasting to be fulfilled human beings and one short life to fight the good fight of faith as good soldiers of the cross. We need to quit chasing soap bubbles we cannot keep and start laying up treasure we cannot lose. We need to get dead serious about the things of God. As Paul wrote, according to my paraphrase, "Stop being a wimp and man-up." Put your toys away, put your armor on, take up the sword of the Word, and fight the good fight of faith.

The Mystic Plane

Peregrinus—One last question before we head for home. What is the Mystic Plane? I have been meaning to ask you this for a while. I know that it stands in contrast to the Daily Grind, but I just haven't been able to wrap my mind around it.

Plowman—Well, you really can't wrap your mind around it. The Mystic Plane is the nearly infinite expanse of pretend that stretches out in every direction from the Daily Grind.

Peregrinus—And men turn there when they don't find the facts or arguments they need in the Daily Grind?

Plowman—You got it. Does a man need axioms, principles, theories, definitions, distinctions, associations, facts of history, doctrines, or exegetical treatments that are not available in the Daily Grind? Not to worry. For a modest effort they can be his. All that he needs is a little twistification with the wonderful silly putty of the Mystic Plane and he can fabricate anything he needs that doesn't exist, never happened, or isn't true.

Peregrinus—What an awful tool in the hands of men.

Plowman—It is downright terrifying. The Mystic Plane gives men everything they need to deceive and be deceived. It gives them everything they need to establish, propagate, and defend classic religion. They can have pretend truth, pretend authority, pretend faith, and pretend acceptance with God. And it gives them everything they need to validate the newfangled religion of pseudoscience. They can twist the facts of history, geology, archaeology, biology, chemistry, physics, cosmology, or any other field, so they can deny the claims of God in the Bible, or even pretend he doesn't exist at all. In short, they can pretend whatever they want for any reason they want.

The Evening Draws to a Close

Peregrinus—Brother, I'm going to bail out. I sure appreciate your thoughts tonight. They gave me lots of light on some difficult questions.

Plowman—Thanks. I appreciate the hunger you show for the truth of God and the Sacred Trust.

As they were standing up and turning for the door, Peregrinus snuck in one more observation.

Peregrinus—You know, it's amazing how much of the so-called "truth" I was taught in the Glorious Salvation Machine and the Half-Havens has been untaught by the Sacred Trust.

Plowman—Yep. When a man starts studying the Sacred Trust in earnest, he soon discovers that much of what he was taught is not the teaching of the Sacred Trust. Over the months the "truth" that he holds is transformed from a collection of Invincible Dogmas and Ironclad Interpretations to a collection of Sacred Trust teachings that have been illuminated by the entire body of relevant testimony in the Sacred Trust.

As our friends stepped through the door and into the brisk evening air, Peregrinus ventured one more question.

Peregrinus—Hey, tell me about the Great Murky Revival.
Plowman—Another book, my friend.
Peregrinus—Aw, dude!

Made in the USA
Middletown, DE
06 January 2023

21577138R00203